The
Unicorn
Expedition

Satyajit Ray

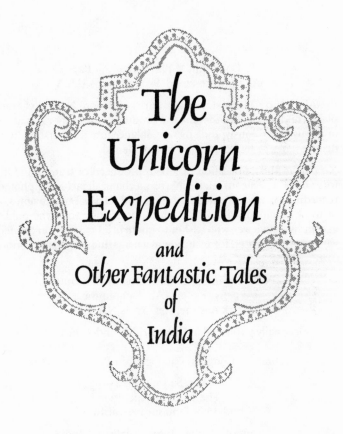

The Unicorn Expedition

and
Other Fantastic Tales
of
India

E. P. DUTTON · NEW YORK

Published in the United States by E. P. Dutton,
a division of NAL Penguin Inc.,
2 Park Avenue, New York, N.Y. 10016.

Originally published in Great Britain under the title *Stories*.

Library of Congress Cataloging-in-Publication Data

Ray, Satyajit, 1922–
The unicorn expedition,
and other fantastic tales of India.

1. Fantastic fiction, India (English) 2. India—
Fiction. I. Title.
PR9499.3.R397U5   1987   891'.4437   87-8932

ISBN: 0-525-24544-8

OBE

1   3   5   7   9   10   8   6   4   2

First American Edition

CONTENTS

Introduction	vii
Glossary	ix
Khagam	1
Patol Babu, Film Star	17
Big Bill	31
Ashamanja Babu's Dog	47
Ratanbabu and That Man	63
Night of the Indigo	79
The Duel	93
Corvus	103
Tellus	119
The Sahara Mystery	137
The Unicorn Expedition	155

INTRODUCTION

In 1913, my grandfather Upendrakisore Ray launched a children's monthly magazine called *Sandesh*. Sandesh is the name of a popular Bengali sweetmeat; but the word also means 'information'. Upendrakisore Ray had a formidable talent as a children's writer, having already published a delightful collection of Bengali folk tales as well as children's versions of the two famous Indian epics *Ramayana* and *Mahabharata*. All three were embellished with his own beautiful illustrations. The books and the magazine were published from his own press, U. Ray & Sons; my grandfather was a process engraver of the highest eminence.

Upendrakisore Ray died in 1915, six years before I was born. In the two years that he edited *Sandesh*, he filled its pages with stories, articles and illustrations. After his death, his eldest son, my father Sukumar Ray, took over. Sukumar Ray, too, had unique gifts as a children's writer and comic illustrator. Apart from school stories, plays and articles, he wrote a series of nonsense rhymes for the magazine which went on to win a permanent place in Bengali literature.

Sandesh folded four years after my father's death. Soon, U.

Ray & Sons too closed down. My mother and I moved to my maternal uncle's house where I grew up, finished my education and, in 1943, joined a British advertising agency as a junior visualiser. I had no literary bent at all, and never thought that I might one day write stories. What interested me besides advertising was films, although advertising seemed more dependable as a profession. I was in advertising for twelve years before I relinquished it to brave the hazards of a career in films.

It was in 1961, after I had established myself as a film-maker, that a poet friend of mine and I hit upon the idea of reviving *Sandesh*. The idea soon became a reality. The first issue of the revived *Sandesh* came out in the Bengali new year, in May 1961, on my fortieth birthday. As one of the two editors, I felt I had to contribute something. I produced a Bengali version of Edward Lear's *The Jumblies*. The second issue of *Sandesh* carried my first short story with my own illustration. Since then I have been writing and illustrating regularly for *Sandesh*, which celebrated its twenty-fifth anniversary this year.

Some of the stories I have written reflect my love of Verne and Wells and Conan Doyle whose works I read as a schoolboy. Professor Shonku, the scientist–inventor, may be said to be a mild- mannered version of Professor Challenger, where the love of adventure takes him to remote corners of the globe. Four of his adventures are included here. I don't think the other stories in this volume show any marked influence. Among these are straightforward tales as well as tales of the fantastic and the supernatural for which I have a special fascination.

I enjoy writing stories for its own sake and derive a pleasure from it which is quite distinct from the pleasure of the vastly more intricate business of making a film. I have written stories both during the making of a film and in the free period – usually lasting about six months – between films.

GLOSSARY

KHAGAM

3 *Ramayana* and *Mahabharata* – the two famous epics of India

PATOL BABU, FILM STAR

20 Esplanade – a locality in the heart of Calcutta
23 *Dhoti* – loin cloth worn by men
   Panjabi – a collarless, long-sleeved tunic worn with the dhoti

ASHAMANJA BABU'S DOG

53 *King of Bombardia* – the title of a well-known Bengali nonsense verse

RATANBABU AND THAT MAN

63 *Puja* – worship of a deity
65 *Dal barfi* – a confection made with lentil

NIGHT OF THE INDIGO

81 *Paan* – leaf of the betel tree commonly chewed with a mixture of spices
84 Dak bungalow – a house for travellers in India

THE DUEL

95 Nawabs – acting like a prince or noble; pertaining to titled aristocrats

THE UNICORN EXPEDITION

158 Kailas – a mountain in the Himalayas in Tibet supposed to be
the home of the Indian god Siva
174 Gita – one of the sacred books of the Hindus

Babu when used as a suffix to a name, takes the place of Mr

The
Unicorn
Expedition

KHAGAM

We were having dinner by the light of the petromax lamp. I had just helped myself to some curried egg when Lachhman, the cook and caretaker of the rest house, said, 'Aren't you going to pay a visit to Imli Baba?'

I had to tell him that since we were not familiar with the name of Imli Baba, the question of paying him a visit hadn't arisen. Lachhman said the driver of the Forest Department jeep which had been engaged for our sight-seeing would take us to the Baba if we told him. Baba's hut was in a forest and the surroundings were picturesque. As a holy man he was apparently held in very high regard; important people from all over India came to him to pay their respects and seek his blessings. What really aroused my curiosity was the information that the Baba kept a king cobra as a pet which lived in a hole near his hut and came to him every evening to drink goat's milk.

Dhurjati Babu's comment on this was that the country was being overrun by fake holy men. The more scientific knowledge was spreading in the west, he said, the more our people vere heading towards superstition. 'It's a hopeless situation, sir. It puts my back up just to think of it.'

As he finished talking, he picked up the fly swatter and brought it down with unerring aim on a mosquito which had settled on the dining-table. Dhurjati Babu was a short, pale-looking man in his late forties, with sharp features and grey eyes. We had met in the rest house in Bharatpur; I came here by way of Agra before going to my elder brother in Jaipur to spend a fortnight's holiday with him. Both the Tourist Bungalow and the Circuit House being full, I had to fall back on the Forest Rest House. Not that I regretted it; living in the heart of the forest offers a special kind of thrill along with quiet comfort.

Dhurjati Babu had preceded me by a day. We had shared the Forest Department jeep for our sight-seeing. Yesterday we had been to Deeg, twenty-two miles to the east from here, to see the fortress and the palace. The fortress in Bharatpur we saw this morning, and in the afternoon we saw the bird sanctuary at Keoladeo. This was something very special: a seven-mile stretch of marshland dotted with tiny islands where strange birds from far corners of the globe come and make their homes. I was absorbed in watching the birds, while Dhurjati Babu grumbled and made vain efforts to wave away the tiny insects buzzing around our heads. These *unkis* have a tendency to settle on your face, but they are so small that most people can ignore them. Not Dhurjati Babu.

Finishing dinner at half past eight, we sat on cane chairs on the terrace admiring the beauty of the forest in moonlight. 'That holy man the servant mentioned,' I remarked, 'what about going and taking a look at him?'

Flicking his cigarette towards a eucalyptus tree, Dhurjati Babu said, 'King cobras can never be tamed. I know a lot about snakes. I spent my boyhood in Jalpaiguri, and killed many snakes with my own hand. The king cobra is the deadliest, most vicious snake there is. So the story of the holy man feeding it goat's milk must be taken with a pinch of salt.'

I said, 'We see the fortress at Bayan tomorrow morning. In the afternoon we have nothing to do.'

'I take it you have a lot of faith in holy men?'

I could see the question was a barbed one. However, I answered in a straightforward way.

'The question of faith doesn't arise because I've never had anything to do with holy men. But I can't deny that I am a bit curious about this one.'

'I too was curious at one time, but after an experience I had with one. . .'

It turned out that the Dhurjati Babu suffered from high blood pressure. An uncle of his had persuaded him to try a medicine prescribed by a holy man. Dhurjati Babu had done so, and as a result had suffered intense stomach pain. This had caused his blood pressure to shoot up even more. Ever since then he had looked upon ninety per cent of India's holy men as fakes.

I found this allergy quite amusing, and just to provoke him I said, 'You said it wasn't possible to tame king cobras; I'm sure ordinary people like us couldn't do it, but I've heard of sadhus up in the Himalayas living in caves with tigers.'

'You may have heard about it, but have you seen it with your own eyes?'

I had to admit that I hadn't.

'You never will,' said Dhurjati Babu. 'This is the land of tall stories. You'll hear of strange happenings all the time, but never see one yourself. Look at our *Ramayana* and *Mahabharata*. It is said they're history, but actually they're no more than a bundle of nonsense. The ten-headed Ravana, the Monkey-God Hanumana with a flame at the end of his tail setting fire to a whole city, Bhima's appetite, Ghatotkacha, Hidimba, the flying chariot Pushpaka, Kumbhakarna – can you imagine anything more absurd than these? And the epics are full of fake holy men. That's where it all started. Yet everyone – even the educated – swallows them whole.'

We lunched in the rest house after visiting the fortress at Bayan and, after a couple of hours' rest, reached the holy man's hermitage a little after four. Dhurjati Babu didn't object to the trip. Perhaps he too was a little curious about the Baba. The hermitage was in a clearing in the forest below a huge tamarind tree, which is why he was called Imli Baba by the local people, *Imli* being the Hindi word for tamarind. His real name was not known.

In a hut made of date palm leaves, the Baba sat on a bearskin with a lone disciple by his side. The latter was a young fellow, but it was impossible to guess the Baba's age. There was still an hour or so until sunset, but the dense covering of foliage made the place quite dark. A fire burnt before the Baba, who had a *ganja* pipe in his hand. We could see by the light of the fire a clothes-line stretched across the wall of the hut from which hung a towel, a loin cloth, and about a dozen sloughed-off snake skins.

Dhurjati Babu whispered in my ear: 'Let's not beat about the bush; ask him about the snake's feeding time.'

'So you want to see Balkishen?' asked the Baba, reading our minds and smiling from behind his pipe. The driver of the jeep, Din Dayal, had told us a little while ago that the snake was called Balkishen. We told Baba that we had heard of his pet snake and we were most anxious to see it drink milk. Was there any likelihood of our wish being fulfilled?

Imli Baba shook his head sadly. He said, as a rule Balkishen came every day in the evening in answer to Baba's call, and had even come two days ago. But since the day before he had not been feeling well. 'Today is the day of the full moon,' said the Baba, 'so he will not come. But he will surely come again tomorrow evening.'

That snakes too could feel indisposed was news to me. And yet, why not? After all, it was a tame snake. Weren't there hospitals for dogs, horses and cows?

The Baba's disciple gave us another piece of news: red ants had got into the snake's hole while it lay ill, and had been pestering it. Baba had exterminated them all with a curse. Dhurjati Babu gave a sidelong glance at me at this point. I turned my eyes towards Baba. With his saffron robe, his long, matted hair, his iron earrings, *rudraksha* necklaces and copper amulets, there was nothing to distinguish him from a host of other holy men. And yet in the dim light of dusk, I couldn't take my eyes away from the man on the bearskin.

Seeing us standing, the disciple produced a pair of reed mats and spread them on the floor in front of the Baba. But what was the point of sitting down when there was no hope of seeing the pet snake? Delay would mean driving through the forest in the dark, and we knew there were wild animals about; we had seen herds of deer while coming. So we decided to leave. We bowed in *namaskar* to the Baba who responded by nodding without taking the pipe away from his mouth. We set off for the jeep parked about two hundred yards away on the road. Only a little while ago, the place had been alive with the call of birds coming home to roost. Now all was quiet.

We had gone a few steps when Dhurjati Babu suddenly said, 'We could at least have asked to see the hole where the snake lives.'

I said, 'For that we don't have to ask the Baba; our driver Din Dayal said he had seen the hole.'

'That's right.'

We fetched Din Dayal from the car and he showed us the way. Instead of going towards the hut, we took a narrow path by an almond tree and arrived at a bush. The stone rubble which surrounded the bush suggested that there had been some sort of an edifice here in the past. Din Dayal said the hole was right behind the bush. It was barely visible in the failing light. Dhurjati Babu produced from his pocket a small electric torch, and as the light from it hit the bush we saw the hole. But what about the snake? Was it likely to crawl out just to show its face to a couple of curious visitors? To be quite honest, while I was ready to watch it being fed by the Baba, I had no wish to see it come out of the hole now. But my companion seemed devoured by curiosity. When the beam from the torch had no effect, he started to pelt the bush with clods of dirt.

I felt this was taking things too far, and said, 'What's the matter? You seem determined to drag the snake out, and you didn't even believe in its existence at first.'

Dhurjati Babu now picked up a large clod and said, 'I still don't. If this one doesn't drag him out, I'll know that a cock-and-bull story about the Baba has been spread. The more such false notions are destroyed the better.'

The clod landed with a thud on the bush and destroyed a part of the thorny cluster. Dhurjati Babu had his torch trained on the hole. For a few seconds there was silence but for a lone cricket which had just started to chirp. Now there was another sound added to it: a dry, soft whistle of indeterminate pitch. Then there was a rustle of leaves and the light of the torch revealed something black and shiny slowly slipping out of the hole.

Now the leaves of the bush stirred, and the next moment, through a parting in them emerged the head of a snake. The light showed its glinting eyes and its forked tongue flickering out of its mouth again and again. Din Dayal had been pleading with us to go back to the jeep for some time; he now said, 'Let it be, sir. You have seen it: now let us go back.'

It was perhaps because of the light shining on it that the snake had its eyes turned towards us and was flicking its tongue from time to time. I have seen many snakes, but never a king cobra at such close quarters. And I have never heard of a king cobra making no attempt to attack intruders.

Suddenly the light of the torch trembled and was whisked away from the snake. What happened next was something I was not prepared for at all. Dhurjati Babu swiftly picked up a stone and hurled it with all his force at the snake. Then he followed it in quick succession with two more such missiles. I was suddenly gripped by a horrible premonition and cried out, 'Why on earth did you have to do that, Dhurjati Babu?'

The man shouted in triumph, panting, 'That's the end of at least one vicious reptile!'

Din Dayal was staring open-mouthed at the bush. I took the torch from Dhurjati Babu's hand and flashed it on the hole. I could see a part of the lifeless form of the snake. The leaves around were spattered with blood.

I had no idea that Imli Baba and his disciple had arrived to take their place right behind us. Dhurjati Babu was the first to turn round, and then I too turned and saw the Baba standing with a staff in his hand a dozen feet behind us. He had his eyes fixed on Dhurjati Babu. It is beyond me to describe the look in them. I can only say that I have never seen such a mixture of surprise, anger, and hatred in anyone's eyes.

Now Baba lifted his right arm towards Dhurjati Babu. The index finger now shot out to pinpoint the aim. I now noticed for the first time that Baba's fingernails were over an inch long. Who did he remind me of? Yes, of a figure in a painting by Ravi Varma which I had seen as a child in a framed reproduction in my uncle's house. It was the sage Durbasha cursing the hapless Sakuntala. He too had his arm raised like that, and the same look in his eyes.

But Imli Baba said nothing about a curse. All he said in Hindi in his deep voice was: 'One Balkishen is gone; another will come to take his place. Balkishen is deathless. . . '

Dhurjati Babu wiped his hands with his handkerchief, turned to me and said, 'Let's go.' Baba's disciple lifted the lifeless snake from the ground and went off, probably to arrange for its cremation. The length of the snake made me gasp; I had no idea king cobras could be that long. Imli Baba slowly made his way towards the hut. The three of us went back to the jeep.

On the way back, Dhurjati Babu was gloomy and silent. I asked him why he had to kill the snake when it was doing him no harm. I thought he would burst out once more and fulminate against snakes and Babas. Instead he put a question which seemed to have no bearing on the incident.

'Do you know who Khagam was?'

Khagam? The name seemed to ring a bell, but I couldn't think where I had heard it. Dhurjati Babu muttered the name two or three times, then lapsed into silence.

It was half past six when we reached the guest house. My mind went back again and again to Imli Baba glowering at Dhurjati Babu with his finger pointing at him. I don't know why my companion behaved in such a fashion. However, I felt that we had seen the end of the incident, so there was no point in worrying about it. Baba himself had said Balkishen was deathless. There must be other king cobras in the jungles of Bharatpur. I was sure another one would be caught soon by the disciples of the Baba.

Lachhman had prepared curried chicken, lentil and chapatis for dinner. One feels hungry after a whole day's sight-seeing. I find I eat twice as much here as I eat at home. Dhurjati Babu, although a small man, is a hearty eater; but today he seemed to have no appetite. I asked him if he felt unwell. He made no reply. I now said, 'Do you feel remorse for having killed the snake?'

Dhurjati Babu was staring at the petromax. What he said was not an answer to my question. 'The snake was whistling,' he said in a soft, thin voice. 'The snake was whistling. . . '

I said, smiling, 'Whistling, or hissing?'

Dhurjati Babu didn't turn away from the light. 'Yes, hissing,' he said. 'Snakes speak when snakes hiss. . . yes,

Snakes speak when snakes hiss
I know this. I know this. . . '

Dhurjati Babu stopped and made some hissing noises himself. Then he broke into rhyme again, his head swaying in rhythm.

'Snakes speak when snakes hiss
I know this. I know this,
Snakes kill when snakes kiss
I know this. I know this. . .

What is this? Goat's milk?'

The question was directed at the pudding in the plate before him.

Lachhman missed the 'goat' bit and answered, 'Yes, sir – there is milk and there is egg.'

Dhurjati Babu is by nature whimsical, but his behaviour today seemed excessive. Perhaps he himself realised it, because he seemed to make an effort to control himself. 'Been out on the sun too long these last few days.' he said. 'Must go easy from tomorrow.'

It was noticeably chillier tonight than usual; so instead of sitting out on the terrace, I went into the bedroom and started to pack my suitcase. I was going to catch the train next evening. I would have to change in the middle of the night at Sawai-Madhopur and arrive in Jaipur at five in the morning.

At least that was my plan, but it came to nothing. I had to

send a wire to my elder brother saying that I would be arriving a day later. Why this was necessary will be clear from what I'm about to say now. I shall try to describe everything as clearly and accurately as possible. I don't expect everyone will believe me, but the proof is still lying on the ground fifty yards away from the Baba's hut. I feel a cold shiver just to think of it, so it is not surprising that I couldn't pick it up and bring it as proof of my story. Let me now set down what happened.

I had just finished packing my suitcase, turned down the wick of my lantern and got into my pyjamas when there was a knock on the door on the east side of the room. Dhurjati Babu's room was behind that door.

As soon as I opened the door the man said in a hoarse whisper: 'Do you have some Flit, or something to keep off mosquitoes?'

I asked: 'Where did you find mosquitoes? Aren't your windows covered with netting?'

'Yes, they are.'

'Well, then?'

'Even then something is biting me.'

'How do you know that?'

'There are marks on my skin.'

It was dark at the mouth of the door, so I couldn't see his face clearly. I said, 'Come into my room. Let me see what kind of marks they are.'

Dhurjati Babu stepped into my room. I raised the lantern and could see the marks immediately. They were greyish, diamond-shaped blotches. I had never seen anything like them before, and I didn't like what I saw. 'You seem to have caught some strange disease.' I said. 'It may be an allergy, of course. We must get hold of a doctor first thing tomorrow morning. Try and go to sleep and don't worry about the marks. And I don't think they're caused by insects. Are they painful?'

'No.'

'Then don't worry. Go back to bed.'

He went off. I shut the door, climbed into bed and slipped under the blanket. I'm used to reading in bed before going to sleep, but this was not possible by lantern-light. Not that I needed to read. I knew the day's exertions would put me to sleep within ten minutes of putting my head on the pillow.

But that was not to be tonight. I was about to drop off when there was the sound of a car arriving, followed soon by English voices and the bark of a dog. Foreign tourists obviously. The dog stopped barking at a sharp rebuke. Soon there was quiet again except for the crickets. No, not just the crickets; my neighbour was still awake and walking about. And yet through the crack under the door I had seen the lantern either being put out, or removed to the bathroom. Why was the man pacing about in the dark?

For the first time I had a suspicion that he was more than just whimsical. I had known him for just two days. I knew nothing beyond what he had himself told me. And yet, to be quite honest, I had not seen any signs of what could be called madness in him until only a few hours ago. The comments that he had made while touring the forts at Bayan and Deeg suggested that he was quite well up on history. Not only that: he also knew quite a bit about art, and spoke knowledgebly about the work of Hindu and Moslem architects in the palaces of Rajasthan. No – the man was obviously ill. We must look for a doctor tomorrow.

The radium dial on my watch said a quarter to eleven. There was another rap on the east side door. This time I shouted from the bed.

'What is it, Dhurjati Babu?'

'S–s–s–s– '

'What?'

'S–s–s–s– '

I could see that he was having difficulty with his speech. A fine mess I had got myself into. I shouted again: 'Tell me clearly what the matter is.'

'S-s-s-sorry to bother you, but – '

I had to leave the bed. When I opened the door, the man came out with such an absurd question that it really annoyed me.

'Is s-s-s-snake spelt with one "s"?'

I made no effort to hide my annoyance.

'You knocked on the door at this time of the night just to ask me that?'

'Only one "s"?' he repeated.

'Yes, sir. No English word begins with two s's.'

'I s-s-see. And curs-s-s-e?'

'That's one "s" too.'

'Thank you. S-s-s-sleep well.'

I felt pity for the poor man. I said, 'Let me give you a sleeping pill. Would you like one?'

'Oh no. I s-s-s-sleep s-s-s-soundly enough. But when the s-s-sun was s-s-s-setting this evening –'

I interrupted him. 'Are you having trouble with your tongue? Why are you stammering? Give me your torch for a minute.'

I followed Dhurjati Babu into his room. The torch was on the dressing table. I flashed it on his face and he put out his tongue.

There was no doubt that something was wrong with it. A thin red line had appeared down the middle.

'Don't you feel any pain?'

'No. No pain.'

I was at a loss to know what the matter was with him.

Now my eye fell on the man's bed. Its clean appearance made it clear that he hadn't got into bed at all. I was quite stern about it. I said, 'I want to see you turn in before I go back. And I urge you please not to knock on my door again. I know I won't have any sleep in the train tomorrow, so I want to have a good night's rest now.'

But the man showed no signs of going to bed. The lantern being kept in the bathroom, the bedroom was in semi-darkness. Outside there was a full moon. Moonlight flooded in through the north window and fell on the floor. I could see Dhurjati Babu in the soft reflected glow from it. He was standing in his nightclothes, making occasional efforts to whistle through parted lips. I had wrapped the blanket around me when I left my bed, but Dhurjati Babu had nothing warm on him. If he caught a chill then it would be difficult for me to leave him alone and go away. After all, we were both away from home; if one was in trouble, it wouldn't do for the other to leave him in the lurch and push off.

I told him again to go to bed. When I found he wouldn't, I realised I should have to use main force. If he insisted on behaving like a child, I had no choice but to act the stern elder.

But the moment I touched his hand I sprang back as if from an electric shock.

Dhurjati Babu's body was as cold as ice. I couldn't imagine that a living person's body could be so cold.

It was perhaps my reaction which brought a smile to his lips. He now regarded me with his grey eyes wrinkled in amusement. I asked him in a hoarse voice: 'What is the matter with you?'

Dhurjati Babu kept looking at me for a whole minute. I noticed that he didn't blink once during the whole time. I also noticed that he kept sticking out his tongue again and again. Then he dropped his voice to a whisper and said, 'Baba is calling me – "Balkishen! . . . Balkishen! . . . " I can hear him call.' His knees now buckled and he went down on the floor. Flattening himself on his chest, he started dragging himself back on his elbows until he disappeared into the darkness under the bed.

I was drenched in a cold sweat and shivering in every limb. It was difficult for me to keep standing. I was no longer worried about the man, all I felt was a mixture of horror and disbelief.

I came back to my room, shut the door and bolted it. Then I got back into bed and covered myself from head to toe with the blanket. In a while the shivering stopped and I could think a little more clearly. I tried to realise where the matter stood, and the implication of what I had seen with my own eyes. Dhurjati Babu had killed Imli Baba's pet cobra by pelting it with stones. Immediately after that Imli Baba had pointed to Dhurjati Babu with his finger and said; 'One Balkishen is gone. Another will come to take his place.' The question is: was the second Balkishen a snake or a man?

Or a man turned into a snake?

What were those diamond-shaped blotches on Dhurjati Babu's skin?

What was the red mark on his tongue?

Did it show that his tongue was about to be forked?

Why was he so cold to the touch?

Why did he crawl under the bed?

I suddenly recalled something in a flash. Dhurjati Babu had asked about Khagam. The name had sounded familiar, but I couldn't quite place it. Now I remembered. A story I had read in the *Mahabharata* when I was a boy. Khagam was the name of a sage. His curse had turned his friend into a snake. Khagam – snake – curse – it all fitted. But the friend had turned into a harmless non-poisonous snake, while this man. . .

Somebody was knocking on the door again. At the foot of the door this time. Once, twice, thrice. . . I didn't stir out of the bed. I was not going to open the door. Not again.

The knocking stopped. I held my breath and waited.

A hissing sound now, moving away from the door.

Now there was silence, except for my pounding heartbeat.

What was that sound now? A squeak. No, something between a squeak and a screech. I knew there were rats in the bungalow. I saw one in my bedroom the very first night. I had told Lachhman, and he had brought a rat-trap from the pantry to show me a rat in it. 'Not only rats, sir; there are moles too.'

The screeching had stopped. There was silence again. Minutes passed. I glanced at my watch. A quarter to one. Sleep had vanished. I could see the trees in the moonlight through my window. The moon was overhead now.

The sound of a door opening. It was the door of Dhurjati Babu's room which led to the verandah. The door was on the same side as my window. The line of trees was six or seven yards away from the edge of the verandah.

Dhurjati Babu was out on the verandah now. Where was he going? What was he up to? I stared fixedly at my window.

The hissing was growing louder. Now it was right outside my window. Thank God the window was covered with netting!

Something was climbing up the wall towards the window. A

head appeared behind the netting. In the dim light of the lantern shone a pair of beady eyes staring fixedly at me.

They stayed staring for a minute; then there was the bark of a dog. The head turned towards the bark, and then dropped out of sight.

The dog was barking at the top of its voice. Now I heard its owner shouting at it. The barking turned into a moan, and then stopped. Once again there was silence. I kept my senses alert for another ten minutes or so. The lines of a verse I had heard earlier that night kept coming back to me –

> *Snakes speak when snakes hiss*
> *I know this. I know this,*
> *Snakes kill when snakes kiss*
> *I know this. I know this. . .*

And then the rhyme grew dim in my mind and I felt a drowsiness stealing over me.

I woke up to the sound of agitated English voices. My watch showed ten minutes to six. Something was happening. I got up quickly, dressed and came out on the verandah. A pet dog belonging to two English tourists had died during the night. The dog had slept in the bedroom with its owners who hadn't bothered to lock the door. It was surmised that a snake or something equally venomous had got into the room and bitten it.

Instead of wasting my time on the dog, I went to the door of Dhurjati Babu's room at the other end of the verandah. The door was ajar and the room empty. Lachhman gets up every morning at five to light the oven and put the tea-kettle on the boil. I asked him. He said he hadn't seen Dhurjati Babu.

All sorts of anxious thoughts ran in my head. I had to find Dhurjati Babu. He couldn't have gone far on foot. But a thorough search of the woods around proved abortive.

The jeep arrived at half past ten. I couldn't leave Bharatpur without finding out what had happened to my companion. So I sent a cable to my brother from the post office, got my train ticket postponed for a day and came back to the rest house to learn that there was still no sign of Dhurjati Babu. The two Englishmen had in the meantime buried their dog and left.

I spent the whole afternoon exploring around the rest house. Following my instruction, the jeep arrived again in the afternoon. I was now working on a hunch and had a faint hope of success. I told the driver to drive straight to Imli Baba's hermitage.

I reached it about the same time as we did yesterday. Baba was seated with the pipe in hand and the fire burning in front of him. There were two more disciples with him today.

Baba nodded briefly in answer to my greeting. The look in his eyes today held no hint of the blazing intensity that had appeared in them yesterday. I went straight to the point: did the Baba have any information on the gentleman who came with me yesterday? A gentle smile spread over Baba's face. He said, 'Indeed I have! Your friend has fulfilled my hope. He has brought back my Balkishen to me.'

I noticed for the first time the stone pot on Baba's right-hand side. The white liquid it contained was obviously milk. But I hadn't come all this way to see a snake and a bowl of milk. I had come in quest of Dhurjati Babu. He couldn't simply have vanished into thin air. If I could only see *some* sign of his existence!

I had noticed earlier that Imli Baba could read one's mind. He took a long pull at the pipe of *ganja,* passed it on to one of his disciples and said, 'I'm afraid you won't find your friend in the state you knew him, but he has left a memento behind. You will find that fifty steps to the south of Balkishen's home. Go carefully; there are thorny bushes around.'

I went to the hole where the king cobra lived. I was not the least concerned with whether another snake had taken the place of the first one. I took fifty steps south through grass, thorny shrubs and rubble, and reached a *bel* tree at the foot of which lay something the likes of which I had seen hanging from a line in Baba's hut a few minutes ago.

It was a freshly sloughed-off skin marked all over with a pattern of diamonds.

But was it really snake skin? A snake was never that broad, and a snake didn't have arms and legs sticking out of its body. It was actually the sloughed-off skin of a man. A man who had ceased to be a man. He was now lying coiled inside that hole. He is a king cobra with poison fangs.

There, I can hear him hissing. The sun has just gone down. I can hear the Baba calling – 'Balkishen – Balkishen – Balkishen.'

PATOL BABU, FILM STAR

Patol Babu had just hung his shopping-bag on his shoulder when Nishikanto Babu called from outside the main door. 'Patol, are you in?'

'Oh, yes,' said Patol Babu. 'Just a minute.'

Nishikanto Ghosh lived three houses away from Patol Babu in Nepal Bhattacharji Lane. He was a genial person.

Patol Babu came out with the bag. 'What brings you here so early in the morning?'

'Listen, what time will you be back?'

'In an hour or so. Why?'

'I hope you'll stay in after that – today being Tagore's birthday. I met my youngest brother-in-law in Netaji Pharmacy yesterday. He is in the film business, in the production department. He said he was looking for an actor for a scene in a film they're now shooting. The way he described the character – fiftyish, short, bald-headed – it reminded me of you. So I gave him your address and asked him to get in touch with you directly. I hope you won't turn him away. They'll pay you, of course.'

Patol Babu hadn't expected such news at the start of the day.

17

That an offer to act in a film could come to a fifty-two-year-old nonentity like him was beyond his wildest dreams.

'Well, yes or no?' asked Nishikanto Babu. 'I believe you did some acting on the stage at one time?'

'That's true,' said Patol Babu. 'I really don't see why I should say no. But let's talk to your brother-in-law first and find out some details. What's his name?'

'Naresh. Naresh Dutt. He's about thirty. A strapping young fellow. He said he would be here around ten-thirty.'

Buying provisions in the market, Patol Babu mixed up his wife's orders and bought red chillies instead of onion seeds. And he quite forgot about the aubergines. This was not surprising. At one time Patol Babu had a real passion for the stage; in fact, it verged on obsession. In *Jatras*, in amateur theatricals, in plays put up by the club in his neighbourhood, Patol Babu was always in demand. His name had appeared in handbills on countless ocasions. Once it appeared in bold type near the top: 'Sitalakanto Ray (Patol Babu) in the role of Parasar.' Indeed, there was a time when people bought tickets especially to see him.

That was when he used to live in Kanchrapara. He had a job in the railway factory there. In 1934, he was offered higher pay in a clerical post with Hudson and Kimberley, in Calcutta, and was also lucky to find a flat in Nepal Bhattacharji Lane. He gave up his factory job and came to Calcutta with his wife. It was quite smooth sailing for some years, and Patol Babu was in his boss's good books. In 1943, when he was just toying with the idea of starting a club in his neighbourhood, sudden retrenchment in his office due to the war cost him his nine-year-old job.

Ever since then Patol Babu had struggled to make a living. At first he opened a variety store which he had to wind up after five years. Then he had a job in a Bengali firm which he gave up in disgust when his boss began to treat him in too high-handed a fashion. Then, for ten long years, starting as an insurance salesman, Patol Babu tried every means of earning a livelihood without ever succeeding in improving his lot. Of late he has been paying regular visits to a small establishment dealing in scrap iron where a cousin of his has promised him a job.

And acting? That has become a thing of the remote past; something which he recalls at times with a sigh. Having a good memory, Patol Babu still remembers lines from some of his better parts. 'Listen, O listen to the thunderous twang of the mighty bow Gandiva engaged in gory conflict, and to the angry roar of the mountainous club whizzing through the air in the hands of the great Brikodara!' It sent a shiver down his spine just to think of such lines.

Naresh Dutt turned up at half past twelve. Patol Babu had given up hope and was about to go for his bath when there was a knock on the front door.

'Come in, come in, sir!' Patol Babu almost dragged the young man in and pushed the broken-armed chair towards him. 'Do sit down.'

'No, thanks. I–er–I expect Nishikanto Babu told you about me?'

'Oh yes. I must say I was quite taken aback. After so many years . . . '

'I hope you have no objection?'

'You think I'll be all right for the part?' Patol Babu asked with great diffidence.

Naresh Dutt cast an appraising look at Patol Babu and gave a nod. 'Oh yes,' he said. 'There is no doubt about that. By the way, the shooting takes place tomorrow morning.'

'Tomorrow? Sunday?'

'Yes, and not in the studio. I'll tell you where you have to go. You know Faraday House near the crossing of Bentinck Street and Mission Row? It's a seven-storey office building. The shooting takes place outside the office in front of the entrance. We'll expect you there at eight-thirty sharp. You'll be through by midday.'

Naresh Dutt prepared to leave. 'But you haven't told me about the part,' said Patol Babu anxiously.

'Oh yes, sorry. The part is that of a – a pedestrian. An absent-minded, short-tempered pedestrian. By the way, do you have a jacket which buttons up to the neck?'

'I think I do. You mean the old-fashioned kind?'

'Yes. That's what you'll wear. What colour is it?'

'Sort of nut-brown. But woollen.'

'That's okay. The story is supposed to take place in winter, so that would be just right. Tomorrow at 8.30 am sharp. Faraday House.'

Patol Babu suddenly thought of a crucial question.

'I hope the part calls for some dialogue?'

'Certainly. It's a speaking part. You have acted before, haven't you?'

'Well, as a matter of fact, yes . . .'

'Fine. I wouldn't have come to you for just a walk-on part. For that we pick people from the street. Of course there's dialogue and you'll be given your lines as soon as you show up tomorrow.'

After Naresh Dutt left, Patol Babu broke the news to his wife.

'As far as I can see, the part isn't a big one. I'll be paid, of course, but that's not the main thing. The thing is – remember how I started on the stage? Remember my first part? I played a dead soldier! All I had to do was lie still on the stage with my arms and legs spread. And remember how I rose from that position? Remember Mr Watts shaking me by the hand? And the silver medal which the chairman of our municipality gave me? Remember? This is only the first step on the ladder, my dear better-half ! Yes – the first step that would – God willing – mark the rise to fame and fortune of your beloved husband!'

'Counting your chickens again before they're hatched, are you? No wonder you could never make a go of it.'

'But it's the real thing this time! Go and make me a cup of tea, will you? And remind me to take some ginger juice tonight. It's very good for the throat.'

The clock in the Metropolitan building showed seven minutes past eight when Patol Babu reached Esplanade. It took him another ten minutes to walk to Faraday House.

There was a big crowd outside the building. Three or four cars stood on the road. There was also a bus which carried equipment on its roof. On the edge of the pavement there was an instrument on three legs around which there was a group of busy people. Near the entrance stood – also on three legs – a pole which had a long arm extending from its top at the end of which was suspended what looked like a small oblong beehive. Surrounding these instruments was a crowd of people among which Patol Babu noticed some non-Bengalis. What they were supposed to do he couldn't tell.

But where was Naresh Dutt? He was the only one who knew him.

With a slight tremor in his heart, Patol Babu advanced towards the entrance. It was the middle of summer, and the warm jacket buttoned up to his neck felt heavy. Patol Babu could feel beads of perspiration forming around the high collar.

'This way, Atul Babu!'

Atul Babu? Patol Babu spotted Naresh Dutt standing at the entrance and gesturing towards him. He had got his name wrong. No wonder, since they had only had a brief meeting. Patol Babu walked up, put his palms together in a *namaskar* and said, 'I suppose you haven't yet noted down my name. Sitalakanto Ray – although people know me better by my nickname Patol. I used it on the stage too.'

'Good, good. I must say you're quite punctual.'

Patol Babu rose to his full height.

'I was with Hudson and Kimberley for nine years and wasn't late for a single day.'

'Is that so? Well, I suggest you go and wait in the shade there. We have a few things to attend to before we get going.'

'Naresh!'

Somebody standing by the three-legged instrument called out.

'Sir?'

'Is he one of our men?'

'Yes, sir. He is – er – in that shot where they bump into each other.'

'Okay. Now, clear the entrance, will you? We're about to start.'

Patol Babu withdrew and stood in the shade of a *paan* shop.

He had never watched a film shooting before. How hard these people worked! A youngster of twenty or so was carrying that three-legged instrument on his shoulder. Must weigh at least sixty pounds.

But what about his dialogue? There wasn't much time left, and he still didn't know what he was supposed to do or say.

Patol Babu suddenly felt a little nervous. Should he ask somebody? There was Naresh Dutt there; should he go and remind him? It didn't matter if the part was small, but, if he had to make the most of it, he had to learn his lines beforehand. How small he would feel if he muffed in the presence of so many people! The last time he acted on stage was twenty years ago.

Patol Babu was about to step forward when he was pulled up short by a voice shouting 'Silence!'

This was followed by Naresh Dutt loudly announcing with hands cupped over his mouth: 'We're about to start shooting. Everybody please stop talking. Don't move from your positions and don't crowd round the camera, please!'

Once again the voice was heard shouting 'Silence! Taking!' Now Patol Babu could see the owner of the voice. He was a stout man of medium height, and he stood by the camera. Around his neck hung something which looked like a small telescope. Was he the director? How strange! – he hadn't even bothered to find out the name of the director!

Now a series of shouts followed in quick succession – 'Start sound!' 'Running!' 'Camera!' 'Rolling!' 'Action!'

Patol Babu noticed that as soon as the word 'Action' was said, a car came up from the crossing and pulled up in front of the office entrance. Then a young man in a grey suit and pink make-up shot out of the back of the car, took a few hurried steps towards the entrance and stopped abruptly. The next moment Patol Babu heard the shout 'Cut!' and immediately the hubbub from the crowd resumed.

A man standing next to Patol Babu now turned to him. 'I hope you recognised the young fellow?' he asked.

'Why, no,' said Patol Babu.

'Chanchal Kumar,' said the man. 'He's coming up fast. Playing the lead in four films at the moment.'

Patol Babu saw very few films, but he seemed to have heard the name Chanchal Kumar. It was probably the same boy Koti Babu was praising the other day. Nice make-up the fellow had on. If he had been wearing a Bengali *dhoti* and *panjabi* instead of a suit, and given a peacock to ride on, he would make a perfect God Kartik. Monotosh of Kanchrapara – who was better known by his nickname Chinu – had the same kind of looks. He was very good at playing female parts, recalled Patol Babu.

Patol Babu now turned to his neighbour and asked in a whisper, 'Who is the director?'

The man raised his eyebrows and said, 'Why, don't you know? He's Baren Mullick. He's had three smash hits in a row.'

Well, at least he had gathered some useful information. It wouldn't have done for him to say he didn't know if his wife had asked in whose film he had acted and with which actor.

Naresh Dutt now came up to him with tea in a small clay cup.

'Here you are, sir – the hot tea will help your throat. Your turn will come shortly.'

Patol Babu now had to come out with it.

'If you let me have my lines now. . . '

'Your lines? Come with me.'

Naresh Dutt went towards the three-legged instrument with Patol Babu at his heels.

'I say, Sosanko.'

A young fellow in a short-sleeved shirt turned towards Naresh Dutt. 'This gentleman wants his lines. Why don't you write them down on a piece of paper and give it to him? He's the one who –'

'I know, I know.'

Sosanko now turned to Patol Babu.

'Come along, Grandpa. I say, Jyoti, can I borrow your pen for a sec? Grandpa wants his lines written down.'

The youngster Jyoti produced a red-dot pen from his pocket and gave it to Sosanko. Sosanko tore off a page from the notebook he was carrying, scribbled something on it and handed it to Patol Babu.

Patol Babu glanced at the paper and found that a single word had been scrawled on it – 'Oh!'

Patol Babu felt a sudden throbbing in his head. He wished he could take off his jacket. The heat was unbearable.

Sosanko said, 'What's the matter, Grandpa? You don't seem too pleased.'

Were these people pulling his leg? Was the whole thing a gigantic hoax? A meek, harmless man like him, and they had to drag him into the middle of the city to make a laughing stock out of him. How could anyone be so cruel?

Patol Babu said in a hardly audible voice, 'I find it rather strange.'

'Why, Grandpa?'

'Just "Oh"? Is that all I have to say?'

Sosanko's eyebrows shot up.

'What are you saying, Grandpa? You think that's nothing? Why, this is a regular speaking part! A speaking part in a Baren Mullick film – do you realise what that means? Why, you're the luckiest of actors. Do you know that till now more than a hundred persons have appeared in this film who have had *nothing* to say? They just walked past the camera. Some didn't even walk; they just stood in one spot. There were others whose faces didn't register at all. Even today – look at all those people standing by the lamp-post; they all appear in today's scene but have nothing to say. Even our hero Chanchal Kumar has no lines to speak today. You are the only one who has – see?'

Now the young man called Jyoti came up, put his hand on Patol Babu's shoulder and said, 'Listen, Grandpa. I'll tell you what you have to do. Chanchal Kumar is a rising young executive. He is informed that an embezzlement has taken place in his office, and he comes to find out what has happened. He gets out of his car and charges across the pavement towards the entrance. Just then he collides with an absent-minded pedestrian. That's you. You're hurt in the head and say "Oh!", but Chanchal Kumar pays no attention to you and goes into the office. The fact that he ignores you reflects his extreme preoccupation – see? Just think how crucial the shot is.'

'I hope everything is clear now,' said Sosanko. 'Now, if you just move over to where you were standing . . . the fewer people crowd around here the better. There's one more shot left before your turn comes.'

Patol Babu went slowly back to the *paan* shop. Standing in the shade, he glanced down at the paper in his hand, cast a quick look around to see if anyone was watching, crumpled the paper into a ball and threw it into the roadside drain.

Oh. . .

A sigh came out of the depths of his heart.

Just one word – no, not even a word; a sound – 'oh!'

The heat was stifling. The jacket seemed to weigh a ton. Patol Babu couldn't keep standing in one spot any more; his legs felt heavy.

He moved up to the office beyond the *paan* shop and sat down on the steps. It was nearly half past nine. On Sunday mornings, songs in praise of the Goddess Kali were sung in Karali Babu's house. Patol Babu went there every week and enjoyed it. What if he were to go there now? What harm would there be? Why waste a Sunday morning in the company of these useless people, and be made to look foolish on top of that?

'Silence!'

Stuff and nonsense! To hell with your 'silence'! They had to put up this pompous show for something so trivial! Things were much better on the stage.

The stage. . . the stage. . .

A faint memory was stirred up in Patol Babu's mind. Some priceless words of advice given in a deep, mellow voice: 'Remember one thing, Patol; however small a part you're offered, never consider it beneath your dignity to accept it. As an artist your aim should be to make the most of your opportunity, and squeeze the last drop of meaning out of your lines. A play involves the work of many and it is the combined effort of many that makes a success of the play.'

It was Mr Pakrashi who gave the advice. Gogon Pakrashi, Patol Babu's mentor. A wonderful actor, without a trace of vanity in him; a saintly person, and an actor in a million.

There was something else which Mr Pakrashi used to say. 'Each word spoken in a play is like a fruit in a tree. Not everyone in the audience has access to it. But you, the actor, must know how to pluck it, get at its essence, and serve it up to the audience for their edification.'

The memory of his guru made Patol Babu bow his head in obeisance.

Was it really true that there was nothing in the part he had been given today? He had only one word to say – 'Oh!', but was that word so devoid of meaning as to be dismissed summarily?

Oh, oh, oh, oh, oh – Patol Babu began giving the exclamation a different inflection each time he uttered it. After doing it for a number of times he made an astonishing discovery. The same exclamation, when spoken in different ways, carried different shades of meaning. A man when hurt said 'Oh' in quite a different way. Despair brought forth one kind of 'Oh', while sorrow provoked yet another kind. In fact, there were so many kinds of Oh's – the short Oh, the long-drawn Oh, Oh shouted and Oh whispered, the high-pitched Oh and the low-pitched Oh, and the Oh starting low and ending high, and the Oh starting high and ending low . . . Strange! Patol Babu suddenly felt that he could write a whole thesis on that one monosyllabic exclamation. Why had he felt so disheartened when this single word contained a gold-mine of meaning? The true actor could make a mark with this one single syllable.

'Silence!'

The director had raised his voice again. Patol Babu could see the young Jyoti clearing the crowd. There was something he had to ask him. He went quickly over to him.

'How long will it be before my turn comes, brother?'

'Why are you so impatient, Grandpa? You have to learn to be patient in this line of business. It'll be another half an hour before you're called.'

'That's all right. I'll certainly wait. I'll be in that side street across the road.'

'Okay – so long as you don't sneak off.'

'Start sound!'

Patol Babu crossed the road on tiptoe and went into the quiet little side street. It was good that he had a little time on his hands. While these people didn't seem to believe in rehearsals, he himself would rehearse his own bit. There was no one about. These were office buildings, so very few people lived here. Those who did – such as shopkeepers – had all gone to watch the shooting.

Patol Babu cleared his throat and started enunciating the syllable in various ways. Along with that he worked out how he would react physically when the collision took place – how his features would be twisted in pain, how he would fling out his arms, how his body would crouch to express pain and surprise – all these he performed in various ways in front of a large glass window.

Patol Babu was called in exactly half an hour. Now he had completely got over his apathy. All he felt now was a keen anticipation and suppressed excitement. It was the feeling he used to feel twenty years ago just before he stepped on to the stage.

The director Baren Mullick called Patol Babu to him. 'I hope you know what you're supposed to do?' he asked.

'Yes, sir.'

'Very good. I'll first say "Start sound". The recordists will reply by saying "Running". That's the signal for the camera to start. Then I will say "Action". That will be your cue to start walking from that pillar, and for the hero to come out of the car and make a dash for the office. You work out your steps so that the collision takes place at this spot, here. The hero ignores you and strides into the office, while you register pain by saying "Oh!", stop for a couple of seconds, then resume walking – okay?'

Patol Babu suggested a rehearsal, but Baren Mullick shook his head impatiently 'There's a large patch of cloud approaching the sun', he said. 'This scene must be shot in sunlight.'

'One question please.'

'Yes?'

An idea had occurred to Patol Babu while rehearsing; he now came out with it.

'Er – I was thinking – if I had a newspaper open in my hand, and if the collision took place while I had my eyes on the paper, then perhaps –'

Baren Mullick cut him short by addressing a bystander who was carrying a Bengali newspaper. 'D'you mind handing your paper to this gentleman, just for this one shot? Thanks . . . Now you take your position beside the pillar. Chanchal, are you ready?'

'Yes, sir.'

'Good. Silence!'

Baren Mullick raised his hand, then brought it down again, saying, 'Just a minute. Kesto, I think if we gave the pedestrian a moustache, it would be more interesting.'

'What kind, sir? Walrus, Ronald Colman or Butterfly? I have them all ready.'

'Butterfly, butterfly – and make it snappy!'

The elderly make-up man went up to Patol Babu, took out a small grey moustache from a box, and stuck it on with spirit-gum below Patol Babu's nose.

Patol Babu said, 'I hope it won't come off at the time of the collision?'

The make-up man smiled. 'Collision?' he said. 'Even if you were to wrestle with Dara Singh, the moustache would stay in place.'

Patol Babu had a quick glance in a mirror which the man was holding. True enough, the moustache suited him very well. Patol Babu inwardly commended the director's perspicacity.

'Silence! Silence!'

The business with the moustache had provoked a wave of comments from the spectators which Baren Mullick's shout now silenced.

Patol Babu noticed that most of the bystanders' eyes were turned towards him.

'Start sound!'

Patol Babu cleared his throat. One, two, three, four, five – five steps would take him to the spot where the collision was to take place. And Chanchal Kumar would have to walk four

steps. So if both were to start together, Patol Babu would have
to walk a little faster than the hero, or else –

'Running!'

Patol Babu held the newspaper open in his hand. What he
had to do when saying 'Oh!' was mix sixty parts of irritation
with forty parts of surprise.

'Action!'

Clop, clop, clop, clop, clop – Wham!

Patol Babu saw stars before his eyes. The hero's head had
banged against his forehead, and an excruciating pain had
robbed him of his senses for a few seconds.

But the next moment, by a supreme effort of will, Patol Babu
pulled himself together, and mixing fifty parts of anguish with
twenty-five of surprise and twenty-five of irritation, cried 'Oh!'
and, after a brief pause, resumed his walk.

'Cut!'

'Was that all right? asked Patol Babu anxiously, stepping
towards Baren Mullick.

'Jolly good! Why, you're quite an actor! Sosanko, just take a
look at the sky through the dark glass, will you.'

Jyoti now came up to Patol Babu and said, 'I hope Grandpa
wasn't hurt too badly?'

'My God!' said Chanchal Kumar, massaging his head, 'You
timed it so well that I nearly passed out!'

Naresh Dutt elbowed his way through the crowd, came up to
Patol Babu and said, 'Please go back where you were standing.
I'll come to you in a short while and do the necessary.'

Patol Babu took his place once again by the *paan* shop. The
cloud had just covered the sun and brought down the
temperature. Nevertheless, Patol Babu took off his woollen
jacket, and then heaved a sigh of relief. A feeling of total
satisfaction swept over him.

He had done his job really well. All these years of struggle
hadn't blunted his sensibility. Gogon Pakrashi would have
been pleased with his performance. But all the labour and
imagination he had put into this one shot – were these people
able to appreciate that? He doubted it. They just got hold of

some people, got them to go through certain motions, paid them for their labours and forgot all about it. Paid them, yes, but how much? Ten, fifteen, twenty rupees? It is true that he needed money very badly, but what was twenty rupees when measured against the intense satisfaction of a small job done with perfection and dedication?

Ten minutes or so later Naresh Dutt went looking for Patol Babu near the *paan* shop and found that he was not there. That's odd – the man hadn't been paid yet. What a strange fellow!

'The sun has come out,' Baren Mullick was heard shouting. 'Silence! Silence! – Naresh, hurry up and get these people out of the way!'

BIG BILL

By Tulsi Babu's desk in his office on the ninth floor of a building in Old Court House Street there is a window which opens onto a vast expanse of the western sky. Tulsi Babu's neighbour Jaganmoy Dutt had just gone to spit betel juice out of the window one morning in the rainy season when he noticed a double rainbow in the sky. He uttered an exclamation of surprise and turned to Tulsi Babu. 'Come here, sir. You won't see the like of it every day.'

Tulsi Babu left his desk, went to the window, and looked out.

'What are you referring to?' he asked.

'Why, the double rainbow!' said Jaganmoy Dutt. 'Are you colour-blind?'

Tulsi Babu went back to his desk. 'I can't see what is so special about a double rainbow. Even if there were twenty rainbows in the sky, there would be nothing surprising about that. Why, one can just as well go and stare at the double-spired church in Lower Circular Road!'

Not everyone is endowed with the same sense of wonder, but there is good reason to doubt whether Tulsi Babu possesses any at all. There is only one thing that never ceases to surprise him, and that is the excellence of the mutton *kebab* at Mansur's. The only person who is aware of this is Tulsi Babu's friend and colleague, Prodyot Chanda.

Being of such a sceptical temperament, Tulsi Babu was not particularly surprised to find an unusually large egg while looking for medicinal plants in the forests of Dandakaranya.

Tulsi Babu had been dabbling in herbal medicine for the last fifteen years; his father was a well-known herbalist. Tulsi Babu's main source of income is as an upper division clerk in Arbuthnot & Co but he has not been able to discard the family profession altogether. Of late he has been devoting a little more time to it because two fairly distinguished citizens of Calcutta have benefited from his prescriptions, thus giving a boost to his reputation as a part-time herbalist.

It was herbs again which had brought him to Dandakaranya. He had heard that thirty miles to the north of Jagdalpur there lived a holy man in a mountain cave who had access to some medicinal plants including one for high blood pressure which was even more efficacious than *rawolfia serpentina*. Tulsi Babu suffered from hypertension; *serpentina* hadn't worked too well in his case, and he had no faith in homeopathy or allopathy.

Tulsi Babu had taken his friend Prodyot Babu with him on this trip to Jagdalpur. Tulsi Babu's inability to feel surprise had often bothered Prodyot Babu. One day he was forced to comment, 'All one needs to feel a sense of wonder is a little imagination. You are so devoid of it that even if a full-fledged ghost were to appear before you, you wouldn't be surprised.' Tulsi Babu had replied calmly, 'To feign surprise when one doesn't actually feel it, is an affectation. I do not approve of it.'

But this didn't get in the way of their friendship.

The two checked into a hotel in Jagdalpur during the Autumn vacation. On the way, in the Madras Mail, two foreign youngsters had got into their compartment. They turned out to be Swedes. One of them was so tall that his head nearly touched the ceiling. Prodyot Babu had asked him how tall he was and the young man had replied, 'Two metres and seven centimetres.' Which is nearly seven feet. Prodyot Babu couldn't take his eyes away from this young giant during the rest of the journey; and yet Tulsi Babu was not surprised. He said such extraordinary height was simply the result of the diet of the Swedish people, and therefore nothing to be surprised at.

They reached the cave of the holy man Dhumai Baba after walking through the forest for a mile or so then climbing up about five hundred feet. The cave was a large one, but since no sun ever reached it, they only had to take ten steps to be engulfed in darkness, thickened by the ever-present smoke from the Baba's brazier. Prodyot Babu was absorbed in watching, by the light of his torch, the profusion of stalactites and stalagmites while Tulsi Babu enquired after his herbal medicine. The tree that Dhumai Baba referred to was known as *chakraparna*, which is the Sanskrit for 'round leaves'. Tulsi Babu had never heard of it, nor was it mentioned in any of the half-dozen books he had read on herbal medicine. It was not a tree, but a shrub. It was found only in one part of the forest of Dandakaranya, and nowhere else. Baba gave adequate directions which Tulsi Babu noted down carefully.

Coming out of the cave, Tulsi Babu lost no time in setting off in quest of the herb. Prodyot Babu was happy to keep his friend company; he had hunted big game at one time – conservation had put an end to that, but the lure of the jungle persisted.

The holy man's directions proved accurate. Half an hour's walk brought them to a ravine which they crossed and in three minutes they found the shrub seven steps to the south of a *neem* tree scorched by lightning – a waist-high shrub with round green leaves, each with a pink dot in the centre.

'What kind of a place is this?' asked Prodyot Babu, looking around.

'Why, what's wrong with it?'

'But for the *neem*, there isn't a single tree here that I know. And see how damp it is. Quite unlike the places we've passed through.'

It *was* moist underfoot, but Tulsi Babu saw nothing strange in that. Why, in Calcutta itself, the temperature varied between one neighbourhood and another. Tollygunge in the south was much cooler than Shambazar in the north. What was so strange about one part of a forest being different from another? It was nothing but a quirk of nature.

Tulsi Babu had just put the bag down on the ground and stooped towards the shrub when a sharp query from Prodyot Babu interrupted him.

'What on earth is that?'

Tulsi Babu had seen the thing too, but was not bothered by it. 'Must be some sort of egg,' he said.

Prodyot Babu had thought it was a piece of egg-shaped rock, but on getting closer he realised that it was a genuine egg, yellow, with brown stripes flecked with blue. What could such a large egg belong to? A python?

Meanwhile, Tulsi Babu had already plucked some leafy branches off the shrub and put them in his bag. He wanted to take some more but something happened then which made him stop.

The egg chose this very moment to hatch. Prodyot Babu had jumped back at the sound of the cracking shell, but now he took courage to take a few steps towards it.

The head was already out of the shell. Not a snake, nor a croc or a turtle, but a bird.

Soon the whole creature was out. It stood on its spindly legs and looked around. It was quite large; about the size of a hen. Prodyot Babu was very fond of birds and kept a mynah and a bulbul as pets; but he had never seen a chick as large as this, with such a large beak and long legs. Its purple plumes were unique, as was its alert behaviour so soon after birth.

Tulsi Babu, however, was not in the least interested in the chick. He had been intent on stuffing his bag with as much of the herb as would go into it.

Prodyot Babu looked around and commented, 'Very surprising; there seems to be no sign of its parents, at least not in the vicinity.'

'I think that's enough surprise for a day,' said Tulsi Babu, hoisting his bag on his shoulder. 'It's almost four. We must be out of the forest before it gets dark.'

Somewhat against his wish, Prodyot Babu turned away from the chick and started walking with Tulsi Babu. It would take at least half an hour to reach the waiting taxi.

A patter of feet made Prodyot Babu stop and turn round. The chick was following them.

'I say –' called out Prodyot Babu.

Tulsi Babu now stopped and turned. The chick was looking straight at him.

Then it padded across and stopped in front of Tulsi Babu where it opened its unusually large beak and gripped the edge of Tulsi Babu's *dhoti.*

Prodyot Babu was so surprised that he didn't know what to say, until he saw Tulsi Babu pick up the chick and shove it into his bag. 'What d'you think you're doing?' he cried in consternation. 'You put that nameless chick in your bag?'

'I've always wanted to keep a pet,' said Tulsi Babu, resuming his walk. 'Even mongrels are kept as pets. What's wrong with a nameless chick?'

Prodyot Babu saw the chick sticking its neck out of the swinging bag and glancing around with wide-open eyes.

Tulsi Babu lived in a flat on the second floor of a building in Masjidbari Street. Besides Tulsi Babu, who was a bachelor, there was his servant Natobar and his cook Joykesto. There was another flat on the same floor, and this was occupied by Tarit Sanyal, the proprietor of the Nabarun Press. Mr Sanyal was a short-tempered man made even more so by repeated power failures in the city which seriously affected the working of his press.

Two months had passed since Tulsi Babu's return from Dandakaranya. He had put the chick in a cage which he had specially ordered immediately upon his return. The cage was kept in a corner of the inner verandah. He had found a Sanskrit name for the chick: *Brihat-Chanchu,* or Big Bill; soon the Big was dropped and now it was just Bill.

The very first day he had acquired the chick in Jagdalpur, Tulsi Babu had tried to feed it grain. The chick had refused.

Tulsi Babu had guessed, and rightly, that it was probably a meat eater; ever since he has been feeding it insects. Of late the bird's appetite seems to have grown, and Tulsi Babu has been obliged to feed it meat; Natobar buys meat from the market regularly, which may explain the bird's rapid growth in size.

Tulsi Babu had been far-sighted enough to buy a cage which was several sizes too large for the bird. His instinct had told him that the bird belonged to a large species. The roof of the cage was two and a half feet from the ground, but only yesterday Tulsi Babu had noticed that when Bill stood straight its head nearly touched the roof; even though the bird was only two months old, it would soon need a larger cage.

Nothing has so far been said about the cry of the bird, which made Mr Sanyal choke on his tea one morning while he stood on the verandah. Normally the two neighbours hardly spoke to each other; today, after he had got over his fit of coughing, Mr Sanyal demanded to know what kind of an animal Tulsi Babu kept in his cage that yelled like that. It was true that the cry was more beast-like than bird-like.

Tulsi Babu was getting dressed to go to work. He appeared at the bedroom door and said, 'Not an animal, but a bird. And whatever its cry, it certainly doesn't keep one awake at night the way your cat does.'

Tulsi Babu's retort put an end to the argument, but Mr Sanyal kept grumbling. It was a good thing the cage couldn't be seen from his flat; a sight of the bird might have given rise to even more serious consequences.

Although its looks didn't bother Tulsi Babu, they certainly worried Prodyot Babu. The two met rarely outside office hours, except once a week for a meal of *kebab* and *paratha* at Mansur's. Prodyot Babu had a large family and many responsibilities. But since the visit to Dandakaranya, Tulsi Babu's pet was often on his mind. As a result he had started to drop in at Tulsi Babu's from time to time in the evenings. The bird's astonishing rate of growth and the change in its appearance were a constant source of surprise to Prodyot Babu. He was at a loss to see why Tulsi Babu should show no concern about it. Prodyot

Babu had never imagined that the look in a bird's eye could be so malevolent. The black pupils in the amber irises would fix Prodyot Babu with such an unwavering look that he would feel most uneasy. The bird's beak naturally grew as well as its body; shiny black in colour, it resembled an eagle's beak but was much larger in relation to the rest of the body. It was clear, from its rudimentary wings and its long sturdy legs and sharp talons, that the bird couldn't fly. Prodyot Babu had described the bird to many acquaintances, but no one had been able to identify it.

One Sunday Prodyot Babu came to Tulsi Babu with a camera borrowed from a nephew. There wasn't enough light in the cage, so he had come armed with a flash gun. Photography had been a hobby with him once, and he was able to summon up enough courage to point the camera at the bird in the cage and press the shutter. The scream of protest from the bird as the flash went off sent Prodyot Babu reeling back a full yard, and it struck him that the bird's cry should be recorded; showing the photograph and playing back the cry might help in the identification of the species. Something rankled in Prodyot Babu's mind; he hadn't yet mentioned it to Tulsi Babu but somewhere in a book or a magazine he had seen a picture of a bird which greatly resembled this pet of Tulsi Babu's. If he came across the picture again, he would compare it with the photograph.

When the two friends were having tea, Tulsi Babu came out with a new piece of information. Ever since Bill had arrived, crows and sparrows had stopped coming to the flat. This was a blessing because the sparrows would build nests in the most unlikely places, while the crows would make off with food from the kitchen. All that had stopped.

'Is that so?' asked Prodyot Babu, surprised as usual.

'Well, you've been here all this time; have you seen any other birds?'

Prodyot Babu realised that he hadn't. 'But what about your two servants? Have they got used to Bill?'

'The cook never goes near the cage, but Natobar feeds it meat with pincers. Even if he does have any objection, he hasn't come out with it. And when the bird turns nasty, one sight of me calms it down. By the way, what was the idea behind taking the photograph?'

Prodyot Babu didn't mention the real reason. He said, 'When it's no more, it'll remind you of it.'

Prodyot Babu had the photograph developed and printed the following day. He also had two enlargements made. One he gave to Tulsi Babu and the other he took to the ornithologist Ranajoy Shome. Only the other day an article by Mr Shome on the birds of Sikkim had appeared in the weekly magazine *Desh*.

But Mr Shome failed to identify the bird from the photograph. He asked where the bird could be seen, and Prodyot Babu answered with a bare-faced lie. 'A friend of mine has sent this photograph from Osaka. He wanted me to identify the bird for him.'

Tulsi Babu noted the date in his diary: February the fourteenth, 1980. Big Bill, who had been transferred from a three and a half foot cage to a four and a half foot one only last month, had been guilty of a misdeed last night.

Tulsi Babu had been awakened by a suspicious sound in the middle of the night. A series of hard, metallic twangs. But the sound had soon stopped and had been followed by total silence.

Still, the suspicion that something was up lingered in Tulsi Babu's mind. He came out of the mosquito net. Moonlight fell on the floor through the grilled window. Tulsi Babu put on his slippers, took the electric torch from the table, and came out onto the verandah.

In the beam of the torch he saw that the meshing on the cage had been ripped apart and a hole large enough for the bird to escape from had been made. The cage was now empty.

Tulsi Babu's torch revealed nothing on this side of the verandah. At the opposite end, the verandah turned right towards Mr Sanyal's flat.

Tulsi Babu reached the corner in a flash and swung his torch to the right.

It was just as he had feared.

Mr Sanyal's cat was now a helpless captive in Bill's beak. The shiny spots on the floor were obviously drops of blood. But the cat was still alive and thrashing its legs about.

Tulsi Babu now cried out 'Bill' and the bird promptly dropped the cat from its beak.

Then it advanced with long strides, turned the corner, and went quietly back to its cage.

Even in this moment of crisis, Tulsi Babu couldn't help heaving a sigh of relief.

A padlock hung on the door of Mr Sanyal's room; Mr Sanyal had left three days ago for a holiday, after the busy months of December and January when school books were printed in his press.

The best thing to do with the cat would be to toss it out of the window on to the street. Stray cats and dogs were run over every day on the streets of Calcutta; this would be just one more of them.

The rest of the night Tulsi Babu couldn't sleep.

The next day Tulsi Babu had to absent himself from work for an hour or so while he went to the railway booking office; he happened to know one of the booking clerks which made his task easier. Prodyot Babu had asked after the bird and Tulsi Babu had replied he was fine. Then he had added after a brief reflection – 'I'm thinking of framing the photo you took of it.'

On the twenty-fourth of February, Tulsi Babu arrived in Jagdalpur for the second time. A packing case with Bill in it arrived in the luggage van in the same train. The case was provided with a hole for ventilation.

From Jagdalpur, Tulsi Babu set off in a luggage caravan with two coolies and the case, for the precise spot in the forest where he had found the bird.

At a certain milepost on the main road, Tulsi Babu got off the vehicle and, with the coolies carrying the packing case, set off for the scorched *neem* tree. It took nearly an hour to reach the spot. The coolies put the case down. They had already been generously tipped and told that they would have to open the packing case. This was done, and Tulsi Babu was relieved to see that Bill was in fine fettle. The coolies, of course, bolted screaming at the sight of the bird, but that didn't worry Tulsi Babu. His purpose had been served. Bill was looking at him with a fixed stare. Its head already touched the four and a half foot high roof of the cage.

'Good-bye, Bill.'

The sooner the parting took place the better.

Tulsi Babu started on his journey back to the Tempo.

Tulsi Babu hadn't told anybody in the office about his trip, not even Prodyot Babu, who naturally asked where he had been when he appeared at his desk on Monday. Tulsi Babu replied briefly that he had been to a niece's wedding in Naihati.

About a fortnight later, on a visit to Tulsi Babu's place, Prodyot Babu was surprised to see the cage empty. He asked about the bird. 'It's gone,' said Tulsi Babu.

Prodyot Babu naturally assumed that the bird was dead. He felt a twinge of remorse. He hadn't meant it seriously when he had said that the photo would remind Tulsi Babu of his pet when it was no more; he had no idea the bird would die so soon. The photograph he had taken had been framed and was hanging on the wall of the bedroom. Tulsi Babu seemed out of sorts; altogether the atmosphere was gloomy. To relieve the gloom, Prodyot Babu made a suggestion. 'We haven't been to Mansur's in a long while. What about going tonight for a meal of *kebab* and *paratha?*'

'I'm afraid I have quite lost my taste for them.'

Prodyot Babu couldn't believe his ears. 'Lost your taste for *kebabs?* What's the matter? Aren't you well? Have you tried the herb the holy man prescribed?'

Tulsi Babu said that his blood pressure had come down to normal since he tried the juice of the *chakra-parna*. What he didn't bother to mention was that he had forgotton all about herbal medicines as long as Bill had been with him, and that he had gone back to them only a week ago.

'By the way,' remarked Prodyot Babu, 'the mention of the

herb reminds me – did you read in the papers today about the forest of Dandakaranya?'

'What did the papers say?'

Tulsi Babu bought a daily newspaper all right, but rarely got beyond the first page. The paper was near at hand. Prodyot Babu pointed out the news to him. The headline said 'The Terror of Dandakaranya'.

The news described a sudden and unexpected threat to the domestic animals and poultry in the village around the forests of Dandakaranya. Some unknown species of animal had started to devour them. No tigers are known to exist in that area, and proof has been found that something other than a feline species has been causing the havoc. Tigers usually drag their prey to their lairs; this particular beast doesn't. The shikaris engaged by the Madhya Pradesh government had searched for a week but failed to locate any beasts capable of such carnage. As a result, panic has spread amongst the villagers. One particular villager claims that he had seen a two-legged creature running away from his cowshed. He had gone to investigate, and found his buffalo lying dead with a sizeable portion of his lower abdomen eaten away.

Tulsi Babu read the news, folded the paper, and put it back on the table.

'Don't tell me you don't find anything exceptional in the story?' said Prodyot Babu.

Tulsi Babu shook his head. In other words, he didn't.

Three days later a strange thing happened to Prodyot Babu.

At breakfast, his wife opened a tin of Digestive biscuits and served them to her husband with his tea.

The next moment Prodyot Babu had left the dining-table and rushed out of the house.

By the time he reached his friend Animesh's flat in Ekdalia Road, he was trembling with excitement.

He snatched the newspaper away from his friend's hands, threw it aside and said panting: 'Where d'you keep your copies of *Readers' Digest?* Quick – it's most important!'

Animesh shared with millions of others a taste for *Readers'
Digest*. He was greatly surprised by his friend's behaviour but
scarcely had the opportunity to show it. He went to a book-case
and dragged out some dozen issues of the magazine from the
bottom shelf.

'Which number are you looking for?'

Prodyot Babu took the whole bunch, flipped through the
pages of issue after issue, and finally found what he was looking
for.

'Yes – this is the bird. No doubt about it.'

His fingers rested on a picture of a conjectural model of a bird
kept in the Chicago Museum of Natural History. It showed an
attendant cleaning the model with a brush.

'*Andalgalornis*', said Prodyot Babu, reading out the name.
The name meant terror-bird. A huge prehistoric species,
carnivorous, faster than a horse, and extremely ferocious.

The doubt which had crept into Prodyot Babu's mind was
proved right when in the office next morning Tulsi Babu came
to him and said that he had to go to Dandakaranya once again,
and that he would be delighted if Prodyot Babu would join him
and bring his gun with him. There was too little time to obtain
sleeping accommodation in the train, but that couldn't be
helped as the matter was very urgent.

Proydyot Babu agreed at once.

In the excitement of the pursuit, the two friends didn't mind
the discomfort of the journey. Prodyot Babu said nothing about
the bird in the *Readers' Digest*. He could do so later; there was
plenty of time for that. Tulsi Babu had in the meantime told
everything to Prodyot Babu. He had also mentioned that he
didn't really believe the gun would be needed; he had suggested
taking it only as a precaution. Prodyot Babu, on the other hand,
couldn't share his friend's optimism. He believed the gun was
essential, and he was fully prepared for any eventuality.
Today's paper had mentioned that the Madhya Pradesh
government had announced a reward of 5,000 rupees to
anyone who succeeded in killing or capturing the creature,
which had been declared a man-eater ever since a woodcutter's
son had fallen victim to it.

In Jagdalpur, permission to shoot the creature was obtained from the conservator of forests, Mr Tirumalai. But he warned that Tulsi Babu and Prodyot Babu would have to go on their own as nobody could be persuaded to go into the forest any more.

Prodyot Babu asked if any information had been received from the shikaris who had preceded them. Tirumalai turned grave. 'So far four shikaris have attempted to kill the beast. Three of them had no success. The fourth never returned.'

'Never returned?'

'No. Ever since then shikaris have been refusing to go. So you had better think twice before undertaking the trip.'

Prodyot Babu was shaken, but his friend's nonchalance brought back his courage. 'I think we will go,' he said.

This time they had to walk a little further because the taxi refused to take the dirt road which went part of the way into the forest. Tulsi Babu was confident that the job would be over in two hours, and the taxi agreed to wait that long upon being given a tip of fifty rupees. The two friends set off on their quest.

It being springtime now, the forest wore a different look from the previous trips. Nature was following its course, and yet there was an unnatural silence. There were no bird calls; not even the cries of cuckoos.

As usual, Tulsi Babu was carrying his shoulder bag. Prodyot Babu knew there was a packet in it, but he didn't know what it contained. Prodyot Babu himself was carrying his rifle and bullets.

As the undergrowth was thinner they could see farther into the forest. That is why the two friends were able to see from a distance the body of a man lying spread-eagled on the ground behind a jackfruit tree. Tulsi Babu hadn't noticed it, and stopped only when Prodyot Babu pointed it out to him. Prodyot Babu took a firm grip on the gun and walked towards the body. Tulsi Babu seemed only vaguely interested in the matter.

Prodyot Babu went half-way, and then turned back.

'You look as if you've seen a ghost,' said Tulsi Babu when his friend rejoined him. 'Isn't that the missing shikari?'

'It must be,' said Prodyot Babu hoarsely. 'But it won't be easy to identify the corpse. The head's missing.'

The rest of the way they didn't speak at all.

It took one hour to reach the *neem* tree, which meant they must have walked at least three miles. Prodyot Babu noticed that the medicinal shrub had grown fresh leaves and was back to its old shape.

'Bill! Billie!'

There was something faintly comic about the call, and Prodyot Babu couldn't help smiling. But the next moment he realised that for Tulsi Babu the call was quite natural. That he had succeeded in taming the monster bird, Prodyot Babu had seen with his own eyes.

Tulsi Babu's call resounded in the forest.

'Bill! Bill! Billie!'

Now Prodyot Babu saw something stirring in the depths of the forest. It was coming towards them, and at such a speed that it seemed to grow bigger and bigger every second.

It was the monster bird.

The gun in Prodyot Babu's hand suddenly felt very heavy. He wondered if he would be able to use it at all.

The bird slowed down and approached them stealthily through the vegetation.

Andalgalornis. Prodyot Babu would never forget the name. A bird as tall as a man. Ostriches were tall too; but that was largely because of their neck. This bird's back itself was as high as an average man. In other words, the bird had grown a foot and a half in just about a month. The colour of its plumes had changed too. There were blotches of black on the purple. And the malevolent look in its amber eyes which Prodyot Babu found he could confront when the bird was in captivity, was now for him unbearably terrifying. The look was directed at its ex-master.

There was no knowing what the bird would do. Thinking its stillness to be a prelude to an attack, Prodyot Babu had made an attempt to raise the gun with his shaking hands. But the moment he did so, the bird turned its gaze at him, its feathers puffing out to give it an even more terrifying appearance.

'Lower the gun', hissed Tulsi Babu in a tone of admonition.

Prodyot Babu obeyed. Now the bird lowered its feathers too and transferred its gaze to its master.

'I don't know if you are still hungry,' said Tulsi Babu, 'but I hope you will eat this because I am giving it to you.'

Tulsi Babu had already brought out the packet from the bag. He now unwrapped it and tossed the contents towards the bird. It was a large chunk of meat.

'You've been the cause of my shame. I hope you will behave yourself from now on.'

Prodyot Babu saw that the bird picked up the chunk with its huge beak, and proceeded to masticate it.

'This time it really is good-bye.'

Tulsi Babu turned. Prodyot Babu was afraid to turn his back on the bird, and for a while walked backwards with his eyes on the bird. When he found that the bird was making no attempt to follow him or attack him, he too turned round and joined his friend.

A week later the news came out in the papers of the end of the terror in Dandakaranya. Prodyot Babu had not mentioned anything to Tulsi Babu about *Andalgalornis*, and the fact that the bird had been extinct for three million years. But the news in the papers today obliged him to come to his friend. 'I'm at a loss to know how it happened,' he said. 'Perhaps you may throw some light on it.'

'There's no mystery at all,' said Tulsi Babu. 'I only mixed some of my medicine with the meat I gave him.'

'Medicine?'

'An extract of *chakra-parna*. It turns one into a vegetarian. Just as it has done me.'

ASHAMANJA BABU'S DOG

On a visit to a friend in Hashimara, Ashamanja Babu had one of his long cherished wishes fulfilled. Ashamanja Babu lives in a room and a half, in a flat on Mohini Mohan Road in Bhowanipore. As a clerk in the registry department of Lajpat Rai Post Office, Ashamanja Babu is able to avoid the hassle of riding in trams and buses, because it takes him only seven minutes to walk to work. Not being one to sit and brood about what might have been or done had Fate been kinder to him, Ashamanja Babu is quite content with his lot. Two Hindi films, a dozen packets of cigarettes a month, and fish twice a week – these are enough to keep him happy. But being a bachelor and lacking friends, he has often wished to possess a pet dog. Not a large dog like the Talukdar's Alsatian, two houses away to the east, but a medium-sized dog which would keep him company, wag its tail when he came home from work and show love and devotion by obeying his orders. One of Ashamanja Babu's pet conceits was that he would speak to his dog in English. 'Stand up,' 'Sit down,' 'Shake hands' – how nice it would be if his dog obeyed such commands! Ashamanja Babu liked to believe that dogs belonged to the English race. Yes, an English dog, and he

47

would be its master. That would make him really happy.

On a cloudy day marked by a steady drizzle, Ashamanja Babu had gone to the market in Hashimara to buy some oranges. At one end of the market sat a Bhutanese by a stunted *kul* tree holding a cigarette between his thumb and forefinger. As their eyes met, the man smiled. Was he a beggar? His clothes made him seem like one, for there were five patches on his jacket and trousers. But the man didn't have a begging bowl. Instead, by his side was a shoe-box with a little pup sticking its head out from it.

'Good morning!' said the Bhutanese in English, his eyes reduced to slits in a smile. Ashamanja Babu was obliged to return the greeting.

'Buy dog? Dog buy? Very good dog.' The man had taken the pup out of the box and put it down on the ground. 'Very cheap. Very good. Happy dog.'

The pup shook itself free of the raindrops, looked at Ashamanja Babu and wagged its two-inch tail. Nice pup.

Ashamanja Babu moved closer to the pup, crouched on the ground and put his hand towards it. The pup gave his ring finger a lick with his pink tongue. Nice, friendly pup.

'How much? What price?'

'Ten rupees.'

A little haggling, and the price came down to seven-fifty. Ashamanja Babu paid the money, put the pup back in the shoe-box, closed the lid to save it from the drizzle, and turned homewards, forgetting all about the oranges.

Biren Babu, who worked in the Hashimara State Bank, didn't know of his friend's wish to own a dog. He was naturally surprised and a bit alarmed to see what the shoe-box contained. But when he heard the price, he heaved a sigh of relief. He said in a tone of mild reprimand, 'Why come all the way to Hashimara to buy a mongrel? You could easily have bought one in Bhowanipore.'

That was not true. Ashamanja Babu knew it. He had often seen mongrel pups in the streets in his neighbourhood. None of them had ever wagged their tail at him or licked his fingers. Whatever Biren might say, this dog was something special. But the fact that the pup was a mongrel was something of a disappointment to Ashamanja Babu, and he said so. But Biren Babu's retort came sharp and quick.'But do you know what it means to keep a pedigree dog as a pet? The vet's fees alone would cost you half a month's salary. With this dog you have no worries. You don't even need a special diet for him. He'll eat what you eat. But don't give him fish. Fish is for cats; dogs have trouble with the bones.'

Back in Calcutta, it occurred to Ashamanja Babu that he had to think of a name for the pup. He wanted to give it an English name, but the only one he could think of was Tom. Then, looking at the pup one day, it struck him that since it was brown in colour, Brownie would be a good name for it. A cousin of his had a camera of an English make called Brownie, so the name must be an English one. The moment he decided on the name and tried it on the pup, it jumped off a wicker stool and padded up to him wagging its tail. Ashamanja Babu said, 'Sit down.' Right away the pup sat on its haunches and opened its mouth in a tiny yawn. Ashamanja Babu had a fleeting vision of Brownie winning the first prize for cleverness in a dog show.

It was lucky that his servant Bipin had also taken a fancy to the dog. While Ashamanja Babu was away at work, Bipin gladly took it upon himself to look after Brownie. Ashamanja Babu had warned Bipin against feeding the dog rubbish. 'And see that he doesn't go out into the street. The car drivers these days seem to wear blinkers.' But however much he might instruct his servant, his worry would linger until, after returning from work, he would be greeted by Brownie with his wagging tail.

The incident took place three months after returning from Hashimara. It was a Saturday, and the date was November the twenty-third. Ashamanja Babu had just got back from work and sat down on the old wooden chair – the only piece of furniture in the room apart from the bed and the wicker stool – when it suddenly gave under him and sent him sprawling on the floor. He was naturally hurt and, in fact, was led to wonder if, like the rickety leg of the chair, his right elbow was also out of commission, when an unexpected sound made him forget all about his pain.

The sound had come from the bed. It was the sound of laughter or, more accurately, a giggle, the source of which was undoubtedly Brownie, who sat on the bed and whose lips were still curled up.

If Ashamanja Babu's general knowledge had been wider, he would surely have known that dogs never laughed. And if he had a modicum of imagination, the incident would have robbed him of his sleep. In the absence of either, what Ashamanja Babu did was to sit down with the book *All About Dogs* which he had bought for two rupees from a second-hand book shop in Free School Street. He searched for an hour but found no mention in the book about laughing dogs.

And yet there wasn't the slightest doubt that Brownie had laughed. Not only that, he had laughed because there had been cause for laughter. Ashamanja Babu could clearly recall an incident from his own childhood. A doctor had come on a visit to their house in Chandernagore and had sat on a chair which had collapsed under him. Ashamanja Babu had burst out laughing, and had his ears twisted by his father for doing so.

Ashamanja Babu shut the book and looked at Brownie. As their eyes met, Brownie put his front paws on the pillow and wagged his tail, which had grown an inch and a half longer in three months. There was no trace of a smile on his face now. Why should there be? To laugh without reason was a sign of madness. Ashamanja Babu felt relieved that Brownie was not a mad dog.

On two more occasions within a week of this incident, Brownie had occasion to laugh. The first took place at night, at nine-thirty. Ashamanja Babu had just spread a white sheet on the floor for Brownie to sleep on when a cockroach came fluttering into the room and settled on the wall. Ashamanja Babu picked up a slipper and flung it at the insect. But it missed its target, landed on a hanging mirror, and sent it crashing to the floor. This time Brownie's laughter more than compensated for the loss of his mirror.

The second time it was not laughter, but a brief snicker. Ashamanja Babu was puzzled, because nothing had really happened. So why the snicker? The servant Bipin provided the answer. He came into the room, glanced at his master and said, smiling, 'There's shaving-soap right by your ears, sir.' With his mirror broken, Ashamanja Babu had to use one of the window panes for shaving. He now felt with his fingers and found that Bipin was right.

That Brownie should laugh even when the reason was so trifling surprised Ashamanja Babu a great deal. Sitting at his desk in the post office he found his thoughts turning again and again to the smile on Brownie's face and the sound of the snicker. *All About Dogs* may say nothing about a dog's laughter, but if he could get hold of something like an encyclopaedia of dogs, there was sure to be a mention of laughter in it.

When four book shops in Bhowanipore – and all the ones in the New Market – failed to produce such an encyclopaedia, Ashamanja Babu wondered whether he should call on Mr Rajani Chatterji. The retired professor lived not far from his house on the same street. Ashamanja Babu didn't know what subject Rajani Babu had taught, but he had seen through the window of his house many fat books in a book-case in what appeared to be the professor's study.

On a Sunday morning, Ashamanja Babu invoked the name of the goddess Durga for good luck and turned up at Professor Chatterji's. He had seen him several times from a distance, and had no idea he had such thick eyebrows and a voice so grating. But since the professor hadn't turned him away, Ashamanja Babu took courage in occupying a seat on a sofa across the room from him. Then he gave a short cough and waited. Professor Chatterji put aside the newspaper and turned his attention to the visitor.

'Your face seems familiar.'

'I live close by.'

'I see. Well?'

'I have seen a dog in your house; that is why . . .'

'So what? We have two dogs, not one.'

'I see, I have one too.'

'Are you employed to count the number of dogs in the city?'

Being a simple man, Ashamanja Babu missed the sarcasm in the question. He said, 'I have come to ask if you have something I've been looking for.'

'What is it?'

'I wonder if you have a dog encyclopaedia.'

'No, I don't. Why do you need one?'

'You see, my dog laughs. So I wanted to find out if it was natural for dogs to laugh. Do your dogs laugh?'

Throughout the time it took the wall clock in the room to strike eight, Professor Chatterji kept looking at Ashamanja Babu. Then he asked: 'Does your dog laugh at night?'

'Well, yes – even at night.'

'And what are your preferences in drugs? Only *ganja* can't produce such symptoms. Perhaps you take charas and hashish as well?'

Ashamanja Babu meekly answered that his only vice was smoking – and even that he had had to reduce from four packets a week to three ever since the arrival of his dog.

'And yet you say your dog laughs?'

'I have seen and heard him laugh, with my own eyes and ears.'

'Listen.' Professor Chatterji took off his spectacles, cleaned them with his handkerchief, put them on again and fixed Ashamanja Babu with a hard stare. Then he declaimed in the tones of a classroom lecture. 'I am amazed at your ignorance concerning a fundamental fact of nature. Of all the creatures created by God, only the human species is capable of laughter. This is one of the prime differences between *homo sapiens* and other creatures. Don't ask me why it should be so, because I do not know. I have heard that a marine species called the dolphin has a sense of humour. Dolphins may be the single exception. Apart from them there are none. It is not clearly understood why human beings should laugh. Great philosophers have racked their brains to find out why; but have not succeeded. Do you understand?'

Ashamanja Babu understood, and he also understood that it was time for him to take his leave because the professor had once again taken up his newspaper.

Doctor Sukhomoy Bhowmick – some called him Doctor Bhow-wowmick – was a well-known vet. In the belief that if ordinary people didn't listen to him a vet might, Ashamanja Babu made an appointment with him on the phone and turned up at his residence on Gokhale Road. Brownie had laughed seventeen times during the last four months. One thing Ashamanja Babu had noticed is that Brownie didn't laugh at funny remarks; only at funny incidents. Ashamanja Babu had recited the *King of Bombardia* to Brownie, and it had produced no effect on him. And yet when a potato from a curry slipped from Ashamanja Babu's fingers and landed on a plate of curd, Brownie had almost choked with laughter. Professor Chatterji had said that none of God's creatures laughed except human beings, and yet here was proof that the learned gentleman was wrong.

So Ashamanja Babu went to the vet in spite of knowing that the latter charged twenty rupees per visit.

Even before he had heard of the dog's unique trait, its very appearance had the vet's eyebrows shooting up. 'I've seen mongrels, but never one like this.'

The vet lifted the dog and placed him on the table. Brownie sniffed at the brass paperweight at his feet.

'What do you feed him?'

'He eats what I eat, sir. He has no pedigree, you see . . .'

Doctor Bhowmick frowned. He was observing the dog with great interest. 'We can tell a pedigree dog when we see one. But sometimes we are not so sure. This one, for instance. I should hesitate to call him a mongrel. I suggest that you stop feeding him rice and *dal*. I'll make a diet chart for him.'

Ashamanja Babu now made an attempt to come out with the real reason for his visit. 'I – er, my dog has a speciality – which is why I have brought him to you.'

'Speciality?'

'The dog laughs.'

'Laughs – ?'

'Yes. Laughs, like you and me.'

'You don't say! Well, can you make him laugh now so I can see?'

And now Ashamanja Babu was in a quandary. As it is he was a very shy person, so he was quite unable to make faces at Brownie to make him laugh, nor was it likely that something funny should happen here at this very moment. So Ashamanja Babu had to tell the doctor that Brownie didn't laugh when asked to, but only when he saw something funny happening.

After this Doctor Bhowmick didn't have much time left for Ashamanja Babu. He said, 'Your dog looks distinctive enough; don't try to make him more so by claiming that he laughs. I can tell you from my twenty-two years' experience that dogs cry, dogs feel afraid, dogs show anger, hatred, distrust and jealousy. Dogs even dream, but dogs don't laugh.'

After this encounter, Ashamanja Babu decided that he would never tell anyone about Brownie's laughter. When immediate proof was not forthcoming, to talk about it was to court embarrassment. What did it matter if others never knew? He himself knew, Brownie was his own dog, his own property. Why drag outsiders into their own private world?

But man proposes, God disposes. Even Brownie's laughter was one day revealed to an outsider.

For some time now, Ashamanja Babu had developed the habit of taking Brownie for a walk in the afternoon near the Victoria Memorial. One April day, in the middle of their walk, a big storm came up suddenly. Ashamanja Babu glanced at the sky and decided that it wasn't safe to try and get back home as it might start raining any moment. So he ran with Brownie and took shelter below the marble arch with the black equestrian statue on it.

Meanwhile, huge drops of rain had started to fall and people were running this way and that for shelter. A stout man in white bush shirt and trousers, twenty paces away from the arch, opened his umbrella and held it over his head when a sudden strong gust of wind turned the umbrella inside out with a loud snap.

To tell the truth, Ashamanja Babu was himself about to burst out laughing, but Brownie beat him by a neck with a canine guffaw which rose above the sound of the storm and reached the ear of the hapless gentleman. He stopped trying to bring the umbrella back to its original shape and stared at Brownie in utter amazement. Brownie was now quite helpless with laughter, Ashamanja Babu had given up trying to suppress it by clapping his hand over the dog's mouth.

The dumbfounded gentleman now walked over to Ashamanja Babu as if he had seen a ghost. Brownie's paroxysm was now subsiding, but it was still enough to make the gentleman's eyes pop out of his head.

'A laughing dog!'

'Yes, a laughing dog,' said Ashamanja Babu.

'But how extraordinary!'

Ashamanja Babu could make out that the man was not a Bengali. Perhaps he was a Gujrati or a Parsi. Ashamanja Babu braced himself to answer in English the questions he knew he would soon be bombarded with.

The rain had turned into a heavy shower. The gentleman took shelter alongside Ashamanja Babu, and in ten minutes had found out all there was to know about Brownie. He also took Ashamanja Babu's address. He said his name was Piloo Pochkanwalla, that he knew a lot about dogs and wrote about them occasionally, and that his experience today had surpassed everything that had ever happened to him, or was likely to happen in the future. He felt something had to be done about it, since Ashamanja Babu himself was obviously unaware of what a priceless treasure he owned.

It wouldn't be wrong to say that Brownie was responsible for Mr Pochkanwalla being knocked down by a minibus while crossing Chowringhee Road soon after the rain had stopped – it was the thought of the laughing dog running through his head which made him a little unmindful of the traffic. After spending two and half months in hospital, Pochkanwalla had gone off to Naini Tal for a change. He had come back to Calcutta after a month in the hills, and the same evening had described the incident of the laughing dog to his friends Mr Balaporia and Mr Biswas at the Bengal Club. Within half an hour, the story had reached the ears of twenty-seven other members and three bearers of the Club. By next morning, the incident was known to at least a thousand citizens of Calcutta.

Brownie hadn't laughed once during these three and a half months. One good reason was that he had seen no funny incidents. Ashamanja Babu didn't see it as cause for alarm; it had never crossed his mind to cash in on Brownie's unique gift. He was happy with the way Brownie had filled a yawning gap in his life, and felt more drawn to him that he had to any human being.

Among those who got the news of the laughing dog was an executive in the office of the *Statesman*. He sent for the reporter Rajat Chowdhury and suggested that he should interview Ashamanja Babu.

Ashamanja Babu was greatly surprised that a reporter should think of calling on him. It was when Rajat Chowdhury mentioned Pochkanwalla that the reason for the visit became clear. Ashamanja Babu asked the reporter into his bedroom. The wooden chair had been fitted with a new leg, and Ashamanja Babu offered it to the reporter while he himself sat on the bed. Brownie had been observing a line of ants crawling up the wall; he now jumped up on the bed and sat beside Ashamanja Babu.

Rajat Chowdhury was about to press the switch on his recorder when it suddenly occurred to Ashamanja Babu that a word of warning was needed. 'By the way, sir, my dog used to laugh quite frequently, but in the last few months he hasn't laughed at all. So you may be disappointed if you are expecting to see him laugh.'

Like many a young, energetic reporter, Rajat Chowdhury exuded a cheerful confidence in the presence of a good story.

Although he was slightly disappointed he was careful not to show it. He said, 'That's all right. I just want to get some details from you. To start with, his name. What do you call your dog?'

Ashamanja Babu bent down to reach closer to the mike. 'Brownie.'

'Brownie. . .' The watchful eye of the reporter had noted that the dog had wagged his tail at the mention of his name. 'How old is he?'

'A year and a month.'

'Where did you f-f-find the dog?'

This had happened before. The impediment Rajat Chowdhury suffered often showed itself in the middle of interviews, causing him no end of embarrassment. Here too the same thing might have happened but for the fact that the stammer was unexpectedly helpful in drawing out Brownie's unique trait. Thus Rajat Chowdhury was the second outsider after Pochkanwalla to see with his own eyes a dog laughing like a human being.

The morning of the following Sunday, sitting in his air-conditioned room in the Grand Hotel, Mr William P. Moody of Cincinnati, USA, read in the papers about the laughing dog and at once asked the hotel operator to put him through to Mr Nandy of the Indian Tourist Bureau. That Mr Nandy knew his way about the city had been made abundantly clear in the last couple of days when Mr Moody had occasion to use his services. The *Statesman* had printed the name and address of the owner of the laughing dog. Mr Moody was very anxious to meet this character.

Ashamanja Babu didn't read the *Statesman*. Besides, Rajat Chowdhury hadn't told him when the interview would come out, or he might have bought a copy. It was in the fish market that his neighbour Kalikrishna Dutt told him about it.

'You're a fine man,' said Mr Dutt. 'You've been guarding such a treasure in your house for over a year, and you haven't breathed a word to anybody about it? I must drop in at your place some time this evening and say hello to your dog.'

Ashamanja Babu's heart sank. He could see there was trouble ahead. There were many more like Mr Dutt in and around his neighbourhood who read the *Statesman* and who would want 'to drop in and say hello' to his dog. A most unnerving prospect.

Ashamanja Babu made up his mind. He decided to spend the day away from home. Taking Brownie with him, he took a taxi for the first time, went straight to the Ballygunge station and boarded a train to Port Canning. Half-way through, the train pulled up at a station called Palsit. Ashamanja Babu liked the look of the place and got off. He spent the whole day in quiet bamboo groves and mango orchards and felt greatly refreshed. Brownie, too, seemed to enjoy himself. The gentle smile that played around his lips was something Ashamanja Babu had never noticed before. This was a benign smile, a smile of peace and contentment, a smile of inner happiness. Ashamanja Babu had read somewhere that a year in the life of a dog equalled seven years in the life of a human being. And yet he could scarcely imagine such tranquil behaviour in such sylvan surroundings from a seven-year-old human child.

It was past seven in the evening when Ashamanja Babu got back home. He asked Bipin if anyone had called. Bipin said he had to open the door to callers at least forty times. Ashamanja Babu couldn't help congratulating himself on his foresight. He had just taken off his shoes and asked Bipin for a cup of tea when there was a knock on the front door. 'Oh, hell!' swore Ashamanja Babu. He went to the door and opened it, and found himself facing a foreigner. 'Wrong number' he was at the point of saying, when he caught sight of a young Bengali standing behind the foreigner. 'Whom do you want?'

'You,' said Shyamol Nandy of the Indian Tourist Bureau, 'in case the dog standing behind you belongs to you. He certainly looks like the one described in the papers today. May we come in?'

Ashamanja Babu was obliged to ask them into his bedroom. The foreigner sat in the chair, Mr Nandy on the wicker stool, and Ashamanja Babu on his bed. Brownie, who seemed a bit ill

at ease, chose to stay outside the threshold; probably because
he had never seen two strangers in the room before.

'Brownie! Brownie! Brownie!' The foreigner had leaned
forward towards the dog and called him repeatedly by name to
entice him into the room. Brownie, who didn't move, had his
eyes fixed on the stranger.

Who were these people? The question had naturally
occurred to Ashamanja Babu when Mr Nandy provided the
answer. The foreigner was a wealthy and distinguished citizen
of the United States whose main purpose in coming to India
was to look for old Rolls-Royce cars.

The American had now got off the chair and, sitting on his
haunches, was making faces at the dog.

After three minutes of abortive clowning, the man gave up,
turned to Ashamanja Babu and said, 'Is he sick?'

Ashamanja Babu shook his head.

'Does he really laugh?' asked the American.

In case Ashamanja Babu was unable to follow the American's speech, Mr Nandy translated it for him.

'Brownie laughs,' said Ashamanja Babu, 'but only when he
feels amused.'

A tinge of red spread over the American's face when Nandy
translated Ashamanja Babu's answer to him. Next, he let it be
known that he wasn't willing to squander any money on the dog
unless he had proof that the dog really laughed. He refused to
be saddled with something which might later cause embarrassment. He further let it be known that in his house he had
precious objects from China to Peru, and that he had a parrot
which spoke only Latin. 'I have brought my chequebook with
me to pay for the laughing dog, but only if it laughed.'

The American now pulled out a blue chequebook from his
pocket to prove his statement. Ashamanja Babu glanced at it
out of the corner of his eyes. CitiBank of New York, it said on
the cover.

'You would be walking on air,' said Mr Nandy temptingly.
'If you know a way to make the dog laugh, then out with it. This
gentleman is ready to pay up to 20,000 dollars. That's two lakhs
of rupees.'

The Bible says that God created the universe in six days. A human being, using his imagination, can do the same thing in six seconds. The image that Mr Nandy's words conjured up in Ashamanja Babu's mind was of himself in a spacious air-conditioned office, sitting in a swivel chair with his legs up on the table, with the heady smell of *hasu-no-hana* wafting in through the window. But the image vanished like a pricked balloon at a sudden sound.

Brownie was laughing,

This was like no laugh he had ever laughed before.

'But he *is* laughing!'

Mr Moody had gone down on his knees, tense with excitement, watching the extraordinary spectacle. The cheque-book came out again and, along with that, his gold Parker pen.

Brownie was still laughing. Ashamanja Babu was puzzled because he couldn't make out the reason for the laughter. Nobody had stammered, nobody had stumbled, nobody's umbrella had turned inside out, and no mirror on the wall had been hit with a slipper. Why then was Brownie laughing?

'You're very lucky,' commented Mr Nandy. 'I think I ought to get a percentage on the sale – wouldn't you say so?'

Mr Moody had now risen from the floor and sat down on the chair. He said, 'Ask him how he spells his name.'

Although Mr Nandy had relayed the question in Bengali, Ashamanja Babu didn't answer, because he had just seen the light, and the light filled his heart with a great sense of wonder. Instead of spelling his name, he said, 'Please tell the foreign gentleman that if he only knew why the dog was laughing, he wouldn't have opened his chequebook,'

'Why don't you tell me?' Mr Nandy snapped in a dry voice. He certainly didn't like the way events were shaping. If the mission failed, he knew the American's wrath would fall on him.

Brownie had at last stopped laughing. Ashamanja Babu lifted him up on his lap, wiped his tears and said, 'My dog's laughing because the gentleman thinks money can buy everything.'

'I see,' said Mr Nandy. 'So your dog's a philosopher, is he?'

'Yes, sir.'

'That means you won't sell him?'

'No, sir.'

To Mr Moody, Shyamol Nandy only said that the owner had no intention of selling the dog. Mr Moody put the chequebook back in his pocket, slapped the dust off his knees and, on his way out of the room, said with a shake of his head, 'The guy must be crazy!'

When the sound of the American car had faded away, Ashamanja Babu looked into Brownie's eyes and said, 'I was right about why you laughed, wasn't I?'

Brownie chuckled in assent.

RATANBABU AND THAT MAN

Stepping out of the train on the platform, Ratanbabu heaved a
sigh of relief. The place seemed quite inviting. A *shirish* tree
reared its head from behind the station house, and there was a
spot of red in its green leaves where a kite was caught in a
branch. The few people around seemed relaxed and there was a
pleasant earthy smell in the air. All in all, he found the
surroundings most agreeable.

As he had only a small holdall and a leather suitcase, he
didn't need a coolie. He lifted his luggage with both hands and
made for the exit.

He had no trouble finding a cycle rickshaw outside.

'Where to, sir?' asked the young driver in striped shorts.

'You know the New Mahamaya hotel?' asked Ratanbabu.

The driver nodded. 'Hop in, sir.'

Travelling was almost an obsession with Ratanbabu. He
would go out of Calcutta whenever the opportunity came, not
that it came so often. Ratanbabu had a regular job. For
twenty-four years, he had been a clerk in the Calcutta Office of
the Geological Survey. He could really get away only once a
year, when he would latch his yearly leave on to the *Puja*

holidays and set off all by himself. He never took anyone with him, nor would it have occurred to him to do so. There was a time when he had felt the need of companionship; in fact, he had once talked about it to Keshabbabu who occupied the adjacent desk in his office. It was a few days before the holidays; in the planning stage. 'You're pretty much on your own, like me,' he had said. 'Why don't we go off together somewhere this time?'

Keshabbabu had stuck his pen in his ear, put his palms together and said with a wry smile, 'I don't think you and I have the same tastes, you know. You go to places no one has heard of, places where there's nothing much to see, nor any decent places to stay or eat at. No sir, I'd sooner go to Harinabhi and visit my brother-in-law.'

In time, Ratanbabu had come to realise that there was virtually no one who saw eye to eye with him. His likes and dislikes were quite different from the average person's, so it was best to give up hopes of finding a suitable companion.

There was no doubt that Ratanbabu possessed traits which were quite unusual. Consider these trips of his. Keshabbabu had been quite right: Ratanbabu was never attracted to places where people normally went for vacations. 'All right', he would say, 'so there is the sea in Puri and there is the temple of Jagannath; and you can see the Kanchanjungha from Darjeeling, and there are hills and forests in Hazaribagh and the Hundroo falls in Ranchi. So what? You've heard them described so many times that you almost feel you've seen them yourself.'

What Ratanbabu looked for was a little town somewhere with a railway station not too far away. Every year before the holidays he would open the timetable, pick such a town and sally forth. No one bothered to ask where he was going and he never told anyone. In fact, there had been occasions when he had gone to places he had never even heard of, and whenever he had gone he had discovered things to delight him. To others, such things might appear trivial, like the old fig tree in Rajabhatkhaoa which coiled itself around a *kul* and a coconut tree: or the ruins of the indigo factory in Maheshgunj: or the delicious *dal barfi* sold in a sweet shop in Moina. . .

This time Ratanbabu has come to a town called Shini, fifteen miles from Tatanagar. Shini was not picked from the timetable; it was his colleague Anukul Mitra who had mentioned it. The New Mahamaya hotel, too, was recommended by him.

To Ratanbabu, the hotel seemed quite adequate. His room wasn't large, but that didn't matter. There were windows to the east and the south with pleasant views of the countryside. The servant Pancha seemed an amiable sort. Ratanbabu was in the habit of bathing twice a day in tepid water throughout the year, and Pancha had assured him that there would be no trouble about that. The cooking was passable, and this was all right too, because Ratanbabu was not fussy about food. There was only one thing he insisted on: he needed to have rice with the fish curry and *chapati* with *dal* and vegetables. He had informed Pancha about this as soon as he had arrived, and Pancha had passed on the information to the manager.

Another habit of Ratanbabu's when he arrived in a new place was to go for a walk in the afternoon. The first day at Shini was no exception. He finished the cup of tea brought by Pancha and was out by four.

After a few minutes' walk he found himself in open country. The terrain was uneven and criss-crossed with paths. Ratanbabu chose one at random and after half an hour's walk, discovered a charming spot. It was a pond with water lilies growing in it and a large variety of birds in and around it. Of these there were some – cranes, snipes, kingfishers, magpies – which Ratanbabu recognised, the others were unfamiliar.

Ratanbabu could cheerfully have spent all his afternoons sitting beside this pond, but on the second day he took a different path in the hope of discovering something new. Having walked a mile or so, he had to stop for a herd of goats to cross his path. As the road cleared, he went on for another five minutes until a wooden bridge came into view. Going a little further, he realised it had railway lines passing below it. He went and stood on the bridge. To the east could be seen the railway station; to the west the parellel lines stretched as far as the eye could see. What if a train were suddenly to appear and go thundering underneath? The very thought thrilled Ratanbabu.

Perhaps because he had his eyes on the tracks, he failed to notice another man who came and stood beside him. Ratanbabu looked around and gave a start.

The stranger was clad in a *dhoti* and shirt, carried a snuff-coloured wrapper on his shoulder, wore bifocals and brown canvas shoes. Ratanbabu had an odd feeling. Where had he seen this person before? Wasn't there something familiar about him? Medium height, medium complexion, a pensive look in his eyes. . . How old could he be? Surely not over fifty.

The stranger smiled and folded his hands in greeting. Ratanbabu was about to return the greeting when he realised in a flash why he had that odd feeling. No wonder the stranger's face seemed familiar. He had seen that face many, many times – in his own mirror. The resemblance was uncanny. The squarish jaw with the cleft chin, the way the hair was parted, the carefully trimmed moustache, the shape of the earlobes – they were all strikingly like his own. Only the stranger seemed a shade fairer, his eyebrows a little bushier and the hair at the back a trifle longer.

Now the stranger spoke, and Ratanbabu had another shock. Sushanto, a boy from his neighbourhood, had once recorded his voice in a tape recorder and played it back to him. There was no difference between that voice and the one that spoke now.

'My name is Manilal Majumdar. I believe you're staying at the New Mahamaya?'

Ratanlal – Manilal. . . the names were similar too. Ratanbabu managed to shake off his bewilderment and introduced himself.

The stranger said, 'I don't suppose you'd know, but I have seen you once before.'

'Where?'

'Weren't you in Dhulian last year?'

Ratanbabu's eyebrows shot up. 'Don't tell me you were there too!'

'Yes, sir. I go off on trips every *Puja*. I'm on my own. No friends to speak of. It's fun to be in a new place all by yourself. A collegue of mine recommended Shini to me. Nice place isn't it?'

Ratanbabu swallowed, and then nodded assent. He felt a strange mixture of disbelief and uneasiness in his mind.

'Have you seen the pond on the other side where a lot of birds gather in the evening?' asked Manilalbabu.

Ratanbabu said yes, he had.

'Some of the birds I could recognise', said Manilalbabu, 'others I have never seen before in Bengal. What d'you think?'

Ratanbabu had recovered somewhat in the meantime. He said, 'I had the same feeling; some birds I didn't recognise either.'

Just then a booming sound was heard. It was a train. Ratanbabu saw a point of light growing bigger as it approached from the east. Both Ratanbabu and Manilalbabu moved up close to the railing of the bridge. The train hurtled up and passed below them, causing the bridge to shake. Both men now crossed to the other side and kept looking until the train disappeared from view. Ratanbabu felt the same thrill as he did as a small boy. 'How strange!' said Manilalbabu, 'Even at this age watching trains never fails to excite me.'

On the way back Ratanbabu learnt that Manilalbabu had arrived in Shini three days ago. He was staying at the Kalika Hotel. His home was in Calcutta where he had a job in a trading company. One doesn't ask another person about his salary, but an indomitable urge made Ratanbabu throw discretion to the wind and put the question. The answer made him gasp in astonishment. How was such a thing possible? Both Ratanbabu and Manilalbabu drew exactly the same salary – four hundred and thirty-seven rupees a month – and both had received exactly the same *Puja* bonus.

Ratanbabu found it difficult to believe that the other man had somehow found out all about him beforehand and was playing some deep game. No one had ever bothered about him before; he had kept very much to himself. Outside his office he spoke only to his servant and never made calls on anyone. It was just possible for an outsider to find out about his salary, but such details as when he went to bed, his tastes in food, what newspapers he read, what plays and films he had seen lately – these were known only to himself. And yet everything tallied exactly with what this man was saying.

He couldn't tell this to Manilalbabu. All he did was listen to what the man had to say and marvel at the extraordinary similarity. He revealed nothing about his own habits.

They came to Ratanbabu's hotel first, and stopped in front of it. 'What's the food here like?' asked Manilalbabu.

'They make a good fish curry,' replied Ratanbabu, 'the rest is just adequate.'

'I'm afraid the cooking in my hotel is rather indifferent,' said Manilalbabu, 'I've heard they make very good *luchis* and *chholar dal* at the Jagannath Restaurant. What about having a meal there tonight?'

'I don't mind,' said Ratanbabu, 'shall we meet around eight then?'

'Right. I'll wait for you, then we'll walk down together.'

After Manilalbabu left, Ratanbabu roamed about in the street for a while. Darkness had fallen. It was a clear night, indeed, so clear that the Milky Way could be seen stretching from one end of the star-filled sky to the other. What a strange thing to happen! All these years Ratanbabu had regretted that he couldn't find anyone to share his tastes and become friends with him. Now at last in Shini he has run into someone who might be said to be an exact replica of himself. There was a slight difference in looks, perhaps, but in every other respect such identity was rare even amongst twins.

Did it mean that he had found a friend at last?

Ratanbabu couldn't find a ready answer to the question. Perhaps he would find it when he got to know the man a little better. One thing was clear – he no longer had the feeling of being isolated from his fellow men. All along there had been another person exactly like him, and he had quite by chance come to know him.

In the Jagannath Restaurant, sitting face-to-face across the table, Ratanbabu observed that, like him, Manilalbabu ate with a fastidious relish; like him, didn't drink any water during the meal; and like him, he squeezed lemon into the *dal*. Ratanbabu always had sweet curd to round off his meals, and so did Manilalbabu.

While eating, Ratanbabu had the uncomfortable feeling that diners at other tables were watching them. Did they observe how alike they were? Was the identity so obvious to onlookers?

After dinner, Ratanbabu and Manilalbabu walked for a while in the moonlight. There was something which Ratanbabu wanted to ask, and he did so now. 'Have you turned fifty yet?'

Manilalbabu smiled. 'I'll soon be doing so,' he said, 'I'll be fifty on the twenty-ninth of December.'

Ratanbabu's head swam. They were both born on the same day: the twenty-ninth of December, 1916.

Half an hour later, as they were taking leave, Manilalbabu said, 'It has been a great pleasure knowing you. I don't seem to get on very well with people, but you're an exception. I can now look forward to an enjoyable vacation.'

Usually, Ratanbabu was in bed by ten. He would glance through a magazine, and gradually feel drowsiness stealing over him. He would put down the magazine, turn off the bedlamp and within a few minutes would start snoring softly. Tonight he found that sleep wouldn't come. Nor did he feel like reading. He picked up the magazine and put it down again.

Manilal Majumdar. . .

Ratanbabu had read somewhere that of the billions of people who inhabited the earth, no two looked exactly alike. And yet every one had the same number of features – eyes, ears, nose, lips and so on. But even if no two persons looked alike, was it possible for them to have the same tastes, feelings, attitudes – as in the present case? Age, profession, voice, gait, even the power of their glasses – were identical. One would think such a thing impossible, and yet here was proof that it was not, as Ratanbabu had learnt again and again in the last four hours.

At about midnight, Ratanbabu got out of bed, poured some water from the carafe and splashed it on his head. Sleep was impossible in his feverish state. He passed a towel lightly over his head and went back to bed. At least the wet pillow would keep his head cool for a while.

Silence had descended over the neighbourhood. An owl went screeching overhead. Moonlight streamed in through the window and onto the bed. Presently, Ratanbabu's mind regained its calm and his eyes closed of their own accord.

As sleep had come late, it was almost eight when Ratanbabu woke up next morning. Manilalbabu was supposed to come at nine. Today was Tuesday – the day when the weekly market or *haat* was held at a spot a mile or so away. The night before the two had almost simultaneously expressed a wish to visit the *haat*, more to look around than to buy anything.

It was almost nine when Ratanbabu finished breakfast. He helped himself to a pinch of *mouri* from the saucer on the table, came out of the hotel and saw Manilalbabu approaching.

'I couldn't sleep for a long time last night,' were Manilalbabu's first words. 'I lay thinking how alike you and I were. It was five to eight when I woke this morning. I am usually up by six.'

Ratanbabu refrained from comment. The two set off towards the *haat*. They had to pass some youngsters standing in a cluster by the roadside. 'Hey, look at Tweedledum and Tweedledee!' one of them cried out. Ratanbabu tried his best to ignore the remark and went on ahead. It took them about twenty minutes to reach the *haat*.

The *haat* was a bustling affair. There were shops for fruits and vegetables, for utensils, clothes and even livestock. The two men wove their way through the milling crowd casting glances at the goods on display.

Who was that there? Wasn't it Pancha? For some reason, Ratanbabu couldn't bring himself to face the hotel servant. That remark about Tweedledum and Tweedledee had made him realise it would be prudent not to be seen alongside Manilalbabu.

As they jostled through the crowd, a thought suddenly occurred to Ratanbabu. He realised he was better off as he was – alone, without a friend. He didn't need a friend. Or, at any rate, not someone like Manilalbabu. Whenever he had spoken to Manilalbabu, it had seemed as if he was carrying on a conversation with himself. It was as if he knew all the answers before he asked the questions. There was no room for argument, no possibility of misunderstanding. Were these signs of friendship? Two of his colleagues, Kartik Ray and Mukunda Chakravarty, were bosom friends. Did that mean they had no arguments? Of course they did. But they were still friends – close friends.

It struck him again and again that it would have been better if Manilalbabu hadn't come into his life. Even if there existed two identical men, it was wrong that they should meet. The very thought that they might continue to meet even after returning to Calcutta made Ratanbabu shudder.

One of the shops was selling cane walking sticks. Ratanbabu had always wanted to possess one, but seeing Manilalbabu haggling with the shopkeeper, he checked himself. Manilalbabu bought two sticks and gave one to Ratanbabu saying, 'I hope you won't mind accepting this as a token of our friendship.'

On the way back to the hotel, Manilalbabu spoke a lot about himself – his childhood, his parents, his school and college days. Ratanbabu felt that his own life story was being recounted.

The plan came to Ratanbabu in the afternoon as the two were on their way to the railway bridge. He didn't have to talk much, so he could think. He had been thinking since midday of getting rid of this man, but he couldn't decide on a method. Ratanbabu had just turned his eye to the clouds gathering in the west when the method suddenly appeared to him with a blazing clarity. The vision he saw was of the two of them standing by the railing of the bridge. In the distance the mail train was approaching. When the engine approached to within twenty yards, Ratanbabu gathered his strength and gave a hefty push –

Ratanbabu inadvertently closed his eyes. Then he opened them again and shot a glance at his companion. Manilalbabu seemed quite unconcerned. But if the two had so much in common, perhaps he too was thinking of a way to do him in?

But his looks didn't betray any such thoughts, as a matter of fact, he was humming a Hindi film tune which Ratanbabu himself was in the habit of humming from time to time.

The dark clouds had just covered the sun which would in any case set in a few minutes. Ratanbabu looked about and saw they were quite alone. Thank God for that. Had there been anyone else, his plan wouldn't have worked.

It was strange that even though his mind was bent on murder, Ratanbabu couldn't think of himself as a culprit. Had Manilalbabu possessed any traits which endowed him with a personality different from his own, Ratanbabu could never have thought of killing him. He believed that there was no sense in both of them being alive at the same time. It was enough that he alone should continue to exist.

The two arrived at the bridge.

'Bit stuffy today,' commented Manilalbabu. 'It may rain tonight, and that could be the start of a cold spell.'

Ratanbabu stole a glance at his wrist-watch. Twelve minutes to six. The train was supposed to be very punctual. There wasn't much time left. Ratanbabu contrived a yawn to ease his tension. 'Even if it does rain,' he said, 'it is not likely to happen for another four or five hours.'

'Care for a betel nut?'

Manilalbabu had produced a small round tin box from his pocket. Ratanbabu too was carrying a metal box with betel nuts in it, but didn't mention the fact to Manilalbabu. He helped himself to a nut and tossed it into his mouth.

Just then was heard the sound of the train.

Manilalbabu advanced towards the railing, glanced at his watch and said, 'Seven minutes before time.'

Because of the thick cloud in the sky, it had grown a little darker than usual. This made the headlight seem brighter in contrast. The train was still far away but the light was growing brighter every second.

'Krrrring. . . . Krrring. . '

A cyclist was approaching from the road towards the bridge. Good God! Was he going to stop?

No. Ratanbabu's apprehension proved baseless. The cyclist rode swiftly past them and disappeared into the gathering darkness down the other side of the road.

The train was hurtling up at great speed. It was impossible to gauge the distance owing to the blinding glare of the headlight. In a few seconds the bridge would start shaking.

Now the sound of the train was deafening.

Manilalbabu was looking down with his hands on the railings. A flash of lightning in the sky – and Ratanbabu gathered all his strength, flattened his palms against the back of Manilalbabu, and heaved. Manilalbabu's body vaulted over the four-foot high railing and plummeted down towards the on-rushing engine. That very moment the bridge began to shake.

Ratanbabu didn't wait to see the train vanishing into the horizon. Like the bridge, he too felt a tremor within himself. The cloud had spread from the west and there were occasional flashes of lightning.

Ratanbabu wound his wrapper tighter and started on his way back.

Towards the end of his journey he had to break into a run in a vain effort to avoid being pelted by the first big drops of rain. Panting with the effort, he rushed into the hotel.

As soon as he entered he felt there was something wrong.

Where had he come? The lobby of the New Mahamaya was not like this at all – the tables, the chairs, the pictures on the wall. . .

Looking around, his eye was suddenly caught by a signboard on the wall. What a stupid mistake! He had come into the Kalika Hotel instead. Isn't this where Manilalbabu was staying?

'So you couldn't avoid getting wet?'

Somebody had put the question to him. Ratanbabu turned round and saw a man with curly hair and a green shawl –

probably a resident of the hotel – looking at him with a cup of tea in his hand. 'Sorry,' said the man, seeing Ratanbabu's face, 'for a moment I thought you were Manilalbabu.'

It was this mistake which raised the first doubts in Ratanbabu's mind. Had he been careful enough about the crime he had committed? Many must have seen the two of them going out together, but had they really noticed? Would they remember what they had seen? And if they did, would the suspicion then fall on him? That no one had seen them after they had reached the outskirts of the town he was sure of. And after reaching the bridge – oh, yes, the cyclist. He must have seen them both. But by that time it had turned quite dark. The cyclist passed by at a high speed. Was it likely that he would remember their faces? Certainly not.

The more Ratanbabu pondered, the more reassured he felt. There was no doubt that Manilalbabu's dead body would be discovered. But that it would lead to him being suspected of the crime, that he would be tried, found guilty, and brought to the gallows – all this he just could not believe.

Since it was still raining, Ratanbabu stayed for a cup of tea. Around seven-thirty the rain stopped and Ratanbabu went directly to the New Mahamaya. He found it almost funny the way he had blundered into the wrong hotel.

At dinner, he ate well and with relish; then he slipped into bed with a magazine, read an article on the aborigines of Australia, turned off the bedlamp and closed his eyes with not a worry in his mind. Once again he was on his own; and unique. He didn't have a friend, and didn't need one. He would spend the rest of his days in exactly the same way he had done so far. What could be better?

It had started to rain again. There were flashes of lightning and peals of thunder. But none of it mattered. Ratanbabu had already started to snore.

'Did you buy that stick from the *haat*, sir?' asked Pancha when he brought Ratanbabu his morning tea.

'Yes', said Ratanbabu.

'How much did you pay for it?'

Ratanbabu mentioned the price. Then he asked casually, 'Were you at the *haat* too?'

Pancha broke into a broad smile. 'Yes, sir,' he said, 'and I saw you. Didn't you see me?'

'Why, no.'

That ended the Pancha episode.

Finishing tea, Ratanbabu made his way to the Kalika Hotel. The curly-haired man was talking to a group of people outside the hotel. Ratanbabu heard Manilalbabu's name and the word 'suicide' mentioned several times. He edged closer to hear better. Not only that, he was bold enough to put a question.

'Who has committed suicide?'

The curly-haired man said, 'It was the same man I had mistaken you for yesterday.'

'Suicide, was it?'

'It looks like that. The dead body was found by the railway tracks below the bridge. Looks as if he threw himself from it. An odd character, he was. Hardly spoke to anyone. We used to talk about him.'

'I suppose the dead body. . . ?'

'In police custody. Came here for a change of air from Calcutta. Didn't know anyone here. Nothing more has been found out.'

Ratanbabu shook his head, made a few clucking noises and went off.

Suicide! So nobody had thought of murder at all. Luck was on his side. How simple it was, this business of murder! He wondered what made people quail at the thought.

Ratanbabu felt quite light-hearted. After two whole days he would now be able to walk alone again. The very thought filled him with pleasure.

It was probably while he pushed Manilalbabu yesterday that a button from his shirt had come off. He found a tailor's shop and had the button replaced. Then he went into a store and bought a tube of Neem toothpaste.

Walking a few steps from the store he heard the sound of

Kirtan coming from a house. He stood for a while listening to the song, then made for the open terrain outside the town. He walked a mile or so along a new path, came back to the hotel about eleven, had his bath and lunch, and took his afternoon nap.

As usual he woke up around three, and realised almost immediately that he had to pay another visit to the bridge that evening. For obvious reasons he had not been able to enjoy the sight of the train yesterday. The sky was still cloudy but it didn't seem that it would rain. Today he would be able to watch the train from the moment it appeared till it vanished into the horizon.

He had his afternoon tea at five and went down into the lobby. The manager Shambhubabu sat at his desk by the front door. He saw Ratanbabu and said, 'Did you know the man who was killed yesterday?'

Ratanbabu looked at Shambhubabu, feigning surprise. Then he said, 'Why do you ask?'

'Well, it's only that Pancha mentioned he had seen you two together in the *haat*.'

Ratanbabu smiled. 'I haven't really got to know anyone here,' he said calmly. 'I did speak to a few people in the *haat*, but the fact is, I don't even know which person was killed.'

'I see,' said Shambhubabu, laughing. He was prone to laughter, being jovial by nature. 'He too had come for a change,' he added. 'He put up at the Kalika.'

'I see.'

Ratanbabu went out. It was a two-mile walk to the bridge. If he didn't hurry he might miss the train.

In the street nobody cast suspicious glances at him. Yesterday's youngsters were not in their usual place. That remark about Tweedledum and Tweedledee had nettled him. He wondered where the boys were. The sound of drums could be heard from somewhere close by. There was a *puja* on in the neighbourhood. That's where the boys must have gone. Good.

Today he was all by himself on the path in the open field. He was a contented person even before he had met Manilalbabu; but today he felt more relaxed than ever before.

There it was – the *babla* tree. A few minutes' walk from the tree was the bridge. The sky was still overcast, but not with thick black clouds like yesterday. These were grey clouds, and there being no breeze, the whole sky stood ashen and still.

Ratanbabu's heart leaped with joy at the sight of the bridge. He quickened his pace. Who knows, the train might turn up even earlier than yesterday. A flock of cranes passed overhead. Migratory cranes? He couldn't tell.

As he stood on the bridge, Ratanbabu became aware of the stillness of the evening. Straining his ears, he could hear faint drumbeats from the direction of the town. Otherwise all was quiet.

Ratanbabu moved over to the railing. He could see the signal, and beyond that, the station. What was that now? Lower down the railing, in a crack in the wood was lodged a shiny object. Ratanbabu bent down and prised it out. A small round tin box with betel nuts in it. Ratanbabu smiled and tossed it over the railing. A metallic clink was heard as it hit the ground. Who knows how long it would lie there?

What was that light?

Ah, the train. No sound yet, just an advancing point of light. Ratanbabu stood and stared fascinated at the headlight. A sudden gust of wind whipped the wrapper off his shoulder. Ratanbabu wrapped it properly around him once more.

Now he could hear the sound. It was like the low rumble of an approaching storm.

Ratanbabu suddenly had the feeling that somebody had come and stood behind him. It was difficult to take his eyes away from the train, but even so he cast a quick glance around. Not a soul anywhere. Being not so dark as yesterday, the visibility was much better. No, except for himself and that approaching train, there was no one for miles around.

The train had now approached within a hundred yards. Ratanbabu edged further towards the railing. Had the train been an old-fashioned one with a steam engine, he couldn't have gone so close to the edge as the smoke would have got into his eyes. This was a smokeless diesel engine. There was only a deep, earthshaking rumble and the blinding glare of the headlight.

Now the train was about to go under the bridge.

Ratanbabu placed his elbows on the railing and leaned forward to watch.

At that very moment a pair of hands came up from behind and gave him a savage push. Ratanbabu went clean over the four-foot high railing.

As usual, the train made the bridge shudder as it passed under it and sped towards the west where the sky had just begun to turn purple.

Ratanbabu is no longer on the bridge, but as a token of his presence a small shining object is stuck in a crack in the wooden railing.

It is an aluminium box with betel nuts in it.

NIGHT OF THE INDIGO

My name is Aniruddha Bose. I am twenty-nine and a bachelor. For the last eight years I've been working in an advertising agency in Calcutta. With the salary I get I live in reasonable comfort in a flat in Sardar Shankar Road. It consists of two rooms on the first floor facing south. Two years ago I bought an Ambassador car which I drive myself. I do a bit of writing in my spare time. Three of my stories have been published in magazines and have earned the praise of my acquaintances, but I know I cannot make a living by writing alone. The last few months I haven't written at all, but have read a lot about indigo plantations in Bengal and Bihar in the nineteenth century. I am something of an authority on the subject now: how the English started the cultivation of indigo here; how they exploited the poor peasants; how the peasants rose in revolt, and how, finally, with the invention of synthetic indigo in Germany, the cultivation of indigo was wiped out from our country – all this I know by heart. It is to describe the terrible experience which instilled in me this interest in indigo that I have taken up my pen today.

At this point I must tell you something about my past.

My father was a well-known physician in Monghyr, a town in Bihar. That is where I was born and that is where I went to a missionary school. I have a brother five years older than me. He studied medicine in England and is now attached to a hospital in a suburb of London called Golders Green. He has no plans to return to India.

My father died when I was sixteen. Soon after his death, my mother and I left Monghyr and came to Calcutta where we stayed with my maternal uncle. I went to St Xavier's College and took my bachelor's degree. Soon after that I got my job with the advertising agency. The backing of my uncle helped, but I wasn't lacking in qualities as a candidate myself. I had been a good student, I spoke English fluently, and I had the ability to carry myself well in an interview.

The fact that I had spent my early years in Monghyr will help to explain one of my traits. From time to time I long to get away from the hectic life of Calcutta. I have done so several times ever since I bought my car. On weekends I have made trips to Diamond Harbour, to Port Canning, to Hassanabad along the Dum Dum Road. Each time I have gone alone because, to be quite honest, I don't really have a close friend in Calcutta. That is why Promode's letter made me so happy. Promode had been my classmate in Monghyr. After I came away to Calcutta, we continued to keep in touch for three or four years. Then, perhaps it was I who stopped writing. Suddenly the other day when I came back from work, I found a letter from Promode waiting for me on my desk. He had written from Dumka – 'I have a job in the Forest Department here. I have my own quarters. Why don't you take a week's leave and come over. . . ?'

Some leave was due to me, so I spoke to my boss, and on the twenty-seventh of April – I shall remember the date as long as I live – I packed my bags and set off for Dumka.

Promode hadn't suggested that I go by car; it was my idea. Dumka was 200 miles away, so it would take about five or six hours at the most. I decided to have an early lunch, set off by ten and reach there before dusk.

At least that was the plan, but there was a snag right at the start. I had my meal and was about to toss a *paan* into my mouth when my father's old friend Uncle Mohit suddenly turned up – a man of grave deportment whom I was meeting again after ten years. So there was no question of giving him short shrift. I had to offer him tea and listen to him chat for over an hour.

I saw Uncle Mohit off and shoved my suitcase and my bedding into the back seat of my car. Just then I saw my ground floor neighbour Bhola Babu walking up with his four-year-old son Pintu in tow.

'Where are you off to all by yourself?' Bhola Babu asked.

When I told him, he said with some concern, 'But that's a long way. Shouldn't you have arranged for a driver?'

I said I was a very cautious driver myself, and that I had taken such care of my car that it was still as good as new – 'So there's nothing to worry about.'

Bhola Babu wished me luck and went into the house. I glanced at my wrist-watch before turning the ignition key. It was ten minutes past eleven.

Although I avoided Howrah and took the Bally Bridge road, it took me an hour and a half to reach Chandernagore. Driving through dingy towns, these first thirty miles were so dreary that the fun of a car journey was never in evidence. But from here on, as the car emerged into open country, the effect was magical. When did one see such clear blue sky free from chimney smoke, and breathe air so pure and so redolent of the smell of earth?

At about half past twelve, when I was nearing Burdwan, I began to feel the consequence of having an early lunch. I felt hungry. I pulled up by the station which fell on the way, went into the restaurant and had a light meal consisting of toast, omelette and coffee. Then I resumed my journey. I still had a hundred and thirty-five miles to go.

Twenty miles from Burdwan was the small town of Panagarh. There I should have to leave the Grand Trunk Road and take the road to Ilambazar. From Ilambazar the road went via Suri and Massanjore to Dumka.

The military camp at Panagarh had just come into view

when there was a bang from the rear of my car. I had a flat tyre.

I got down from the car. I had a spare tyre and could easily fit it. The thought that other cars would go whizzing by and that their occupants would laugh at my predicament was not a pleasant one. Nevertheless I brought out the jack from the boot and set to work.

By the time I finished putting the new tyre on, I was dripping with sweat. My watch showed half past two. It had turned muggy in the meantime. The cool breeze which was blowing even an hour ago, and which made the bamboo trees sway, had stopped. Now everything was still. As I got back into the car I noticed a blue-black patch in the west above the tree tops. Cloud. Did it portend a storm? A nor'wester? It was useless to speculate. I must drive faster. I helped myself to some hot tea from the flask and resumed my journey.

Before I had crossed Ilambazar, I was caught in the storm. I had enjoyed such nor'westers in the past, sitting in my room, and had even recited Tagore poems to chime with the mood. I had no idea that, driving through open country, such a nor'wester could strike terror into the heart. Thunderclaps always make me uncomfortable. They seem to show a nasty side of nature; a vicious assault on helpless humanity. It seemed as if the shafts of lightning were all aimed at my poor Ambassador, and one of them was sure to find its mark sooner of later.

In this precarious state I passed Suri and was well on my way to Massanjore when there was yet another bang which no one could mistake for a thunderclap, I realised that one more of my tyres had decided to call it a day.

I gave up hope. It was now pouring with rain. My watch said half past five. For the last twenty miles I had had to keep the speedometer down to fifteen, or I would have been well past Massanjore by now. Where was I? Up ahead nothing was visible through the rainswept windscreen. The wiper was on but its efforts were more frolicsome that effective. Being April, the sun should still be up, but it seemed more like late evening.

I opened the door on my right slightly and looked out. What

I saw didn't suggest the presence of a town, but I could make out a couple of buildings through the trees. There was no question of getting out of the car and exploring, but one thing was clear enough: there were no shops along the road as far as the eye could see.

And I had no more spare tyres.

After waiting in the car for a quarter of an hour, it struck me that no other vehicles had passed in all this time. Was I on the right road? There had been no mistake up to Suri, but suppose I had taken a wrong turning after that? It was not impossible in the blinding rain.

But even if I had made a mistake, it was not as if I had strayed into the jungles of Africa or South America. Wherever I was, there was no doubt that I was still in the district of Birbhum, within fifty miles of Santiniketan, and as soon as the rain stopped my troubles would be over – I might even find a repair shop within a mile or so.

I brought out my packet of Wills from my pocket and lit a cigarette. I recalled Bhola Babu's warning. He must have been through the same trying experience, or how could he have given me such sound advice? In future –

'Honk! Honk! Honk!'

I turned round and saw a truck standing behind. But why was it blowing its horn? Was I standing right in the middle of the road?

The rain had let up a little. I opened the door, got out and found that it was no fault of the truck's. When my tyre burst the car had swerved at an angle and was now blocking most of the road. There was no room for the truck to pass.

'Take the car to one side, sir.'

The Sikh driver had by now come out of the truck.

'What's the matter?' he asked. 'A puncture?'

I shrugged to convey my state of helplessness. 'If you could lend a hand,' I said, 'we could move the car to one side and let you pass.'

The Sikh driver's helper too came out. The three of us pushed the car to one side of the road. Then I found out by asking that this was not the road to Dumka at all. I had indeed taken a wrong turning. I should have to drive back three miles to get back on the right track. I also learnt that there were no repair shops nearby.

The truck went on its way. As its noise faded away, the truth struck me like a hammer blow.

I had reached an impasse.

There was no way I could reach Dumka tonight, and there was no knowing how and where I would spend the night.

The roadside puddles were alive with the chorus of frogs. The rain had now been reduced to a light drizzle.

I got back into the car. I was about to light a second cigarette when I spotted a light through the window on my side. I opened the door again. Through the branches of a tree I saw a rectangle of orange light. A window. Just as smoke meant the presence of fire, a kerosene lamp meant the presence of a human being. There was a house nearby and there were occupants in it.

I got out of the car with my torch. The window wasn't too far away. I had to go and investigate. There was a narrow footpath branching off from the main road which seemed to go in the direction of the house with the window.

I locked the door of the car and set off.

I made my way avoiding puddles as far as possible. As I passed a tamarind tree, the house came into view. Well, hardly a house. It was a small cottage with a corrugated tin roof. Through an open door I could see a hurricane lantern and the leg of a bed.

'Is anybody there?' I called out.

A stocky, middle-aged man with a thick moustache came out of the room and squinted at my torch. I turned the spot away from his face.

'Where are you from, sir?' the man asked.

In a few words I described my predicament. 'Is there a place here where I can spend the night?' I asked, 'I shall pay for it, of course.'

'In the dak bungalow, you mean?'

Dak bungalow? I didn't see any dak bungalow.

But immediately I realised my mistake. Because of the presence of the lantern, I had failed to look around. Now I turned the torch to my left and immediately a large, one-storey bungalow came into view, 'You mean that one?' I asked.

'Yes sir, but there is no bedding. And you can't have meals here.'

'I'm carrying my own bedding,' I said, 'I hope there's a bed there?'

'Yes sir. A *charpoy*.'

'And I see there's an oven lighted in your room. You must be cooking your own meal?'

The man broke into a smile and asked if I would care for coarse *chapati* prepared by him and *urut-ka-dal* cooked by his wife. I said they would do very nicely. I liked all kinds of chapatis, and *urut* was my favourite *dal*.

I don't know what it was like in its heyday, but now it was hardly what one understood by a dak bungalow. But belonging to the time of the Raj, the bedroom was large and the ceiling was high. The furniture consisted of a *charpoy*, a table set against the wall on one side, and a chair with a broken arm.

The *chowkidar*, or the caretaker, had in the meantime lighted a lantern for me. He brought it and put it on the table. 'What is your name?' I asked.

'Sukhanram, sir.'

'Has anybody ever lived in this bungalow or am I the first one?'

'Oh, no sir, others have come too. There was a gentleman who stayed here two nights last winter.'

'I hope there are no ghosts here,' I said in a jocular tone.

'God forbid!' he said, 'No one has ever complained of ghosts.'

I must say I found his words reassuring. If a place is spooky, and old dak bungalows have a reputation for being so, it will be so at all times. 'When was this bungalow built?' I asked.

Sukhan began to unroll my bedding and said, 'This used to be a sahib's bungalow, sir.'

'A sahib?'

'Yes sir. An indigo planter. There used to be an indigo factory close by. Now only the chimney is standing.'

I knew indigo was cultivated in these parts at one time. I had seen ruins of indigo factories in Monghyr too in my childhood.

It was ten-thirty when I went to bed after dining on Sukhan's coarse *chapatis* and *urut-ka-dal*. I had sent a telegram to Promode from Calcutta saying that I would arrive this afternoon. He would naturally wonder what had happened. But it was useless to think of that now. That I had found a shelter, and that too without much trouble, was something I could congratulate myself on. In future I would do as Bhola Babu had advised. I had learnt a lesson, and a lesson learnt the hard way goes deeper.

I put the lantern in the adjoining bathroom. The little light that seeped through the door which I kept slightly ajar was enough. I can't sleep if there's a light on in my room, and yet what I most badly needed now was sleep. I was worried about my car which I had left standing on the road, but it was certainly safer to do so in a village than in the city.

The sound of drizzle had stopped. The air was now filled with the croaking of frogs and the shrill chirping of crickets. Lying in this ancient bungalow in this remote village, the city seemed to belong to another planet. Indigo. . . I thought of the play by Dinabandhu Mitra – *The Mirror of Indigo*. As a college student I had watched a performance of it in a theatre in Cornwallis Street.

I didn't know how long I had slept, but I was suddenly awakened by a sound. It was a sound of scratching which came from the door. The door was bolted. Must be a dog or a jackal. In a minute or so the sound stopped.

I shut my eyes in an effort to sleep, but only for a short while. The barking of a dog put an end to my efforts. This was not the bark of a stray village dog, but the unmistakable bay of a hound. I was familiar with it. Two houses away from us in Monghyr lived Mr Martin. He had a hound which bayed just like this. Who on earth kept a pet hound here? I thought of opening the door to find out because the sound came from quite near. But then I thought; why bother? It was better to get some more sleep. What time was it now?

A faint moonlight came in through the window. I raised my left hand to glance at the wrist-watch, and gave a start. There was no wrist-watch.

And yet, because it was an automatic watch, I always wore it to bed. Where did it disappear? And how? Are there thieves around? What will happen to my car then?

I felt beside my pillow for my torch and found that was gone too.

I jumped out of bed, knelt on the floor and looked underneath it. My suitcase too had disappeared.

My head started spinning. Something had to be done about it. I called out: '*Chowkidar!*'

There was no answer.

I went to the door and found it was still bolted. The window had bars. So how did the thief enter?

As I was about to unfasten the bolt, I glanced at my hand and experienced an odd feeling.

Had whitewash from the wall got on to my hand? Or was it white powder? Why did it look so pale?

I had gone to bed wearing a vest; why then was I wearing a long-sleeved silk shirt?

I felt a throbbing in my head. I opened the door and went out on the verandah.

'*Chowkidar!*'

The word that came out was spoken with the unmistakable accent of an Englishman. And where was the *chowkidar,* and where was his little cottage? There was now a wide open field in front of the bungalow. In the distance was a building with a high chimney. The surroundings were unusually quiet.

And they had changed.

And so had I.

I came back into the bedroom in a sweat. My eyes had got used to the darkness. I could now clearly make out the details. The bed was there, but it was covered with a mosquito net. I hadn't been using one. The pillow too was unlike mine. This one had a border with frills; mine didn't. The table and the chair stood where they did, but they had lost their aged look.

The varnished wood shone even in the soft light. On the table stood not a lantern but a kerosene lamp with an ornate shade.

There were other objects in the room which gradually came into view: a pair of steel trunks in a corner, a folding bracket on the wall from which hung a coat, an unfamiliar type of headgear and a hunting crop. Below the bracket, standing against the wall was a pair of galoshes.

I turned away from the objects and took another look at myself. Till now I had only noticed the silk shirt: now I saw the narrow trousers and the socks. I didn't have shoes on, but saw a pair of black boots on the floor by the bed.

Now I passed my right hand over my face and realised that not only my complexion but my features too had changed. I didn't possess such a sharp nose, nor such thin lips or narrow chin. I felt the hair on my head and found that it was wavy and that there were sideburns which reached below my ears.

Along with surprise and terror, I felt a great urge to find out what I looked like. But where to find a mirror?

I strode towards the bathroom, opened the door with a sharp push and went in.

I had earlier noticed that there was nothing there but a bucket. Now I saw a metal bath tub, and a mug kept on a stool beside it. The thing I was looking for was right in front of me: an oval mirror fixed to a dressing-table. Although I stood facing the mirror, the person reflected in it was not me. By some devilish trick I had turned into a nineteenth-century Englishman, with a sallow complexion, blond hair and light eyes which showed a strange mixture of hardness and suffering. How old would the Englishman be? Not more than thirty, but it looked as if either illness or hard work or both had aged him prematurely.

I went closer and had a good look at 'my' face. As I looked a deep sigh rose from the depths of my heart.

The voice was not mine. The sigh, too, expressed not my feelings but those of the Englishman.

What followed made it clear that all my limbs were acting of their own volition. And yet it was surprising that I – Aniruddha

Bose – was perfectly aware of the change in identity. But I didn't know if the change was temporary or permanent or if there was any way to regain my lost self.

I came back to the bedroom.

Now I glanced at the table. Below the lamp was a notebook bound in leather. It was open at a blank page. Beside it was an inkwell with a quill pen dipped in it.

I walked over to the table. Some unseen force made me sit in the chair and pick up the pen with my right hand. The hand with the pen now moved towards the left-hand page of the notebook. Now the silent room was filled with the scratching noise of a quill pen writing on the blank page. This is what I wrote:

April 27, 1868

Those fiendish mosquitoes are singing in my ears again. So that's how the son of a mighty Empire had to meet his end – at the hands of a tiny insect. What strange will of God is this? Eric has made his escape. Percy and Tony too left earlier. Perhaps I was greedier than them. So in spite of repeated attacks of malaria I couldn't resist the lure of indigo. No, not only that. One mustn't lie in one's diary. My countrymen know me only too well. I didn't lead a blameless life at home either; and that they surely have not forgotten. So I do not dare go back home. I know I will have to stay here and lay down my life on this alien soil. My place will be beside the graves of my wife Mary and my dear little son Toby. I have treated the natives here so badly that there is no one to shed a tear at my passing away. Perhaps Mirjan would miss me – my faithful trusted bearer Mirjan.

And Rex? My real worry is about Rex. Alas, faithful Rex! When I die, these people will not spare you. They will either stone you or club you to death. If only I could do something about you!'

I could write no more. The hands were shaking. Not mine, but the diarist's.

I put down the pen.

Now my right hand came down from the table, moved to the right and made for the handle of the drawer.

The drawer opened.

Inside there was a pin cushion, a brass paperweight, a pipe and some papers.

Now the drawer opened a little more. A metal object glinted in the half-light.

It was a pistol, its butt inlaid with ivory.

The hand brought out the pistol. The shaking stopped.

A group of jackals cried out. It was as if in answer to the jackal's cry that the hound bayed again.

I left the chair and advanced towards the door. Then through the door out onto the verandah.

The field in front was bathed in moonlight.

About ten yards from the verandah stood a large greyhound. He wagged his tail as he saw me.

'Rex!'

It was the same deep English voice. The echo of the call came floating back from the faraway factory and bamboo grove – Rex! Rex!

Rex came up towards the verandah.

As he stepped from the grass on to the cement, my right hand rose to my waist, the pistol pointing towards the hound. Rex stopped in his tracks, his eye on the pistol. He gave a low growl.

My right forefinger pressed the trigger.

As the gun throbbed with a blinding flash, smoke and the smell of gunpowder filled the air.

Rex's lifeless, blood-spattered body lay partly on the verandah and partly on the grass.

The sound of the pistol had wakened the crows in the nearby trees. A hubbub now rose from the direction of the factory.

I came back into the bedroom, bolted the door and sat on the bed. The shouting drew near.

I placed the still hot muzzle of the pistol by my right ear.

That is all I remember.

*

I woke up at the sound of knocking.

'I've brought your tea, sir.'

Daylight flooded in through the window. Out of sheer habit my eyes strayed to my left wrist.

Thirteen minutes past six. I brought the watch closer to my eyes to read the date, April the twenty-eighth.

I now opened the door and let Sukhanram in.

'There's a car repair shop half an hour down the road, sir,' he said, 'it'll open at seven.'

'Very good,' I said, and proceeded to drink my tea.

Will anyone believe me when they hear of my experience on the one hundredth anniversary of the death of an English indigo planter in Birbhum?

THE DUEL

'Do you know what the word "duel" means?' asked Uncle Tarini.

'Oh yes,' said Napla. 'Dual means double. Some actors play dual roles in films.'

'Not that kind of dual,' Uncle Tarini said, laughing. 'D-U-E-L, not D-U-A-L. Duel means a fight between two persons.'

'Yes, yes, of course,' we all shouted together.

'I once read up on duels out of curiosity,' went on Uncle Tarini. 'The practice of duelling spread from Italy to the rest of Europe in the sixteenth century. Swords were then part of a gentleman's dress, and sword-play or fencing was part of their education. If a person was insulted by someone, he would immediately challenge the other to a duel in order to save his own honour. Whether the honour was saved or not depended on the challenger's skill as a swordsman. But even when the skill was lacking, the duel took place because to swallow an insult was looked upon in those days as the height of cowardice.

'In the eighteenth century the pistol replaced the sword as the duelling weapon. This led to so many deaths that there was a move to pass a law against duelling. But if one ruler banned it, the next one would relax the law and duelling would rear its head again.'

Uncle Tarini took a sip of milkless tea, cleared his throat and continued.

'A duel was fought according to a set of strict rules. Such as identical weapons to be used by both parties, each to have his "second" or referee to see that no rules were broken: the obligatory gap of twenty yards between the two opponents, and both pistols to be fired the moment the challenger's second gave the command.'

As usual we were impressed with Uncle Tarini's fund of knowledge, which was little short of his fund of experience. We knew that all this rigmarole – or 'instructive information', as Uncle Tarini called it – was a prelude to yet another episode from his colourful life. All we had to do was bide our time before we would be regaled with what Uncle Tarini called fact but which struck us as being more fiction-like than fiction.

'I don't know if you are aware,' resumed Uncle Tarini, 'that a famous duel took place in our country – in fact, in Calcutta itself – two hundred years ago.'

Even Napla didn't know, so we all shook our heads.

'One of the two who fought was a world-famous person: the Govenor General Warren Hastings. His adversary was Philip Francis, a member of the Viceroy's Council. Hastings had written an acrimonious letter to Francis which made the latter challenge him to a duel. You know the National Library in Alipur – the duel took place in an open spot not far from it. Since Francis was the challenger, a friend of his procured the pistols and served as his second. The pistols were both fired at the same time, but only one of the two men was felled by a bullet: Philip Francis. Luckily the wound was not fatal.'

'That's history,' said Napla. 'It's time we had a story, Uncle Tarini. Of course, living in the twentieth century, *you* couldn't possibly have taken part in a duel.'

'No,' said Uncle Tarini, 'but I watched one.'

'Really?'

Uncle Tarini took another sip of milkless tea, lighted an export-quality *bidi* and began his story.

I was then living in Lucknow. I had no regular job and no need for one because a couple of years earlier I had won a lakh and a half rupees in the Rangers Lottery. The interest on it was enough to keep me in clover. This was in 1951. Everything cost less then and, being a bachelor, one could live in comfort on six or seven hundred rupees a month. I lived in a small bungalow on La Touche Road, wrote occasional pieces for the *Pioneer*, and paid regular visits to an auction house in Hazratgunj. In those days one could still pick up objects belonging to the time of the great Nawabs. One made a sizeable profit by buying them cheap and selling them at a good price to American tourists. I was both a dealer and a collector. Although my sitting-room was small, it was crowded with objects bought at this auction house.

Going to the auction house one Sunday morning, I saw a brown mahogany box lying amongst the items to be sold. It was a foot and a half long, about eight inches wide and three inches high. I couldn't guess what it contained, and this made me very curious indeed. There were other things being auctioned, but I had my eyes only on the mahogany box.

After an hour of disposing of other objects, the auctioneer picked up the box. I sat up expectantly. The usual praises were sung. 'May I now present to you something most attractive and unique. Here you are, ladies and gentlemen, as good as new although more than a hundred years old. A pair of duelling pistols made by the famous firm of Joseph Manton. A pair without compare!'

I was immediately hooked. I had to possess those pistols. My imagination had started working. I could see the duellists facing each other, the bullets flying, and the bloody conclusion.

As my mind worked and the bidding went on, I suddenly heard a Gujerati gentleman cry out 'Seven hundred and fifty!' I at once topped it with a bid of a thousand rupees. This ended the bidding and I found myself the owner of the pistols.

Back home, I opened the box and found that the pistols were even more attractive than I thought they were in the auction house. They were truly splendid specimens of the gunsmith's art. The name of the maker was carved on the butt of each pistol. From the little I had read about weapons, I knew that Joseph Manton was a most distinguished name among the gunsmiths of eighteenth-century Britain.

I had arrived in Lucknow three months earlier. I knew there were many Bengalis living there, but I hadn't met any so far. In the evenings, I usually stayed at home writing or listening to music on the gramophone. I had just sat down at my desk to write a piece on the Hastings–Francis encounter when the doorbell rang. Perhaps a customer? I had already built up a small reputation as a supplier of antiques.

I opened the door and found a sahib standing outside. He was in his mid-forties and looked clearly like someone who had spent a long time in India. Indeed, he could well have been an Anglo-Indian.

'Good evening.'

I returned his greeting, and he said, 'Do you have a minute? There's something I wanted to discuss with you.'

'Please come in.'

There was no trace of an Indian accent in the man's speech. He came in, and I could see him more clearly in the light of the lamp. He was a good-looking man with blue eyes, reddish-brown hair and a stout moustache. I apologised for not being able to offer him any liquor, but perhaps he would care for a cup of tea or coffee? The sahib refused saying that he had just had dinner. Then he went straight to the reason for his visit.

'I saw you at the auction house in Hazratgunj this morning.'

'Were you there too?'

'Yes, but you were probably too preoccupied to see me.'

'The fact is, my mind was on something which had caught my eye.'

'And you succeeded in acquiring it. A pair of duelling pistols made by Joseph Manton. You were very lucky.'

'Did they belong to someone you know?'

'Yes, but he has been dead for a long time. I don't know where the pistols went after his death. D'you mind if I take a look at them? I happen to know an interesting story about them . . .'

I handed him the mahogany box. He opened the lid, took out one of the pistols and held it in the light of the lamp. I could see that his eyebrows had gone up and a faraway look had come into his eyes. 'Do you know,' he said, 'that these pistols were used in a duel which was fought in this very city?'

'A duel in Lucknow!'

'Yes. It took place a hundred years ago. In fact, it will be exactly a hundred years three days from now – on October the sixteenth!'

'How extraordinary! But who fought the duel?'

The sahib returned the pistols and sat down on the sofa. 'The whole thing was so vividly described to me that I can almost see it before my eyes. There was a very beautiful woman in Lucknow in those days. She was called Annabella, the daughter of Doctor Jeremiah Hudson. She was not only beautiful but also formidable in that she could ride a horse and wield a gun as well as any man. Besides this she was an accomplished singer and dancer. A young portrait painter, John Illingworth by name, had just arrived in Lucknow hoping for a commission for the Nawab himself. When he heard of Annabella's beauty, he turned up in the house of Doctor Hudson with an offer to paint her portrait. Illingworth got the commission, but before the portrait was finished he had fallen deeply in love with the sitter.

'Some time earlier, Annabella had been to a party where she had met Charles Bruce, a captain in the Bengal Regiment. Bruce too had lost his heart to Annabella at first sight.

'Soon after the party, Bruce called on Annabella at her residence. He found her seated on the verandah posing for her portrait to a stranger. Illingworth was an attractive young man and it took little time for Bruce to realise that he had a rival in the painter.

'Now, Bruce regarded painters with scant respect. On this occasion he chose to make a remark to Illingworth in the presence of Annabella which clearly showed his attitude of disdain.

'As befits the practitioner of a gentle art, Illingworth was of a mild disposition. Nevertheless, the insult in the presence of the woman he loved was something he couldn't swallow. He challenged Bruce to a duel forthwith. Bruce took up the challenge, and the date and time of the duel were settled on the spot. Now, I suppose you know that each participant in a duel has to have a second?'

I nodded.

'Usually the second is a friend of the challenger,' said the sahib. 'Illingworth's circle of acquaintances in Lucknow was not very large, but there was one whom he could call a friend. This was a government employee by the name of George Drummond. Drummond agreed to be his second and to procure a pair of identical pistols. On the opposite side, Charles Bruce asked his friend Philip Moxon to be his second.

'The day of the duel drew near. Everyone knew what the outcome would be, because Charles Bruce was a superb marksman while Illingworth was not nearly as adept with the gun as with the paint brush.'

The sahib stopped. I asked him eagerly, 'Well, what *was* the outcome?'

The sahib smiled and said, 'You can find that out for yourself.'

'How?'

'Every year on October the sixteenth the duel is re-enacted.'

'Where?'

'In the same spot where it took place. To the east of Dilkhusha, below a tamarind tree by the river Gumti.'

'What do you mean by re-enacted?'

'Just what I say. If you were to come at six in the morning the day after tomorrow, you will see the whole incident before your eyes.'

'But that is impossible! Do you mean to say –'

'You don't have to take my word for it. All you have to do is go and see for yourself.'

'I would very much like to, but I don't think I could find my way there. I haven't been here long, you know.'

'Do you know Dilkhusha?'

'Yes, I do.'

'I will wait outside the gate of Dilkhusha at a quarter to six in the morning of October the sixteenth.'

'Very well.'

The sahib bade good-night and left. It was then that it struck me that I hadn't asked his name. But then he didn't ask mine either. Anyway, the name wasn't important; it was what he had said that mattered. It was hard to believe that Lucknow had been the scene of such chivalry and romance, and that I was in possession of a pair of pistols which had played such an important part in it. But who really won the hand of Annabella in the end? And which of the two did she really love?

The alarm clock woke me up at five on the morning of the sixteenth. I had a cup of tea, wrapped a muffler around my neck and set off for Dilkhusha in a *tonga*. Dilkhusha had been at one time Nawab Sadat Ali's country house. There used to be a spacious park around it where deer roamed and into which an occasional leopard strayed from the forests nearby. Now only the shell of the house remained and a garden which was tended and open to the public.

At twenty to six I reached my destination. In my best Urdu, I told the *tongawallah* to wait as I would be going back home in half an hour's time.

I had to walk only a few steps from the *tonga* to find the sahib waiting for me below an *arjun* tree. He said he had arrived only five minutes ago. We started to walk.

In a few minutes we found ourselves in an open field. The view ahead was shrouded in mist. Perhaps it had been misty on the morning of the duel too.

Another minute's walk brought us to a dilapidated cottage which must have belonged to some sahib in the last century.

We stood with our backs to the ruins and faced east. In spite of the mist I could clearly make out the huge tamarind tree at some distance from us. To our right, about twenty yards away, stood a large bush. Beyond the tree and the bush I could dimly discern the river; its water reflecting the eastern sky just beginning to turn pink. The surroundings were eerily quiet.

'Can you hear it?' asked my companion suddenly.

Yes, I could. The sound of horses' hooves. I can't deny that I felt a chill in my bones. At the same time, I was gripped by the keen anticipation of a unique experience.

Now I saw the two riders. They rode down our left, pulled up below the tamarind tree and dismounted.

'Are those the two duellists?' I asked in a whisper.

'Only one of them,' said my companion. 'The taller of the two is John Illingworth, the challenger. The other is his friend and second, George Drummond. You can see Drummond is carrying the mahogany box.'

Indeed he was. I couldn't make out the faces in the mist, but I could clearly see the box. It gave me a very strange feeling to see it in the hands of someone when I knew the same box was at this very moment lying in my house locked up in my trunk.

Presently two more riders arrived and dismounted.

'The blond one is Bruce,' whispered my companion.

Drummond now consulted a pocket-watch and nodded to the two protagonists. The two took their positions face-to-face. Then they turned right about and each took fourteen paces in the opposite direction from the other. Then they stopped, swung round and faced each other again.

The protagonists now raised their pistols and took aim. The next moment the silence was broken by Drummond's command: 'FIRE!'

The shots rang out, and I was astonished to see both Bruce and Illingworth fall to the ground.

But there was something else that caught my eye now. It was the hazy figure of a woman running out from behind the bush and disappearing into the mist away from the group around the tamarind tree.

'Well, you saw what happened,' said my companion. 'Both men were killed in the duel.'

I said, 'Very well, but who was the woman I saw running away?'

'That was Annabella.'

'Annabella?'

'Annabella had realised that Illingworth's bullet wouldn't kill Bruce, and yet she wanted both of them out of the way. So she hid behind the bush with a gun which she fired at Bruce the moment the command was given. Illingworth's bullet went wide of the mark.'

'But why did Annabella behave like that?'

'Because she loved neither of the two men. She realised that Illingworth would be killed in the duel leaving Bruce free to court her against her will. She didn't want that because she loved someone else – someone she went on to marry and find happiness with.'

I could see the scene of a hundred years ago swiftly fading before my eyes. The mist was growing thicker by the minute. I was thinking of the extraordinary Annabella when a woman's voice startled me.

'George! Georgie!'

'That's Annabella,' I heard my companion saying.

I turned to him and froze. Why was he suddenly dressed in the clothes of a hundred years ago?

'I haven't had a chance to introduce myself,' he said in a voice which seemed to come floating across a vast chasm. 'My name is George Drummond. It was me, Illingworth's friend, that Annabella really loved. Good-bye . . .'

On getting back home, I opened the mahogany box and took out the pistols once more. Their muzzles were warm to the touch, and an unmistakable smell of gunpowder assailed my nostrils.

CORVUS

August 15

Birds have fascinated me for a long time. When I was a boy, we had a pet mynah which we taught to pronounce clearly more than a hundred Bengali words. I knew, of course, that although some birds could talk, they didn't understand the meaning of what they said. But one day our mynah did something so extraordinary that I was forced to revise my opinion. I had just got back from school, Mother had brought me a plate of *halwa*, when the mynah suddenly screeched, 'Earthquake! Earthquake!' We had felt nothing but next day the papers reported that a slight tremor had indeed been recorded by the seismograph.

Ever since then I have felt a curiosity about the intelligence of birds, although in my preoccupation with various scientific projects, I have not been able to pursue it in any way. My cat, Newton, contributed to this neglect. Newton doesn't like birds, and I don't wish to do anything that would displease him. Lately, however – perhaps because of age – Newton has grown increasingly indifferent to birds. Which is probably why my laboratory is being regularly visited by crows, sparrows and *shaliks*. I feed them in the morning, and in anticipation of this they begin to clamour outside my window from well before sunrise.

Every creature is born with skills peculiar to its species. I believe such skills are more pronounced and more startling in birds than in other creatures. Examine a weaver-bird's nest, and it will make you gasp with astonishment. Given the ingredients to construct such a nest, a man would either throw up his hands in despair or take months of ceaseless effort to do so.

There is a species of birds in Australia called the Malle Fowl which builds its nest on the ground. Sand, earth and vegetable matter go into the making of this hollow mound which is provided with a hole for entry. The bird lays its eggs inside the mound but doesn't sit on them to hatch. Yet without heat the eggs won't hatch, so what is the answer? Simply this: by some amazing and as yet unknown process, the Malle Fowl maintains a constant temperature of seventy-eight degrees Fahrenheit inside the mound regardless of whether it is hot or cold outside.

Nobody knows why a bird called the Grebe should pluck out its feathers to eat them and feed their young with them. The same Grebe while floating in water can, by some unknown means, reduce its own specific gravity at the sight of a predator so that it floats with only its head above the water.

We all know of the amazing sense of direction of the migratory birds, the hunting prowess of eagles and falcons, the vultures' keen sense of smell, and the enchanting gift of singing possessed by numerous birds. It is for this reason that I have been wanting for some time to devote a little more time to the study of birds. How much can a bird be taught beyond its innate skills? Is it possible to instil human knowledge and intelligence in one? Can a machine be constructed to do this?

September 20

I believe in the simple method, so my machine will be a simple one. It will consist of two sections: one will be a cage to house the bird; the other will transmit intelligence to the bird's brain by means of electrodes.

For the past month I have been carefully studying the birds which come into my laboratory for food. Apart from the ubiquitous crows and sparrows and *shaliks*, birds such as pigeons, doves, parakeets, and bulbuls also come. Amongst all these, one particular bird has caught my attention, a crow. Not the jet black raven, but the ordinary crow. I can easily make him out from the other crows. Apart from the tiny white spot below the right eye which makes him easily recognisable, his behaviour, too, marks him out from other crows. For instance, I have never seen a crow hold a pencil in its beak and make marks on the table with it. Yesterday he did something which really shook me. I was working on my machine when I heard a soft rasping noise. I turned round and saw that the crow had taken a matchstick from a half-open matchbox and, holding it in his beak, was scraping it against the side of the box. When I shooed him away, he flew across, sat on the window and proceeded to utter some staccato sounds which bore no resemblance to the normal cawing of a crow. In fact, for a minute I thought the crow was laughing!

September 27

I finished assembling my Ornithon machine today. The crow has been in the lab since morning, eating breadcrumbs and hopping from window to window. As soon as I placed the cage on the table and opened the door, the crow flew over and hopped inside, a sure sign that he is extremely eager to learn. Since a familiarity with language is essential for the bird to follow my instructions, I have started with simple Bengali lessons. All the lessons being pre-recorded, all I have to do is press buttons. Different lessons are in different channels, and each channel bears a different number. I have noticed a strange thing; as soon as I press a button the crow's eyes close and his movements cease. For a bird as restless as a crow this is unusual indeed.

A conference of ornithologists is being held in November in Santiago, the capital of Chile. I have written to my ornithologist friend Rufus Grenfell in Minnesota. If my feathered friend is able to acquire some human intelligence, I should like to take him to the conference for a lecture-demonstration.

October 4

Corvus is the Latin name for the genus crow. I have started calling my pupil by that name. In the beginning he used to answer my call by a turn of the head in my direction. Now he responds vocally. For the first time I heard a crow saying 'ki' (what?) instead of 'caw'. But I don't expect speech will ever be his forte. Corvus will never turn into a talking crow. Whatever intelligence he acquires will show in his actions.

Corvus is learning English now; if I do go abroad for a demonstration, English would help. Lessons last an hour between eight and nine in the morning. The rest of the day he hangs around the lab. In the evening he still prefers to go back to the mango tree in the north-east corner of my garden.

Newton seems to have accepted Corvus. After what happened today, I shouldn't be surprised if they end up friends. It happened in the afternoon. Corvus for once was away somewhere, I sat in the armchair scribbling in my notebook, and Newton was curled up on the floor alongside when a flapping sound made me turn towards the window. It was Corvus. He had just come in with a freshly cut piece of fish in his beak. He dropped it in front of Newton, went back to the window, and sat surveying the scene with little twists of his neck.

Grenfell has replied to my letter. He says he is arranging to have me invited to the ornithologists' conference.

October 20

Unexpected progress in the last two weeks. With a pencil held in his beak, Corvus is now writing English words and numerals.

The paper is placed on the table, and Corvus writes standing on it. He wrote his own name in capital letters: C-O-R-V-U-S. He can do simple addition and subtraction, write down the capital of England when asked to, and can even write my name. Three days ago I taught him the months, days, and dates: when asked what day of the week it was today, he wrote in clear letters: F-R-I-D-A-Y.

That Corvus is clever in his eating habits too was proved today. I had kept some pieces of toast on one plate and some guava jelly on another in front of him; each time he put a piece in his mouth, he smeared some jelly on it first with his beak.

October 22

I had clear proof today that Corvus now wants to stay away from other crows. There was a heavy shower and after an earsplitting thunderclap I looked out of the window and saw the *simul* tree outside my garden smouldering. In the afternoon, after the rain stopped, there was a tremendous hue and cry set up by the neighbourhood crows who had all gathered around the *simul* tree. I sent my servant Prahlad to investigate. He came back and said, 'Sir, there's a dead crow lying at the foot of the tree; that's why there is such excitement.' I realised the crow had been struck by lightning. But strangely enough, Corvus didn't leave my room at all. He held a pencil in his beak and was absorbed in writing the prime numbers: 1,2,3,5,7,11, 13...

November 7

Corvus can now be proudly displayed in scientific circles. Birds can be taught to do small things, but a bird as intelligent and educated as Corvus is unique in history. The Ornithon has done its job well. Questions which can be answered in a few words, or with the help of numbers, on subjects as diverse as mathematics, history, geography and the natural sciences, Corvus is now able to answer. Along with that Corvus has spontaneously acquired what can only be termed human intelligence, something which has never been associated with birds. I shall give an example. I was packing my suitcase this morning in preparation for my trip to Santiago. As I finished and closed the lid, I found Corvus standing by with the key in his beak.

Another letter from Grenfell yesterday. He is already in Santiago. The organisers of the conference are looking forward to my visit. Till now these conferences have only dealt with birds in the abstract; never has a live bird been used as an illustration. The paper I have written is based on the priceless knowledge I have gathered in the last two months about bird behaviour. Corvus will be there in person to silence my critics.

November 10

I'm writing this on the plane to South America. I have only one incident to relate. As we were about to leave the house, I found Corvus greatly agitated and obviously anxious to get out of the cage. I couldn't make out the reason for this; nevertheless, I opened the cage door. Corvus hopped out, flew over to my desk and started pecking furiously at the drawer. I opened it and found my passport still lying in it.

I have had a new kind of cage built for Corvus. It maintains the temperature that best suits the bird. For his food, I have prepared tiny globules which are both tasty and nutritious. Corvus has aroused everyone's curiosity on the plane as they have probably never seen a pet crow before. I haven't told anyone about the uniqueness of my pet – I prefer to keep it secret. Corvus too, probably sensing this, is behaving like any ordinary crow.

November 14

Hotel Excelsior, Santiago, 11 pm. I have been too busy these last couple of days to write. Let me first describe what happened at the lecture, then I shall come to the disconcerting events of a little while ago. To cut a long story short, my lecture has been another feather in my cap. My paper took half an hour to read; then followed an hour's demonstration with the crow. I had released Corvus from the cage and put him down on the table as soon as I ascended the podium. It was a long mahogany table behind which sat the organisers of the conference, while I stood to one side speaking into the microphone. As long as I spoke, Corvus listened with the utmost attention, with occasional nods to suggest that he was getting the drift of my talk. To the applause that followed my speech, Corvus made his own contribution by beating a tattoo with his beak on the surface of the table.

The demonstration that followed gave Corvus no respite. All that he had learnt in the past two months he now demonstrated to the utter amazement of the delegates who all agreed that they had never imagined a bird could be capable of such intelligent behaviour. The evening edition of the local newspaper *Correro de Santiago* splashed the news on the front page with a picture of Corvus holding a pencil in his beak.

After the meeting, Grenfell and I went on a sight-seeing tour of Santiago with the chairman Signor Covarrubias. It is a bustling, elegant metropolis to the east of which the Andes range stands like a wall between Chile and Argentina. After an hour's drive Covarrubias turned to me and said, 'You must have noticed in our programme that we have made various arrangements for the entertainment of our delegates. I should particularly like to recommend the show this evening by the Chilean magician Argus. His speciality is that he uses a lot of trained birds in his repertory.'

I was intrigued, so Grenfell and I have been to the Plaza theatre to watch Senor Argus. It is true that he uses a lot of birds. Ducks, parrots, pigeons, hens, a four-foot-high crane, a flock of humming birds – all these Argus deploys with much evidence of careful training. But none of these birds comes anywhere near Corvus. Frankly, I found the magician himself far more interesting than his birds. Over six feet tall, he has a parrot-like nose, and his hair, parted in the middle, is slick and shiny as a new gramophone record. He wears spectacles so high-powered that they turn his pupils into a pair of tiny black dots, and out of the sleeves of his jet-black coat emerges a pair of hands whose pale, tapering fingers cast a spell on the audience with their sinuous movements. Not that the conjuring was of a high order, but the conjuror's presence and personality were well worth the price of admission. As I came out of the theatre, I remarked to Grenfell that it wouldn't be a bad idea to show Senor Argus some of Corvus's tricks now that he had shown us his.

Dinner was followed by excellent Chilean coffee and a stroll in the hotel garden with Grenfell. It was past ten when I returned to my room. I changed into my nightclothes, put out the lamp and was about to turn in when the phone rang.

'Senor Shonku?'

'Yes – '

'I'm calling from the reception. Sorry to trouble you at this hour, sir, but there's a gentleman here who is most anxious to see you.'

I said I was too tired to see anybody, and that it would be better if the gentleman could make an appointment over the phone next morning. I was sure it was a reporter. I had already been interviewed by four of them. Some of the questions they asked tried the patience of even a placid person like me. For instance, one of them asked if crows too, like cows, were held sacred in India!

The receptionist spoke to the caller and came back to me.

'Senor Shonku, the gentleman says he wants only five minutes of your time. He has another engagement tomorrow morning.'

'This person – is he a reporter?' I asked.

'No sir. He is the famous Chilean magician Argus.'

When I heard the name, I was left with no choice but to ask him to come up. I turned on the bedside lamp. Three minutes later the buzzer sounded.

The man who confronted me when I opened the door had seemed like a six-footer on stage; now he looked a good six inches taller. In fact, I had never seen anyone so tall before. Even when he bowed he remained a foot taller than me.

I asked him in. He had discarded his stage costume and was now dressed in an ordinary suit, but this one too was black. When he entered, I saw the evening edition of the *Correro* sticking out of his pocket. We took our seats after I had congratulated him on his performance. 'As far as I can recall,' I said, 'there was a gifted person in Greek mythology who had eyes all over his body and who was called Argus. An apt name for a magician, I think.'

Argus smiled, 'Then I'm sure you also remember that this person had some connection with birds.'

I nodded, 'The Greek goddess Hera had plucked out Argus's eyes and planted them on the peacock's tail – which is supposed to account for the circular markings on the tail. But what I'm curious about are your eyes. What is the power of your glasses?'

'Minus twenty,' he replied. 'But that doesn't bother me. None of my birds are short-sighted.'

Argus laughed loudly at his own joke, then suddenly froze open-mouthed. His eyes had strayed to the plastic cage kept on a shelf in a corner of the room. Corvus was asleep when I came in, but was now wide-awake and staring fixedly at the magician.

Argus, his mouth still open, left his chair and tiptoed towards the cage. He stared at the crow for a full minute. Then he said, 'Ever since I read about him in the evening papers, I've been anxious to meet you. I haven't had the privilege of hearing you speak. I'm not an ornithologist, you know, but I too train birds.'

The magician looked worried as he returned to his seat. 'I can well appreciate how tired you must be,' he said, 'but if you could just let your bird out of the cage . . . just one sample of his intelligence. . . '

I said, 'It's not just I who is tired; Corvus is too. I shall open the cage door for you, but the rest is up to the bird. I can't force him to do anything against his wish.'

'All right, fair enough.'

I opened the cage door. Corvus came out, flapped up to the bedside table, and with an unerring peck of his beak, switched off the lamp.

The room was plunged into darkness. Intermittent flashes of pale green light from the neon sign of the Hotel Metropole across the street glared through the open window. I sat silent. Corvus flew back to his cage and pulled the door shut with his beak.

The green light played rhythmically across Argus's face making his snake-like eyes look even more reptilian through the thick lenses of his gold-rimmed spectacles. I could see that he was struck dumb with amazement, and that he could read the meaning behind Corvus's action. Corvus wanted to rest. He didn't want light in the room. He wanted darkness; he wanted to sleep.

From under his thin moustache a soft whisper escaped his lips – 'Magnifico!' He had brought his hands below his chin with his palms pressed together in a gesture of frozen applause.

Now I noticed his nails. They were unusually long and shiny. He had used nail polish – silver nail polish – the kind that would under glaring stage lights heighten the play of his fingers. The green light was now reflected again and again on those silver nails.

'*I want that crow!*'

Argus spoke in English in a hoarse whisper. All this time he had been speaking in Spanish. Although, as I write this down, I realise that it probably sounds like unashamed greed, but in fact Argus was pleading with me.

'I want that crow!' Argus repeated.

I regarded him in silence. There was no need to say anything just now. I waited instead to hear what else he had to say.

Argus had been looking out of the window. Now he turned to me. I was fascinated by the alternation of darkness and light on his face. Now he was there, now he wasn't. Like magic again.

Argus moved his fingers and pointed them at himself.

'Look at me, Professor. I am Argus. I am the world's greatest magician. In every city of North and South America, anyone who knows about magic knows me. Men, women and children – they all know me. Next month I go on a world tour. Rome, Madrid, Paris, London, Athens, Stockholm, Tokyo. . . Every city will acclaim my genius. But do you know what can make my wonderful magic a thousand times more wonderful? It is that crow – that Indian crow. I want that bird, Professor, I want that bird! I do. . . '

As Argus spoke, he waved his hands before my eyes like snakes swaying to a charmer's flute, his silver nails catching the green light from the neon flashing on and off. I couldn't help being amused. If it had been anyone else in my place, Argus would have accomplished his object and got his hands on the bird. I now had to tell Argus that his plan wouldn't work with me.

I said: 'Mr Argus, you're wasting your time. It is useless to try to hypnotise me. I cannot accede to your request. Corvus is not only my pupil, he is like a son to me, and a friend – a product of my tireless effort and experiment.'

'Professor!' – Argus's voice was much sharper now, but he softened it the very next moment and said, 'Professor, do you realise that I am a millionaire? Do you know that I own a fifty-room mansion in the eastern end of this city? That I have twenty-six servants and four Cadillacs? Nothing is too expensive for me, Professor. For that bird I am willing to pay you ten thousand escudos right now.'

Ten thousand escudos meant about fifteen thousand rupees. Argus did not know that just as expenses meant nothing to him, money itself meant nothing to me. I told him so. Argus made one last attempt.

'You're an Indian. Don't you believe in mystic connections? Argus – Corvus. . . how well the two names go together! Don't you realise that the crow was fated to belong to me?'

I couldn't bear with him any more. I stood up and said, 'Mr Argus, you can keep your cars, houses, wealth and fame to yourself. Corvus is staying with me. His training is not over yet, I still have work left to do. I am extremely tired today. You had asked for five minutes of my time, and I have given you twenty.

I can't give you any more. I want to sleep now and so does my bird. Therefore, good-night.'

I must say I felt faint stirrings of pity at the abject look on his face; but I didn't let them surface. Argus bowed once again in continental style and, muttering good-night in Spanish, left the room.

I closed the door and went to the cage to find Corvus still awake. Looking at me, he uttered the single syllable 'kay' (who?) in a tone which clearly suggested a question.

'A mad magician,' I told him, 'with more money than is good for him. He wanted to buy you off, but I turned him down. So you may sleep in peace.'

November 16

I wanted to record the events of yesterday last night, but it took me the better part of the night to get over the shock.

The way in which the day began held no hint of impending danger. In the morning there was a session of the conference in which the only notable event was the stupendously boring extempore speech by the Japanese ornithologist Morimoto. After speaking for an hour or so, Morimoto suddenly lost the thread of his argument and started groping for words. It was at this point that Corvus, whom I had taken with me, decided to start an applause by rapping with his beak on the arm of my chair. This caused the entire audience to burst out laughing, thus putting me in an acutely embarrassing position.

In the afternoon there was lunch in the hotel with some delegates. Before going there, I went to my room, number 71, put Corvus into the cage, gave him some food and said, 'You stay here. I'm going down to eat.'

The obedient Corvus didn't demur.

By the time I finished lunch and came up, it was two thirty. As I inserted the key into the lock, a cold fear gripped me. The door was already open. I burst into the room and found my worst fears confirmed: Corvus and his cage were gone.

I was back in the corridor in a flash. Two suites down was the room-boys' enclosure. I rushed in there and found the two of them standing mutely with glazed looks in their eyes. It was clear that they had both been hypnotised.

I now ran to 107 – Grenfell's room. I told him everything and we went down to the reception together. 'No one had asked us for your room keys, sir,' said the clerk. 'The room-boys have the duplicate keys. They might have given them to someone.'

The room-boys didn't have to give the keys to anyone. Argus had cast his spell over them and helped himself to the keys.

In the end we got the real story from the concierge. He said Argus had arrived half an hour earlier in a silver Cadillac and gone into the hotel. Ten minutes later he had come out carrying a cellophane bag, got into his car and driven off.

A silver Cadillac. But where had Argus gone from here? Home? Or somewhere else?

We were now obliged to turn to Covarrubias for help. He said, 'I can find out for you in a minute where Argus lives; but how will that help? He is hardly likely to have gone home. He must have gone into hiding somewhere with your crow. But if he wants to leave the city, there's only one road leading out. I can fix up a good car and driver and police personnel to go with you. But time is short. You must be out in half an hour and take the highway. If you're lucky, you may still find him.'

We were off by three fifteen. Before leaving I made a phone call from the hotel and found out that Argus had not returned home. We went in a police car with two armed policemen. One of them, a young fellow named Carreras, turned out to be quite well-informed about Argus. He said Argus had several hide-outs in and around Santiago; that he had at one time hobnobbed with gypsies, and that he had been giving magic shows from the age of nineteen. About four years ago he had decided to include birds in his repertory, and this had given his popularity a great boost.

I asked Carreras if Argus was really a millionaire.

'So it would seem,' Carreras replied. 'But the man's a tightwad, and trusts nobody. That's why he has few friends left.'

As we left the city and hit the highway we ran into a small problem. The highway branched into two – one led north to Los Andes, and the other west to the port of Valparaiso. There was a petrol station near the mouth of the fork. We asked one of the attendants there and he said, 'A silver Cadillac? Senor Argus's Cadillac? Sure, I saw it take the road to Valparaiso a little while ago.'

We shot off in pursuit. I knew Corvus would not come to any harm, as Argus needed him badly. But Corvus's behaviour last night had clearly indicated that he hadn't liked the magician at all. So it pained me to think how unhappy he must be in the clutches of his captor.

We came across two more petrol stations on the way, and both confirmed that they had seen Argus's Cadillac pass that way earlier.

I am an optimist. I have emerged unscathed from many a tight corner in the past. To this day none of my ventures has ever been a failure. But Grenfell, sitting by my side, kept shaking his head and saying, 'Don't forget, Shonku, that you're up against a fiendishly clever man. Now that he's got his hands on Corvus, it's not going to be easy for you to get your bird back.'

'And Senor Argus may be armed,' added Carreras. 'I've known him use real revolvers in his acts.'

The highway sloped downwards. From Santiago's elevation of 1,600 feet we were now down to a thousand. Behind us the mountain range was becoming progressively hazier. We had already done forty miles; another forty and we would be in Valparaiso. Grenfell's glum countenance was already beginning to make a dent in my armour of optimism. If we did not find Argus on the highway, we would have to look for him in the city, and it would then be a hundred times more difficult to track him down.

The road now rose sharply. Nothing could be seen beyond the hump. We sped along, topped the rise, and saw the road ahead dipped gently down as far as the eye could see. A few trees dotted its sides; a village could be made out in the distance; buffaloes grazed in a field. Not a human being in sight anywhere. But what was that up ahead? It was still quite far away, whatever it was. At least a quarter of a mile.

Not more than four hundred yards away now. A car, gleaming in the sunlight, parked at an angle by the roadside.

We drew nearer.

A Cadillac! A silver Cadillac!

Our Mercedes drew up alongside. Now we could see what had happened: the car had swerved and dashed against a tree. Its front was all smashed up.

'It is Senor Argus's car,' said Carreras. 'There is only one other silver Cadillac in Santiago. It belongs to the banker, Senor Galdames. I can recognise this one by its number.'

The car was there; but where was Argus?

What was that next to the driver's seat?

I poked my head through the window. It was Corvus's cage. Its key was in my pocket. I hadn't locked it that afternoon – merely put the door to. Corvus had obviously come out of the cage by himself. But after that?

Suddenly we heard someone scream in the distance. Carreras and the other policeman raised their weapons, but our driver turned out to be a milksop. He dropped on his knees and started to pray. Grenfell's face had fallen too. 'Magicians as a tribe make me most uncomfortable,' he groaned. I said, 'I think you'd better stay in the car.'

The screams came closer. They seemed to be coming from behind some bushes a little way ahead to the left of the road. It took me some time to recognise the voice, because last night it had been dropped to a hoarse whisper. It was the voice of Argus. He was pouring out a string of abuse in Spanish. I clearly heard 'devil' in Spanish a couple of times along with the name of my bird.

'Where is that devil of a bird? Corvus! Corvus! Damn that bird to hell! Damn him!'

Suddenly Argus stopped, for he had seen us. We could see him too. He stood with a revolver in each hand near some bushes some thirty yards away.

Carreras shouted, 'Lower your weapons, Senor Argus, or – '

With an earsplitting sound a bullet came crashing into the door of our Mercedes. This was followed by three more shots, the bullets whizzing over our heads. Carreras now raised his voice threateningly. 'Senor Argus, we are fully armed. We are the police. If you don't drop your guns, we'll be forced to hurt you.'

'Hurt me?' moaned Argus in a hoarse voice. 'You are the police? I can't see anything!'

Argus was now within ten yards of us. Now I realised his plight. He had lost his spectacles, and that is why he was shooting at random.

Argus now threw down his weapons and came stumbling forward. The policemen advanced towards him. I knew that none of Argus's tricks would work in this crisis. He was in a pitiful state. Carreras retrieved the revolvers from the ground, while Argus kept groaning, 'That bird is gone – that Indian crow! That devil of a bird! But how damnably clever!'

Grenfell had been trying to say something for some time. Now at last I could make out what he was saying.

'Shonku, that bird is here.'

What did he mean? I couldn't see Corvus anywhere.

Grenfell pointed to the top of a bare acacia tree across the road.

I looked up – and sure enough – there he was: my friend, my pupil, my dear old Corvus, perched on the topmost branch of the tree and looking down at us calmly.

I beckoned, and he swooped gracefully down like a free-floating kite and alighted on the roof of the Mercedes. Then, carefully, as if he was fully aware of its worth, he placed before us the object he had been carrying in his beak: Argus's high-powered, gold-rimmed spectacles.

TELLUS

There was a demonstration of Tellus today in the presence of more than three hundred scientists and a hundred journalists from all over the world. Tellus was placed on a three-foot-high pedestal of transparent pellucidite on the stage of the hall of the Namura Technological Institute. When two of the workers of the Institute came in carrying the smooth, elegant platinum sphere, the hall echoed with spontaneous applause. That an apparatus which can answer a million questions should be only as large as a football, weigh forty-two kilos and bear no resemblance to a machine, came as a complete surprise to the audience. The fact is, in this age of microminiaturisation, no instrument, however complicated, need be very large. Fifty years ago, in the age of cabinet radios, could anyone have imagined that one would one day be watching television programmes on one's wrist-watch?

There is no doubt that Tellus is a triumph of modern technology. But it is also true that in the making of intricate instruments, man comes nowhere near nature yet. The machine we have constructed contains ten million circuits. The human brain is one fourth the size of Tellus, and contains about one hundred million neurons. This alone indicates how intricate is its construction.

Let me make it clear that our computer is incapable of mathematical calculations. Its job is to answer questions which would normally require a person to consult an encyclopedia. Another unique feature of the computer is that it gives its answers orally in English, in a clear, bell-like tone. The first question has to be preceded with the words 'Tell us', which activate the instrument and which gives it its name. At the end the words 'Thank you' turn it off. The battery, whose life is one hundred and twenty hours is of a special kind, and is housed in a chamber inside the sphere. There are two hundred minute holes on the surface of the sphere covering an area of one square inch; these allow the questions to enter and the answers to come out. The questions have to be of a nature which calls for short answers. For instance, although the delegates were briefed before today's demonstration, a journalist from the Philippines asked the instrument to talk about ancient Chinese civilisation. Naturally no answer came out. And yet when the same journalist asked about certain specific aspects of specific Chinese civilisations, the instrument astonished everyone by answering instantly and precisely.

Tellus can not only supply information, but is also capable of reasoning logically. The biologist Doctor Solomon from Nigeria asked the instrument whether it would be safer to keep a young baboon before a hungry deer or a hungry chimpanzee. Tellus answered in a flash! 'A hungry deer'. 'Why?' asked Doctor Solomon. Came the answer in a sharp, ringing voice: 'Because the chimpanzee is carnivorous.' This is a fact which has only recently come to light; even ten years ago everyone thought that monkeys and apes of all species were vegetarian.

Besides these, Tellus is able to take part in games of bridge and chess, point out a false note or a false beat in music, identify *ragas,* name a painter from a verbal description of one of his paintings, prescribe medicines and diets for particular kinds of ailments, and even indicate the chances of survival from the description of a patient's condition.

What Tellus lacks are abilities to think and feel, and supernatural powers. When Professor Maxwell of Sydney University asked it if a man would still be reading books a hundred years from now, Tellus was silent because prognostication is beyond it. In spite of these deficiencies, Tellus surpasses human beings in one respect: the information fed into its brain suffers no decay. The most brilliant of men often suffer from a loss of faculties with age. Even I, only the other day in Giridih, found myself addressing my servant Prahlad as Prayag. This is the kind of mistake which Tellus will never make. So, in a way, although it is a creation of human beings, it is more dependable than man.

The original idea for the instrument came from the famous Japanese scientist Matsue, one of the great names in electronics. The Japanese Government approved of his scheme and agreed to bear the expenses of constructing it. The technicians of the Namura Institute put in seven years of hard labour to construct Tellus. In the fourth year, just before the preliminary work was over, Matsue invited seven scientists from five continents to help feed information into the computer. Needless to say, I was one of the seven. The other six were: Doctor John Kensley of Britain, Doctor Stephen Merrivale of the Massachusetts Institute of Technology, Doctor Stassof of USSR, Professor Stratton of Melbourne, Doctor Ugati of West Africa, and Professor Kuttna of Hungary. Of these, Merrivale died of a heart attack three days before leaving for Japan. He was replaced by Professor Marcus Wingfield from the same MIT. Some of these scientists have stayed the full stretch of three years as guests of the Japanese Government. Others, such as myself, have come for short stretches at regular intervals. I have been here eleven times in the last three years.

I should like to mention an extraordinary event. The day before yesterday, on March the tenth, there was a solar eclipse. Japan fell in the zone of totality. Because it was a special day, we had already decided to finish our work before the tenth. We thought we had done so on the eighth of March when we discovered that no speech was coming out of the machine. The sphere was built so that it could be taken apart down the middle. We did that. Now we had to find out which of the ten million circuits was at fault.

We searched for two days and two nights. On the tenth, just as the eclipse was about to begin – at one thirty-seven in the afternoon – a high-pitched whistle issued from Tellus' speaker. This indicated that the fault had been repaired. We heaved a sigh of relief and went out to watch the eclipse. I wondered if there was any significance in the fact that the beginning of the eclipse coincided exactly with the coming to life of the instrument.

Tellus has been kept in the Institute. A special room has been built for it to keep it under controlled temperature. The room is a most elegant one. Tellus rests on the concave surface of the pellucidite pedestal in the middle of one side of the room against the wall. On the ceiling is a hole through which a concealed light sends a powerful beam to illuminate the sphere. The light is kept on all the time. Because Tellus is a national treasure, the room is guarded by watchmen. One musn't forget that even nations can be jealous of one another; I have already heard Wingfield grumble twice about the USA losing the race to Japan in computer technology. A word about Wingfield here. There is no question that he is a qualified man; but nobody likes him very much. One probable reason is that Wingfield is among the most glum-faced of individuals. Nobody in Osaka remembers seeing him laugh in the last three years.

Three of the scientists from abroad are going back home today. Those who are staying behind are Wingfield, Kensley, Kuttna and myself. Wingfield suffers from gout and is getting himself treated by a specialist in Osaka. I hope to travel around a bit. I'm going to Kyoto with Kensley tomorrow. A physicist by profession Kensley's interests range wide. He is something of an authority on Japanese art. He is most anxious to go to Kyoto if only to see the Buddhist temples and the Zen gardens.

The Hungarian biologist, Krzystoff Kuttna, does not much care for art, but there is one thing that interests him which only I know of, because I am the only person he discusses it with. The subject does not come strictly under the province of science. An example will make it clear.

We were having breakfast together this morning. Kuttna took a sip of coffee and said quite unexpectedly, 'I didn't watch the eclipse the other day.'

I wasn't aware of this. For me the total solar eclipse is a phenomenon of such outstanding importance. The corona around the sun at the time of totality is for me such an extraordinary sight, that I never notice who else is watching besides me. I was amazed that Kuttna could deprive himself of such an opportunity. I said, 'Do you have any superstition about watching an eclipse?'

Instead of answering, Kuttna put a question to me: 'Does a solar eclipse exert any influence on platinum?'

'Not that I know of,' I said. 'Why do you ask?'

'Why then did the sphere lose its lustre during those two and a half minutes of totality? I clearly noticed a pall descending on the sphere as soon as totality began. It lifted the moment totality ended.'

I didn't know what to say. 'What do you think?' I asked at last, wandering how old Kuttna was and whether it was a symptom of senility.

'I have no thoughts,' he said, 'because the experience is completely new to me. All I can say is that if it turns out to be an optical illusion, I would be happy. I am not superstitious about an eclipse, but I am about mechanical brains. When Matsue asked me to come, I told him about it. I said, if man continues to use machines to serve human functions, there may come a time when machines will take over.'

The discussion couldn't go on because of the arrival of Kensley and Wingfield. What Kuttna felt about machines was nothing new. That man may one day be dominated by machines has been a possibility for quite some time. As a simple example, consider man's dependence on vehicles. Even city dwellers, before the days of mechanical transport, used to walk seven or eight miles a day with ease, now they feel helpless without transport. But this doesn't mean that one should call a halt to scientific progress. Machines *will* be made to lighten the work of man. There is no going back to primitive times.

March 14, Kyoto

Whatever I have read or heard in praise of Kyoto is no exaggeration. I wouldn't have believed that the aesthetic sense of a people could permeate a whole city in such a way. This afternoon we had been to see a famous Zen temple and the garden adjoining it. It is hard to imagine a more peaceful atmosphere. We met the famous scholar Tanaka in the temple. A saintly character, his placidity harmonises perfectly with his surroundings. When he heard about our computer, he smiled gently and said, 'Can your machine tell us whose will works behind the sun and the moon coinciding so perfectly for a solar eclipse?'

A true philosopher's question. The moon is so much smaller than the sun, and yet its distance from the earth is such that it appears to be exactly the same size as the sun. I had realised the magnitude of the coincidence as a small boy. Ever since then I have had a feeling of profound wonder at the phenomenon of total eclipse. How can Tellus know the answer to the question when we don't know it ourselves?

We will spend another day here and then go to Kamakura. I have benefited a lot from Kensley's company. Good things seem even better when you are with someone who appreciates them.

March 15

I am writing this in the compartment of our train in the Kyoto station. There was a severe earthquake here last night at two-thirty am. Tremors are common in Japan, but this one was of a great magnitude and lasted for nine seconds. But this is not the only reason we are returning. The earthquake has precipitated an incident which calls for our immediate return to Osaka. Matsue phoned at five this morning and gave me the news.

Tellus has disappeared.

It wasn't possible to talk at length over the telephone. Matsue speaks in broken English anyway. In his agitation he could barely make himself understood. This much he told us: immediately after the earthquake it was seen that the pellucidite pedestal was lying on the floor and Tellus was missing. Both the guards were found lying unconscious and both had had their legs broken. They are in the hospital now, and haven't yet regained consciousness. So it is not yet known what brought them to this state.

In Kyoto, ninety people were killed by houses collapsing. In the station everybody is talking of the earthquake. To be honest, when the tremor started last night, I too felt helpless and uneasy. I had run out of the hotel along with Kensley, and we could make out from the vast crowd outside that everybody had come out.

What a calamity! So much money, labour and experience gone into the making of the world's most sophisticated apparatus, and in three days it disappears.

March 15, Osaka, 11 pm

I am sitting in my room in the International Guest House which faces the Namura Institute across a public park. From the window could be seen the tower of the Institute. It is no longer there; it came down during yesterday's earthquake.

Matsue came to the station with his car to receive us. The car took us straight to the Institute. One of the guards has regained consciousness. His story goes like this: his friend and he had both considered running out into the open when the earthquake started, but hearing a sound from Tellus' room they had unlocked the door and gone in to investigate.

The guard's version of what happened thereafter is wholly unbelievable. He says, what they saw upon entering the room was that the pedestal was lying on the floor while Tellus was rolling from one end of the room to the other. By then the tremor had abated in intensity. Both the guards had advanced towards the sphere to capture it. At this the sphere had come charging towards them and hit them in their legs with force enough to break their bones and render them unconscious.

If the story of the ball rolling by itself is not true, then the other possibility is theft. That both the guards were a little drunk has been admitted by Konoye, the one who has regained consciousness. In that state it was not unnatural that they would both dash out of the building; there were people working in the Institute laboratory that night, and everybody had run out into the compound. This means that most of the doors were open. There was nothing to prevent outsiders from entering the Institute. A clever thief could easily have taken advantage of the panic and made off with a forty-two-kilogram sphere without anybody noticing.

Theft or no theft, Tellus was no longer in its place. Who has taken it, where it is at the moment, whether there is any possibility of retrieving it – are questions which remain unanswered. The Government has already announced that whoever finds Tellus will get a reward of 500,000 yen. The police have started their investigations. Meanwhile the second guard has regained consciousness and vehemently asserts that the sphere was not stolen but, guided by some mysterious force, had assaulted its protector and made its escape.

Only Kuttna amongst us has believed the guards' story, although unable to support it by any rational explanation. Kensley and Wingfield both believe that theft is the only possible explanation. Platinum is a most precious metal. These days the younger generation of Japanese are quite capable of doing reckless things under the influence of drugs. Some of the more radical amongst them would be quite prepared to undertake such a robbery if only to embarrass the Government. If such a group has made off with Tellus, they will surely extract a high price before giving it up.

The search will not be easy, for the agitation over the

earthquake hasn't subsided yet. More than a hundred and fifty people have been killed in Osaka, while the number of those injured exceeds two thousand. And there is no guarantee that there will be no more tremors.

Kuttna was here till a little while ago. Although he believes that Tellus escaped on its own, he cannot find a reason for its doing so. He believes that crashing on the floor during the tremor has done something to its innards. In other words Tellus has lost its mind.

I myself feel wholly at a loss. This is an unprecedented experience for me.

March 16, 11.30 pm

Let me set down the nerve-racking experiences of today.

Of the four of us, only Kuttna is able to hold his head high because his guess has turned out to be largely correct. I doubt if any one will have the temerity to work on artificial intelligence after this.

Last night, after I had finished writing my diary, I found it difficult to go to sleep. Finally, I decided to take one of my Somnolin pills. As I left my bed to get the phial, my eye was drawn to the north window. This is the window which looks out over the park and faces the Namura Institute. What had caught my eye was the light from a torch in the park. The torch was being turned off and on and roved over a fairly large area.

This went on for about fifteen minutes. It was clear that the owner of the torch was searching for something. Whether he succeeded or not I do not know, but I saw him picking out his way with the help of the torch as he finally left the park.

This morning I described the incident to my three colleagues. We all decided to take a look in the park after breakfast.

At about eight the four of us set off. Like most other cities of Japan, Osaka is not flat, and one has to climb up a slope before reaching the park. The path in the park winds through flowering trees and bushes. Maple, birch, oak and chestnut abound. The Japanese had started a long time ago to uproot their own trees and plant English ones instead.

After walking for about fifteen minutes, we met our first stranger: a Japanese schoolboy, about ten years old, with pink cheeks, close cropped hair, and his satchel around his shoulder. The boy halted in his tracks, and was now looking at us with an expression of alarm. Kuttna knew Japanese. 'What is your name?' he asked the boy.

'Seiji.'

'What are you doing here?'

'I'm going to school.'

'What were you looking for in the bush?'

The boy said nothing.

Meanwhile Kensley had moved over to the right. 'Come here Shonku,' he called out.

Kensley was looking down at the grass. Wingfield and I joined him and found that a patch of grass and a sprig of wild-flower had been flattened by something rolling over them. A few feet away we saw a flattened lizard.

This time the boy had to answer. He said he had seen a metal ball behind a bush on his way back from school yesterday. As he had approached it, the ball had rolled away. He had kept chasing the ball for a long time but had failed to catch it. Coming back home he had heard on the television about the reward. So he had looked for the ball with a torch the night before but had not found it.

We told the boy that if we found the ball in the park, we would see that he got his prize. The boy looked relieved, left his address and ran off to school. The four of us split up and went off in four directions to look for the sphere. Anybody finding it would call out to the others.

I left the beaten track and started looking behind bushes. If Tellus had really become mobile, it was doubtful whether it would surrender. On top of that, if it has developed an antipathy to human beings, it would be hard to predict what it might do.

Casting wary looks around, I walked on for another five minutes when I found a couple of butterflies lying on the grass. One of them was dead, while the other's wings still flapped weakly. It was clear that something heavy had passed over them only a little while ago.

I now proceeded slowly and with great caution when I was pulled up short by a sudden sharp sound. If one were to describe it in words, it would be – 'Coo-ee!'

I was trying to locate the source of the sound when I heard again – 'Coo-ee!'

This was unmistakably Tellus, and the sound could only mean one thing: it was playing hide-and-seek with us.

I didn't have to go far. Tellus was behind a geranium tree, glistening in the sunlight. It didn't move at my approach. It must have been the 'Coo-ee' which had told the others of Tellus' proximity. All three converged on the same spot. The smooth metal sphere made a strange contrast with the surrounding vegetation. Was there a slight change in Tellus' appearance? That we can tell only if we removed the dust and grass from the surface.

'Tell us – tell us – tell us . . .'

Kensley knelt on the grass and called out the two words to activate Tellus. We were all anxious to find out if it still functioned.

'In which battles was Napoleon victorious?'

The question came from Wingfield. The same question had been asked by one of the journalists on the day of the demonstration, and Tellus had answered instantly.

But no answer came today. We exchanged glances. My heart filled with a deep foreboding. Wingfield moved up closer to the sphere and repeated the question.

'Tell us what battles Napoleon won.'

This time there was an answer. No, not an answer, but a counter-question.

'Don't you know?'

Wingfield was flabbergasted. Kuttna's mouth had fallen open. The fear that was mixed with his look of surprise was characteristic of someone confronted by a supernatural event.

Whatever the cause, Tellus was no longer the same. By some unknown means it had surpassed the skill human beings had endowed it with. I was sure that one could converse with it now. I asked it:

'Did someone bring you here or did you come by yourself?'

'I came by myself.'

Kuttna put the next question. He was excited to the point where his hands trembled and beads of perspiration showed on his forehead.

'Why did you come?'

The answer came like a flash.

'To play.'

'To play?' I asked in great surprise.

Wingfield and Kensley were now squatting on the grass.

'A child must play,' said Tellus.

What kind of talk was this? The four of us now spoke almost in unison.

'A child? You are a child?'

'I am a child because you are all children.'

I don't know how the others felt, but I could see what Tellus was trying to say. Even towards the end of the twentieth century man has to admit that what he knows is very little compared with what he doesn't know. Gravity, which pervades the universe and whose presence we feel every moment of our existence, is to this day a mystery to us; we are indeed children if we take such things into account.

The question now was: what to do with Tellus. Now that it had a mind of its own, it would be best to ask it. I said, 'Have you finished playing?'

'Yes, I am growing older.'

'What will you do now?'

'Think.'

'Will you stay here, or come with us?'

'Go with you.'

'Thank you.'

We picked up Tellus and started on our way back.

On reaching the guest house, we sent for Matsue. We explained to him that it wouldn't do to keep Tellus in the Institute any longer because one would have to keep an eye on him all the time. At the same time, it wouldn't be wise to make any public statement about his present state.

In the end, it was Matsue who decided on the course of action. There were two trial spheres made before the one that was actually used. One of them would be kept in the Institute and an announcement made to the effect that the sphere had been retrieved. The real Tellus could be kept in the guest house where there were no other residents apart from the four of us. It was a two-storey building with sixteen rooms. The four of us were occupying four rooms on the first floor. We could communicate with each other by phone.

Within a few hours a glass case arrived in my room from Matsue. Tellus has been placed in it in a bed of cotton. While wiping the dust from the sphere I noticed that its surface was not as smooth as before. Platinum is a metal of great hardness, so that in spite of all the rolling the sphere had done, there was no reason for it to lose its smoothness. In the end I asked Tellus. After a few moments' pause it answered:

'I do not know. I am thinking.'

In the afternoon, Matsue arrived with a tape recorder. The speciality of this particular model is that it starts recording the moment a sound is produced, and stops as the sound stops. The recorder has been kept in front of Tellus. It'll work by itself.

Matsue is overcome by a feeling of helplessness. All his mastery over electronics is of no use in the present situation. He wanted to take apart the sphere and examine the circuit but I dissuaded him. I said, 'Whatever may have gone wrong inside it is important that we shouldn't interfere with what is happening now. Man is able to build a machine, and will do so in future too, but no human skill can produce an object like Tellus as it is now. So all we do now is keep observing it and communicating with it.

In the evening the four of us were sitting in our room having coffee when we heard a sound from the glass cage. A well-known, high-pitched, flutey sound. And yet nobody had said the two words to switch it on. Tellus was obviously able to activate itself. I went over to the cage and asked: 'Did you say anything?'

The reply came: 'I know now. It is age.'

Tellus had found the answer to the question I had asked in the morning. The roughness of the sphere was a sign of ageing.

'Are you old now?' I asked.

'No,' said Tellus. 'I am in my youth.'

Among the four of us, only Wingfield's behaviour seems a little odd to me. When Matsue suggested taking Tellus apart, it was only Wingfield who supported him. He regrets that Tellus is no longer serving the purpose for which it was built. Whenever Tellus starts to talk on its own, Wingfield appears to feel ill at ease. I agree Tellus' behaviour has something of the supernatural about it, but why should a scientist react like that? In fact, today it gave rise to a most unpleasant incident. Within a minute of Tellus' talking to me, Wingfield left his chair, strode up to the glass cage and said, 'What battles did Napoleon win?'

The answer came like a whiplash.

'To want to know what you already know is a sign of an imbecile.'

I can't describe the effect the answer had on Wingfield. The words that came out of his mouth were of a nature one would scarcely associate with an aged scientist. Yet the fault was Wingfield's. That he could not accept Tellus' transformation was only an indication of his stubbornness.

The most extraordinary thing, however, was Tellus' reaction to Wingfield's boorishness. 'Wingfield, I warn you!' I heard it say in a clear voice.

It was not possible for Wingfield to stay in the room any longer. He strode out, shutting the door behind him with a bang.

Kensley and Kuttna stayed on for quite a while. Kensley feels Wingfield is a psychopathic case who shouldn't have accepted to come to Japan. As a matter of fact, Wingfield has made the least contribution among the seven of us. Had Merrivale been alive things might have been different.

We had dinner in my room. None of us spoke, nor did Tellus. All of us noticed that the sphere was getting rougher by the hour.

After my two colleagues left, I shut the door and sat down on the bed. Just then, Tellus' voice set the tape recorder in motion again. I moved up to the glass cage. Tellus' voice was no longer high-pitched; a new solemnity had come into it.

'Are you going to sleep?' asked Tellus.

'Why do you ask?'

'Do you dream?' came the second question.

'I do sometimes. All human beings do.'

'Why sleep? Why dream?'

Difficult questions to answer. I said, 'The reasons are not clear yet. There is a theory about sleep. Primitive man used to hunt for food all day and then sit in the darkness of his cave and fall asleep. Daylight would wake him up. Perhaps we still retain that primal habit.'

'And dreaming?'

'I don't know. Nobody knows.'

'I know.'

'Do you?'

'I know more. I know how memory works. I know the mystery of gravity. I know when man first appeared on earth. I know about the birth of the universe.'

I was watching Tellus tensely. The recorder was turning. Was Tellus about to explain all the mysteries of science?

No, not so.

After a pause, Tellus said, 'Man has found the answer to many questions. These too he will find. It will take time. There is no easy way.'

Then, after another pause: 'But one thing man will never know. I too do not know it yet, but I will. I am not a man; I am a machine.'

'What are you talking about?'

But Tellus was silent. The recorder had stopped. After about a minute it turned again, only to record two words: 'Goodnight'.

March 18

I am writing my diary in the hospital. I feel much better now. They say they will release me this afternoon. I had no idea such an experience awaited me. I realise what a mistake I had made in not taking Tellus' advice.

The day before yesterday, I went straight to bed after saying good-night to Tellus. I fell asleep within a few minutes. Normally I sleep very lightly and wake up at every sound. So when the phone rang I was up at once. The time on my travelling clock with the luminous dial was 2.33 am.

It was Wingfield calling.

'Shonku, I've run out of sleeping pills. Can you help me?'

I said I'd be over in a minute with the pill. Wingfield said he would come himself.

I had brought out the phial from my suitcase when the door bell rang. Almost at once came the voice from the glass cage: 'Don't open the door.'

I was startled. 'Why not?' I asked.

'Wingfield is evil.'

'What kind of talk is that, Tellus?'

The doorbell rang again, and was followed by Wingfield's anxious voice.

'Have you fallen asleep, Shonku? I've come for the sleeping pills.'

Tellus had given its warning and fallen silent.

I was in a dilemma. How could I not open the door? How could I explain my action? What if Tellus' warning was baseless?

I opened the door. Something descended with force on my head and I lost consciousness.

When I came to, I was in a hospital. Three scientists stood at my bedside – Kensley, Kuttna and Matsue. It was they who provided me with the details.

Having knocked me out, Wingfield had taken Tellus apart and taken the hemispheres into his room. He had put them in his suitcase, waited until dawn, and then gone down and asked the manager to arrange a car for him to take him to the airport. Meanwhile the porter who had brought Wingfield's luggage down had been suspicious about the great weight of the suitcase, and had informed the policeman on duty at the gate. The policeman had challenged Wingfield, and the latter had desperately pulled out his revolver. But he wasn't quick enough. He was now in custody. It is suspected that he may be responsible for his colleague Merrivale's death in Massachusetts. He was afraid that Tellus, with his supernatural abilities, would reveal unpleasant facts about him. This is why he was anxious to run away with the sphere, hoping to dispose of it somewhere on the way to the airport.

'Where is Tellus now?' I asked after I had listened to the extraordinary story.

'It is back in the Institute,' replied Matsue. 'You see, it was no longer safe to keep it in the guest house. It is back in his place on the pedestal. I put it together again.'

'Has it said anything since?'

'It has asked to see you,' said Matsue.

I couldn't contain myself any more. To hell with the pain in my head – I had to go to the Institute.

'Can you make it?' asked Kuttna.

'I'm sure I can.'

Within half an hour we were in the elegant room once again. Tellus was seated on its throne on the pedestal, bathed in the shaft of light from the ceiling. I could see there were cracks all over the sphere. There was no question that these four days have aged Tellus considerably.

I went over and stood near it. Before I said anything, I heard its calm, grave voice.

'You have come at the right time. There will be an earthquake in three and a half minutes. A mild tremor. You will feel it, but it will do no damage. As the tremor ends, I will know the answer to my last question.'

There was nothing to do except wait with bated breath. A few feet above Tellus was the electric clock whose second hand moved steadily along.

One minute ... two minutes ... three minutes ... We watched with amazement a glow beginning to pervade Tellus as the cracks widened. The colour of the sphere was changing. Yes, it was turning into gold!

Fifteen seconds ... twenty seconds ... twenty-five seconds.

Just at the stroke of the half hour, the floor under our feet shook, and in that very instant, the sphere exploded into a thousand bits and scattered on the floor. Then, from the ruins was heard an eerie, disembodied voice declaiming –

'*I know what comes after death!*'

THE SAHARA MYSTERY

January 3

Distressing news in the New Year: Demetrius is missing, Professor Hektor Demetrius, the famous Greek biologist. Demetrius lived in Iraklion, the largest city in the island of Crete. I had never met him, but had written to him when I came to know that he was doing research on ancient medicine. When I sent him some information on our own Ayurvedic medicine, he replied at once, thanking me profusely, with elegant handwriting and considerable command of English. I later learned from my friend John Summerville that Demetrius had studied in Cambridge. It was Summerville's letter which informed me yesterday of Demetrius's disappearance and this is what the letter revealed.

On the thirty-first of December, at nine in the morning, Demetrius had left his home with a suitcase in his hand. His servant had seen him go out, but didn't know where he was going. When his master hadn't returned by evening, he had informed the police. Investigations had revealed that Demetrius had taken a taxi to the airport and caught a plane at ten-thirty in the morning. The plane was bound for Cairo. In Cairo, Demetrius had checked into the Alhambra hotel and stayed there one night. After that the police had drawn a blank.

Summerville, who had written from Iraklion, was a friend of Demetrius. He had gone to Athens to give a lecture, and had decided to go back by way of Crete. He heard of Demetrius's disappearance while still in Athens, had dropped everything and gone straight to Iraklion. Now he has decided to carry on his own investigation and wants me to help him. I have been to Greece twice before but not to Crete. The urge to go is strong.

January 8

I arrived in Iraklion this morning. The town is situated on the northern coast of the island. Demetrius's home is in the outskirts of the town at the foot of a hill, surrounded on three sides by an olive orchard. At the back of the house, beyond the orchard, is a forest of cypress and fir. On the whole a picturesque setting.

Summerville is worried, and there is plenty of cause for that. Firstly, there has been no further news from Cairo. Secondly, no reason has been found for Demetrius's sudden disappearance. Examination of the papers in his laboratory has given no indication of what he had been working on. A notebook has been found which, it appears, he had been using of late. It is filled with writing, but the strange script has baffled us completely. Some of the letters look English, but the whole thing makes no sense at all. I asked Summerville if there was any possibility of it being a code. Summerville replied, 'I shouldn't be surprised. He had a special interest in languages. Are you familiar with Linear A?'

I knew that Cretan stone inscriptions dating back to 2000 BC have been christened Linear A by archaeologists; Summerville said Demetrius had been studying this script for a long time. Perhaps the notebook contains important conclusions drawn from that study. Demetrius's servant Mikhaili says his master had been making frequent trips to ancient Cretan cities. He would stay a week or so in each place and come back with stone slabs bearing inscriptions. We have, of course, seen quite a few of these slabs strewn about the house.

Something else which Mikhaili said caused Summerville much concern. The day before Demetrius left, Mikhaili had heard a gunshot in the evening. It came from the direction of the forest behind the house. Demetrius was not at home then, but had returned a little later. Demetrius himself possessed a gun which hadn't been used for a long time. That gun was missing.

Mikhaili has a son about ten years old. I don't know if one can trust his words, but he says that a little before the gunshot, he had heard the roar of a tiger from the forest. Since the presence of tigers was impossible in Crete, I asked the boy how he could recognise the roar. He said he had once heard a tiger roaring in a circus which had come to Iraklion. There was no reason to doubt the truth of this.

We have decided to make a trip to the forest after lunch; it is important to find out what happened there.

January 9

I am writing this in the lounge of the Iraklion airport. They have announced that the Cairo flight will be delayed by two hours, so I am taking this opportunity to record yesterday's event.

Yesterday after lunch Summerville and I went out to explore the forest.

Although walking through the forest for twenty minutes revealed nothing suspicious, I detected a smell that raised my hopes. Summerville had a cold which had blocked his nostrils, but I could clearly make out the presence of a dead animal in the vicinity. I proceeded in the direction of the smell with Summerville following on my heels. Soon enough Summerville too became aware of the smell.

He asked in a whisper, 'Are you carrying a weapon?' I produced my Stun Gun from my pocket and showed it to him. It was obvious that Summerville was apprehensive of the presence of live animals as well as the dead one.

We advanced cautiously. It was Summerville who spotted the vultures first. In a clearing amidst the cypresses, a dozen or so of these ungainly birds were making a meal of a dead animal. We were still about thirty yards away, so we couldn't make out what the animal was except that it was black in colour. A few paces later, my eyes fell on a tuft of jet black fur lying on the grass beside a cluster of white wild flowers.

'Bear?' I asked tentatively.

'Most unlikely,' said Summerville. I too was aware that the presence of a bear in this region was an impossibility.

Meanwhile Summerville had picked up some of the fur.

As we advanced another ten yards or so, the head of the animal came into view. Although part of the head had been devoured by the vultures, it was clear that the animal belonged to the tiger species.

One of the vultures hopped aside with a flapping of wings at our approach, revealing the white of the exposed bones and the black of the pelt sticking to the angry red of the raw flesh. The vultures were having a great time. Have they ever tasted the flesh of a black panther in Crete? Although I am using the term panther, I know that no panther ever possessed such long and thick fur.

Summerville finally said, 'I suppose we'll have to call it a brand new species of tiger.'

'But was this the one killed with the gun?'

'So it would seem. But the question is whether it was Demetrius who used the gun.'

When we later described the beast to Mikhaili, he was quite surprised. 'A black beast looking like a tiger? The only black beasts I have seen around here are a cat and a dog.'

In the evening we found something very valuable in a drawer of Demetrius's desk: a brand new diary bound in leather containing two entries in Greek on December the twenty-seventh and the twenty-eighth, and in Demetrius's own hand. Between the two of us we soon translated it. Although brief, the comments were as mysterious as they were intriguing. The entry for December the twenty-seventh runs:

'I have always noticed that in my life happiness and sorrow go hand in hand. Which is why even success brings me no peace. I must never again undertake any experiment without first considering its possible consequences.'

The entry for December twenty-eight says:

'In a fair at Knossos ten years ago, a gypsy woman told me my fortune. She said that some danger might befall me on my sixty-fifth birthday, and that it might prove fatal. There are only sixteen days to my sixty-fifth birthday on the thirteenth of January. When the gypsy's other prophecies have come true, I can assume that this one too will. Perhaps the experiment I am about to undertake will be the cause of my death. If I achieve success before I die, I will have no regrets. But this small, crowded island is most unsuitable for what I am about to do. I need the vast open spaces. I need the – *Sahara!*'

There is a double underline below the word Sahara. This makes the reason for the trip to Cairo clear; but the nature of the experiment, and why a desert should be needed for it, are not clear. Perhaps our trip to Cairo will shed some light.

January 9, 5 pm

Cairo. We are staying in the same hotel as Demetrius – the Alhambra. I noticed Demetrius's name when I was writing my own in the register. Summerville did something very sleuth-like: he asked for us the same room – No 313 – in which Demetrius had stayed. Luckily the room was free. The possibility of the existence of any clues is remote, because in the last eleven days many guests have occupied the room, and it has been cleaned many times. But in the end it has turned out to be a very lucky decision. The room-boy who came and made our beds a little while ago provided us with some useful information. It was Summerville who questioned him.

'How long have you been working in this hotel?'

'Four years, sir.'

'Do you remember the guests who come here for short stays?'

'I certainly remember the ones who tip me well.'

I could see the boy had a sense of humour. Summerville said, 'A Greek gentleman came and stayed here for a night ten days ago. He was a man of about sixty-five, bald-headed, with thick black eyebrows and a high pointed nose. Can you recall him?'

Although I had never met Demetrius, a photo on the mantelpiece in his study had familiarised me with his features.

The boy grinned broadly. 'He tipped me seventy-five piastres; how can I forget him?'

Seventy-five piastres is almost fifteen rupees. No wonder the boy was happy.

'The gentleman was here for just one night, wasn't he?' asked Summerville.

'Yes, sir, and he had the *Do Not Disturb* sign hanging on his door-knob most of the time.'

'Did he say where he was going from here?'

'He asked me about camels. He said he wanted to go to the desert and asked me where he could hire camels. I said there was a caravan track from El Giza which runs a thousand miles into the desert. I said he could hire a camel in El Giza.'

That's all the information we could elicit from the room-boy. The news about Giza was most important. Cairo was on the eastern bank of the Nile, while at Giza, on the west, were the famous pyramids and the Sphinx.

We shall make a few more enquiries in Cairo, then proceed to Giza tomorrow morning.

January 10, 12.30 pm

We are with a caravan of about five hundred camels on our way to the Baharia oasis. The caravan consists almost entirely of traders. They are taking wool and other products from the city into the villages in the deep interior of the desert. They will exchange their wares mainly for dates. This has been going on for centuries.

We halted by an oasis about ten minutes ago, and will continue after a brief rest. This is a valley. An occasional limestone hill rears its head from an endless stretch of sand. There is a pool nearby surrounded by date palms and tents set up by the Bedouins. Strewn about are ruined fragments of ancient Egyptian architecture. I am leaning against a headless pillar as I write.

We left the hotel at seven-thirty this morning after an early breakfast. It took us half an hour to reach Giza. We hired our camels in a market place, where we also got news of Demetrius from an old fruit-seller. I know Arabic, which is why I was able to describe Demetrius to a shop-keeper and ask him if he had seen him. He pointed to the old fruit-seller. 'Ask Mehmood, he might know.' As soon as we questioned the old man, he burst into an angry tirade against Demetrius. Apparently, Demetrius had bought dates from him and paid him in coins which contained two Greek leptas. Later he had looked for Demetrius and found that he was gone. Summerville was obliged to make good his loss by paying him in local currency. Well, it is clear that we have done the right thing by coming to Giza. Demetrius had obviously set off from here on a camel towards the desert. The question is whether he has gone all the way with the caravan or had veered off on his own.

I have taken with me enough of my nutriment pills to last us a fortnight. I hope our mission will be over by then, and that we will find Demetrius alive. The gypsy woman's prophecy keeps rankling in my mind. I have found such prophecies coming true at times, although I have never found a rational explanation for it. January the thirteenth is Demetrius's birthday; today is the tenth.

January 11, 6.30 pm

I don't know how far we have travelled in thirty-six hours. My guess is about a hundred miles. We have now halted for the day, and will resume our journey tomorrow morning. The travellers have pitched their tents and lit fires. The camels are all seated around making occasional gurgling noises. The cry of jackals can be heard; once I heard what sounded like a hyena's laughter. On the way we have seen wild hare and field rats darting out of the bushes. The only birds we have seen so far are hawks and kites.

We are now seated in our tent, lit by my Luminimax lamp; the fuel is a naphthalene-like ball which when set alight gives off the same amount of light as a two hundred watt bulb. One ball lasts the whole night.

Let me now describe what happened this afternoon.

It had been a bit stuffy during the day, although not too warm. Clouds had gathered in the west, and I thought it would rain. The two or three days' rain that takes place in this region every year usually does so in winter. But it didn't rain. Instead, a wind rose from the direction of the clouds. We were thankful for it, as it can be very hot in the desert in the daytime. But the wind brought with it a sound which greatly perplexed us. It went 'dub – thump . . . dub – thump . . . dub – thump . . .' as if a gigantic drum was being beaten, although to produce a sound so deep and low, the drum would have to be the size of a pyramid.

In a little while it was clear that the sound had produced a commotion among both men and beasts comprising the caravan. A dozen or so of the camels flopped down on the ground with the riders on their backs. As long as the wind held up the eerie sound continued 'dub – thump . . . dub – thump . . . dub – thump . . . ' I worked out that there was a gap of two seconds between the 'dub' and the 'thump', and three seconds between the 'thump' and the next 'dub'. The rhythm and timing were maintained right through.

Both of us dismounted.

'What do you make of it?' I asked Summerville.

Summerville listened intently for a while. 'It seems to have a subterranean quality,' he said.

I too had the same feeling. The sound had strength and body, but lacked clarity. But there was no way of finding out the distance of the source.

Meanwhile, great agitation seemed to have spread among the Bedouins. An old wool merchant with a coppery skin and a heavily wrinkled face came up to me and started talking about demons and ogres. Not only that, he started a whispering campaign against us, accusing us of having brought them bad luck. If all the five hundred traders suddenly took it into their heads that we were responsible for those infernal drumbeats, there would be real trouble.

I could feel the wind dropping and the beats becoming fainter. I decided to cash in on it. I turned towards the wind, stretched my arms forward, and with various appropriate gestures started intoning Sanskrit verses. Around the middle of the fifth verse the wind stopped, and along with it the drumbeats too. We had no more trouble from our fellow travellers after this.

But there is no denying that the drumming has caused both of us great bewilderment. Not that this is likely to have any connection with Demetrius. Summerville thinks it could be large tribal tom-toms distorted and magnified by the vagaries of the desert atmosphere. Perhaps he is right. Whatever it was, I don't think we have to worry about it any more.

January 12, 10.30 am

We were forced to break away from the caravan which proceeded south-west to Baharia while we went west. Let me explain.

This morning, after travelling from six o'clock for four and a half hours, we suddenly noticed, some two hundred yards to our right, a group of vultures gathered over a sand dune. I caught my breath. I didn't like the sight. I looked behind and found Summerville too surveying the same scene. Our caravan was by-passing it, but I felt a burning desire to find out what the birds were up to. I turned to our camel drivers and said, 'We should like to go and take a look at those vultures. We'll rejoin the caravan afterwards.'

The men readily agreed, doubtless because they too were

impressed with my performance yesterday and had taken me for a prophet.

We left the caravan and headed towards the vultures.

It took five minutes for our curiosity to be satisfied. The vultures were making a meal of a dead camel.

No, not just a camel. There was another carcase lying alongside, and this was human. Like the two men with us, this too was a camel driver. Man and beast had strayed from a caravan and met their end. But was it natural death, or was somebody else responsible for it?

What was that lying on the sand a couple of yards away?

I dismounted and walked over to investigate. What was shining in the midday sun was the barrel of a rifle, the rest of it being buried in the sand.

I picked up the weapon. It was a Mauser. There was no doubt that bullets from it had killed these two creatures, and there was every reason to believe that the man who had done the killing was none other than Professor Hektor Demetrius. I was also sure that the same gun had been used by the same man to kill the unnamed black beast in the forest in Iraklion.

So this was the camel that Demetrius hired. At this point, he had no more use for his mount; so he had killed it as well as its owner. Wherever Demetrius had gone from here, he must have gone on foot.

We now looked at the two Arabs. Their faces had turned white. This was not only because of the scene of carnage, but because gusts of wind had started blowing from the west again, bringing with them the eerie sound – 'dub – thump . . . dub – thump . . . dub – thump. . .'

We realised we should have to mount our camels again and follow the sound to its source. Both of us now believed that it must have some connection with Demetrius.

The camelmen agreed after some persuasion backed by baksheesh.

For three hours we travelled while the sound grew louder and louder, until a strange sight obliged us to stop and dismount.

In the middle of the desert stood a huge sand-covered mound

shaped somewhat like a pyramid. If it was a relic of ancient Egypt, neither of us had ever seen it mentioned in any book.

We have pitched our tent at a considerable distance from the mound. We shall get a proper idea of its dimensions when we go closer to it. We have asked the camel drivers about it, but they seem to have been struck dumb; perhaps the insistent drumming has made them speechless. From here the deep pounding can be heard all the time, even when there is no wind blowing. It is as if the sound was part of the ambience of the place. We have been here an hour; not once has the pounding stopped or its rhythm changed.

Summerville's guess is that the mound is an ancient monument. We have decided to take a little rest and then go up to it to take a close look. Summerville seems just as puzzled as I am about the pounding, but he was right about one thing: the source of the sound *is* subterranean. It was proved when we placed our ears on the sand. This incessant pounding may disturb our concentration. We can only wait and see what happens.

Clouds have gathered in the west again, and a wind is raising the sand.

January 12, 4 pm

A terrible sandstorm nearly blew away our tents. On top of that there was an earthquake.

I noticed something strange about the tremor: it was not sideways like an ordinary earthquake. At the first impact, it felt as if the ground had suddenly subsided. It was like pulling a chair from under someone. I know that some earthquakes are accompanied by a rumbling sound; I myself heard it in the Bihar earthquake of 1934. But I doubt if anything like the sound which accompanied the earthquake today had ever been heard before. It was as if the whole earth was groaning in unbearable agony. Even I found myself breaking out in a cold sweat. Murad and Suleiman, our two camelmen, both fainted from sheer fright. They were revived with medication, but I doubt if they'll ever be able to speak again. The two camels seem petrified with their looks fixed towards the mysterious edifice. I feel quite confused. The only constant thing in all this is the great, pounding drumbeats.

We shall wait for some time. If no other calamity takes place we shall go out. We must get close to the mound to investigate.

5.15 pm

I am writing this sitting by the sand-hill, which now seems twice as high as it did from the camp. Its highest point is certainly higher than the highest pyramid at Giza. The drumbeat here is deafening. We have to use a sign language to communicate with each other. But the strange thing is that one begins to get used to a sound of even such deafening intensity. It doesn't bother me any more nor does it interfere with my thoughts.

First let me try to explain what the hill looks like. Here is a diagram of it –

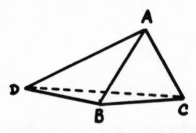

ABC, the northern face, is vertical, and roughly the shape of an equilateral triangle. ABD and ACD are respectively the eastern and western faces, while BCD is the base – in the shape of an isosceles triangle – on which the structure stands. We both believe that removing the sand would reveal a solid structure, probably of sandstone, representing an ancient Egyptian monument as yet unknown to the civilized world.

On the way to the mound we discovered two highly interesting and mysterious objects. Summerville is now busy with one of them. What we first came across looked like a length of very stout brown cable sticking out of the sand. We had never seen anything like it before, and it was impossible to guess what it was made of. Both of us pulled hard at it, but it stuck fast. In the end Summerville sliced off a portion of the cable with his knife with a view to testing it.

What baffled us even more was something which looked like the segment of a disc-like object, pink in colour, and with furrows on its curved surface. This too proved impossible to dislodge. My guess is that, had the whole surface been revealed, it would have proved large enough to hold a tennis court.

Both the objects were so out of place in the desert and so unlikely in their connection with ancient Egypt, that it has set a new problem for us.

I wonder if the two objects, the colossal mound, and the pounding drumbeats, have an extra-terrestrial origin? They all seem to be on a superhuman scale. Perhaps the pounding emanates from an underground factory or laboratory where Demetrius is working under the guidance of an alien intelligence?

Summerville is making for the vertical northern face of the mound. I must go with him. If something should happen to one of us, the other would feel very helpless indeed.

11.20 pm

A great many strange happenings in the last five hours.

First of all, let me say that by digging with our hands we have been able to locate a tunnel on the vertical northern face of the mound. The inside of it is pitch dark. We flashed a powerful torch into it and looked through binoculars. There was nothing to see. Great gusts of wind blew out of the tunnel every so often and it made our work very difficult, but we persisted. We gave up only after it became too dark to work, and came back to our tent. Tomorrow, if we find that the layer of sand has thinned down a bit, we shall make an attempt to enter the tunnel. I strongly believe that the answer to the mystery lies in the depths of that darkness.

Back at camp, we made ourselves some coffee. My pills take care of both our thirst and hunger, but don't provide the satisfaction of a cup of hot coffee at the end of a day's work. Summerville has brought some excellent Brazilian coffee, which is what we drank. But let me now describe what happened after coffee.

Summerville was sitting with Demetrius's notebook open before him. Half an hour's effort to decipher the script had failed. I too sat beside him recalling the strange events of the past few days, when my eyes fell on the notebook. Summerville's spectacles were resting on it on their rims. I noticed that Demetrius's writing was reflected in the glasses as in a mirror. The very next moment, I saw that I could read the writing and that it was a language we both knew. It was not Greek, but the all too familiar English! Demetrius had guarded himself against others having access to his notes by using mirror writing. I recalled that Da Vinci also wrote his notes in this fashion. In the last couple of hours, we have been able to read most of Demetrius's notes with the help of Summerville's shaving mirror. Here is what the notes have revealed –

In Knossos, in the ruins of a 5,000-year-old temple, Demetrius had found a stone inscription. On deciphering it, he had found that it was the formula for a miraculous drug which was supposed to induce a god's power into a human being. Demetrius had proceeded to prepare the drug, and the note suggests that he had succeeded in doing so. Not only that; on the twenty-sixth of December he had tried out the drug on someone called Felix. Demetrius does not say who this Felix was, but both Summerville and I know that although some people are called Felix, it can also be the name for a cat, *felis* being the Latin term for the genus cat. Does that name – no, it is not possible to continue writing. A storm seems to be building up.

January 16

It is about two hours since we arrived in Cairo. My hands are not steady, yet I must write down the terrible events of the last two days. We have lost a whole day waiting for a caravan. Our own camels, along with their owners, are missing, probably dead. We had to trek three and half hours across the desert in our pitiful state to reach the caravan track. My Miracurol has worked wonders to the extent of mending Summerville's broken elbow. But the state of our minds is far from normal. By great good fortune, my two phials of medicine, my diary, fountain pen, wallet, duplicate spectacles and my pistol were all in the pockets of my jacket. Everything else, including Demetrius's notebook, has been blown away without trace.

I have already recorded how on January the twelfth a storm interrupted my writing. As a matter of fact, it was a combination of rain and storm, the like of which I have never experienced in all my life. The first thing to go was the Luminimax lamp. The camels had started to scream at the top of their voices, and I peeped out of the tent and saw in three successive flashes of lightning, Murad and Suleiman lying prostrate on the sand desperately invoking the name of Allah.

About a quarter to midnight – the radium dial on my watch could at least tell me the time – the storm seemed to subside a little. Our tents had, of course, collapsed long ago, and were now wrapped around us. We clung on to them in the hope that we would be able to set them up again when the weather cleared.

Precisely at midnight, after an earsplitting thunderclap, the convusions of a terrible earthquake started. With the very first shock, I found that I was no longer on the ground but had been hoisted skyward like a cricket ball from a mighty drive. I sailed for a full five seconds through the air before landing on wet sand as cold as a slab of ice. I had nothing over my head now, nor was Summerville by my side. Where Summerville was, whether he was still alive, where the camels and the camelmen were, whether *they* were alive – there was no way of knowing.

And now there was a sudden jolt, and the earth was still.

The rain too had stopped, and there was silence.

No sound at all? Not even the drumbeats?

No, not even those. Incredibly enough, the pounding had stopped.

Instead of that there was an almost palpable silence.

I raised my head and looked around. It wasn't dark any more. How could there be so much light? How was it that I could see everything clearly?

Now I realised that the sky was clear but for a wisp of cloud which was slowly revealing the moon – the full moon.

And now the moon was out. Never had I seen such resplendent moonlight.

Who was that to my left – about a couple of yards away? Wasn't it Summerville?

Yes, Summerville. He was standing. I shouted, 'John! John!'

No answer. Had he turned deaf? Or mad? What was he staring at so intently?

I too turned my eyes in the same direction, towards the mound.

The mound was clear of sand now. But what was it that was revealed in its nakedness?

I staggered towards Summerville. I could not take my eyes off the mound. The incredibility of it all took my breath away. I could see that the enormous thing that raised itself towards the sky was something well known to me. And the two enormous cavities on the vertical northern face, those which we thought were tunnels into a subterranean factory, they were known to me too. The cavities were nostrils, and the mound was the nose of a man lying on the ground, and the two dense semi-circles of dark foliage were the two eyebrows on the two sides of the bridge, and the huge convexities below them were the two closed eyelids.

'Demetrius!'

Summerville's whispered utterance seemed to echo in the stillness of the vast moonlit expanse of the Sahara.

'Demetrius! Demetrius!'

Yes, Demetrius. I know that now from his photo. Those eyes I have seen open; now they were closed in death. Now I know that the brown cable was a hair of his body, and the pink segment of a disc was one of his fingernails.

'Do you realise the reason for the earthquake?' asked Summerville.

I said, 'Yes. They were caused by Demetrius in the throes of death.'

'And the pounding drumbeats?'

'Demetrius's heartbeat, of course. . .He had first tried out his drug on his black cat Felix. The cat grew to an enormous size, forcing Demetrius to use the gun.'

'But he didn't wish to stop his own growth. Like a true scientist, he wanted to find out the limit of the drug's power.'

'Yes. He believed he would grow into a Colossus. So he wanted the limitless expanse of the Sahara for his experiment.'

'Have you tried to work out how big he had grown?'

I said, 'If the vertical wall with the nostrils is a hundred feet high, then the whole body should be at least sixty times more.'

'That is more than a mile.'

Summerville sighed.

'So the old gypsy woman wasn't wrong,' he said.

'In fact, she was dead right. Today is the thirteenth. The pounding stopped exactly at midnight.'

We had to wait for the day.

As soon as it turned light, I saw a horrible sight. The sky was filled with hundreds of vultures circling slowly down. It was as if all the vultures in the world had joined forces to devour the six thousand-foot-long carcase.

I took out my pulverising pistol from my pocket, aimed it at the swarm and pressed the trigger.

In a few seconds the swarm disappeared and the spotless, rain-washed blue sky of the Sahara smiled down at us.

THE UNICORN EXPEDITION

July 1

Exciting news. A diary belonging to Charles Willard has been found. Only a year ago, while on his way back from Tibet, this English explorer was waylaid by a gang of Khampa robbers who made off with most of his belongings. By a supreme effort, Willard was able to reach the town of Almora in India in a state of near collapse. He died there soon after. All this I had read in the papers. Today I had a letter from London from my geologist friend Jeremy Saunders. He says that among the few personal effects that Willard left behind was a diary which is now in Saunders' possession. The diary mentions a most unusual event. Knowing of my great interest in Tibet and the Tibetan language, Saunders has passed the information on to me. Here is an extract from his letter:

'You know that Willard had been an old friend of mine. I called on his widow Edwina a couple of days back. She mentioned that among Willard's possessions sent her from Almora was a diary. I borrowed the diary from her. Unfortunately, much of the writing has been washed away, but the very last entry is quite legible. It records an incident which took place on March the nineteenth. Only two lines describe it: "*I saw a herd of unicorns today. I write this in full possession of my senses.*" Seeing a storm coming up, Willard had stopped writing at this point. I am most curious to know what you feel about the extraordinary statement."

Willard had to assert that he was in his right senses; like the dragon of the east and the west, the unicorn has been known as a product of human imagination. But I have some hesitation in using the word imagination. I have a book open before me on my desk which is about the ancient civilisation of Mohenjo-daro. Apart from pottery, toys, figurines and ornaments, diggings at Mohenjo-daro have revealed a large number of rectangular clay and ivory seals bearing carvings of, amongst other things, animals such as elephants, tigers, bulls and rhinoceroses. In addition to these familiar animals, there are representations of a beast unknown to us. It is shown as a bull-like creature with a single curved horn growing out of its forehead. Archaeologists have taken it to be a creature of fantasy, although I see no point in depicting an imaginary creature when all the others shown are real.

There is another reason for thinking that the unicorn may not, after all, be a fantastic animal. Two thousand years ago, the Roman scholar Pliny clearly stated in his famous treatise on animals that in India there exist cows and donkeys with a single horn. Aristotle, too, maintained that there were unicorns in India. Would it be wrong to conclude from this that in India there did exist, in ancient times, a species of unicorn which became extinct here, but which still survives in some parts of Tibet? What if Willard had accidentally stumbled upon a herd of them? It is true that in the last two hundred years many foreign explorers have visited Tibet none of whom mention the unicorn. But what does that prove? There are still many unexplored regions in Tibet. Who knows what species of animal may exist there?

I must pass my thoughts on to Saunders.

July 15

Here is Saunders' reply to my letter:

Dear Shonku:

Thanks for your letter. I have managed to decipher some of Willard's entries towards the end of his diary, and am even more astonished. On March the sixteenth he writes: '*Today I flew with the two hundred-year-old lama.*' What on earth does he mean? Flying in an aeroplane? That sounds most unlikely when Tibet lacks even railways. Does he mean flying without the aid of an aircraft? Like a bird? But is such a thing possible? Such a statement raises doubts about Willard's sanity. And yet the doctor – Major Horton – who examined Willard in Almora categorically stated that Willard's brain had not been affected. The entry of March the thirteenth mentions a monastery called Thokchum-Gompa. According to Willard: '*A wonderful monastery. No European has ever been here before*'. Have you heard of this monastery? Anyway, the upshot is that Willard's diary has fired me with a great impulse to visit Tibet. My German friend Wilhelm Kroll is also enthusiastic. He has been particularly intrigued by the mention of the flying lama. I suppose you know that Kroll has done important research on magic and witchcraft. He is also an excellent mountaineer. It goes without saying that it would be wonderful if you too could come with us. Let me know what you decide.

With best wishes,

Yours,

Jeremy Saunders

A flying lama! I have read the autobiography of the Tibetan saint Milarepa. He was able to perform supernatural feats by Tantra and yogic meditation. One of the feats he became adept at was flying. Did Willard fly with the help of such a yogi?

I haven't been to Tibet; but I have read about it and learned the Tibetan language. Willard's diary has raised my curiosity to a high pitch. That is why I'm thinking of joining Saunders' party. It would actually help them if I did, because I have inventions of mine which would considerably reduce the strain of such a journey.

July 27

My friend and neighbour Mr Abinash Mazumdar threw up his hands when I told him I was going to Tibet. Having accompanied me twice on my trips abroad, his wanderlust had been aroused. I had to tell him about the hazards of such a journey. He replied, 'So what? What more could a devout Hindu like me want than to have a glimpse of Lord Siva's own mountain Kailas?' Although Mr Mazumdar knew about Kailas, he didn't know about the holy lake at its foot. 'What!' he exclaimed, 'Lake Mansarovar in Tibet? I always thought it was in Kashmir.'

I didn't mention the unicorn and the flying lama to Mr Mazumdar because I do have doubts about them, but when I mentioned the Khampa bandits, Mr Mazumdar calmly said, 'Don't worry, Lord Siva will protect you from harm.'

We have decided to start our journey from Kathgodam. I have sent a wire to Saunders saying that I shall arrive in Kathgodam on the first of August. We will, of course, have to travel light. When I told this to Mr Mazumdar, he said, 'What about my pillows? I can't sleep without them.' I have promised to make him a couple of inflatable ones. For high altitude wear I'm taking vests made of Shanklon fabric. In case anyone has breathing trouble, we are taking small portable oxygen cylinders. In all, the luggage shouldn't weigh more than ten kilograms. Suitable footwear we could buy on the way in Almora.

It has been quite stuffy here these last few days. Possibly a portent of heavy rains. Once we cross over into Tibet, we shall be out of reach of the monsoon.

August 10, Garbayang

I haven't had any time for my diary these last few days. We left Kathgodam on the third by taxi for Almora. Thereafter we have travelled a hundred and fifty miles on horseback to reach Garbayang yesterday evening.

Garbayang is a Bhutiya village at an altitude of 10,000 feet. We are still in India. To our east runs the river Kali. Across the river one can see the dense pine forests of Nepal. Twenty miles to the north one has to negotiate a pass in order to reach Lipudhura. Beyond Lipudhura is Tibet.

Mount Kailas and the Lake Mansarovar are about forty miles from the Tibetan border. Not a great distance, but the terrain is difficult and the cold bitter. Besides, there are other unforeseen hazards which have discouraged ninety-nine per cent of Indians from venturing into this region. And yet the landscape we have passed through even at this early stage gives a foretaste of the grandeur that lies ahead.

Let me describe our party now. Besides Saunders and Kroll, a third European has joined us. His name is Ivan Markovitch; he is a Russian by birth but lives in Poland. He speaks English quite well but with an accent. He is the youngest in our group, and the tallest. He has blue eyes, a headful of unruly brown hair, thick eyebrows and a drooping moustache. We met him in Almora. He was also bound for Tibet, the reason being sheer wanderlust. He joined our party as soon as he learnt that we were also headed the same way. He seems a reasonably decent individual, although I have noticed that he seldom smiles, and even when he does, his lips curl up but his eyes remain unsmiling: a sure sign of a closed mind, which is probably why Kroll has taken a dislike to him.

Wilhelm Kroll is a round, ruddy individual no taller than five foot six inches, and with no hair on his head except for a few golden tufts about the ears. It is impossible to guess by looking at him that he has climbed the Matterhorn four times. A highly qualified anthropologist, Kroll makes no secret of his deep interest in the occult. He fully believes that the unicorn and flying lamas may well exist in Tibet. I have noticed that Kroll has a habit of lapsing into absentmindedness, so that you have to call him thrice before he answers.

Saunders is five years younger than me. He is a well-built handsome man with intelligent blue eyes and a broad forehead. He has read about a dozen books on Tibet in the last couple of weeks to prepare himself for the journey. He doesn't believe in magic or yogic powers; even reading about Tibet hasn't converted him. There is nothing he relishes more than a lively argument with Kroll and he indulges in it at every opportunity.

My neighbour Mr Mazumdar has come for the sole purpose of pilgrimage. He is now seated a few yards away from us sipping Tibetan tea from a copper bowl, with his eyes on a yak tethered to a nearby pole. Only this morning he remarked, 'All our lives we have seen the yak's tail at the end of a silver handle being waved at religious ceremonies. Now, for the first time, I see where it really belongs.' Actually, it is the tail of the white yak which is used in rituals. The ones here are mostly black. They are invaluable as carriers of luggage. We are taking with us four yaks, six ponies and eight porters.

Mr Mazumdar has warned me that I shouldn't expect him to hobnob with my foreign friends. 'You may know sixty-four languages; I know only one. I can say "good-morning" and "good-evening" all right; and if one of them should slip and fall into an abyss I could even say "good-bye". But that is all. You can tell them I am one of those Indian sadhus who observe a vow of silence, and my only purpose in coming is pilgrimage.'

The three Europeans and myself are now seated in front of a Bhutiya shop, having our breakfast of tea and *sampa*. *Sampa* is a ball of ground wheat which you soak in tea or water and eat. The tea is not like our Indian tea at all. It comes from China and is known as brick tea. Instead of milk and sugar, this tea is taken with butter and salt. It is poured into a cylindrical bamboo cup and stirred with a bamboo stump till the three ingredients are thoroughly mixed. Tibetans drink it at least thirty times a day. They also eat the meat of goat and yak. We are carrying with us a large stock of rice, lentils, vegetables, coffee and tinned food. If and when we run out of stock, we shall have to fall back on my nutriment pills.

Having now read Willard's diary myself, my curiosity has increased a hundredfold. A group of Tibetan wool merchants has arrived here. I asked one of them about unicorns. He only grinned at me as if I was a child asking a stupid question. When asked about flying lamas, he said all lamas could fly. I don't think anything will come out of talking to these people. We doubt if we will have Willard's luck, but we're all hoping that we will. In his entry for March the eleventh, Willard talks about a place whose name he doesn't mention, but whose geographical position he gives as Lat. 33′3 N and Long. 84 E. The map shows it to be roughly one hundred miles north-east of Mount Kailas in a region called Chang Thang. This is supposed to be a particularly hostile terrain, quite bereft of vegetation. Some nomadic tribes pass through it once in a while, but no one lives here. The place is also known for blizzards which bore through seven layers of woollens to freeze one's bones.

We are prepared to put up with everything provided we achieve our goal. Mr Mazumdar says, 'You mustn't worry. My faith in the Lord of Mount Kailas will guarantee the success of your mission.'

August 14, Purang Valley

We have set up camp beside a torrential river at an altitude of about 12,000 feet. It is afternoon now, and the sun is about to go down behind the high, snow-clad mountains which surround us, making the atmosphere chillier by the minute. Surprisingly enough, although the nights here can be extremely cold, in the daytime the temperature often rises to ninety degrees Fahrenheit.

Since I knew we would be climbing high, I reminded everyone that we were carrying oxygen. Saunders and Mr Mazumdar needed it. Kroll didn't since he was from the mountain resort of Meiningen, and therefore used to heights.

Markovitch too said he was used to heights. He was to realise later that he had done something very foolish. We were proceeding quite peacefully with five of us up front on our ponies, followed by our porters and the yaks loaded with our baggage. As we crossed the Gurup-la pass at 16,000 feet we heard a strange noise above the clatter of hooves and the whistling of the wind. Someone amongst us had broken out in wild laughter.

I looked about and realised that the laughter emanated from the man at the head of the group, Mr Ivan Markovitch. We all stopped.

Markovitch had pulled up too. He now dismounted, still laughing, and stood swaying perilously close to the edge of the road which dropped 2,000 feet into a gorge. If he went over, Mr Mazumdar would surely have an opportunity to say 'goodbye'.

Saunders, Kroll and myself dismounted and hurried towards Markovitch. The man's eyes looked glazed and, like his laughter, suggested a mind bereft of sense. It was clear what had happened. Above 12,000 feet, the oxygen content in the atmosphere begins to thin. This causes some people to feel no more than a slight discomfort in breathing, others faint, or show symptoms of insanity by weeping or laughing hysterically. Markovitch belonged to the last category. Our porters had probably never encountered such an exhibition before, for they too had started to laugh. The mountains around now echoed with the laughter of nine men.

Kroll suddenly came up to me and said, 'What about giving him a sock on the jaw?'

I was bewildered. 'Why sock him?' I asked. 'It is lack of oxygen which is making him laugh like that.'

'Precisely,' said Kroll. 'You can't make him take any oxygen in this state. If I knock him out, you can force it down his nose.'

Before I could answer him, Kroll had turned round and delivered a mighty blow on the man's jaw. I got busy with the medication, and in ten minutes Markovitch had regained consciousness. He looked about with a puzzled expression, rubbed his jaw, and got back onto his pony without any more fuss. We resumed our journey.

Sitting around the fire, we fell to talking about fantastic creatures. What strange beings the human imagination had concocted in past ages! Of course, some scholars say that they are not wholly imaginary. Remnants of the memory of creatures seen in prehistoric times are said to persist for ages in the collective human consciousness. By adding his imagination to such shreds of memory, man creates new species. Perhaps the pterodactyl and the aepyornis are really the progenitors of our mythical Garuda and Jatayu, and the Roc in the tale of Sinbad, a giant bird whose young fed on elephants. In the folk tales of Egypt one reads of the bird Ti-Bennu which became the Phoenix of later European myths. Then there is the dragon which occurs both in the myths of the east and the west. The difference is that the dragon of western mythology is a malignant demon, while that of the Far East is a benevolent god.

It was I who finally changed the subject and raised the question of Markovitch, who was away resting in his tent. We hadn't yet told him the real reason for our expedition; it was my feeling that we should tell him now. We should also make clear to him the terrible hazards of the Chang Thang region. If after knowing of the risks involved he still wants to come with us, then let him do so. If not, he should either branch off on his own or get back to India.

'You're right,' said Kroll. 'Why should we burden ourselves with someone who can't even mix properly? Let's have it out with him right now.'

The three of us went into Markovitch's tent. He sat crouching on the far side dimly visible in the half-light. Without beating about the bush, Saunders told him about Willard's diary and our search for the unicorn. Even before he had finished, Markovitch blurted out, 'Unicorns? Why, I have seen dozens of unicorns. Even today I saw one. Didn't you see it?'

We exchanged glances. It didn't seem as if Markovitch was being facetious. Kroll left the tent humming a German tune. He had obviously given up Markovitch as a bad case. Now the two of us came out too. Kroll lit his pipe and said in a mocking tone, 'You don't think it's lack of oxygen that makes him talk like that, do you?' Saunders and I were both silent. 'I haven't the slightest doubt that we have a loony in our midst,' said Kroll, and walked off with his camera towards a large boulder which had the Tibetan mantra *Om Mani Padme Hum* inscribed on it.

Is Markovitch really a madman? Or is he just pretending? I have an uneasy feeling in my mind.

Mr Mazumdar seems to be the least worried person in our group. I have known him for forty years. I never suspected that he had any imagination. He has always pooh-poohed my scientific experiments, and my epoch-making inventions have never produced any admiration or wonder in his mind. But the trips abroad that he made with me – once to Africa and once across the Pacific – seem to have brought about a change in him. There is an English saying that travel broadens the mind. This certainly has been more than true in the case of Mr Mazumdar. Today he came up to me and whispered in my ears an old poem about Mount Kailas which compares it with a million moons and describes it as the home of heavenly beings. It is clear that Mr Mazumdar still believes the age-old legends about Kailas. I'm afraid he will be disappointed when he comes face-to-face with the real thing. Just now he is observing the porters cooking their meal; they're going to have wild goat for dinner.

In the far distance I can see a group of men on horseback coming down the path which we shall take tomorrow. Till a little while ago, the group had seemed like a conglomeration of moving dots. Now I can see them clearly. The sight of them seems to have excited our porters. Who are those people?

The temperature is dropping. We can't stay out much longer.

August 14, 7 pm

A momentous event took place a little while ago.

The group we had seen approaching was a gang of Khampa

robbers. We now have proof that this was the very group which waylaid Willard.

Twenty-two men on horseback, everyone with swords and daggers tucked in their belts around their thick tunics, and old-fashioned blunderbusses slung across their shoulders. Besides the men and horses, there were five woolly Tibetan dogs.

When the gang was about a hundred yards away from us, two of our porters, Rabsang and Tundup, rushed up to us and said, 'Please bring out all your weapons, sir.' I asked him if we were supposed to turn them over to the bandits. 'No, no!' said Rabsang, 'They have great respect for foreign weapons. If you don't bring them out, they will just run away with everything we have.'

We had three firearms with us – an Enfield and two Austrian Mannlichers. Besides, I had my own invention – the Stun Gun. This was actually a pistol which produced a 'ping' instead of a 'bang' when the trigger was pressed, and injected a needle which instantly stunned the victim. Saunders and Kroll brought out their guns from the tent. There was no sign of Markovitch. I had to keep my hands free in case the Stun Gun was needed, and yet three guns in the hands of two men seemed odd, so I handed the third to Mr Mazumdar. He first made a show of protest, then took the gun, turned his back on the bandits and stood facing the river, ramrod straight.

The bandits arrived. The huge shaggy dogs started barking at us as if they were bandits too. These gangs usually raid the encampments of the nomads and make off with all their belongings. To turn against them without proper arms means certain death. It is not easy to run these gangs to ground in the wild, snow-bound country, but when the Tibetan police do get their hands on them, the robbers have their heads and right hands chopped off and sent to Lhasa. I have also heard that the bandits are so afraid of retribution in hell that after each raid they undergo a spell of absolution by either circumambulating Mount Kailas, or climbing a cliff and loudly proclaiming their misdeeds for all the world to hear.

The bandit in front seemed to be the leader. A snub nose, ringed ears, and a deeply lined face belied his youth. His slit eyes now regarded the four of us with deep suspicion. The others held on to their reins, obviously waiting for the word from their chief.

Now the chief dismounted, strode up to Kroll and said in a thick voice: '*Peling?*' *Peling* is the Tibetan word for a European. I answered for Kroll. 'Yes', I said, '*Peling.*' But how did he guess Kroll was a European?

The deep croak of a rook could be heard from somewhere. Apart from that, the only sound came from the swiftly flowing river. The bandit went up to Mr Mazumdar. I'm not sure why my friend thought fit to bow in greeting to the robber, but it was obvious that the latter found the gesture highly comic. He gave a sharp prod to the butt of the gun in Mr Mazumdar's hand and burst into an unseemly guffaw.

I was now alarmed to see Kroll slowly raising his gun towards the bandit, the veins in his forehead standing out in reckless rage. I was forced to restrain him with a sharp gesture. Meanwhile Saunders had moved up to my side. 'They have an Enfield too,' he whispered through clenched teeth.

I turned towards the bandits and found that one of them, a particularly fierce-looking individual, was indeed carrying an Enfield. We know from Willard's diary that he had an Enfield. The gun wasn't among his personal effects when he came to Almora. That and the fact that the chief could recognise a European, made it obvious that this was the gang that had plagued Willard.

But there was nothing that we could do about it. The gang far outnumbered us. I could see that they were just biding their time before getting down to the serious business of plunder.

I was wondering how long this cat-and-mouse game was to go on when a diversion occurred. Markovitch suddenly emerged from his tent, staggered towards the gang and pointing with outstretched arms at the Tibetan dogs, cried out jubilantly, 'Unicorns! Unicorns!'

At this, one of the huge mastiffs suddenly took a menacing

stance and with a nasty growl leaped at Markovitch.

But before he could reach his target he had dropped down on the ground senseless. The reason for this was, of course, my pistol. My right hand had for some time been gripped around its butt in my pocket. At the crucial moment the hand had come out and performed the conjuring trick.

Markovitch suddenly seemed to lose grip on himself and collapsed on the ground. Kroll and Saunders lifted him up between them and bore him back into his tent.

And the bandits? There was an incredible transformation in them. Some of them dismounted and were down on their knees, while others who were still on their ponies made repeated gestures of obeisance towards me. The chief too had in the meantime thought it prudent to get back on his mount. That the combined threat of twenty-two bandits would vanish so quickly, I had never imagined.

I approached the man with the Enfield and said, 'Either you hand over that gun or I'll make the whole lot of you suffer the fate of the dog.' He immediately offered the gun to me with shaking hands. I now addressed the whole gang: 'You took this gun from a *peling*; I want you to turn over to me whatever else you took from him.'

Within a minute various objects were produced from the bag of the robbers – two tins of sausages, a Gillette safety-razor, a mirror, a pair of field-glasses, a torn map of Tibet, an Omega watch and a leather bag. I opened the bag and found in it two standard books on Tibet by Morecraft and Tiffenthaler, both bearing Willard's name in his own handwriting.

Having confiscated the objects, I was about to command the bandits to go away when they themselves turned tail and, in the gathering dusk, disappeared the way they came.

I now relieved Mr Mazumdar of the Mannlicher and went to see how Markovitch was faring.

He was lying on a rug on the ground with his eyes closed. As I flashed my torch on his face, he slowly opened them. One look at his pupils told me that he was under the influence of some potent drug, perhaps the source of his unicorns. Drugs like cocaine, heroin and morphine may well lead to hallucinations.

An addict like Markovitch would be a great handicap to our expedition. Either we must get rid of him or of his addiction.

August 15, 7 am

When last night Markovitch went without dinner even when we urged him to join us, I was even more convinced about his addiction. Drugs tend to deaden one's appetite. When I told Saunders, he blew his top. 'He must be questioned at once,' he insisted. Kroll said 'You two are too gentlemanly. Let me do the questioning.'

After dinner, Kroll dragged Markovitch out of his tent and taking him by the scruff of his neck, hissed into his ears: 'Come on, out with your drugs, or we'll bury you in the snow and leave you to rot. No one will ever know.'

I could see that, although groggy, Markovitch had turned pale. He wriggled himself free, put his hand in his valise and pulled out a hair-brush which he handed Kroll. At first I thought this was another sympton of the Russian's addiction; but Kroll could, with his German astuteness, immediately make out that Markovitch had given up the real thing. With a little pressure, the wooden back of the brush opened like a lid, revealing a store of white powdered cocaine. In a few moments the powder had become part of the Himalayan atmosphere.

That Markovitch's craving too had disappeared with the cocaine was made clear when this morning at breakfast, the Russian helped himself to four glasses of tea, nearly a pound of goat's meat, and a considerable amount of *sampa*.

August 17, beyond Sangchan

It is two-thirty in the afternoon now. We are taking rest outside a monastery on the way to Lake Mansarovar. We have passed many monasteries on the way, each of them built on a cliff and each affording a splendid view of the mountains. One must admit that the lamas have a fine sense of atmosphere.

To the north stands the proud peak of Gurla Mandhata, 25,000 feet high. Beside this, many other snow peaks can be seen from here. A little further on are the great lake and Mount Kailas, the goals for which Mr Mazumdar is gamely striving.

Needless to say, no sight of unicorns so far. Animals can be seen frequently, but they consist of wild goats, sheep, donkeys and yaks. Occasionally one can see a hare or a field rat. We know there are deer and bears, but we haven't seen any yet. Last night hyenas were prowling near our camp; I could see their glowing eyes in the light of my torch.

Saunders has almost given up hope. He now believes that Willard too was under the influence of drugs; that flying lamas and unicorns were both drug-induced hallucinations. He seems to forget that we had met Major Horton at Almora, and seen his report concerning Willard. There was no mention of drugs in that.

There is only a single lama living in the monastery outside which we are now resting. We met him a little while ago. A strange experience. We had no intention of going into the monastery; but when Rabsang told us about the solitary lama, and that he hadn't spoken for fifty years, our curiosity was aroused. We climbed the hundred steps from the road and entered the sacred building.

Built of granite, the monastery was dark and clammy inside. In the main hall were seven or eight Buddha statuettes ranged on a shelf at the back. At least three were made of solid gold. A lamp was burning on the shelf. Alongside was a pot with a dollop of butter in it. This, and not oil, was used to light the lamps in the monasteries. Mr Mazumdar pointed to an object on the shelf and said, 'I'm sure that is used for tantric rites.' It was a human skull.

I said, 'Not only that; lamas are known to drink tea from such skulls.' Mr Mazumdar gave a slight shiver.

The mute lama was in a small room on the eastern wing of the monastery. He sat cross-legged on the floor beside a small window, slowly and patiently turning his prayer-wheel – a lean, shaven-headed man whose arms and legs had grown unusually thin from sitting down for hours at a stretch. One by one, we paid our respects to him. He gave each one of us a red thread as a sign of benediction.

We sat on a low bench facing him while he looked expectantly at us. Since the lama won't speak, we should have to put questions which could be answered in sign language. I went straight to the crucial question.

'Are there any unicorns in Tibet?'

The lama kept smiling at us for a minute or so. Five pairs of eyes were tensely fixed on him. Now the lama moved his head up and down – once, twice, three times. In other words, there were. But now he moved his head again, this time from side to side, meaning there weren't.

What kind of an answer was that? Could it mean that there were unicorns at one time, but not any more? Kroll turned to me and whispered, 'Ask him where they are.' Markovitch too was all attention.

I put the question Kroll had suggested. In reply, the lama raised his shrivelled left hand and pointed towards north-west. That was the direction we were going – to Chang Thang beyond Mount Kailas. I now felt impelled to put a third question.

'You are a yogi; you can see into the future. Please tell us if we will be able to see this wonderful creature.'

The lama again smiled and moved his head up and down three times.

Kroll was now in the throes of intense excitement. He now said quite loudly in English; 'Ask him if he knows about flying lamas.'

I turned to the lama. 'I have read about your great saint Milarepa,' I said.'He says he was able to travel from one place to another through the air. Are there any Tibetan saints still living who are capable of such a feat?'

I noticed a hardening of the look of the silent lama. He shook his head sideways quite emphatically, meaning there were none.

Before leaving the monastery, we left some tea and *sampa* for the mute lama. Among travellers and nomads in these parts, whoever knows about the mute lama leaves some provisions for him when they pass the monastery.

Coming outside, Kroll and Saunders fell into an argument. Saunders was not prepared to give any credence to the lama's statements. He said: 'One moment he says yes, the next moment no. When you're contradicting yourself like that, you're making no statement at all. I think we have only wasted our time.'

Kroll, by the way, had a totally different interpretation of the lama's answers. He said: 'To me the meaning is crystal clear: "Yes" means that the unicorn exists, and "No" means that he is asking us not to look for it because of the danger involved. But naturally we shall ignore his warning.'

For the first time Markovitch joined in our conversation. He said: 'Suppose we do come across a unicorn; have we decided what we're going to do with it?'

Kroll said, 'We haven't thought of that yet. The first thing is to track down the creature.'

Markovitch lapsed into silence. It seemed that he has some plans of his own. Now that he is rid of the cocaine habit, he seems much more energetic. I have also been observing in him a great interest in lamaseries. When we left the monastery after our talk with the mute lama, Markovitch stayed back to explore the place a little more thoroughly. Is the drug addict turning religious? I wonder.

August 19, 10 am

Just now we crossed the Chusung-la pass and had a glimpse of the Lake Ravana and the white dome of Mount Kailas behind it. Lake Ravana is called Rakshasa Tal in Tibetan, and Mount Kailas is Kang Rimpoche. The lake isn't a particularly holy one, but the first sight of Kailas made our porters prostrate themselves. Mr Mazumdar was a little perplexed at first, but the moment he realised what the dome was, he reeled off a dozen names of Lord Siva, fell on his knees and touched the ground again and again with his head. The holy Mansarovar is to the east of Lake Ravana. We expect to be there by tomorrow.

August 20, 2.30 pm

We have halted by a hot spring to the north-west of Mansarovar. We shall reach the lake as soon as we are over the hump to our left.

Today for the first time in over a week we all had a bath. A pall of vapour hangs over the spring which contains sulphur, and is very warm. One feels remarkably refreshed after a bath in it.

I wouldn't have opened my diary now but for an incident which took place a little while ago.

Mr Mazumdar and I were using the west side of the spring while the others bathed in the north side. I had finished my bath and Kroll walked over and, as if he had come for a casual tête-à-tête, said in a low voice, 'A messy affair.'

I said, 'Why, what's the matter?'

'Markovitch.'

'Markovitch?'

'A snake in the grass.'

'What has he done now?' I knew Kroll had a particular dislike for Markovitch.

Kroll kept up that smiling, chatty tone and said, 'We had taken off our coats and kept them behind a boulder before we got into the water. I was up after a dip or two. Markovitch's coat was lying next to mine. I could see the inside pocket, and couldn't resist the temptation of looking what was in it. There were three letters. All with British postage stamps, and all addressed to a Mr John Markham.'

'Markham?'

'Markham – Markovitch, John – Ivan, don't you see?'

'Where were the letters sent?' I asked.

'To an address in New Delhi.'

John Markham. . . .John Markham. . . .the name seemed to ring a bell. Where had I heard it before? Yes. It was in the papers some three years back. A man caught smuggling gold. John Markham. He got a prison sentence too, but had managed to escape by killing a guard. The man was British, but had been living in India for a long time. Used to run a hotel in Naini Tal. An escaped convict. Now he has teamed up with us and is trying to pass himself off as a Russian living in Poland. He wants Tibet to be his hideout. A swindler all right, and perhaps with more villainy up his sleeve. I had to praise Kroll's sleuthing. I told him of Markham and his dark deeds.

Kroll has kept up his toothy smile simply because Markovitch can see us from where he is. He mustn't suspect that we are talking about him.

Kroll laughed out loudly at nothing, dropped his voice, kept smiling and said: 'I suggest that we leave him behind. Let him freeze to death in the blizzard. That would be his punishment.'

I didn't like the idea. I said, 'No. Let him come with us. We will hand him over quietly to the police when we return.'

In the end Kroll agreed to my proposal. Must find an opportunity to tell Saunders, and must keep a sharp watch over Markovitch.

August 20, 5.30 pm

In the famous Sanskrit poem *Meghdoot* of Kalidasa, there is a description of swans and lotuses in the Mansarovar. We have seen flocks of wild geese but no swans or lotuses as yet. Apart from that I can say that the descriptions of the lake one reads in travel books come nowhere near the real thing. I cannot ever begin to describe how one feels at the sudden sight of the vast expanse of vivid and transparent blue in a terrain of sand and rocks. To the north of the lake stands the 22,000 foot Mount Kailas, and to the south, rising almost straight out of the water, stands Gurla Mandhata. All round are mountains dotted with monasteries, their golden domes glistening in the sun.

We have pitched our tents about thirty feet from the edge of the lake. There are many pilgrims around. Some of them are doing their circumambulation of the lake by crawling, while others are doing it on foot with prayer-wheels in their hands. Mansarovar is sacred to both Hindus and Buddhists. Geographically, the place is important because the sources of four great rivers lie close by. They are Brahmaputra, Sutlej, Indus and Karnali.

Apart from doing obeisance by lying prone on the ground, Mr Mazumdar made our foreign friends get down on their knees by repeatedly saying, 'Sacred, sacred – more sacred than cow!' But what he did after that was far from prudent. He went to the edge of the lake, threw away his overcoat, put his palms together and plunged straight into the water. The icy water numbed him instantly. However, Kroll managed to drag him out and force some brandy down his throat, thus bringing some warmth back into his body.

Mr Mazumdar is up and about again. He says he has had arthritis in his left thumb for the last twenty-six years which the water of the lake has completely cured. He has filled three empty Horlicks bottles with the holy water which he says he will sprinkle on us from time to time to keep us from trouble.

Nearby in Gianima there is a large market from which we have bought dried fruits, cakes of frozen yak milk and woollen tents. Kroll has bought an assortment of bones, one of which – a human thigh bone – can be played like a flute. He says they will be useful for his research on witchcraft. Markovitch had strayed from the group in the bazaar for a while. He got back only ten minutes ago. We haven't found out what he brought back in his bag. Saunders has managed to get rid of some of his pessimism. He has realised that even if he cannot find a unicorn, the unearthly beauty of Mansarovar and the extra-ordinarily clear and invigorating atmosphere of the place make the trip more than worthwhile.

We shall set off for the dreaded Chang Thang tomorrow. Our destination will be Lat. 33′3 N, and Long. 84 E.

Mr Mazumdar is now sitting on the sand with the sun on his back, his face turned towards Mount Kailas and the pocket *Gita* open in his hand. We shall now find out how far his faith is able to tide us over travails.

August 22, Chang Thang, Lat. 30′5 N, Long 81′8 E

It is eight-thirty in the morning now. We have set up camp beside a small lake.

A strange occurrence last night. At midnight, with the temperature well below freezing point, Kroll came into my tent, woke me up and announced that he had found highly suspicious objects among Markovitch's belongings. I was amazed. 'But didn't he find out that you were rummaging amongst his things?' I asked.

'How could he? I had mixed some barbiturate in his tea last night. It's not for nothing that I learned sleight-of-hand. He's now fast asleep.'

'What did you find?'

'Come and have a look.'

I wrapped myself in a thick blanket, left my tent and crawled into Kroll's. The moment I entered, a strong, vaguely familiar odour assailed my nostrils. 'What's this smell?' I asked.

Kroll said, 'Well, this is just one of the things I found. It is in this tin.'

I took the tin and took off the cap. My mouth fell open.

'But this is musk!' I exclaimed in a shocked voice.

'No question about it,' said Kroll.

I knew there were musk deer in Tibet – a species which was fast becoming extinct from the rest of the world. A deer the size of an average dog which carried the extraordinary substance in its stomach. Musk is used in perfumery. A gram of musk costs nearly thirty rupees. In India, soon after the start of our journey, I met a musk dealer in Askot who alone had exported under government licence nearly 400,000 rupees worth of musk. I said, 'Is this something which Markovitch bought from the bazaar at Gianima?'

'Bought it?' The question was put by Saunders, his voice oozing sarcasm. 'You think these were all *bought* by Markovitch?'

Saunders opened a bag and brought out from its depths a mass of black yak wool, five gold statuettes of Buddha, a gold *vajra* set with precious stones, and some twenty or thirty loose gems.

'We have a real robber in our midst,' said Saunders. 'I'm absolutely sure that he filched the musk from some shop in Gianima just as he filched the other objects from the monastery.'

Now I realised why Markovitch stayed back in the monastery. What a daredevil the man is!

This morning, Markovitch's behaviour suggested that he hadn't yet found out about last night's raid. Everything was put back in place before we left. We had also discovered that Markovitch was carrying a weapon with him – a .45 Colt automatic. Markovitch hadn't mentioned this to us. Not that the weapon is going to serve him any purpose now, because Kroll has made off with all the bullets.

August 25, Chang Thang, Lat. 32'5 N, Long. 82 E, 4.30 pm

The terrifying aspect of Chang Thang is gradually revealing itself to us. The elevation here is 16,500 feet. We are now in an uneven terrain. Sometimes we have to climb four or five hundred feet to negotiate a pass, and then descend again.

We haven't seen a single tree or shrub since yesterday morning. All around us are sand, rock and snow. Even here the Tibetans have carved their mantra *Om Mani Padme Hum* on rock faces. There are no monasteries here, although we do come across an occasional *chorten*. Of human habitation there is no sign at all.

The day before yesterday we suddenly found ourselves in a nomad encampment. Nearly five hundred men, women, children, goats, sheep, donkeys, dogs and yaks occupying a large territory with woollen tents pitched everywhere. The people were jolly, with a smile on everyone's face, obviously happy in their rootless, wandering state. We asked one or two about unicorns but got no satisfactory answer.

When they heard that we were going further north, they vehemently advised us against it. 'In the north there is Dung-lung-do,' they said. 'Beyond that you cannot go.' From their description it sounded as if Dung-lung-do was a place surrounded by a high wall which is impossible to scale. Nobody knows what lies beyond the wall. These people have never seen it, but Tibetans have always known about it. In earlier times, some lamas are said to have gone there, but no one in the last three or four hundred years.

When the mute lama's warnings hadn't discouraged us, why should we listen to these nomads? We have Charles Willard's diary with us. We must follow in his footsteps.

August 28, Chang Thang, Lat. 32'8 N, Long. 82'2 E

I am writing my diary sitting in my camp beside a lake. A strange experience today. We were crossing a valley with dark clouds in the sky threatening a storm when Saunders suddenly cried out, 'What are those?'

Further up, where the valley ascended, we could discern a dozen or so dark forms. They did seem like a herd of animals. We asked Rabsang, but he couldn't say what they were. The strange thing is that whatever they were, they all stood rooted to the same spot.

At Kroll's instigation I looked through the omniscope. 'Do you see horns?' Kroll asked breathlessly. I had to admit I didn't.

In another ten minutes the mystery was solved. They were wild donkeys, nearly twenty in number, all standing stiff and lifeless in the snow. Rabsang explained what had happened. They got buried in the snow in the blizzard and died. Summer has since melted the snow and exposed them again.

Our stock of foodstuff is dwindling. We had bought some tea and butter from the nomads with Indian money; they will last for a while. We are all heartily sick of eating meat. But vegetables are in short supply too. Everyone has had to take my food-and-drink pills from time to time. Soon there will be nothing left but these pills. Kroll has been using spells and incantations learnt all over the world from Mexico to Borneo to find out whether we will have the luck to stumble upon a herd of unicorns. Five spells said 'Yes', six said 'No'.

Thirty or forty miles to the north of where we have camped in the direction we are heading, the land seems to rise abruptly. It has the appearance of a table mountain through binoculars. Is that Dung-lung-do? We are actually near the location mentioned by Willard in his diary.

But where is Willard's monastery – Thokchum Gompa? Where is the two hundred-year-old flying lama?

And where is the herd of unicorns?

August 29

An electrifying experience in a wonderful monastery.

There is no doubt that this is the Thokchum Gompa of Willard's diary. And we have proof of that too. Three minutes before reaching the monastery we found carved on a rock face by the roadside the letters CRW, which obviously stood for Charles Roxton Willard. I must mention that all our porters except Rabsang and Tundup have absconded. I doubt if Rabsang will ever desert us. He is not only trustworthy, but there's not a trace of superstition in him. He is a rare exception among Tibetans. The others have taken away with them all our ponies and four yaks. Only two yaks are left. Our tents and some of our heavy baggage can go on their backs. The rest we will have to carry ourselves. And since our ponies are gone, we will have to do the rest of the journey on foot. The high plateau is getting closer by the hour, which is why excitement is running high among the group. We all believe that must be Dung-lung-do, although we still don't know what it is. Saunders believes it is the wall of a fortress, while my feeling is that behind the wall is a lake which is not shown on any map of Tibet.

The monastery I am about to describe was hidden from view till the last moment. It was situated behind a granite hillock. As soon as we crossed the hillock, it came into view, evoking expressions of surprise from all of us. Although the sun was behind the clouds, the splendour of the monastery made it appear paved in gold from base to spire.

As we approached it, we had the impression that there were very few occupants in it. The whole place seemed wrapped in silence. We climbed the slope and made our way through the main entrance. A huge bronze bell hung overhead across the threshold. As Kroll pulled the rope, it rang with a solemn sonority, the reverberations persisting for nearly three minutes.

It was quite clear from the moment of entry that no one had been here for a very long time. There was everything one would expect in a monastery except human beings. When Saunders' loud 'Hellos' produced no replies, we decided to explore. Kroll's behaviour made it clear that he was not going to leave Markovitch alone. There were too many gold objects about. Saunders went over to the door to the left of the hall, while Mr Mazumdar and I went to the door on the right. There was a thick layer of dust on the floor and abundant proof that rats lived here. We had just entered a room when a sudden scream stopped us in our tracks and froze our blood.

It was Saunders' voice. We ran to investigate and were joined by Kroll and Markovitch, the four of us arriving simultaneously at the door of a room on the right of the central hall. Our way was blocked by Saunders who had stopped at the threshold, apparently riveted by something at the back of the low, dank room.

Now I realised the reason for the scream.

An ancient, shaven-headed lama sat cross-legged at a desk on the far side of the room, his body bent forward, his eyes open but unseeing, his shrivelled hands placed on the withered pages of an open manuscript.

The lama was dead. When and how he died there was no way of knowing, nor how his corpse had escaped decay.

We were all inside the room now, Saunders was back to his normal self. He had been suffering from nerves for some time, which explains his extreme fright. I know if our expedition is crowned with success, he will surely regain his health.

Now we turned to the other objects in the room. On one side

was an assortment of brass and copper vessels which almost gave the impression that we were in a kitchen. On inspecting the vessels, we found that they contained powdered, liquid and viscous substances of various kinds and hues. I couldn't recognise any of them.

The opposite wall had shelves overflowing with ancient manuscripts. Below the shelves, on the floor, stood eight pairs of Tibetan high boots, all intricately embroidered and set with gems. Besides these, the floor was strewn with bones, skulls and animal skins. Kroll cried excitedly, 'This is the first monastery where I feel I am in the presence of ancient magic!'

I had no feeling of fright, so I approached the dead lama. I wanted to find out what he was studying when he died. I had already noticed that the manuscript was in Sanskrit, not Tibetan.

I gently tugged at the manuscript and it slipped out from under the corpse's fingers and came into my hands. The lama's hand stayed suspended in the air three inches above the desk.

A quick glance told me that the subject of the manuscript was scientific. I took it with me and the five of us left the gloom of the monastery and came out into the open.

It is two in the afternoon now, I am sitting on a flat rock outside the monastery. I have gone through a considerable portion of the manuscript in the last couple of hours. That the Tibetans had not confined their studies only to religion is now clear. The manuscript is called *Uddayansutram* or *A Treatise on Flying*. It describes how a person can be airborne by purely chemical means. I had heard of the treatise. In Buddhist times there was a great scholar in Taxila in India known as Vidyutdhamani. He was the one who composed the treatise and left for Tibet shortly thereafter. He never came back to India, and no one in India ever learnt about his scientific researches.

The manuscript describes a substance called *ngmung*. With the help of *ngmung* the weight of a person can be reduced to such an extent that a breath of wind can make him soar 'like a feather plucked from the back of a swan'. There is a description of how *ngmung* can be prepared, but the ingredients mentioned are totally unfamiliar to me. The dead lama must have known about these ingredients and must have succeeded in preparing *ngmung*. Doubtless this is the two hundred-year-old lama with whom Willard flew. That the lama should have died within the last six months is our misfortune, or we too might have flown like Willard.

Everybody is preparing to leave, so I must close now.

August 30, Lat. 33′3 N, Long. 84 E

Willard's diary mentions camping on this location. We have done the same thing. We are now reduced to five members including Rabsang. Markham alias Markovitch has disappeared, and he must have persuaded Tundup to go with him. Not only that, they have made off with our two last yaks. I had noticed Markham chatting with Tundop several times. I had paid no attention then; now I realise they had been conspiring.

It happened yesterday afternoon. Within two hours of leaving the monastery we were caught in a blinding storm. We didn't know who was going which way. When after half an hour the storm subsided, we found that we were two members and two yaks short. On top of that, when we found that there was a gun missing, we realised that it was not an accident. Markham had deliberately run away and had no intention of returning. One way to look at it is that it is good riddance, but the regret remains that he has escaped punishment. Kroll is greatly upset. He says this is the result of mollycoddling him. However, there's no use crying over spilt milk; we shall proceed to Dung-lung-do without him.

The wall of Dung-lung-do is now constantly in our sight. There are still another four or five miles to go, but even from this distance, the great height of the wall is apparent. In width it seems at least twenty-five miles. The depth, of course, cannot be guessed from here.

The wind is rising again. Must hurry back into the tent.

August 30, 1.30 pm.

The sky is overcast, and a blizzard is blowing with the sound of
a million shrill flutes. It is a good thing we bought those woollen
tents in Gianima.

It looks as if we will have to spend the whole day in the tent.

August 30, 5 pm.

One of the highlights of our expedition took place a little while
ago.

At three the storm let up a little, and Rabsang brought
butter-tea for the four of us. Although the fury of the storm had
abated, occasional gusts of wind caused the tents to flap.

Mr Mazumdar had just sipped his tea and said 'Aaahh!' in
appreciation when we heard a yelling from somewhere. We
couldn't make out the words, but the tone of panic was clear.
We put down our pots and rushed out of the tent.

'Help! Help! Save me! . . . Help!'

Now it was clear. And we could recognise the voice too. Till
now Markham had been speaking English with a Russian
accent; now, for the first time, he sounded thoroughly British.
But where was he? Rabsang too looked around in a bewildered
way, because one moment the voice seemed to be coming from
the south, and the next moment from the north.

Suddenly Kroll shouted, 'There he is!'

He wasn't looking north or south, but up in the sky, directly
above us.

I looked up and was astounded to see Markovitch come
floating towards us. One moment he plummeted down, and the
next a gust of wind sent him soaring up. It was in such a state
that he waved his arms about and screamed to draw our
attention.

There was no time to think how he had arrived at such a
predicament; the question was how to bring him down, because
the wind kept blowing him this way and that.

'Let him stay there,' Saunders suddenly bawled out. Kroll

promptly dittoed the suggestion. They both thought it was an excellent way to punish the miscreant. And yet the scientist in me said that unless he was brought down, we wouldn't be able to find out how he got airborne in the first place. Rabsang, meanwhile, had used his native intelligence and got down to business. He had tied a stone at the end of a long rope and was ready to fling it at Markham. Kroll stopped him. Markham was now directly above us. Kroll shouted at him, 'Drop that gun first.' I hadn't noticed that Markham was carrying a gun. Like an obedient boy, Markham released his hold on the weapon which dropped with a loud thud on the ground, sending up a spray of snow ten feet away from us.

Now Rabsang sent the stone flying up to Markham with unerring aim. Markham grabbed it, and Rabsang brought him down by vigorous pulls at the rope.

Now I noticed that Markham was wearing the ornate boots of which we saw eight pairs in the dead lama's room. Besides this, the bag he was carrying on his shoulder turned out to contain valuable gold objects pilfered from the monastery. There was no doubt that the robber had been caught red-handed. But, at the same time, he had brought to light something so exciting that we forgot all about reprimanding him.

Markham had run away from us all right, and the first thing he had done was to go to the Thokchum monastery and load himself up with some of the precious objects kept in the central hall. Having done that he had gone to the dead lama's room and helped himself to a pair of the gem-studded boots. Walking in them had made him realise that he was feeling lighter. When he had gone a couple of miles with Tundup, a storm had come up from the south and wrecked all his plans by hoisting him up and blowing him back in our direction.

Kroll and Saunders were naturally astonished to hear the story. It was then that I told them about the manuscript and the substance *ngmung*. 'But what is the connection between the substance and the boots?' asked Kroll.

I said, 'The manuscript mentions a connection between the

substance and the sole, or underside of the foot. I'm sure the lining of the boot has a coating of *ngmung*.'

This might have led to an argument, but having seen Markham aloft with their own eyes, Kroll and Saunders accepted my explanation. Of course, all three of us were now anxious to possess such boots. Rabsang said he would bring them for us from the monastery.

Markham is now completely tamed. We have taken away from him everything he had stolen. We shall put them all back in place on our way back. I do hope Markham will behave himself from now on, although at the back of my mind runs the Sanskrit proverb which says that coal will never shed its blackness however much you may wash it.

August 31

We have pitched our tents about two hundred yards away from the wall of Dung-lung-do. We are going about in our boots, waiting for a strong wind to take us across the wall to the unknown region beyond. The wall rises steeply up to a height of about one hundred and fifty feet. Even the geologist Saunders couldn't tell what kind of stone it was made of. It is remarkably smooth and hard, bluish in colour, and resembles no known variety of stone. Kroll has made a few attempts to scale the wall by leaping with the boots on, but in the absence of a strong wind he couldn't rise beyond twenty or thirty feet. I am consumed with curiosity about what lies beyond the wall. Saunders still insists that it must be a fortress. I have stopped guessing.

September 8

In the far distance, I can see a large group of people approaching. If this turns out to be a bandit gang, then there is no hope for us. It was the magical climate of Dung-lung-do that gave us the energy to walk ten miles on foot and arrive at this spot. But now that energy is ebbing. The wind is blowing from a direction opposite to the way we are going; so the boots are of no help at all. Our stock of food is dangerously depleted, and there are few of my tablets left. In this state, in spite of being armed, a bandit gang could cause no end of trouble. As it is, we have lost one of our members, although he was himself responsible for what happened. It was his excessive greed that spelled his doom.

A little while ago, Mr Mazumdar said, 'I don't know what your omniscope reveals; Kailas, Mansarovar and Dung-lung-do have endowed me with supernatural vision. I can already see those people are nomads. So they will do us no harm.'

Well, if they do turn out to be nomads, they would not only do us no harm, but might actually provide us with ponies, yaks and provisions – in fact, everything we need for our return journey.

After waiting for thirty-seven hours, on the first of September, at one-forty in the afternoon, the state of the sky and a rumble of thunder told us that the kind of wind that we had been waiting for was in fact on its way. Mr Mazumdar had dozed off, and I woke him up. Then we five booted men stood with our backs to the approaching storm and our faces to the wall. In three minutes the storm hit us. Being the lightest of the group, I was the first to get aloft.

It is difficult for me to describe the extraordinary experience. The storm carried us streaking through the air both forwards and upwards, while the wall ahead plunged forward and downward at the same time, revealing more and more of the view beyond. First we could see snowcapped peaks in the far distance beyond the wall on the far side; then came into view a wonderful green world – not a fort, nor a lake – which the wall had kept hidden from us. We were about to enter this world over the top. From behind me I could hear Kroll, Saunders, and Markham expressing their child-like wonder in English and German, while Mr Mazumdar exclaimed, 'Why, this must be the garden of Eden – yes, the garden of Eden!'

As soon as we crossed the wall, the storm magically abated. We landed gently on the green grass, very much like a 'feather plucked from a swan's back'. I said green because of the green colour, but never before have I seen such grass. Saunders shouted, 'Do you know, Shonku – not a single tree here is familiar to me. This is a completely new environment.'

Saunders proceeded immediately to collect specimens of flora, while Kroll got busy with his camera. Mr Mazumdar rolled on the grass saying, 'Let us stay here. Why go back to Giridih? The soil here is wonderful. We can grow anything we want. ' Markham took off his boots and made his way through the tall grass.

Dung-lung-do seemed to be at least as large as Mansarovar. It was a concave valley surrounded by the wall. Although the wall on the outer side dropped steeply, the inner side came down in a gentle slope. Saunders was right; not a single specimen of flora here was known to us. The trees abounded in varicoloured flowers and fruits which we now recognised as the source of the exquisite, heady smell which had drifted across the wall to reach our camp.

The four of us were exploring the place in our boots, advancing by gentle leaps, when we suddenly heard a swishing sound. The next moment something passed across the sun casting a giant shadow. And now we saw it: a colossal bird as large as five hundred eagles put together, with feathers as resplendent as that of a South American macao.

'*Mein Gott!*' cried Kroll in a hoarse whisper. The next moment he was about to raise his gun when I restrained him by raising my hand. Not only was the gun useless against the bird, but my mind told me that the bird would do us no harm.

The bird circled above us three times and then, with a long cry like a foghorn, flew back the way it came. I found myself involuntarily saying, 'Roc.'

'What?' Kroll asked in bewilderment.

I said, 'Roc, or Rukh. The giant bird in Sindbad's tale.'

'But we're not in the land of *Arabian Nights*, Shonku,' said Kroll impatiently. 'This is a real world. There is the ground under our feet, we can touch the leaves with our fingers, smell the flowers with our noses.'

Saunders shook off his wonder and said, 'There isn't a single insect around – which is most surprising.'

The four of us were advancing when we suddenly found ourselves up against an obstacle. For the first time we were faced with an object on the ground which was not a species of flora. A twelve-foot-high boulder, bluish green in colour, obstructed our path. How far it stretched on either side was hard to tell. Kroll suddenly gave a mighty leap which took him soaring and landed him gently on top of the boulder. And then something wholly unexpected happened; the boulder heaved, and then started to move to our left. Kroll too was being borne along with it when he suddenly yelled out, 'My God, it's a dragon!'

Yes, it was a dragon. One of its legs was now passing in front of us. Meanwhile Kroll had jumped off the back of the beast and had joined us. We stared in amazement at what was visible to us of the giant beast. It took it nearly three minutes to pass by us swishing its huge scaly tail, and disappear behind the dense foliage. The smoke which now hung over the forest must have come from the nostrils of the beast.

Saunders had sat down on the grass and was holding his head in his hands. He said, 'I feel like an uneducated boor up against these strange creatures in these unfamiliar surroundings, Shonku.'

I said, 'But I like it. I'm glad to discover that there are still surprises left even for learned men like us in this planet of ours.'

I have lost count of the wonderful things we saw in the next hour of our expedition. We have watched a Phoenix consumed by flames, and a new Phoenix rising from its ashes and flying off towards the sun. We have seen the Gryphon, the Simurgh of Persian legends, the Anka of the Arabs, the Nork of the Russians, and the Feng and the Kirne of the Japanese. Among lizards we have seen the Basilisk whose unblinking stare can reduce anything to ashes, and we have seen the salamander which is proof against fire and which, as if to prove the truth of the legend, was again and again passing through flames and emerging unscathed. We have also seen a four-tusked elephant which could only be Oiravat, the mount of the Indian god Indra. The stately pachyderm stood eating the leaves of a tree whose dazzling brilliance could only mean that it was the celestial tree Parijat of our mythology.

But Dung-lung-do is not just a forest of gorgeous trees. We had proceeded a mile or so along the northern wall when we were suddenly confronted with open country bereft of vegetation. Before us were enormous boulders with caves in them from which emerged blood-curdling roars and snarls. We realised we had come to the region of legendary demons and *rakshasas*, a common feature of fairy tales of all nations. Emboldened by the fact that none of the creatures paid the slightest attention to us, I was debating whether to enter the caves or not when a frenzied, high-pitched cry made us all turn to our left.

'Unicorns! Unicorns! Unicorns!'

It was Markham, and his voice was coming from behind a large boulder.

'Has he been taking cocaine again?' asked Kroll.

'I don't think so,' said I, advancing towards the boulder. As I crossed it, a unique sight nearly stopped my heartbeat.

A big herd of animals, both adult and young, was passing in front of us. Each looked like a cross between a cow and a horse, was pinkish grey in colour, and had a single spiral horn on its forehead. I realised that they were what launched us on our expedition. They were unquestionably unicorns, Pliny's unicorns, the unicorn of western mythology, the unicorn on the seals of Mohenjo-Daro.

Not all the animals were on the move. Some stood chewing grass, some frisked about, while others playfully butted each other with their horns. Like Willard, we too were watching the scene in full possession of our senses.

But where was Markham?

The question had just crossed my mind when we saw a strange sight. Markham had emerged from the herd of unicorns and was running towards the wall behind us. But he was not alone; he was grasping with both hands a unicorn cub.

Saunders cried out, 'Stop that scoundrel! Stop him!'

'Put your boots on! Put your boots on!' screamed Kroll. He

had started running after Markham. We too followed him leaping.

If the warning had reached Markham in time, perhaps he wouldn't have acted the way he did. Running up the grass slope Markham gave a leap as he reached the wall and dropped out of sight behind it.

Later we learnt from Rabsang that as soon as he saw Markham jump over the wall, he had run towards him. But there was nothing for him to do. The two hundred-foot fall had crushed all the bones in his body. When we asked about the unicorn, he shook his head and said he had only found Markham's body; there was no unicorn cub with him.

My conclusions about Dung-lung-do have found favour with both Kroll and Saunders. My feeling is that if a great many people believe in an imaginary creature over a great length of time, the sheer force of that belief may bring to life that creature with all the characteristics human imagination has endowed it with. Dung-lung-do was a repository of such imaginary creatures. Perhaps it was the only place of its kind on earth. To try to bring anything from Dung-lung-do into the world of reality was futile, which is why the unicorn vanished as soon as Markham crossed the limits of the world of fantasy.

The mute lama's saying yes and no almost in the same breath now bears a clear meaning; the unicorn exists, though not in reality. But the lama was wrong when he said no to the question of flight. Perhaps he didn't know about the manuscript.

Mr Mazumdar said at the end of our discussion. 'So there is nothing for us to show when we get back home?'

I said, 'I'm afraid not. Because I doubt if Kroll's photographs will come out, and our boots won't help us to fly, because the manuscript says that *ngmung* melts in the heat of the plains.'

Mr Mazumdar sighed. Now I played my trump card.

'Have you realised that we are going back younger by about twenty years?'

'How's that?'

I wiped the snow flakes off my beard and moustache.

'Why, they're black again!' exclaimed Mr Mazumdar.

'So is your moustache,' I said. 'Look in the mirror.'

At this point Saunders came in. He looked younger too and a weak tooth of his had become stronger again. He heaved a deep sigh of relief.

'Nomads, not robbers,' he said. 'Thank God!'

I can hear the sound of horses' hooves, and the barking of dogs, and the shouting of men, women and children. The cloud has lifted and the sun shines again.

Om Mani Padme Hum!

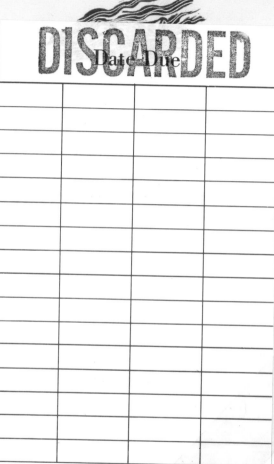

DISCARDED

Date Due

ORCA BOOK PUBLISHERS

National Library of Canada Cataloguing in Publication Data

Bow, Patricia, 1946-
The bone flute / Patricia Bow.

ISBN 1-55143-301-x

I. Title.

PS8553.O8987B65 2004   jC813'.54   C2004-903707-2

Library of Congress Control Number: 2004108678

First Printed in the United States: 2004

Summary: Camrose must find a way to claim an ancient bone flute
and return it to its rightful owner.

Orca Book Publishers gratefully acknowledges the support for its publishing
programs provided by the following agencies: the Government of Canada
through the Book Publishing Industry Development Program (BPIDP),
the Canada Council for the Arts, and the British Columbia Arts Council.

Design and typesetting by Lynn O'Rourke
Cover and interior illustrations by Vladyana Krykorka

In Canada: **In the United States:**
ORCA BOOK PUBLISHERS   ORCA BOOK PUBLISHERS
Box 5626 STN.B   PO Box 468
VICTORIA, BC CANADA   CUSTER, WA USA
V8R 6S4   98240-0468

08 07 06 05 04 • 6 5 4 3 2 1

Printed and bound in Canada

To Eric, James and Erin—*my best of reasons.*

Table of Contents

1 Home before dark 1

2 The limping dog 8

3 Word from the dead 14

4 Terence Castle 19

5 Moonlit shadows 26

6 Music and silence 31

7 Miranda 38

8 The lost house 44

9 The truth about Terence 49

10 Hunted 56

11 The tale of young Diarmid 60

12 Invisible chocolate 65

13 The busker 72

14 The forbidden door 78

15 Plain sight 83

16 Inside the ghost house 88

17 Flute music 95

18 Rhianna's story 103

19 A choice of evils 111

20 The spell battle 117

21 The Wyrde 125

22 The river of time 131

1

Home before dark

Where Camrose stood, on a ledge halfway up a limestone cliff above the Ottawa River, the rocks had already been in shadow for hours. But the light had just lifted from the shoulders of the hills across the river in Quebec and from the white spire of the church on the far shore.

It was sunset, 8:45 p.m., on Friday, July 26, Camrose's twelfth birthday. The date and time were important, but she didn't know that then.

"Don't take all day," Mark said behind her.

"I'm going! Don't rush me." She leaned out a little. Twenty feet below she could see the tops of two heads, one blond, one black: Krystal and Nadia, combing out each other's long hair. Jump wrong from here and she'd land on the rocks beside them.

"You can't miss," Mark said.

"You go first."

"All right." He stepped to the edge, swung out his arms and tipped off. No fuss and nothing fancy. She watched him fade to a ghost in the dark water, then rise again, grow solid and break the surface with a splash. He climbed out onto the rocky ridge thirty feet from shore, the limit of where the swimming was safe.

"Don't wait too long," said a low voice behind her.

"I *said* I …"

It took two seconds to sink in: Mark wasn't behind her. He was down on the ridge. Camrose pivoted on one foot, but no one was there. On a ledge six feet deep by twelve feet wide there was nowhere to hide. She faced front again.

"So, now I'm talking to myself."

"No." The voice was dark and husky. "It's begun. Night's coming. Be ready."

She turned again, slowly. Nobody. Nobody at all.

Stepping to the edge, she took a deep breath and dove. The water smacked her hands and then she was spearing deep. The cold bit into her skin. She kicked and rose, broke into air and sprayed water from her hair.

Climbing onto the ridge beside Mark, she pulled at his arm. "Did anybody jump off the ledge after me?"

"Nope."

"Had to be. There was someone standing behind me. Talking to me."

He turned carefully on his rock, which was just big enough for his feet, and peered back under his hand at the dark cliff against the bright sky. "Can't see anybody."

There were only two ways off that ledge. One was to jump. The other was to pick your way down the steep path, watching out for loose stones. That took time.

There was nobody on the beach but Nadia and Krystal.

"Must've been somebody up on the street. Maybe in the Old Mill Mall," Mark said. "Wind does funny things with sound."

Camrose relaxed. "That must be it." Trust Mark to find a sensible answer. "But who would say creepy things like 'Night's coming. Be ready.'?"

"Lots of strange people around, even in Lynx Landing."

Back on shore, Camrose needed less than twenty seconds to rub her hair into its usual tangle of dark red angles and elbows. Mark took about as long to dry off.

They had to wait another ten minutes while Nadia and Krystal (who hadn't seen anybody either) braided beads into a narrow lock above each other's left ear. Nadia's beads were gold; Krystal's were blue.

Up to a year ago, Nadia had been one of Camrose's two best friends. Nadia Patel, Mark Shoemaker and Camrose Ferguson, they were always together. Then Krystal Spears moved to Lynx Landing.

Lately, Nadia and Krystal had been trying to look and act as much like each other as possible. Mark said it was funny, seeing they weren't a bit alike, Nadia so dark and rounded, Krystal so thin and pale.

They climbed the cliff path and crossed Mill Street and Market Square. Krystal and Nadia were out in front, nudging each other and giggling. "We're playing Spot the Alien," Krystal said over her shoulder. She pointed at Camrose. "Hey! There's one!"

Camrose laughed and pointed back, but it didn't feel like fun. It felt more like being shoved into a corner.

By the time they were walking along McKirdy Street beside the park, she'd made up her mind to tell them about Gilda's parcel. She ignored the nagging voice in the back of her head that told her she was making a mistake.

"This has been a pretty good birthday," she said, off-hand. "Of course, it's not over yet."

Nadia turned back and grabbed her arm. "*And?*"

"There's another present waiting for me at home. A package from Gilda."

"Gilda!" Nadia tossed her hair. "Your great-grandmother?"

"Who else?" Camrose lowered her voice. "And she addressed it to me by name."

"Wait a minute," Mark said. "Gilda's dead."

"That's right." Camrose flicked her towel at a shop window. Nadia shook her arm. "But didn't you say she died before you were born?"

"A year exactly before I was born. The box came in the mail the day after she died." There, that made an impression.

"That's unreal!" Krystal shuddered. "How could she know your name? She couldn't even know you'd ever be alive!"

"Simple," Mark said. "She made a wish. And Cam's parents named her for what was written on the package. Right?"

"Of course!" Nadia laughed. "That explains it. It's not like she could see the future, or anything like that."

Camrose shook her head. "Dad said no. He said they'd already decided on that name, if another daughter was to come along. But they never told Gilda. So how do you explain that?"

"You don't," Krystal said. "Sounds fake to me."

"It's the truth!" Camrose felt her face heating up.

"Then maybe those other stories about Gilda are true too."

"What are you talking about?"

"Well, she was pretty strange," Nadia cut in. "My mother said, if people'd had any sense back then, Gilda Ferguson would've been in the loony bin."

"That's a lie! Gilda was the best mayor this town ever had."

"The weirdest mayor." Krystal laughed. "Maybe it runs in the family! I mean, who's the one who hears spooky whispers when nobody's there?"

She grabbed Nadia's hand and they ran giggling across McKirdy Street to the corner of Grace, where they both lived.

Camrose stood fuming on the sidewalk. "To think I wasted my birthday money paying their way into the movie this afternoon!"

"You shouldn't have mentioned that package. Krystal can smell boasting a mile away."

"I wasn't boasting!"

"No?" He was all seriousness, except for the smile in his brown eyes. "By the way, what was in it?"

She took a few deep breaths to cool her hot cheeks. "The package? I don't know. I haven't opened it yet. I was keeping it back to the end of the day. As a treat."

"Cam, you are kind of strange. Admit it."

She burst out laughing. "Come on, let's go. I'm supposed to be home before dark."

"Bit late for that now."

"We'd better cut through the park."

It was a perfect evening for dawdling. Soft, grass-scented, with a sky the color of peach ice cream. Too bad she'd already broken the home-before-dark rule a few times too many. She trotted onto the mowed lawn of the park and past the baseball diamond.

The game was over. Nobody left but a couple of boys throwing the ball back and forth in the fading afterglow, and a ragged woman leaning against the chain-link backstop. She turned her head and stared as Mark and Camrose walked by.

A strange, sharp face it was. Her eyes shone small and bright through a curtain of hair. Camrose nudged Mark. "Don't like the looks of her."

The trees in the west end of the park cut black scallops out of the bright sky. Camrose looked back. The ragged woman slouched along behind them, a dozen paces back, hands in pockets.

"Hurry up!" She set off bounding over the tussocky ground. Mark came thumping behind her. The skyline bounced as she ran.

When the first gleam flickered through the trees, she thought: Sunset. Then: No, that's done. Then: Windows. Big windows full of yellow light. But there's no house there.

Then she was among the trees, following the cedar-chip path that was almost invisible in the dark under the layered leaves. Through the trunks ahead shone rectangles of light: window-shaped, red-gold and flickering.

Camrose burst through the wall of trees into the hollow and stumbled to a halt. She flung up an arm to shield her eyes.

A house stood there. A tall house made of stone. The lintels over the windows were carved with leaf shapes, and ivy grew up the walls between them. The wide front door was black and polished, with a brass plate fastened across the bottom and an S-shaped brass handle.

And from step to chimneys it was a mass of flames, flames that should have roared but made no noise. A window on the second floor burst outward in a silent spray of glass. Flames licked up, soundless, and curled around the edge of the roof.

"Cam! Wake up! What's the matter?"

Mark was bobbing in front of her. She grabbed at him to yank him back from the flames.

"Watch out!" She tried to pull him around, but he was too heavy to shove. "Look out! The fire!"

"Fire? What are you talking about?"

"The house! It's burning!"

"Oh, I get it. This is one of your games, right?" He took a step back toward the house and stood there, grinning out at her through a sheet of flame.

An outline of treetops formed behind him through the walls of the house. The fire in the windows turned pale yellow, then green, then blue, a watery shadow printed on the trees. And then the house, with its brass, its ivy and its fiery windows, melted into the night.

2

The limping dog

When Camrose could see straight again she found herself sitting in the grass with Mark kneeling beside her.

"What's the matter with you?"

"I ... I saw something."

"You were babbling about some house."

"There was a house on fire." She rubbed her eyes. "Right there." She pointed, though there wasn't anything to see on the dark grass now except her light blue towel.

"Is it there now?"

"No." She lurched to her feet and scooped up her towel.

"So, this wasn't a game?"

"No!"

"I suppose there could have been a house here once." Mark led the way across the hollow into the woods again. The streetlights on Grant Street sent broken gleams through the trees. "I've never heard of one, though."

They walked in silence, Camrose frowning, Mark concentrating on the uneven path under his feet, until the trees were behind them and Grant Street rose up the hill ahead. Camrose stopped in the middle of the sidewalk.

"All right. If I didn't see a house burning back there, what *did* I see? Because I'm telling you, I saw something."

Mark sucked his teeth thoughtfully. "A reflection."

"A reflection! On what?"

"Okay, um ... I know. Fog."

"Fog?"

"Sure." He waved his hand in a loop. "There's often a bit of fog at night. Maybe the light hit it just right, and you imagined the rest."

"There was no fog."

"And you never imagine things."

Camrose closed her mouth tight. She was on the verge of losing her temper, and it didn't help that Mark didn't even seem to notice. She stayed on the verge until they turned up Stone Road. By that time the burning house had faded in her mind. It no longer seemed real. She wondered if maybe he was right.

"See you tomorrow." With a wave of his towel, Mark headed along the sidewalk past the lilac hedge, then cut across the lawn to Number Sixteen. Shrieks rang out as he opened the front door to his house—his little brothers, Ben and Sweeney, fighting again—then the door shut, and silence fell.

Camrose stood by the closed gate of Number Fourteen, trying to decide what to say to avoid getting yelled at. If only her father were home instead of Bronwyn.

The night was so quiet you could hear the hum of traffic on King Street, two blocks east of the park. You could hear ...

Footsteps. On the sidewalk, slow and quiet. Somebody out for a stroll. Hard shoes: the clip–clip of stiff leather on concrete. And alongside, an irregular pattering: clickety–pause–click. Dog toenails. Sounded like it was on three legs.

The footsteps stopped. Camrose looked around, up the street and down, but there was nothing to see.

So? That was nothing special. Just somebody and his dog standing in the dappled darkness under a tree, where you couldn't see them, that was all. No law against it.

But what were they doing? Just standing there? Watching her?

She backed away and pushed at the wooden gate. It stuck, as usual. She slammed it open with her hip, then wedged it shut behind her, turned and ran up the walk toward the front door. Laughter bubbled behind her, so soft it could almost have been the sound of her own quick breathing.

The front door swung open. Bronwyn stood in the doorway. The hall light made a halo of her rust-colored hair, darker than Camrose's but just as thorny. "Where've you been? I was just about to come looking for you."

"It was still light when I started home." Camrose squeezed past her into the hall and looked back. The street was empty.

"Well, make sure you're home before dark after this. There are too many strange characters out there." She scowled out at the night, then shut the door and locked it. "And remember, I'm in charge."

Camrose trailed up the stairs. This was going to be the longest weekend on record. How was she going to figure out what happened to her in the hollow with her father a thousand kilometers away? Why did community college media arts teachers have to have conferences in Halifax anyway?

She couldn't even consider telling Bronwyn, who seemed to think it was her duty to cut a younger sister down to size as often and as short as possible. Camrose couldn't wait till she left for university in the fall.

Once in her room she closed the door. It clicked open again, as it always did. She closed it again and jiggled the handle until the latch caught. There was a keyhole but there'd never been a key, so far as she could remember. The whole house was like that. Dad said he liked old houses, but he never got around to fixing anything.

It took less than two minutes to change from her damp bathing suit into her favorite pajamas, an old T-shirt and briefs. She picked up the parcel from her desk.

"I hope you understand what it cost me not to peek, all these years," her father said that morning at breakfast, just before he'd left for Ottawa International Airport.

The outer brown paper wrapping was torn open at one end. Inside was a package also wrapped in brown paper, but still sealed. On the outer wrapping, in a black, upright, heavily pressed hand was written: "To Miss Camrose Jane Ferguson, c/o Mr. and Mrs. Ian Ferguson, 14 Stone Road, Lynx Landing, Ontario."

Camrose held the package by the corners as if it might bite. She inspected the postmark again. July 26, 1991. A year exactly between Gilda's death and Camrose's birth. That stretch of time was a black chasm, a void that nothing living could cross. Yet here in her hands was something that had crossed. Word from the dead.

She tried to imagine what sort of gift you would send across such a chasm. It would have to be something unique. What would I send if I were Gilda? Camrose wondered. The map to a lost island. A box of jewels. A bottle of moondust.

She pulled the outer wrapping off and dropped it on the desk. The package sat there looking neat and mysterious.

TO MY GREAT-GRANDDAUGHTER
CAMROSE JANE ON HER 12TH BIRTHDAY

was inked across it in thick black capitals. Under that,

NOT TO BE OPENED BY ANYONE ELSE!!!

with two lines scored underneath so fiercely they bit through the paper.

"Imagine waiting all those years without opening it! How could they stand the suspense?" She felt a little sad because her mother, who died when she was two, would never know what was in it.

Stop stalling! Camrose told herself.

She took a deep breath, ripped a layer of sticky tape off one end of the parcel, and peeled off the paper. Inside was a hard, reddish-brown cardboard box with *Tabac Havane Havana Tobacco* printed on the lid. *Tueros*, it said. *Cigares 25 Cigars*.

"Cigars?"

Camrose flipped up the lid. Inside was what looked like a letter, and … She tipped it out, shook the box, and looked at the bottom. And nothing. Only a letter.

But still... word from the dead. All right! She sat down and unfolded the letter. There were three pages, all covered with that stern black handwriting. She smoothed them on the desk.

My dear Camrose, she read. *I'm sorry I can't be there to explain things to you in person...* Her lips moved silently for a few seconds.

Across the room, the door creaked open an inch. Camrose slapped the letter face down on the desk, in case it was Bronwyn sticking her nose in. But Bronwyn didn't appear.

"Darn door." Camrose got up and closed it, then returned to the desk. As she reached for the letter, the door inched open again.

"Bron?" She went and stood in the doorway. The dim upstairs hall was deserted. From downstairs came the crackle of canned laughter from a TV show. It sounded very far away.

Up here, in the quiet, you could hear the cricks and ticks of the old house as it contracted in the cool of the night. Sounded almost like stealthy footsteps, if you let your imagination run wild.

Something gleamed in the stairwell beyond the banister railing. A nail head, maybe. It looked like an eye, watching her.

She stepped back into her room and closed the door firmly. Then she snatched up the pages of the letter and folded them.

"Can't keep this to myself!"

What she really meant, and knew it, was, Don't want to be alone. Not now, not here.

3

Word from the dead

*C*amrose pulled on shorts, shoved her feet into sandals and wedged the folded letter into her back pocket.

The window was open as wide as it would go. Pushing up the two hooks that held the screen to the window frame, she lifted it out, laid it flat on the asphalt shingle roof outside and climbed out herself.

Her room was at the back of the house, overlooking a long shed where the lawnmower and gardening tools and bicycles were stored. To the right of her window was Dad's, now dark. On that side of the shed stood a huge old chestnut tree. One limb snaked over the shed roof, with another, smaller branch reaching out about six feet above it.

Steadying herself with one hand on the branch above her head, she walked quickly along the lower limb to the trunk. On a quiet night like this, the tree was as solid as a house. More solid than our house, she thought. Only the great tent of leaves stirred, with a sound like rain.

A rope lay coiled in a hole in the trunk at the height of her head, just above a limb on the side away from the house. She pulled it out and let it uncoil to the ground. The top end was securely tied to the limb, and triple knots twice as big as her fist ran down the length of it.

She had a good grip on the rope and was feeling downward with one foot when something scrambled up the other side of the tree, something big, with claws that scraped the bark. She yelped and nearly let go.

Leaves thrashed above her head. A triangular face poked through and black eyes in a black mask glittered down at her. She laughed, and her heart stopped thumping. The raccoon chittered furiously.

"Take it easy! I won't bother you."

It ducked back up. Camrose lowered herself down the rope to the ground. It was an easy dash across the lawn, a scramble to the top of the fence and over, landing with a thud on the grass on the other side. Detour around the patch of tomato plants, climb to the top of the lean-to that sheltered the Shoemakers' firewood, and from there to the roof of a shed identical to the one on the Ferguson house.

Two squares of yellow light splashed across the roof. Mark's was the nearest. She scratched on the screen. Mark, who was dressed now in shorts and a T-shirt, came to the window with a colorful brochure in his hands.

"What's that?"

He turned it around and held it out.

WIZARD COMPUTER CAMP

HAVE FUN AND LEARN HOW TO PROGRAM.

"My parents want me to learn something useful this summer instead of hanging around Uncle Wes's wood shop."

"What's wrong with your Uncle Wes? I like him."

"So do I. But I guess they're afraid if I hang around him too much I'll turn out like him."

"What's wrong with that?"

"He works with his hands. They want me to become a respected professional." He looked at his own hands regretfully.

"Why don't you just tell them what you really want to do?"

"I would, if I knew what that was."

"Anyway, I've got something to tell you. Look at this! It's a letter from Gilda." She pulled it from her pocket and waved it. "And Mark, listen! She says I'm an heiress!"

"No kidding."

"That means she left me something special!"

"I know that. But what?"

"Get out here and let's find out."

Mark unhooked the screen from his window, climbed out and placed the screen against the window frame. They sat side by side on the roof. Camrose unfolded the letter and held it up to catch the light from the window.

"*My dear Camrose,*" she read aloud. "*I'm sorry I can't be there to explain things to you in person. I have learned from a reliable source that my time is nearly over. Luckily, this same source has told me that your time will soon begin. And so—this letter. Now that you're twelve years old, you have become an heiress. See?*"

"Well, go on."

"She says, *Of course you want to know what you've inherited.* Of course. *It is something very old and very precious*—Cool!

—an heirloom of our house, though only a few members of our family have ever known of it. And yet it is not yours at all." She stopped and frowned at Mark. "Not mine? This sounds weird."

"Want me to read it for you?" He reached for the letter. She pushed him away.

"No, no. She says, *You are simply its Keeper. When the rightful claimant arrives, you must surrender it. Until that happens, you may be in danger."*

She put the letter down flat on the shingles. "This has got to be a joke."

"Either that or crazy."

"So this is my message from across the chasm. Loony tunes."

"Chasm?"

"Just a stupid idea of mine. I'll read fast through the rest." She squared her shoulders and flexed her fingers and then picked up the letter and started cramming out the words. *"Be very careful. It may be hard to know which of the two is the right one. Seventy-seven years ago, when I was your age and had just learned I was Keeper, I made the wrong decision. It was a terrible mistake, and because of it, everyone I loved was destroyed. But I hadn't lost the heirloom. I hid it—hid it so well, in fact, that you may have some trouble recovering it. Here is how you must go about it. At twilight, go to the . . ."*

She paused to shuffle the first page to the back. As she raised the letter again to the light, Mark raised a hand. "Wait."

"What is it?"

"Thought I heard something in the yard."

They listened. For half a minute there was nothing. No cricket song, no bird cry, no leaf stir, no sound except the distant purr of traffic on Highway 17.

That in itself was strange. Usually you could hear lots of noise at night. A radio, a dog barking, people barbecuing in their backyards, somebody yelling at her kids to get in here _right now!_

Nothing. For a moment, not even traffic.

The chestnut tree broke the spell. It stirred, then swayed with a long, inhaling sound. Camrose relaxed.

"Can't be too careful. I've heard there are some strange people in town these da—"

Quick as that, the wind swooped out of the dark and slapped the letter out of her hand. The pages blew up over their heads, skimmed the roof of the house and were gone.

4

Terence Castle

"Gilda's letter!" Camrose was slithering from the shed roof to the lean-to almost before the words were out. Mark was right behind her. They raced around the house, across the lawn and onto the sidewalk.

Two scraps of white lay flat in the middle of Stone Road. The wind gusted again, skipping the pages along. Camrose galloped after them, nearly cartwheeled off the curb, caught herself and sprinted on. She nabbed one page in midair.

Another page was fluttering against a tree trunk across the street. "Quick!" Camrose screamed. Mark was within arm's length and reaching. It grazed his fingertips and flirted away.

Next moment a man walked briskly around the curve of the street. His hand shot up and snagged the page from the air above his head. Camrose ran up to him, panting.

"This what you're chasing?" He glanced at it in the light from the street lamp, then held it out.

"Yes, thanks." She took the page and stuffed it into her shorts pocket with the other. Mark came up and stood beside her.

The man grinned down at them. He was young, she saw now. His teeth were very white, his skin very tan. He wore a gleaming red leather jacket and had a backpack slung over one shoulder.

"Another page flew by me back there." He waved back at the curve of the street. "I don't think you'll catch it tonight."

Doors were opening left and right along the street. Mark glanced back over his shoulder. "Oh-oh, there's my mother. I better go back in."

"Camrose!" Bronwyn snarled behind them. "What's all the yelling? What are you doing out here?"

"Looking for something."

"We'll never find it tonight." Mark backed toward the crisp footsteps clipping down his front walk. "We'll look tomorrow, first thing, okay?" He turned and jogged away.

"I'll help look," said the stranger.

"And who're you?" Bronwyn demanded.

"You really don't remember? Well, it's been a while. Years. I'm your cousin Terence. One R."

"Um … It rings a bell, but … "

"Terence Castle? Your Aunt Alicia's boy?"

"Oh, that Terence! From New York!"

He laughed. "Yes, that Terence. And you're Bronwyn, and *you* must be little Camrose. Only not so little anymore."

Camrose didn't think she'd ever met him. It occurred to her that it was odd that she couldn't remember if she had or not because he looked like the kind of person you wouldn't forget. She did recall her father talking to Aunt Alicia on the phone one day after dinner, about a year ago. "Um, Terence?"

He tilted his head.

"Aren't you the one who went on a trip around the world?" There was more to it than that, something dramatic had happened to him, but the details escaped her. Must be tired, she thought.

"The very same." He laughed at her, but in a way that made her feel they were sharing a joke. To Bronwyn he said, "Uncle Ian invited me to drop in any time I happened to be near Lynx Landing, so here I am."

"Um…" Bronwyn scrubbed her hands through her hair, making it stand up in tufts. "Thing is, Dad isn't here right now."

"Oh. Well…" He dumped his backpack on the ground, unzipped a side pocket and rummaged through it. "Got the note here somewhere…Aha!" He stood up and held out a postcard.

Peering over Bronwyn's arm, Camrose saw a picture of Lynx Landing's town hall, with its silly brick turrets, on one side of the postcard. On the other was what certainly looked like Dad's handwriting, and he was definitely inviting Terence to stay.

Bronwyn handed it back to him. Even in this light you could see she was red with embarrassment. Imagine making your own cousin prove who he was! But after all, you couldn't let just anybody into the house.

Bronwyn waved toward the house. "Um, please come inside. I guess we can put you in Dad's room."

"If you're sure I won't be any trouble." Terence swung the backpack onto his shoulder. "And I meant what I said just now," he said to Camrose. "In the morning I'll help you find that third page, if we have to turn this town inside out for it."

Something in what he said startled her. Then she yawned and rubbed her bare arms, and the odd thing, whatever it was, slid down into the depths of her tired mind and was lost.

Oh, but Terence could tell a story. Blink, and she was clinging to the side of a fantastic mountain pinnacle in China, the rock gritty under her fingertips and the wind whipping her hair into her eyes. Far below a river twisted like a dragon.

Blink, and she was darting across pavement choked with hooting cars, hemmed in by towers of gilded glass that speared up into a snowy sky. The shop windows were full of things that glittered, and every sign was in five languages.

Blink, and the air was heavy with cloves and cinnamon, dust and heat, and on every side rose stacks of carpets, blue-red-purple, fringed with creamy silk. The sun painted the white stones gold and the shadows inky black.

Blink. The clock on the kitchen wall said ten to midnight. They were still sitting around the table with empty pop cans and torn chip bags in front of them. Bronwyn was leaning forward on her elbows, her eyes wide and shining.

Camrose was pretty sure she'd been gazing at Terence the same way and probably looking just as stupid.

She sat up and looked around, seeing the kitchen with a stranger's eyes. She'd never realized before how shabby it was. The white paint on the cupboard doors was scratched, the linoleum was worn through to bare wood in front of the sink, the fridge door was bristling with take-out pizza coupons and shopping notes stuck on with advertising magnets.

Everything looked tattered and dull by comparison with Terence, with his gleaming dark hair, his eyes the blue-violet of hyacinths, his shining white teeth. He was sleek as a cat and twice as handsome.

"Except for that jacket. That's just plain ugly."

Terence smiled at her and Bronwyn frowned. She had spoken the thought out loud!

But it was ugly. The leather was the dark red of not-very-fresh raw beef, and it looked unpleasantly soft. Rivets winked all over it and steel zippers grinned. A ridge of stiff reddish-brown fur ran along the seams where the shoulders met the sleeves, and another ridge of fur ran down the back. Looking at it made her skin crawl. She closed her eyes.

From a distance someone said, "She's nearly asleep in her chair. It's getting late."

"Oh, right. Sorry I kept you up so late, Terry."

"Terence. Never Terry." That was sharp. Camrose opened her eyes.

"Sorry!" Bronwyn stammered. (That wasn't like Bronwyn, Camrose thought.) "I...I guess you'll want to know where Dad's room is and the bathroom and all that."

She led the way up the creaking stairs. Terence followed. Camrose stumbled at the end of the procession. When she opened the door to her room she leaped back, suddenly wide awake. A mosquito zinged past her ear.

"Camrose, you idiot!" Bronwyn yelled. "You left your screen off!"

Camrose slammed the door, then opened it a crack and peered in. Bugs were everywhere. Moths mobbed the ceiling light and taxied up the walls. Beetles of several varieties barged in and out the open window. The air was loud with the whine of mosquitoes.

"Oh, no!" She slapped at her arm. "I'll never sleep!"

"Well, go close that window, for g—"

"Not yet!" Terence was laughing quietly behind them. "There's a cure for this."

He reached past them and pushed the door all the way open. Then he whistled. Softly at first, a sweet sound, then skimming up to a high, piercing note, and then higher still. Camrose clapped her hands to her ears and screwed her eyes shut to block out the sound. It cut deep into her head, quivered there, and then, just when she couldn't bear it any longer, was gone.

When she opened her eyes the mosquitoes and beetles and moths were streaming out through the window. In seconds the room was clear. Camrose dashed to pull the screen up and slip the hooks into place.

"That was so cool!" Bronwyn's eyes were falling out of her head. "How did you do that?"

"Little trick I learned in Tibet. Folks there call it magic, but really there's no mystery about it. Insects can't stand the pitch of that particular note." He smiled at Camrose. "I'll teach you how to do it, if you like."

"I don't know." She backed away a step.

"Scared? It's not really magic, you know."

"I know that! And of course I'm not scared!"

He laughed as she shut the door, and this time she felt he was laughing at her, not with her. It clicked open, as usual, and she shut it again.

Too tired even to yawn, she sat on the edge of her bed and kicked off her sandals. Pawed at the bedside lamp until it switched off. Slumped sideways, curled up, and fell asleep on top of the white chenille coverlet.

Camrose dreamed of wandering lost through dark streets. It was still dark when she woke. Unlike her usual slow wakening, clinging to dreams, she snapped wide awake with the sure and certain knowledge that she was not alone in her room. Someone was standing there watching her.

5

Moonlit shadows

Camrose lay still with her heart drumming in her ears. Only her eyes moved, straining to see.

Moonlight turned the window into a silver rectangle. Another silver patch stretched across the floor to the left of her bed. The rest of the room was blacker than black.

She held her breath, but that only made her heart thump fit to deafen her. Just when she was ready to tell herself she'd been dreaming, something slid toward her across a corner of the patch of moonlight. She stared at it, unable to shout or move or blink.

Then an angry chittering cry ripped through the night. The sound sprung her loose. She threw herself off the right side of the bed onto the floor.

A moment of silence. Then a faint, irregular pattering: clickety–pause–click. The door swung open, then closed. Then slowly opened again, as it always did.

Camrose fumbled at the bedside table, found the lamp and

switched it on. Nothing was in the doorway. Just a gap of darkness that could have hidden an army of demons.

Before anything could leap out at her she scrambled across the bed to the door, closed it and shoved a sandal between the bottom of the door and the floor. The sandal wasn't quite thick enough, but when she pushed it toward the hinge side where the floor was closer to the door, the sandal wedged in tight.

There. If anyone tried to open that, they'd make a noise she couldn't miss.

Remembering the sudden animal cry from outside, she crossed to the window and looked out. The shed roof was deserted, but a scrabbling noise from the chestnut tree said something had just left.

"Thanks," she whispered to the night.

Still with the light on, Camrose crawled into bed and tried to think about what had just happened in her room. It had to be a dream, of course. Already that sense of *someone there* was fading.

Or I could've been awake and imagined it, she thought. I've imagined worse things in the middle of the night.

And yet, it seemed to her that this was the worst of all, worse than all the rabid tigers and vampires and ghouls she'd ever brewed up from shadows.

Whatever it was that started to cross that patch of moonlight had not been man-high. Dog-high, maybe. And that clickety sound, like toenails, something odd about its rhythm. Like the sound she'd heard on the street this evening.

She shook her head. "It wasn't real. Just one more weird thing. There's an answer to everything weird, so go to sleep!"

After a long time of lying still and listening, Camrose sat up again, pushed her pillow against the headboard, and leaned back. The clock radio on her desk said 3:22 a.m. From the drawer in the bedside table she took a small, spiral-bound notebook and a purple gel pen.

"Some people think better with a pen in their hand," her father told her once. "You and I are like that. If you write things down, often they make better sense."

She opened the notebook to a fresh page and printed **Weird Things—July 26** across the top. Underneath that she drew a line down the page, dividing it into two columns. The left column she headed, **What Happened**, and the right, **Why**.

She worked over it for half an hour, crossing things out, adding words here and there, brooding over what she'd written. Once she nearly tore up the whole thing, then changed her mind and kept working.

Even if it doesn't help, she thought, it might keep me busy until the sun's up. Because I sure won't be sleeping anymore tonight.

When she was finished, the page looked like this:

Weird Things - July 26

What Happened	Why
1. Voice on the ledge	Echo?
2. Burning house	Fog? Imagination?
3. Man and dog under tree	So what?
4. Laughing at me	No wonder—looked like idiot

5. How Gilda knew my name   Good guess?
6. Weird stuff in letter   Crazy? Joke?
7. Wind that grabbed letter   Just wind
8. T. clearing bugs   Science, not magic
9. Something in my room   Dream or imagination

Camrose frowned over the result. It wasn't very useful. There were too many question marks. And there was something else that should be on the list: something Terence said, only she couldn't remember. Funny how many things about him were hard to remember.

Suddenly she threw down the notebook and twisted sideways to get at the pocket of her shorts. All this thinking and writing about Gilda's letter and she'd forgotten all about it! At least two of the pages were safe, and she'd only read one.

Camrose flattened the crumpled pages on the notebook. There was the first page, and there was the last. The middle page was missing. Page three began in the middle of a sentence.

...all this my old friend and helpmate Miranda will be of use, if not much of a comfort. Ask her to tell you the story of how it all began. That will make a great deal clear to you and will help you come to a decision.

Remember, Camrose, you must be absolutely certain that the claimant is the right one. If you make the same mistake I did...

The next two lines were heavily inked out. No matter which way she turned the page, she couldn't make out the words underneath.

Never mind, the letter ended. *There's no point in frightening you out of your wits. I'm sure you'll do well.*

> *Your loving great-grandmother,*
> *Gilda Kilpatrick Ferguson*

Well, if I believed any of this, I'd be so scared I wouldn't have any wits left at all! Camrose thought.

As she was folding up the two pages of the letter, the last strange thing surfaced from the depths of her mind where it had been hiding. She thought about it, then picked up the notebook, drew an arrow to the space between point 7 and point 8, and wrote at the bottom, "How did Terence know there were three pages?"

And then Camrose realized how scared she really was. More scared than she'd ever been in her life before. "I wish Dad was here," she whispered.

Never mind, he'd be back soon. He'd help her figure it out. Until then, there was one thing she could do. She picked up the pen again and printed in large purple letters across the top of the page: **FIND MIRANDA.**

6

Music and silence

At half past noon the next day Camrose and Mark were eating ice cream and following the swirl of the crowd around the town square. It would have been hot if not for a gusty wind that snapped the flags beside the war memorial.

"Listen! There it is again!" Camrose stopped short. From somewhere across the square came a scrap of music, someone playing some kind of reedy instrument. It danced above the noise of the crowd like a red rose petal blown above a stormy sea.

"It's just some busker, Cam, playing for money." Mark pulled at her arm. People were piling up behind them. A baby stroller jabbed her in the back of the knees. She pushed on.

"But it's not like anything I've ever heard before." Another scrap of that windblown music turned her head. "I think it comes from near the war memorial." She went up on tiptoes to try to see over the crowd. But there was no use looking. This was Saturday, market day, and there were twice as many people in Lynx Landing as usual.

And it looked like they were all right here in the square, picking up quart baskets of tomatoes, sniffing bunches of dried thyme and admiring cookie jars shaped like Holstein cows.

The ice cream (chocolate mint for Camrose, honey walnut for Mark, in waffle cones made on a hot iron) was Camrose's treat, paid for with almost the last of her birthday money.

"It just about makes up for spending the whole morning looking for that letter," Mark said. "I don't know why you're so anxious to get it back."

"I just can't stand not knowing the rest. I wish I knew who Miranda is!"

"If she was Gilda's helper, she probably worked at the town hall. You could ask there."

"But they're closed today. I'll have to wait till Monday."

Then the wind died and a dip came in the crowd noise, and the piping sounded clearly, long rippling swaths of it. Camrose started toward it, zigzagging around the knots of people, following the voice that called and called.

In the center of the square the crowd thinned out. A man was sitting by himself on the steps of the war memorial. He was playing something that looked like a small bagpipe but had a sweeter, wilder sound.

A thicket of pipes lay across his knees, and he seemed to be playing them all at once, while pumping air with his arm into a leather bag strapped to his elbow. A little crescent of six or seven people stood around him. Camrose couldn't understand why everybody wasn't over here, listening. Were they deaf?

The piping changed, no longer a dance but a lament. She sat down on the steps around the other side of the war memorial and closed her eyes, the better to hear. In the solitary place behind her eyelids, a landscape took shape.

The skyline at the top of the rocky hillside looked like the edge of the world. Low bushes covered with tiny yellow and purple flowers blanketed the slope and snagged her feet, but there wasn't a tree in sight.

She climbed and climbed. The music pulled her like a rope. On the crest she stopped and looked down. Below lay a valley full of moving cloud-shadows, with a cupful of iron-dark lake at its heart, and in the lake a rocky island, and on the island a gigantic heap of stone.

A thread of smoke rose from one of the pinnacles on the heap of stone, which, Camrose now realized, was a house. And beyond the house and island and lake were more hills—green-purple, violet, blue—and beyond them again the silver line of the sea.

Home, lamented the music of the pipe. So that was what it was, Camrose thought, and why it was pulling her heart into pieces. It's about longing for home, for a home lost forever.

Or was it that simple? For there was someone on that island. Camrose squinted against the sun. She shouldn't have been able to see anything at this distance, but there it was, a tiny figure on the roof of the huge stone house. Its lifted face was a pale speck.

The piping rose to a wail and died away.

Camrose opened her eyes. Mark was clapping, and so were the people around the musician. They were dropping money, loonies and toonies and even a five-dollar bill, into a canvas backpack on the ground.

The piper unstrapped the bag from his arm and bent to slide his pipes into the pack. Then he straightened up and turned around, and Camrose got a good look at him.

Her first thought was surprise that he should be so small and young. Not even as old as Bronwyn, or so he looked, and only a couple of inches taller. What was somebody that age doing on the street, busking for money?

He looked poor too. His jeans were tattered at the heels and worn to holes on the knees. His gray sweatshirt had once been white with printing on it. The only bright, new-looking thing about him was his hair. It was long and pale gold and streamed like silk floss in the wind. Where it caught the sun it shone like glass.

She met his eyes, gray as a November sky in his thin face, and they were old.

Then they lit up. "You!" He took a step toward her.

Camrose wasn't sure, when she thought back, what she would have done if left to herself. But she wasn't left to herself, for a heavy hand pinned her shoulder and Terence stepped in front of her.

"Leave it to me." He gave her one fierce look. "*Don't say anything.*" And turned to face the piper. A policeman stood beside him, hands on hips. The two of them made a wall she couldn't see through.

Mark caught her arm and she turned his way, opening her mouth to say something, but no words came out. He stood with his mouth open and a desperate look on his face. I can't talk, Camrose wanted to say, but couldn't.

Then she realized what was happening in front of her: Terence had got hold of the wrong idea. "I saw him harassing these kids for money," he was saying.

"Aggressive panhandling, eh?" said the policeman. "We've got zero tolerance for that kind of thing in this town."

But he didn't, Camrose shouted silently. She pulled at Terence's red leather sleeve, then quickly let go, hating the fleshy feel of it.

"I'll have to move you on," the policeman was saying. The piper wasn't making a sound.

Mark dodged out of sight and reappeared in front, beside the piper, making urgent signs with his hands.

"What the— Kid, what're you doing?"

"He's pointing at the busker," Terence said. "Obviously he's accusing him."

Camrose took a firm hold of the policeman's arm. He turned and frowned down at her. "What is it?"

He wasn't ... She strained to get it out, ... bothering us!

"What? Speak up!"

Leave him alone! Her throat ached. Tears of frustration started in her eyes.

Terence laughed softly. "Cat's got her tongue."

The policeman turned away. He pointed a finger. "Now, you, mister..."

No! No! She grabbed at Terence's jacket again. Sharp steel raked her knuckles. "Ow!" popped out of her like a cork out of a bottle and a shriek poured out after it.

"LEAVE HIM ALONE!"

"Hey, easy!" said the policeman.

Everybody was looking at her. She hid her bleeding fist in the other hand. "He wasn't bothering us at all," she said firmly. "My cousin made a mistake."

"You sure?"

"Sure!"

"Okay. All right, then." After giving the piper a stern look, the policeman mixed himself into the crowd. The piper shouldered his bag and set off, almost running. He didn't look back.

Terence smiled at the piper's vanishing back. Then he looked at Camrose and his smile faded. "You know, you can't be too careful. It's so easy to make a mistake about strangers."

"Is it your business who I speak to?"

The moment the words popped out they sounded dangerous. Terence's face went still and dark. Camrose held her breath.

Mark eased in beside her. "Besides, you sure made a mistake about a stranger just now, didn't you?"

"Well, well. The stones speak!" Terence raked him with a stare, as if seeing him for the first time. Then he straightened up and squared his shoulders. "No, I don't think I've made a mistake. Not about that one." He sketched a wave and swaggered off across the square, with the sunlight flashing from the studs and zippers of his jacket.

Camrose found a tissue in her pocket and wrapped it around her grazed knuckles. "I didn't like that," Mark said quietly.

"Neither did I."

"What happened to us?"

"Well ...," She didn't like to say it, but there it was, "he said, 'Don't say anything.' And he gave me a *look*. And after that I ... I couldn't ... "

"Me too. When's he leaving?"

"I don't know. This morning Bronwyn invited him to stay till Dad gets back, and he said he would."

"I don't like to think of you stuck in the house with him."

"Bronwyn's there. What's he going to do?"

It took them five minutes to struggle through the crowd to the corner of Market Square and McKirdy Street. Camrose stopped and looked back. "It's funny, how he ran off so quick."

"Who, the busker? I wouldn't have stuck around either, with the cops giving me dirty looks."

"Yes, but he knew me, I'm sure he did." The way his whole face lit up, as if he'd been waiting all his life to meet her. "He knew me, and he wanted to say something, and then he just ran off."

"Well, did you know him?"

She shook her head and started down McKirdy Street. "Never saw him before in my life."

And that was strange, because somewhere in her mind a voice was rejoicing. The long wait is over, it chanted, the task is done; the burden will soon be laid down. She hadn't the faintest idea what it meant.

7

Miranda

They didn't say anything more until they were a block away from Market Square and walking across the park. It was peaceful here, away from the crowds, though not quiet. Small kids played on the swings and splashed in the wading pool, while their parents or grandparents watched from wooden benches near the street.

When they reached the hollow in the patch of woods, Camrose stopped with her foot on a lip of broken stone that nuzzled up through the grass. The burning house flickered in her memory like an old silent movie.

There was nothing to see here now. The hollow was just a green cup of quiet with a big old maple tree growing in the center. The sounds of the children shouting and splashing and the cars rolling by on McKirdy Street had faded away.

The trees kept it quiet by sheltering it from the rest of the park, Camrose guessed. A ragged hedge of purple phlox and lilac bushes ran around the inner edge of the rampart of trees. The loudest thing here would be a blue jay or a cicada.

"I'll bet there was a house here once." She kicked the lip of stone. "I'll bet this was part of it. This could've been the front step."

Mark nodded, squinting from under his hand. "You can see where it used to be, if you look."

He pointed at a shape like a giant footprint in the hollow, a big square dip in the ground twenty long strides across each way. In the dip the silvery seed heads of the grass stood six inches lower than anywhere else.

"You see," Camrose said, though she was just guessing, "they filled in the basement with earth and stuff, but then it settled. I wonder how long ago that was?"

"Oh, fifty years. Probably more."

"How could you know?"

"There's that silver maple in the middle of where the house used to be." He nodded at it. "It took at least that long to get that size."

Camrose accepted that. Ask Mark anything about wood, trees or soccer, and he'd give you the right answer.

She jumped off the stone and went to kneel beside the tree. The earth under the grass was cool against her knees, dark and mysterious.

"Wonder what's down there?"

"Dirt and roots."

"No, if a house used to be here, there could be all kinds of things buried down there. Old coins. Pieces of china. Buttons. Bones."

"Well, we can't dig for them; it's a public park." He looked at his watch. "I have to get home."

"What, and leave me to figure things out by myself?" He was already trotting along the cedar chip path toward Grant Street. "Wait! Where are you going?" she called after him.

"Got to babysit the terrible two. My mom and dad are both showing houses this afternoon."

"I'll help." She caught up and jogged beside him.

"What are you, suicidal?"

"Why? We'll bring them to the playground. It'll be fun."

"Cam, they're monsters!"

She laughed. "Come on, they're just babies. How bad can they be?"

By the time they were back at the playground with Mark's brothers, Camrose was almost wishing she'd gone home by herself. Sweeney was four and Ben was six. They were small, blond kids with round pink faces, and people always fussed over them and said what angels they were.

"It's dinosaurs this week," Mark explained as he pried the two apart. "That's all they talk about. They think they *are* dinosaurs."

Sweeney smiled sweetly up at her. Camrose forced a grin. "What kind of a dinosaur are you?"

"Brontosaurus rex," he said carefully, with the lisp that grownups adored. Then he lunged for her arm with teeth bared. She caught him and held him off.

"I'm a pterodactyl!" Ben screamed. "You're dead, bronto!" He spread his arms and leaped. Mark caught him and dragged him toward the playground.

"Last month it was monster trucks, and they kept running

each other over," he shouted over the shrieks. "Listen, you two! If you're not good, I won't push you on the swings!"

They quieted at once. "I want Camrose to push me," Ben said as he climbed into a swing.

"No, *I* want Camrose."

"*I* want—"

"Quiet! Or Camrose will go home."

The creak of the swings was like sweet music. Push, push, back and forth. The gentle motion seemed to soothe the boys.

"About Terence," Camrose said quietly. "I've been thinking. If he did hypnotize us in the square, he must have had a reason, right?"

"Well, what?"

"Obvious. To stop us talking to that busker. That means he's somebody we *should* be talking to. Maybe he knows something about Terence. Like, that thing I've forgotten."

"What thing?"

"Don't know. There's just something funny about Terence, only I can't remember what it is."

"But if you've forgotten whatever it is, how can you remember you've forgotten it? If you know what I mean."

"Because I can feel it. Down deep, buried. I can feel it scratching to get out."

He shuddered. "Sounds creepy."

"Yeah, it is. All I know is, about a year ago there was a phone call, some news about Terence that was important. Something about Germany." She cuffed the side of her head. "I feel all stuffed up and stupid."

"Never mind. If it's important it'll come ba—"

A terrifying bellow broke out below Camrose's nose and rose to a piercing shriek. They'd forgotten to watch Ben and Sweeney, and they'd let the swings slow down.

"He scratched me!" Ben screamed.

Sweeney growled and made clawing motions. "He kicked me!"

Ben snarled and aimed another kick.

Just as Mark was moving to put a stop to it, someone slipped around in front of the swings and squatted down between the boys. "Oh, it's the fierce monsters they are, all claws and teeth!" Her voice was a strange, rough purr. "Oh, what a pair of hungries they are."

It was the shaggy-haired woman they'd seen yesterday in the park. Ben and Sweeney sat perfectly still and stared at her, wide-eyed. "And *mmrrr*, what a meal they just ate!"

She had the strangest eyes, stony black and bright, shining through the brown tangle of her hair. "A whole crocodile you killed, was it?" She clicked her teeth together. They were sharp and pointed. Broken, Camrose decided.

"Bear," said Sweeney.

"*I* ate a whole elephant," Ben announced. Normally that would have started a fight, but they just sat there smiling at her.

"Then they must sit very, very still and digest, or their bellies will hurt. Very, very soft and still, each on his nest, the good little monsters they are."

They sat there swinging to and fro, making soft clucking noises. They stayed like that as the stranger stood up and stepped away from them.

"Wow," Mark said. "Can you teach me how to do that?"

"Oh, maybe. Depends." She had a strange, foreign way of talking that went with her rough voice. Everything she said rolled up her throat and curled around her tongue a couple of times before it got out into the air.

"Depends on what?" Camrose said. "Be careful, Mark."

The woman grinned with all her pointed teeth. "You're right to be wary. Start early, or else grow wise too late, like Gilda."

"You knew Gilda?"

"I was her right hand, her eyes and ears. Her feet too, sometimes."

"So you're—"

"You have it. I go by the name Miranda."

8

The lost house

"That's kind of hard to believe," Camrose said. You'd never think this woman was ever any kind of a mayor's helper, to look at her now.

"Why?" Miranda growled. "What did you expect?"

"I'm not sure, but I would've thought … I mean …"

"You don't look like the people who work at the town hall," Mark said.

"Oh, them! Shiny shoes and all, eh?" She minced on the spot, pointing her scuffed toes. She was wearing a lot of what looked like coarsely knitted sweaters and vests and a couple of layers of tattered pants, all in half a dozen shades of brown and gray. It was hard to tell what was what because the browns and grays ran together and the ragged bits flapped.

Camrose tried to be firm. "That's right. You don't look like one of them. You look more like … well, um, a street person."

"Of course I'm a street person!" Miranda laughed a croaking laugh. "And a tree person, and a river person, and sometimes an air person." She jumped to catch the bar of the swing frame and swung herself up till she was standing on her hands. They were brown hands with short, dirty fingers and long black nails.

For a moment her strange face jeered at them upside down out of its hedge of hair. "Not a house person, no," Miranda croaked mockingly. "Not a town hall person."

She swung down and dropped onto the grass, but her hair stayed bushed out angrily around her head. "Use your eyes, Keeper!"

"Why do you call me that?"

"If you don't know now, you soon will."

Mark took a look at Ben and Sweeney, who were still swinging contentedly. "Cam? You know how everybody keeps saying Gilda was kind of strange?"

"Mm."

"Well, maybe it fits that her helper wouldn't be exactly nor—I mean, average." He looked encouraging at Miranda. "Do you … you know, need anything? I mean, are you down on your luck?"

She laughed her throaty laugh. "Me? Never! Of luck I've plenty. You might say I *am* luck."

"Well," Camrose said, "if you really are Miranda, you can help me figure out Gilda's letter."

"*Rrrr*, maybe." Miranda turned in a circle on one foot. She seemed to have trouble standing still for more than ten seconds.

"What did she mean when she said she lost everything by making the wrong decision?"

"Everything. Mother, father, sister, house. All burned."

"Burned?" Camrose's eyes widened. "Where did they live?"

"Why ask me? You're the brains here, Keeper. Use them!"

While Camrose stood with her mouth open, too mad to say a word, Miranda added, "I can tell you one thing, at least. Twilight can happen more than once in a day. Remember that."

Then she turned and slouched away.

"Hey! Wait!" Camrose yelled. "Come back!"

Miranda paid no attention. When she came to the white powdered line on the grass that marked the baseball diamond, she walked along it, one foot in front of the other, as if it were a fence rail and she might fall off. They watched till she'd crossed McKirdy Street.

Camrose was still flabbergasted. "I can't believe she just walked off like that! What did she mean about twilight? And why wouldn't she talk about what happened to Gilda?"

"Funny. Did you notice? She looks like she never changes her clothes, but she doesn't smell dirty at all. I got a whiff. She smells like … like cinnamon."

"I don't care how she smells. Big fat help she was!"

Just then Ben and Sweeney turned back into monsters and started clawing at each other. "Time to go!" Mark herded them away. "We're having an early supper because there's soccer tonight," he told Camrose. "You coming to the game?"

"Sure," she said, but her thoughts were busy and far away. The first fight brought her back. After helping him break it up, she said, "You know, I've been thinking about what Miranda said. And what the letter said."

"And?"

"I'm trying to figure out what year Gilda was twelve. I think I remember my dad telling me once ... " She closed her eyes, thought, then opened them again. "Right! She was born in 1902, and she'd be twelve in 1914, right?"

"Works out."

"Mark, can I go home with you for a bit? I want to ask your mom or dad a question. Something about houses."

An hour later, Camrose stood in the cool limestone lobby of the town hall. They kept the archives in the clerk's office, which was closed on a Saturday, but Mrs. Shoemaker was right, there was something worth seeing here. Just opposite the public washrooms, in a glass case set against the stone wall, was a display called *Lynx Landing in Bygone Days*, including things like books and photos and yellowed newspaper ads for corsets and draft horses.

She spotted the house in the hollow right away. The photo was old and brown, but she had no doubt about it. There were the stone lintels with leaf shapes cut into them over the windows. There was the S-shaped door handle and the brass plate across the bottom of the door. Ivy clung to the walls between the windows. The house stood on a smooth green lawn with trees behind it.

And it had a name, which surprised her. It was the first time she'd ever heard that houses in Canada could have names. "Ennismor," they called it.

Next to the picture of the house was a photo of a bearded man in a heavily carved chair with a woman standing behind him, her hand on his shoulder. Two young girls leaned against the chair, one on each side. They wore long white dresses below their knees, their Sunday best, Camrose guessed. All four gazed out at her with water-pale eyes. None was smiling.

How glum they looked! They couldn't have known, could they? Of course not. Camrose pushed the thought aside. People in old photos always looked as if getting your picture taken was a terribly serious business.

A typed label was stuck up under the picture. It said:

Robert Kilpatrick, his wife Lillian, and daughters Olivia (left) and Gilda. Tragically, Ennismor burned down in 1914, with the entire household except for Gilda, then twelve. Gilda Kilpatrick Ferguson later became Lynx Landing's longest serving mayor.

"So that's what the letter meant," Camrose muttered as she turned away. "Gilda became the 'Keeper' of this heirloom, whatever that means, when she turned twelve, and then this awful thing happened. And now I'm twelve and she says I'm *it*."

9

The truth about Terence

Camrose kept her eyes open, hoping the crowd at the soccer game would bring the busker, the way it brought the ice cream cart and the Chip Queen truck, but there was no sign of him. She wondered if he'd left town.

Almost everybody else was there, though. There were no bleachers, but parents and grandparents brought folding lawn chairs and sat along the side lines with pop cans propped askew in the grass and folded newspapers to wave off the gnats and mosquitoes.

Junior soccer was popular in Lynx Landing. Probably, Camrose thought, because the local team almost always won. One big reason they won, everybody agreed, was the goalie, Mark Shoemaker. The ball never surprised him, and he moved faster than you'd think anybody that solid could move.

She followed the action with her eyes without really watching. Every few minutes the people around her would jump up and down and yell. In a faraway space inside her head, that buried memory was working its way up through layers of fuzz. Something about Terence ... Germany ... that phone call ...

Something cold and wet nuzzled her arm. She yelped. Krystal stood there laughing at her, with Nadia giggling beside her, a dripping can of cola in hand.

"Off in dreamland again?" Krystal inquired.

"Why? What's happened?"

"Mark stopped another goal, that's all," Nadia said.

"And," Krystal added sweetly, "best news of all, we've just voted you class dork for next year."

Any other time that would have had Camrose groping for a cutting answer. This time she just shook her head. Don't try too hard, she told herself. Let it come by itself. Terence, Aunt Alicia ... Dad with his hand over the mouthpiece of the phone, his mouth opening ... saying ...

"Oh!"

There it was, out in the open, complete and shocking. The truth about Terence. "Oh my gosh ..."

Krystal snickered. "Completely ga-ga!"

"Oh, come on, it's not worth it," Nadia muttered.

Camrose pushed between them and ran behind the line of lawn chairs to Mark's end. The game was nearly over. Soon as he came off the field she'd grab him ...

"Great game!"

She whirled around. Terence stood right behind her. His jacket was slung over his shoulder, hooked by one finger. She hovered, then decided to stay put. There couldn't be any danger, not here with all these people around. She folded her arms to hide her trembling hands. "Okay, so who are you, really?"

"What? Who on earth do you think I am?"

"I don't know. I just know you're not my cousin Terence."

"Ah...so you remember now." He laughed softly. "Can't fool you for long, can I? Watch it, Camrose, don't get so sharp you cut yourself."

She lifted her chin and tried to look sure of herself. "I think you'd better explain who you are and what you're up to."

"Mm..." He pursed his lips and shook his head. "I think not. You see, I may not be able to fool the Keeper for long, but that won't matter, because I can fool anybody else."

"I'll tell Bronwyn."

"Go ahead. She'll think it over—slo-o-owly—and then say, 'Camrose, you must have made a mistake.'" He pitched his voice high. Camrose felt her face turn red. How dare he make fun of Bronwyn?

"I could call my father."

"Yes, that would be your logical next step. But no matter what you tell him, I guarantee, what he hears will be something different. That's if you can get through. I hear the phone lines out east are pretty bad lately." He dropped his jacket to the grass and applauded. "Hey, great save!"

He folded his arms and settled himself to watch the game. Camrose backed up, but stayed near enough to keep an eye on him.

He was right, of course. She remembered yesterday evening at the kitchen table and today in Market Square. Terence would have no problem wrapping Bronwyn around his finger. He'd probably have no trouble sabotaging the phone line, either.

But why was he doing this? How was he doing it? Who was he? What was he up to?

Then she remembered something else. He'd called her the Keeper. And so had Miranda. Gilda had used the word too.

Keeper. Keeper of what? They all knew more about her than she did herself. That wasn't fair. Her hands curled into fists. Worse: it was just plain wrong, the way Terence had lied and fooled everybody and made fun of them and tried to push them around. Well, if he wouldn't say what he was up to, she'd watch him and find out.

Shouts of victory. Game over, and Lynx Landing had won again. Terence stretched, picked up his jacket, looked at the fading sunset and started off toward the woods.

Mark was in the middle of a crowd of cheering players, all thumping him on the back. They'd be celebrating for a while and Terence was almost out of sight. Camrose bounced on the spot for a moment, then made up her mind and headed for the woods.

On the cedar path under the trees, she crept forward, the soft chips almost silent underfoot. Just before the path entered the hollow she stepped sideways behind an old lilac thicket and crouched down.

Next moment Mark scrunched in beside her, breathing hard. "Hey, why'd you run? What's the—"

"Shh! He's in the hollow."

"Who?"

"Terence. Only he's not Terence."

The ghost house was ablaze. This time Camrose noticed that just as there was no sound, there was no smell of burning either.

And the yellow light didn't touch the trees. It looked like a painting that had come alive: fiery yellow house inside a shell of blue that was nearly black.

Terence had dropped his jacket somewhere, and you could see his white shirt moving around like half a ghost. He was circling the hollow, stopping every few seconds.

"What's he doing?" Mark whispered.

"He's trying all the windows and doors."

"The what?"

"Of the house."

"House?"

"Ennismor!"

Terence stopped and looked around. Camrose crouched lower. Then he went back to his circling and pawing. "The ghost house," she murmured. "That's what it's called."

"You mean it's there?"

"It's there. Burning. Oh, those poor people."

After a moment Mark said, "You actually mean it."

"Think I'm crazy, right? Well, if I am, Terence is too."

"Well," he began cautiously, "you *are* related..."

"No! That's just it, we're not!" She whispered what she'd remembered during the game. The phone call from Aunt Alicia, about a year ago. The news that Terence had been hit by a car while he was hitchhiking across Germany. Hit and killed.

"So, he's not your cousin. How'd he get that postcard from your father, then?"

"I don't think he'd have any trouble faking it."

"He's not moving around anymore."

The house was fading…gone. "He couldn't get in." She drew a sharp breath. "I wonder, is that it?"

Mark waited patiently.

"It's all starting to make a kind of sense," she whispered. "Gilda's house, Ennismor. It burned down in 1914. But somehow she hid this—this heirloom, whatever it is, inside the house, and the only way to get it is to go into the house when it comes back, at twilight."

"I guess that sort of holds together. In a crazy way."

"And Terence knows about the heirloom and he wants it too. It must be something important."

"Know what bothers me? If he can see the house, and you can see it, why can't I see it?"

Camrose put a warning hand on his arm. Terence was turning around, his eyes glinting faintly as they scanned the spot where Camrose and Mark were hiding. He stood still a moment. Then he walked away up the path toward Grant Street.

They gave him a couple of minutes, then crawled out into the hollow. The last of the sunset was gone and the full moon was still tangled in the treetops. You could hardly see a thing, even out in the open.

"I think I know how he found out about the house," Camrose said. "Remember when he came up the street last night?"

"He caught a page of the letter and gave it back to you."

"And maybe he caught the other page too, the one that's missing, and didn't give it back. I bet that's the page that told about the house."

"But he didn't get in."

"I wonder if there's a trick to it. Maybe Miranda knows. If I could only find her and—"

"Shh!"

"What?"

"Thought I heard something."

They both held still. It was so quiet you'd think all the birds were asleep, all the bugs dead.

Then Camrose heard it too. A crackle of dry leaves. *Crunch, crunch, pause, crunch.* Footsteps, with a peculiar uneven rhythm. A limping rhythm.

"Animal," Mark muttered. "Small dog."

Nearer now, less stealthy, louder. A dog, maybe, but not a small one. Lame or not, it wasn't something Camrose wanted to meet face to face.

They backed away, elbow to elbow, toward the western side of the hollow. A few yards away, branches cracked. "Must be the size of a horse," Mark whispered.

"Maybe it is a horse." But somehow she thought not.

A splintering crash came from the other side of the hollow. They turned and ran.

10

Hunted

Something exploded from the trees and pounded across the hollow behind them. They ran and ran, the path unreeling under their flying feet, and it flashed across Camrose's mind that they should be halfway up Grant Street by now. And then the path was gone and the woods were a black-and-white patchwork, confusing the eyes.

Just as Camrose was starting to grasp the idea that something impossible had happened to the woods, Mark's foot caught under a fallen branch. He flailed his arms and fell flat into a nest of brush.

Camrose was beside him right away, pulling at his arm. "Up! Up!" He scrambled up. The footsteps crept nearer. Soft, limping, but they made the ground quiver. How big was this thing?

The crushing sounds stopped. In the silence she looked up and saw a head almost directly above them, black against the stars. An animal head, but with too many things sticking out of it: pointed ears, and thin, curving bristles or horns.

And bigger than a horse, much bigger. You couldn't run from a thing that big. Maybe if they kept still it wouldn't see them. She closed her eyes and hoped it didn't hunt by scent.

For a moment neither of them breathed. The head snuffled at the air above them. It *did* hunt by scent.

A small animal burst from the bushes and charged across their feet. Camrose yelped. Mark lurched backwards. Then they were clutching each other, sliding, rolling downhill. Teeth clashed in the air where their heads had been.

At the bottom of the hill Mark lay flat on his backpack, all the wind knocked out of him. Bushes snapped halfway up the hill, then nearer. Camrose pulled at him. "There's a hole here!"

The hole was a triangle of blackness between two leaning boulders. It didn't look large enough for Mark's shoulders, but he yanked off his pack, and as soon as Camrose had wriggled in, he stuffed it in after her. Then he slid in himself, feet first.

At the last moment he stuck. His head stayed out there like an apple on a plate. Camrose's hands fastened in his shirt and dragged, but she wasn't doing any good.

Then something small and furry hit the ground next to his head and hissed at him. He shrank back and his shoulders were suddenly through the hole. Then his head. He rolled away from the opening and lay gasping on a bed of papery dead leaves.

"We're safe!" Camrose crouched and peered out through the hole. The faint blue light at the entrance darkened. Feet, with claws, scrabbled among the leaves. She threw herself back and banged her head against a hard ceiling.

"It's a raccoon!" Mark said. "Watch out, it may bite."

"Not if we leave it alone. Funny how it came along just in time to scare us into stepping backwards, just there. You could say it saved our lives. And last night, outside my room, there was another raccoon, and I thought..." She heard herself babbling and switched it off.

"I hope it's not rabid."

Rough fur brushed Camrose's hand. Dead leaves rustled. Dust tickled her nose. The third refugee was making itself at home. She edged away. She'd heard they could be vicious even when they weren't rabid.

But she wasn't really thinking of the raccoon. They could hear crunching sounds outside the burrow. The blue triangle darkened over and over again as the thing paced back and forth past the opening.

"I wonder how safe we are here, really? Suppose that what-ever-it-is tries digging us out?" She felt above her head and down the rough wall and was relieved. It felt like solid stone. "What *is* it, anyway?"

"Don't know. Did you see how it grew?" Mark's voice shook. "It started small and got big as a house."

"Bigger."

"At least that means it can't get in."

"But what's to stop it getting small again and coming in after us?"

"Not to worry," said a creaky voice between them. "If it gets small enough to come in, it's small enough for me to handle."

Camrose held her breath. Mark wasn't breathing, either.

"My advice is, stay here till dawn," said the creaky voice. "The hound loves the night."

"Who ..." Camrose cleared her throat. "Who's that?"

"It's Miranda, who else? Use your ears!"

"Miranda?"

"In the flesh. Of a sort. There's still a chance I could be rabid, of course. But most of the time I don't bite."

Camrose tried to put a face to the voice and couldn't come up with anything human, not even as strangely human as Miranda's face.

She flinched as a hand gripped her arm and squeezed. A hard hand with short fingers and long nails that bit into her skin. It was human, though. Almost.

"Okay!" said Mark eagerly. "Now at last we'll get some answers! What was that animal out there? How did it get so big?"

"You want to know too much."

"But isn't that what you're *for*, to give answers?" Camrose broke in. "Gilda's letter said you would. She said, 'Ask Miranda to tell you how this all started, that will make things clear.' Couldn't you at least do *that*?"

"*Mmrrr.*"

"We can use all the help we can get," Mark ventured.

"Mm," she said, more pleasantly. "Well, that creature will be lurking for a while. We have time enough. So curl up, be quiet and don't interrupt, and I will tell you the tale of young Diarmid the bard."

11

The tale of young Diarmid

On the morning of the third day of his journey, young Diarmid came to the river of time. All behind him lay the green and living lands, and before him flowed the dark and starry river, and beyond the river lay a land hidden in everlasting night.

Diarmid stood upon the shore, and he called and called his love by name. "Rhianna!"

And on the far shore she appeared, dressed in a gown of snow-white silk. Smiling, she waded the river, and Diarmid ran to greet her.

But the moment she set her foot upon the living land she became a gaunt white hound with teeth like steel spikes, and leaped at him. He fought for an hour before killing the creature with his sword.

Again he stood upon the shore, and he called and called his love by name. "Rhianna!"

And on the far shore she appeared, dressed all in velvet black as night. Laughing, she waded the river, and Diarmid walked to meet her.

But the moment she set her foot upon the living land she became a huge black hound with claws like iron hooks, and leaped at him. He fought for an hour and then an hour more, before cutting off the creature's head.

A third time he stood upon the shore, and he called and called his love by name. "Rhianna!"

And on the far shore she appeared, in a gown of satin red as blood. Singing for joy, she waded the river, and Diarmid stepped down to meet her.

But the moment she set her foot upon the living land she became a gigantic red hound with eyes of fire, and leaped at him. He fought while the sun rolled up the sky and down the other side, and yet he could neither kill nor hurt the hound.

At last, just when its jaws were snapping at his throat, he cut off its left foreleg. Howling and limping, the creature waded back across the river.

"Now, surely, three times winds up the charm," Diarmid said. He picked up the leg of the hound and from it he took the long bone, and with this bone he made a flute. And on the flute, round and round from lip to tip in an unbroken spiral, he carved words of calling and compelling.

This was the song of the bone flute.

> I call the blood back to the bone,
> I call the spark back to the stone,
> I call the heart back to its own,
> I call the wanderer home.

So it was on the evening of the third day of his journey that young Diarmid stood beside the river of time and played a tune. Over the water the music flew like a flock of singing birds.

And on the far shore she appeared, dressed all in ashen rags. Weeping, she waded the river, and it seemed to Diarmid as he played that she walked upon the music as on a path of flint.

But the moment her foot touched the living land she fell dead at his feet.

When Diarmid saw what he had done he threw down the bone flute, and the river swept it away.

Now Gwyn, son of Nuadu, lord of the Otherworld, had seen Rhianna, and it was he who had stolen her away. Crossing the river like a storm he found Diarmid sitting upon the shore, his sword forgotten on the ground beside him. Of Rhianna there was no sign.

Up went Gwyn's obsidian blade and down it swept, but before it could harm a hair of Diarmid's head it stopped, stuck fast in the air.

When Diarmid looked to see who had worked the spell, he saw before him three sisters robed in black. All in a row they stood, one with a spindle, one with a shuttle and one with a knife as sharp as any sword. They were the Wyrde who spin and weave the lives of women and men and who cut the threads when the web is done.

Diarmid bowed low, for he knew them, but he wasted no words. "Where is my Rhianna?"

"Safe," said the youngest sister, in a voice soft as a summer breeze.

"Changed," said the second sister, in a voice like autumn rain.

"Beyond your reach," added the oldest, in a voice like winter wind.

"But I love her!"

"This is a terrible wrong you have done, young Diarmid," said the youngest. "You made an evil thing, and with it you piped your love back across the river of time."

"No mortal flesh can cross that river twice and live," said the middle sister. "This is your doing, and you must pay."

"Then why not let him kill me?"

"That would be a price too heavy and a penalty too light," the eldest said. She lifted one finger and Gwyn's obsidian blade shattered and fell from his hand.

Then the three sisters spoke together in a voice like the sea, "Hear now your doom, Diarmid the bard. You will search for the bone flute and never will you rest till it's found, though you scour the world over. Find it, prove your right to it, and your doom is done."

"And then will I see Rhianna?"

"Then you will find rest."

"On the other side of darkness, in the land of morning."

"Rhianna may please herself."

Then Gwyn howled with fury. Black clouds boiled, and a tempest threw Diarmid to his knees. "And what of my vengeance? Rhianna was mine! I claim his death for my loss!"

"His death does not belong to you," said the eldest sister, whose hem never stirred no matter how the wind shrieked.

"And neither did Rhianna," said Diarmid, staggering to his feet.

Gwyn smiled, and the wind died. "Then this I swear. I will be the one to first lay hands on the flute. And when I do, I'll pipe you such a tune as will have you dancing in the outer darkness forever!"

Rain fell. When it drew off and the clouds broke, young Diarmid stood alone beside the river of time.

12

Invisible chocolate

*C*amrose crouched in silence for a long time before she realized Miranda had stopped talking. It seemed to her that during the story the husky voice had gone smooth. And in places it sang, and out of the clear notes came images of brave young Diarmid, and the terrible hounds and the three black-robed Wyrde.

"It does explain a lot." She stretched her cramped legs. "So Diarmid's been looking for this flute for ... how many years?"

"More than you could count," said Miranda in her original creaky voice.

"And the heirloom Gilda talked about—that's the bone flute, right? And now it's inside a house that isn't there. How did I get mixed up in this?"

"By birth. You're one of a long line, a line nearly as old as that tale. You are the Keeper of the bone flute."

"Me. The Keeper of the bone flute." She rubbed her eyes, and in the dark behind her eyelids she saw it floating, bright, as if a spotlight was shining on it: an ivory flute with a spiral of letters flowing around and around its length. A beautiful thing, full of power. Evil power, the Wyrde said.

"This can't be right. I'm only twelve. Somebody made a mistake."

"Gilda was only twelve when she became Keeper."

"Yes, and look what happened then!"

"Stop carping! It's in your power to end this tale."

"By giving it to the rightful claimant, you mean, like Gilda said." That was more hopeful.

"But who's the rightful claimant?" Mark put in.

"Easy. It has to be Diarmid, right, Miranda?" Camrose felt almost jaunty now. It was cheering to know the right thing to do.

"*Mmrrr.* That's not for me to say. Just you judge right, and we'll all be happy. Diarmid will find his rest, and you'll lay down your charge, and I—I'll be free!" She laughed with a sound like branches rubbing together.

"Free from what?"

"My bondage. Ask no more of that!"

"Okay, so how do I find Diarmid?"

"That won't be hard. The flute draws him."

"But how will I know him?"

"Think, Keeper—for once! Ask yourself who's new in town."

"Terence?" Mark said in a wondering tone.

"And there's that busker." Camrose remembered his young face with the old eyes. Diarmid's story would explain the eyes.

"Hate this sitting still," Miranda snarled. Feet scrambled across Camrose's legs and a small body darkened the mouth of the burrow.

"Wait! You can't leave us now!"

"It's safe. Go home." She was gone.

Mark crawled to the opening and listened. "I don't hear anything. But it could just be lying in wait."

"No, Miranda's a pain in the neck, but I don't think she'd say it's safe if it isn't. I think we have to trust her."

"Okay. Here goes."

It took a lot of work to get him out. Then Camrose pushed his backpack out after him and slithered out herself.

They stood in a small clearing among the trees, with cool moonlight pouring in. The path glimmered a few steps away. They pushed through to it and in a minute they were heading up Grant Street. At the first bend Camrose turned and looked back, but there was nothing to see but a narrow band of darkness.

"I can't figure out what happened in the woods."

"Me neither."

"It's like it was a much bigger place all of a sudden. Was it just because we were so scared we couldn't think? Were we running around in circles?"

"I don't think it was just that. Remember that hill we fell down? There isn't a hill in those woods." Mark looked at the blue glow of his watch and sucked air through his teeth. "Oh, man. It's past ten! I'm really going to catch it."

Bronwyn had already locked up. Camrose reached up to the ledge above the door where the spare key was hidden and turned it gently in the lock. She replaced the key, eased the door open and slid in, silently closing it behind her.

Get caught coming in this late and there'd be a nasty scene. It was a wonder the police weren't out after her already. Maybe if she could get to her room without being noticed...

Terence was already in. His jacket hung on a hook in the coat alcove. Her hand hovered near the leather, not daring to touch. From inches away she could feel a nimbus of warmth over it. Her spine crawled. She backed toward the stairs.

Her foot was on the bottom step when voices in the kitchen caught her ear. A low murmur—that sounded like Terence— and then Bronwyn in that piercing know-it-all tone that always rubbed Camrose raw.

"I mean, it's not like I really care, but the way Dad encourages her! He actually pretends to take her seriously!" A pause, then she added grumpily, "I don't think he ever paid half that much attention to me."

"I suppose she still has her secret nooks and hiding places, like all young kids."

"Oh, like you wouldn't believe! I'll bet she still thinks that rope ladder in the tree is a secret."

Camrose took her foot from the stairs and walked along the hall toward the kitchen.

"I had one like that when I was a kid. I had some secret caches round the house too."

"I never did. I don't think Camrose does, either. She'd get heck from me if she started prying the place apart."

Camrose stepped into the kitchen. Bronwyn didn't look up. She was sitting at the kitchen table across from Terence, raising a glass to her lips. She sipped and put the glass down. It was empty. An empty plate sat on the table between them.

"Have another chocolate," Terence said.

"I shouldn't, but they're so delicious." Her fingers hesitated over the plate, then chose a piece of nothing and raised it to her lips. She took a delicate bite of air and smiled at him. "Mmm!"

Ice closed around Camrose's heart. She took another step into the room. Terence looked at her, but Bronwyn just raised her empty glass.

"Bronwyn, wake up!"

Bronwyn took another bite of air. Camrose turned on Terence, fists clenched and trembling. "You just stop whatever you're doing to her!"

"Whatever do you mean?" His smile gleamed.

"You've done something. You've hypnotized her!"

"Not even close. But why should you mind? You heard how she's been talking about you."

"I don't care! She's my sister!"

"That matters?"

"Of course it matters!"

Terence leaned forward. "And what will you give me if I set her free?" he purred.

"Give you? I don't have anything to give you!"

"But you will. Soon."

Camrose stared at him and couldn't speak.

He sat back and laughed. "All right, anything to please you, little cousin. Just … " He poised a hand. "Remember this when the time comes to choose." He snapped his fingers.

Bronwyn frowned at her glass and set it down. Then she frowned at Camrose. "When did you get in?"

"Just now."

"Okay, that does it. You're grounded."

"What!"

"You heard me. You can go out during the day, but from now until Dad gets home, you stay in the house after supper."

Terence touched Bronwyn's wrist. "Hey, is that fair?" She looked at him and her eyes went cloudy. He smiled into them.

She blinked. "No, it's not fair. She's not grounded." She rubbed her forehead. "Ow, my head hurts. I think I'll go to bed."

Camrose followed her out of the kitchen and up the stairs and watched her close her door. Then she darted into her own room and closed her own door and wedged it with a sandal.

"If I were grounded, I wouldn't have been able to go into the ghost house again," she muttered. "That was why he did…whatever he did. Not to be nice. He wants me to get the flute."

Remember this when the time comes to choose, he'd said. "If only I didn't have to choose! I never asked for this!"

Half an hour later she stepped out into the dark hallway and tiptoed to the stairs. Down she went, barefoot, stepping at the wall side of the steps so they wouldn't creak.

The light under the buttons of the phone was a dim green glow in the downstairs hall next to the stair wall. Camrose punched "one" for long distance. Then the area code and number written on a piece of paper taped to the phone. It rang once, twice, three times. Stopped.

The receiver filled with a rushing sound like wind or water that went on and on. Camrose hung up and tried again. Three rings, then emptiness and windy sounds.

A small red light flashed on the phone. "Message!" Eagerly she jabbed at the buttons. "Dad?"

Tense silence at the other end. Then an indrawn breath.

"Who's there?" Camrose demanded.

"Who are you?" A breathless, frantic voice. A girl's voice. A...familiar...

The line went dead.

13

The busker

With slippery hands, Camrose clutched a phone cold as bone. It clattered as she hung up. She pressed her hands to her churning stomach.

A stir of the air made her look up. Terence was gazing down at her from the dim landing. His eyes reflected the light with a yellowish sheen like mica.

"Something the matter?" he asked pleasantly.

"Do you think I'd tell you?"

He laughed and went back upstairs. She waited to hear the click of his door closing, then followed. Once in her room again, she curled up in a shivering ball under the covers.

Who was that on the phone? Something strange about that voice. It made her backbone cold.

"Just a wrong number, that's all," she told herself over and over until she fell asleep. It took a long time.

When she woke, the rectangular shape of her window was glimmering in the dark. She stretched. Must be nearly dawn.

She slid out of bed and cat-footed to the window. The sky above the house was violet, but when she pressed her face to the glass she could see a peach glow along the northeast horizon. It's like sunset in reverse, she thought.

Sunset in reverse.

She thumped herself on the forehead. "Why didn't I figure that out before?" She dived for her jeans.

Two minutes later she was racing down the hill past sleeping houses, while the day's first twilight brightened around her. She arrived at the hollow, panting, just in time to see the roofline of Ennismor fade into the morning sky.

"*That's* what Miranda meant. I must be brain-dead, not to've seen it before! I could have gone in there if only I'd got here sooner!" She stood shivering in the cool of the woods, with dew dripping from the leaves down her neck.

But she really couldn't feel sorry. With the bone flute in hand she'd have to make a quick decision. And there were too many things to think about before she could decide anything.

I have to find that busker, she thought.

A car went by as she stepped out onto Grant Street. It was Sunday morning. That meant no Mark until afternoon. His family always got up early on Sunday and went to church, and then to lunch with one or the other set of grandparents.

She'd just have to find the busker by herself.

The old stone building on the brink of the cliff used to be a grist mill. But the giant waterwheel was gone, the roof fallen. All that was left was a shell: outside walls, empty doorways and windows, some of the inner walls and a floor paved with big, flat flagstones.

They called it the Old Mill Mall now. Camrose liked to come here, when she could afford it. It wasn't a good place if you had no money. They expected you to buy things, not just sit and talk with your friends.

At one end of the mall was a coffee shop with a dozen white iron tables and chairs. Tiny stores selling handmade jewelery and glass and pottery ran along the street side. On the other side you could lean on the wide stone window sills and look down the cliff at the river, or across to Quebec.

The mall was always crowded on a Saturday with people from the market. But this early on a Sunday morning, one old couple sat and listened to a lone piper. Or perhaps they were not listening. They were reading newspapers and not looking at him.

Camrose watched from an arched doorway. The music had led her here and it still pulled at her, but this time it didn't waft her away to anyplace strange. After a few minutes the old couple folded their newspapers, got up and walked off. They went out without dropping any money in the busker's bag.

He went on playing to empty chairs and tables. The tune was full of long notes that died away, like birds crying on distant shores. It sounded like all the homesickness in the world.

The last grieving notes faded. Camrose walked stiffly across the flagstones to where he half-sat, half-stood, propped on one of the iron tables. She bent to drop a handful of coins into his canvas backpack.

He gave her a dark look as he untangled himself from his pipes. "So far have I fallen," he muttered.

"Sorry, but it's—it's all I have." She went hot with embarrassment. "It's the last of my birthday money."

"Child, it's a king's ransom!" He scooped up the money and dumped his pipes into the backpack. With a grand sweep of his arm that hardly matched his ragged jeans and faded sweatshirt, he waved around at the ruin. "Come, join me, and we'll sit at our ease in this goodly hall, drinking the blood-red wine."

"Thanks, but—"

"What, you refuse my hospitality?"

"No, but I'm not old enough to drink wine. Besides, they only serve coffee here." She nodded at the Old Mill Coffee Shop.

"Coffee, then. Black as a sinner's heart, my love," he said to the girl behind the counter, who gave him a suspicious look. To Camrose he added, "I've grown to like the stuff, oddly enough. Taste is one of the few pleasures I can still enjoy."

Camrose accepted an iced mocha latte. The sun was pouring into the stone shell and it was already shaping up to be a sultry day. They took their drinks to a table near the cliff side.

A couple of peanut shells were scattered over the tabletop. Camrose pushed them around with her forefinger. How to begin? "You…um, play the bagpipes."

"They're uillean pipes, to name them true."

"Illen pipes," she repeated, because that was how it struck her ear. "You're awfully good. I mean, it sounds like you've been playing them a long, long time."

He studied her for a moment. "No, not so very long."

She sagged. Well, then, this couldn't be Diarmid.

"Only a matter of fifty years or so. I was a true bard once." He held her eyes and let the moment stretch out. "But the kings I harped for have been dust a thousand years."

Her heart thumped. "So you're..."

"Yes, I am Diarmid, once a harpist. Now I pipe on the streets for my bread. I suppose it's better than being dead."

He raised his mug to her and smiled, which changed him for that moment into a shining boy. "Keeper, your health. Long have I sought you, too often lost you. Let this time be the last!"

"I hope so too." She felt her face glowing, reflecting his smile. But a voice niggled at the back of her brain. *Not so fast! Get all the facts. Think before you decide!*

"You want proof." His smile cooled.

"Well, you see, I... It's a big responsibility."

"Of course. The devil of it is, I have no proof at all. You know the tale, I take it? Yes, well... It leaves a lot out. One thing it doesn't tell is that Rhianna and I were to be married. But on the very eve of our wedding she was stolen away."

"You mean she was kidnapped?"

"Just so. Her beauty had caught the eye of the Otherworld prince. Such things have happened before. Those people are drawn to the most beautiful among us, perhaps because their own forms and natures lack substance."

"How d'you mean?"

"They've no true shape. Always changing they are, deceitful to their marrow. You must know: you've met him."

"Him who?"

"Gwyn, of course."

"Gwyn." Gwyn, son of Nuadu, lord of the Otherworld. Sitting at her kitchen table. Sleeping in the bedroom down the hall, if he did sleep. She'd been almost sure, but it was still a shock to hear him named outright.

Diarmid's pale eyes flickered. "Your look is strange. Has he bent you to his will already?"

"No way!"

"Take care he doesn't. You can't trust any of that folk to tell you the least thing truly, not that ice is cold or fire burns, not if they swear by the sun, moon and stars that it's so."

"Don't worry, I don't trust him an inch."

"Good…good. Tell me, will you go to Gilda's house tonight?"

It was on the tip of her tongue to say yes, but there was something too eager in his voice. She studied his face.

He smiled sadly. "Don't you trust me?"

Of course I trust you! I'll give you the flute. The words pressed to spill out. But that voice in the back of her mind niggled at her again: Wait. Don't cave in just yet. So she said nothing and felt mean and guilty. He'd been through such a lot.

"I am growing so weary." Diarmid gazed through the stone arches out over the river and talked on, in a flat, gray voice, as if he were talking to himself. "Weary, not in the body, but in the spirit. So weary. At times I've forgotten about the quest for months, even years, just drifted around the world, piping for my supper, searching…searching…for something…someone…"

14

The forbidden door

"You should have waited for me," Mark said. "It could've been dangerous."

"Dangerous! Mark, this was Diarmid!"

"And that makes him safe?"

They were sitting side by side, cross-legged, at the end of a granite finger that ran out into the river about half a mile downstream from the Old Mill Mall. It was one of Camrose's favorite places to be when she wanted to think without a lot of people around.

The rock was hot under their skin, but the air blowing across the water was cool. The sound and smell and glitter of the river were all around them.

"If you'd only seen him and talked to him, you'd feel sorry for him too," Camrose said.

"It could all be an act. I wouldn't trust him."

"And that might be the smartest thing you've ever said!"

The laughing voice came from right behind them. Camrose leaped to her feet. Mark nearly fell over, untwisting his legs like a corkscrew as he tried to stand up.

Terence settled himself on a low boulder a couple of feet back from the end of the ridge. His jacket was draped over one shoulder.

"I wouldn't trust you, either," Mark said.

Terence ignored him and looked at Camrose, his eyes serious. "Has he sung or played to you? If he has, you may be enspelled."

"What are you talking about?"

"A bard has certain talents. His music puts him in touch with many powers, and not all are what you would call good. Remember, he made the flute and marked it with his spell."

"Good point," Mark said.

"So, I ask, did he sing to you?"

Camrose jammed her hands in her pockets. "He did play the pipes. I mean, it's what he does for a living. But that wasn't for me. It was ... for ... "

Yesterday in Market Square. She could still feel the springy carpet of flowers under her feet and smell smoke on the cool air.

"And while you're thinking about that, here's something else to think about. He knew Rhianna could not cross the river again, not as a living woman. He knew it would kill her. But he forced her to return anyway."

"I don't believe you! He loved her!"

"Did he so?" Terence shrugged. "He was bound and determined no man would have her but himself. Is that love?"

Mark shoved his hair out of his eyes. "You should talk! You're the one who kidnapped her."

"I?"

"Stop playing around," Camrose said. "We know who you are."

He laughed. "All right, then. The truth is, there was no kidnapping. She came willingly, for love of me. What's more, my father made her welcome, and we were married. And then that jealous fool stole her away from me and killed her in doing it. Can you wonder I was in a fury?"

Camrose shook her head. "Why should we believe you? How could Rhianna have been willing to go to such a horrible place?"

"And what place is that?"

"You know, your place. Your world. The Otherworld. Isn't it a kind of hell?"

He threw back his head and laughed. "Oh, my friend! You're thinking of the Underworld, perhaps. Quite a different place altogether, if those old tales of your people are to be believed."

"But the story said … " Camrose groped for the words. "It said, across the river was a land buried under everlasting night."

"A potent argument against trespass. Dark indeed it seemed to your forefathers. Dim and bleak it loomed beyond the river of time."

Camrose shivered. "Cold?" Terence asked.

"No, just—"

But he whirled his jacket in the air and settled it around her shoulders before she could raise a hand to push it away. The roar of the river softened to a silver chiming as he spoke.

"It's not all dark in my world, I promise you. There are sweet green meadows where it's always morning and groves dappled with gold where it's always afternoon. And best of all is my father's hall that lies forever open to the stars. Yet never a tempest comes there and never a drop of rain unless we wish it, and we light the shadows with lamps of dawn and moonlight. Can you see it, Camrose?"

She could see it, spread below as if she hovered like an eagle: a vast hall thronged with dancers. Their clothes were like woven jewels and living flowers. Huge trees grew in that hall, and the pale green glow of their leaves mingled with the rose and silver of the lamps.

And there was music too, clearer every moment. A tangle of pipes and strings and a patter of drums that blew cold down her spine and at the same time made her twitch to join in the dance.

With so much to see, the people so strange and beautiful, and the patterns of the dance so intricate that they teased the eye to follow, Camrose did not stop at first to take a good, close look at any one thing.

And yet one thing did catch her eye in passing. She searched back for it and at last found it, a clot of darkness at the far end of the hall, where there were no rose and silver lamps, no glowing trees, no bright dancers.

There the light reached only far enough to pick out two rows of… soldiers, they must be. Tall figures with golden metal wrapped around their chests and arms and legs and golden helmets shaped like the heads of hawks and lions hiding their faces. They were the only still people in all that hall.

One row of seven faced out toward the dancers. The other row of seven faced in toward the darkness. And in that darkness… Camrose strained to see. The shadowy shape at the end of the hall grew clearer.

It was a door. Not a large door, not much taller than the soldiers who guarded it. But it was massive, made of timber slabs bound with plates of some dull metal. Across its two halves lay a bar of the same metal as thick as a young tree trunk. And all the soldiers stood with swords drawn.

15

Plain sight

Suddenly it was all gone, the hall and the lights and the dancers. Camrose blinked. The jacket sprawled on the rocks at her feet, and Mark stood, hands fisted, scowling past her at Terence.

"Never touch that again," Terence said in a voice like silk.

Mark tried to push past Camrose. "Then keep it to yourself after this!"

She grabbed his wrist. A still moment, then Terence laughed and bent to scoop up the jacket. "So, my Camrose." He smiled down at her. "Can you see things differently now?"

"I don't know." Suppose what he said was true, and Rhianna really had loved him? Suppose what he said about Diarmid was true? Could Terence be the right claimant after all?

His eyes were so blue. They looked … not old, not like Diarmid's, but ageless, as if he'd always been both young and wise. Easy to see how Rhianna could have fallen in love with …

With … Was it the reflected light rippling across his face that made it look so strange?

Ripple, ripple. Then …

Ears long and pointed, eyes a narrow glitter, yellow as a cat's, eyebrows a sharp V, joined in the middle.

And on his shoulder leaned a crimson hound. It raised a horned head to stare at Camrose with eyes that burned red. Its one front paw flexed, showing long, sharp claws.

She took a step back, but the edge of the rock was under her heel. Mark caught her arm. Nowhere to run.

"So you saw." Terence scratched his jaw. He looked human enough now, and the red thing on his shoulder was just a jacket. "I should have known. You're becoming the Keeper, sure enough. Nothing but trouble. If I did not need you to get that flute, Sweetness, I'd have been rid of you long since."

She folded her arms. "Maybe you wouldn't have found that such an easy thing to do."

But her words were hollow, and he knew it. He laughed. Then he stood up and stretched. "Oh, here." He pulled a folded paper from his jeans pocket and handed it to her. "You might as well have this. It's no use to me after all. When you come to make your decision, little cousin, think well on what happened to poor Gilda."

He shrugged the jacket on. It slid up his arms with a deliberate movement and snuggled around his shoulders. After one last cheerful wave, he scrambled along the rocks to the shore.

Mark scowled after Terence's dwindling figure. "Don't ever trust that guy."

"Don't worry, I won't. What … what happened just then?"

"You tell me. He put that jacket on you and for a minute you looked... not all there. I didn't like it, so I grabbed it off you."

"I wasn't all there. I was someplace else."

"What?"

She shook her head. "And then? What did you see after?"

"Don't get you."

"His face. Didn't you see how his face changed?" Mark squinted at her. "Never mind," she said. "It's nothing."

He pointed. "What's that he gave you?"

The paper was still crumpled in her hand. As soon as she unfolded it, the determined black handwriting leaped out at her.

"It's page two of Gilda's letter. So he did have it!"

"Huh. But why give it back now?"

"Not just to be nice, that's for sure." She looked it over. "Remember where the first page ended? At twilight go to the something, it said. So, here goes.

"... *hollow in the woods at the west end of the park on McKirdy Street. That hollow, in case you aren't already aware of this piece of family history, is all that remains of the house where I was born.*

"*Perhaps not quite all. A memory or image of the house on the night it burned, a ghost of that event, returns each time twilight comes to the hollow. I have never gone back inside, because the house is waiting for you, not me. It's your task to take charge of the bone flute and keep it safe for the rightful claimant.*

"*Who are these claimants, and why do they want this heirloom of ours? That story is too long to tell here. You only need to know that they are two, and neither one will show you his true face. Be careful of them both! But so long as you hold the flute safe, you have the upper hand—they depend on you to hand it over willingly. It will be up to you to decide between them.*

"I wish I could tell you how to choose, but the final judgement must be yours alone. In ..."

"In? What?"

"That's the end of the page. I'm not sure it helps much." Camrose wished things were as clear now as they had looked this morning. Then, it was simple. There were two claimants for the flute, one right and one wrong. That was that. "I wonder if it's true, that Diarmid knew it would kill Rhianna to bring her back?"

"Ask him."

"I will. But even if that was true, and even if Gilda was right about him back in 1914, he could have changed since then, couldn't he? It's been a long time."

"Maybe." Mark looked over her shoulder. "Better be getting back. Storm's coming."

Camrose glanced back. Then she jumped up and led the scramble to shore. Thunder castles were building in the west and coming on fast.

It was just before three, the hottest part of the afternoon, and the sunshine was as thick as mustard, the air almost too heavy to breathe. Out on the rocks, surrounded by cool water, they hadn't noticed the change.

"Better get inside before the rain starts!" Camrose said.

By the time they reached Market Square it was nearly deserted, except for storekeepers cranking down awnings, rolling in racks of T-shirts and folding up sandwich boards.

The edge of the cloud mass crossed the sun as they reached McKirdy Street. The thick yellow light shut off and everything went gray. Thunder boomed.

"Better run," Mark said.

Camrose caught his arm. "Wait. Look!" The streetlights were going on all along the street. Streetlights in the middle of the day! "Mark, it's twilight!"

"Yes, but—"

"If the storm lasts, this could work. Don't you see? It could last even longer than a normal twilight!" She jigged with excitement.

"Or it could end any minute."

"Only one way to find out!" She raced across the park to the band of trees and burst into the hollow with Mark close behind her. For a moment she thought she was wrong. The house wasn't there.

And then, as the sky darkened to purple and thunder rumbled, one window appeared, glowing with the warm yellow of lamplight.

16

Inside the ghost house

*I*t grew up out of the grassy hollow, stone on stone, story on story. Its tall windows were capped with carved lintels. Ivy twined beside the wide, front door whose two halves were paneled with dark, polished wood and shod with brass.

Each detail was clear, yet sheer as gauze. Smooth lawns surrounded the house, yet cedar chips crunched under Camrose's sneakers.

"Well?" Mark shook her arm.

"It's almost real. Almost. Can't you see it now?"

"No. Nothing."

It was more solid now. The glow behind the window panes was brighter, but still warm and friendly. The dark green edges of the partly drawn curtains showed inside. A yellow tassel hung next to the glass. A rose bush by the front door carried blooms red as stoplights.

The lawn was a smooth sweep of green, still marked in parallel lines by the mower's wheels. Camrose started forward. The turf was springy under her shoes. She drew in a deep breath and smelled not woods, with their undertone of composting leaves, not flowers run wild, but freshly cut grass and blooming roses.

"Camrose!"

She turned. Mark looked very far away. "I'm going in," she called.

"But if it's burning—"

"It's not burning yet."

She looked up at the house and terror swamped her at the sight of this thing, standing here where it didn't exist, where it had no right to be.

Right ahead lay a path of flagstones, swept clean except for a few fresh grass clippings at the edges. She walked forward and climbed three stone steps to the front door. The brass handle was cold under her hand, and real as … as brass, she thought.

Deep breath. Heart, stop banging!

A click and a push, and the door swung open. She stepped inside. Mark called from the distance. The closing door cut off his voice.

Camrose stood perfectly still. She didn't know what she'd expected. Something more sinister than this, for sure. A wide hallway stretched away from her with closed doors on both sides. The light was the blue of early dusk. To one side she caught a sudden movement and whipped around. Her own white-faced reflection stared back at her from a mirror that hung beside the door.

I'm really here, she thought. I'm inside the ghost house.

She walked on, silent, breathing shallowly. Suppose someone living in the house were to hear her, and come out, and say …

Someone *living?*

She pushed the thought away and concentrated on her task. Gilda said the flute was hidden. It wouldn't be anywhere obvious.

The house was beautiful, what she could see of it. The high ceiling was edged with a border of raised plaster shells and scrolls. To her right on a polished table stood a Chinese vase full of roses, a splash of scarlet in the blue air. Their perfume was so strong it made her feel dizzy. She smelled wood smoke too.

The hall carpet was midnight blue. The thick pile was velvety to the touch, as she found out when she bent down and brushed her fingers over it.

Why was I so afraid? she wondered. Now I'm right inside the house, and it's better than real. It's wonderful.

At the end of the hall a broad staircase curved gracefully up out of sight. She wished she could see what the upstairs rooms were like. Why not go up and take a look? There must be so many beautiful rooms, full of amazing things.

Quick as thought, she found herself at the foot of the staircase. The top of the newel post was carved in the shape of a coiled dragon. She rubbed its polished head—the wood was lighter there—and began to climb. The banister was warm and smooth under her palm.

She was halfway up when a sound caught her ear, the first sound she'd heard in this place. Voices. She looked back. A door stood open in the hallway, though it had been closed before. A fuzzy light streamed from it.

The voices came from there. They had a distorted, echoing

sound, like the noises you hear underwater. They startled the glamor out of Camrose's head.

She walked down the stairs faster than she'd gone up, but still not very fast. There was a thickness in the bluish light that made it impossible to move quickly. And wasn't it a deeper blue than before?

Something in the hall had changed. Camrose looked for it and saw the red roses shriveled and black. Their scent had gone bad. How had that happened so fast?

She stopped just outside the open doorway looking in at a room with silky yellow walls. The tall windows were dark blue with dusk and a chandelier, a blaze of quivering light, hung from the ceiling.

Then she saw the girl and forgot the room. She knew at once who she was: her long, dark red braid hanging down the back of her loose white dress. Gilda stood sideways to the door, her hands wrapped tightly around a wooden box. Her eyes were fixed on someone farther inside the room, someone Camrose couldn't see.

"So you've made your decision." A man's voice, slow and lazy. Camrose almost knew it.

"So she has. Leave her alone," said a second voice, deep and soft, a lovely voice. "Come along, wise child, let's see it."

Gilda looked down at the box. She glanced toward the doorway as if she wished she could run away and escape.

She doesn't see me, Camrose thought. Well, how could she? I'm not there. Or, she's not here. Or …

"Come now, you must choose." An edge in the lazy voice now.

Gilda fumbled at the box with shaking hands.

Camrose watched her anxiously. *She's scared. Just like I would be. I should go in there and back her up,* she thought. But her feet would not cross the threshold.

The box dropped from Gilda's hands, hit the carpet and bounced aside. She held something thin, rolled in white cloth. Then the cloth slipped off and the thing in her hands was brown and smaller than Camrose had expected. It didn't look like much at all. Just an old bone.

"Bring it closer, Keeper!"

"Yes, child. Bring it here. Remember your promise."

Gilda looked down at the thing in her hands, then at the end of the room, at the unseen speakers. "I can't. This isn't right. I need more time!"

She turned toward the door and for the first time looked straight at Camrose. Her eyes went wide. She took a step in that direction and flinched back as a curtain of flame whipped across her path.

Her arm swung. "Take it!" she yelled. "Whoever you are, take it and get out!" And the bone spun through the flames, through the doorway, and smack into Camrose's outstretched hand. It was heavy, hard and cold.

The door slammed in her face. She leaned on the outside of it, coughing. She pounded on the panels. "Gilda!" Smoke seeped from under the door.

Wait a minute, Gilda got out. She lived to be mayor. But the others . . . There were other people in the house: a father, a mother, a sister. All would die.

Camrose ran to the stairs and started up. But the fire was there, too, reaching for her with red hands. She screamed for everyone to get out, but the smoky air sponged up her voice. And she knew they wouldn't hear her because she wasn't there.

The smoke was thicker. The fire had eaten through the wall and red-gold flames were biting chunks out of the ceiling. She fumbled along the wall farthest from the fire.

Now she knew how Gilda's house had burned down. Because it was happening now, this minute. The house was burning down around her.

And she was slowing down. As if the air itself was holding her back. Each step was like pushing through deep water. She could be trudging along the bottom of a lake, drowning. Or would drown soon, if she didn't get out fast.

She looked ahead, toward the doorway. It was closer, but how long had she been struggling toward it?

And then she saw, clear through the billowing smoke and the blue wall, a glimpse of treetops and clouds. The storm dusk was passing. The house was fading.

If it fades with me in it, what happens to me?

Charred walls and ashy carpet blurred into a blue mist around her. Even the flames were sickly looking.

One step, then another. Now it was like dragging her feet though mud. Beyond the wall a branch tossed in the wind. Another step. A sketch of clouds surged above the ceiling. One more sluggish step … The door was closer now.

Sweat rolled down her face and splashed on her hand. At least that showed she was still solid. One more step, and she reached forward to grasp the brass handle of the door. It slid out of her grip like jelly.

She wedged her shoulder against the door and pushed. It inched open.

I'm going to make it, she thought. Her right hand curled around the stubborn nothingness of the door. I'm going to … Time, motion, the whole world trickled to a halt.

Then something stopped her breath. She looked right through her own left arm to the paneling behind it. The bone flute in her hand was opaque, and felt heavier than iron, colder than ice, but her own bones and muscles and skin were shadows.

I'm not going to make it.

17

Flute music

The door melted from her shoulder. At the same moment a hand gripped her fingers and yanked. Stone steps shot up at her. She fell through them, landed hard, and lay face down in long wet grass, too stunned to move. Somebody touched her head.

"I'm all right!" Camrose pushed Mark away, sat up and pulled in a deep lungful of air, cool and moist after the rain. Then she went into a fit of coughing. "'Cept my throat...feels like somebody's been...skiing down it!" She blinked at him with watering eyes. "If you hadn't pulled me out, I wonder where I'd be right now?"

He squatted in front of her. "Better not think about that." He sniffed at her. "You smell like smoke."

She coughed again. "I'm lucky I'm not a cinder!"

"You really were in there. In the ghost house."

"You just figured that out?"

"Still getting my head around it."

"You didn't really believe me before, did you?"

"There's a difference," he said carefully, "between believing somebody and knowing a thing for yourself. You ... you just vanished!"

"Well, here's the real proof!" She held out the flute.

Mark sat back on his heels. "So that's it. Not much to look at, is it? Where's the carving?"

"We'll check it out later." She jumped to her feet and shoved the flute into the waistband of her jeans, under her T-shirt. Her skin shivered away from its cold touch, but there was no way she was going to walk up Grant Street with the bone flute in her hand, plain to see.

As they climbed the street she told Mark what had happened inside the ghost house. "You see, I can't just hand it over. I've got to be sure."

"Which one started the fire? That should tell you."

"It doesn't. I never saw their faces and I'm not sure of their voices. I'm only sure of one thing. I want to get this horrible dead bone away from me!"

"We could be wasting our time," Mark said. "Maybe they don't know you've got it."

It was five o'clock. Mark was sitting on Camrose's desk chair, busy with a handheld electronic game. Camrose was sitting on the bed with her pen and notebook, trying to write down what happened in the ghost house.

"I bet they know. But I can't decide which of them should have the flute. I wish I could just throw it away."

A clinking sound came from behind the closet door. Wire hangers swinging, hitting each other.

Mark bounced from his chair and Camrose leaped from the bed. They exchanged pale-faced looks. Mark nodded, and Camrose yanked open the door.

"You!"

"Surprise, Keeper!" Miranda was squatting with her toes curled around the hanger bar.

"How did you get in there?"

"I get around. I see you found it."

"Does this mean *they* know where it's hidden?"

"No. But they know you've got it. Now everybody waits for you, including me."

Camrose set fists on hips. "Okay, if you're so anxious for me to decide, you can help. I need to know what's going to happen to Diarmid if I give Terence the flute."

"You know the story."

"He swore to make Diarmid dance in the outer darkness forever," Mark said. "Whatever that means."

"*Mmmrr.*" Miranda's lips curled back from her teeth. She jumped down from the bar and prowled around the room.

Camrose closed the closet door and leaned on it. "It means something bad, anyway. Could he do it?"

"Course he could. In his land everything has two faces, every light makes two shadows, and there's a back door to everywhere."

"Door. What does that make me think of? Oh, I know. That time by the river, today," Camrose said slowly, "he made me see his father's hall in the Otherworld."

"So that's why you were looking so out of it," Mark said.

"I guess I was. Anyway, it was a big beautiful room, but there was a door there that..." She shivered. "It looked like they hoped it wasn't going to open any time soon. Miranda?"

"What?" Miranda was scrunched in the corner next to the desk.

"Do you know anything about a do—"

"Brutal thing?" Miranda croaked. She slid down the wall. "Strong, all bound about with bronze, locked tight, guarded?" The lower she slid, the more she shrunk.

"That's it! Where does it go?"

"Nowhere," Miranda whispered.

"But how can that be?"

"Take it easy." Mark frowned at Camrose. "Can't you see how scared she is?"

Miranda was not much more now than a quivering heap of fur. "The door," she muttered from under her hair. "It goes Nowhere. To the place where Nothing is. The Void." She drew a hissing breath and whispered, "The Outer Dark."

In the silence that followed, Camrose thought she heard an answering whisper somewhere far away, like a cold wind in a stony place. Mark glanced around uneasily.

"If Terence gets the flute," Camrose said, "he'll send Diarmid through that door. How can I let that happen?"

"So, give the flute to Diarmid," Mark said.

"But if I do that, Terence might hurt... Bronwyn, and... and other people. If only there was somebody we could tell!"

"Like who?"

"My dad. I could phone..." No, she couldn't. She'd tried again in the last hour, once from a pay phone downtown and once from Mark's house. That time Mark tried to make the call. Same result.

"Anyway, what makes you think he'd believe you?"

"He would, that's all!"

"Never. Not even my Uncle Wes would believe. He's cool about a lot of things, but he wouldn't understand about this."

"If only my dad was here and seeing it all for himself! If only he…" Light dawned. "Okay!" She threw herself at the closet.

"What?"

"What do you think?" She pulled armloads of clothes off the bar and dumped them on the floor. Then lifted the loose steel clamp and swung the bar off its wooden bracket.

"Cam, what're you doing?"

"What did that rhyme say? I bring the blood back to the bone…" The bar was hollow. Camrose reached inside and pulled out something wrapped in a white gym sock. Then she replaced the bar on its bracket.

Miranda was hovering at her shoulder. "It says, 'I call the blood back to the bone, I call the spark back to the stone, I call the heart back to its own, I call the wanderer home.' And it isn't a rhyme, Keeper. It's a spell. One of the strongest."

"Good. I'll bring him home myself."

Mark looked worried. "I don't know. In the story they said it was an evil thing."

"Listen to him, Keeper, he talks sense!"

"Oh, that was just in the story." The more they tried to warn her off, the more they irritated her. "Look, if nothing happens, fine. If it does work … Well, Dad will be here, all of a sudden, all the way from Nova Scotia, and then he'll have to believe, won't he?"

She sat on the bed cross-legged, the flute in her hands. It was nothing like what she'd pictured from the story of Diarmid the bard. It was brown and stained and looked exactly like what it was: an old bone, about ten inches long, with holes in it. You could see where someone had carved something, but the carving had worn down to a spiral line of scratches.

"Just a bone, after all," she muttered. But it wasn't just a bone. It was cold as the earth under a rock and heavy enough for three bones. She didn't like touching it.

For courage, she thought of her father. She pictured him sitting at the kitchen table, waving a finger as he argued with Bronwyn over something on the six o'clock news. "Bring him home," she murmured. "Home." She took a breath, raised the flute to her mouth … then put it down and exhaled.

"Wait, let me think."

"Nobody's stopping you," Miranda growled.

"Suppose I bring him home, and he believes me, and he tries to do something about Terence, and then Terence … Maybe it's not such a good idea."

It gave her a funny feeling when she realized what she was doing. Protecting her father. Wasn't he supposed to protect her? A strange, lonely feeling.

"If only we could find those three women," Mark said. "Those Wyrde. You could just hand the flute back to them."

"They won't come," Miranda said from her new perch on

top of Camrose's dresser. "They don't interfere. They're not allowed."

"Not allowed?" Camrose laughed. "Who'd boss them around?"

"That would be telling—a lot more than I'm allowed."

"I bet you don't know."

"I know this, as Keeper it's your job, and you have to do it, not me. You're the one with the powers."

"Powers?"

"Powers?" Mark echoed.

"Me? What powers have I got?"

"I thought you'd never ask." Miranda interlaced her stubby fingers and recited, "The powers of the Keeper are these: plain sight, far sight, insight and foresight. And unfolding from these gifts of sight, judgement: the power to decide. There."

"You're kidding. When did I ever see…" Camrose stopped, remembering the burning house.

"Just now, when you decided not to call your father home, that was insight."

"And today when I saw what Terence really looks like?"

"Plain sight."

"And when I saw that door?"

Miranda flinched. "Far sight."

"Powers." Mark gave Camrose a strange look and stepped away from her. The desk chair caught him behind the knees and he sat down.

Camrose pushed the flute on the coverlet with her foot. "Well, my insight tells me Mark's right. If I could hand those

Wyrde the flute, everything would be okay. You could tell they could handle Terence and Diarmid rolled up in one, no problem."

"But how can we get to them?" Mark asked.

"Maybe the flute would call them."

Miranda shook herself. "You're asking for trouble. That thing has a will of its own."

"I'll be careful." Camrose grabbed the flute and raised it to her mouth again. "Now, how do I do this?"

"I won't help."

"Cam, I really think you better not."

"I'm telling it where I want to go." Camrose shut her eyes and said firmly, "Take me back to the beginning of this story."

She took a breath, then another, and blew gingerly into the flute. Out came a sour squeak that made Mark grimace, but nothing else happened. "Do I have to play a tune? Miranda?" Miranda turned her back.

A breeze, cool after the storm, swirled in through the window and over her hands. The flute whined. The room blurred.

When her vision cleared she was standing at the window, looking out. In the yard below the gates were open, and a man was riding in on a path of sunset light, like a hero out of a tale.

18

Rhianna's story

The guest rode up from the loch and in through the west gate at sunset. The sun laid down a golden highway through the gate and across the middle of the courtyard, and along that shining path rode Diarmid, fair as the hero of one of his own songs.

The window of Rhianna's room was a perfect place to watch people arriving. Rhianna could see almost the whole front courtyard. Behind the bard on his tall gray horse walked a man leading a mule. Man and mule were equally loaded down.

"Presents for you, lots of them!" Alaric pushed his head under her arm so he could get a bit of window. "And some for me too, maybe."

"Looks more like bedding. Maybe he doesn't trust ours." She watched Diarmid, noting every detail. He was both handsome and young, so far as she could tell from here. He moved like a young man, dismounting with ease, and his hair caught the light and swirled like pale flame to his shoulders.

Shiny things all over him and his belongings reflected the warm light. His horse's bridle and saddle winked with gold and so did the strap of a big leather bag he lifted from the horse and slung over his shoulder. It was the one thing he carried himself. His harp, no doubt.

"He looks rich," Alaric said. "The king must really favor him. Did you know he can sing the deer out of the thickets? It's true! He can lure them out to the hunters' bows, just by singing. Ned said so."

"That doesn't sound very fair to the deer."

Alaric laughed, but Rhianna hardly heard him. She was still watching the courtyard. Her father was out there now to welcome the guest. They'd just turned toward the house together when the servant clumsily let slip some strap on the mule and a pack fell to the stones with a crash.

Quicker than you could blink, Diarmid turned back and cuffed the man to the ground. His head hit the paving stones. Rhianna heard the thud.

Her father put out a hand in protest, but Diarmid laughed, a clear sound that rose like a musical scale to Rhianna's window. He took her father's arm and they walked into the house, disappearing from her view. The servant lay still.

A moment later old Ned from the stables ran across the courtyard and knelt beside the fallen man. He helped him sit up. His eyes were open now, but there was blood on his face.

A babble and bustle broke out in the room behind her and her mother rushed in with two maids and an armload of clothes.

"He's here! Alaric, off you go and put on a clean tunic, that one smells of the stable. Rhianna, come away from that window and off with that dress. Quick now! Sara, where's that comb? Child, your hair's a rat's nest! Never mind, tomorrow you'll outshine the queen. I suppose that's what you've been daydreaming about. There now, stop shaking. Wait till you see him. He looks like a prince!"

This time tomorrow, Rhianna would be Diarmid's wife. She bent her head against the pull of the comb and thought of Alaric's tale of the deer. In her mind's eye she saw them flicking their ears and stepping delicately from their thickets, following the lure of a song, never seeing the archers.

That night the old hall looked brighter than it had since they celebrated Alaric's birth. In honor of the guest, candles burned in all the sconces, and the best silver and linen decked the high table. Someone had even taken a long pole and cleared the cobwebs from the corners of the ceiling. Rhianna wore her second-best dress and her best gold pin, and felt as well decked out as the table, and for the same purpose.

They sat Diarmid at her father's right hand, with Rhianna facing him. "Well, well, well," he said slowly. "Hair of the true red-gold, eyes like the sea, fairest maid in all the west country. So they say, and I see it's no lie."

Rhianna's mother beamed. Her father smiled absently, as if he were calculating something. Perhaps, thought Rhianna, he's figuring by how much he can reduce my dowry.

She was glad custom required her to look sweet and say nothing. She could not have spoken a word for all the king's gold, not with Diarmid's eyes on her face. Eyes as gray and cold as a winter sky.

"So far, I'm pleased," he told Rhianna's father without looking at him, a small piece of rudeness that lit a spark of anger inside her. "But is she fit to live at the king's court? I promise, I won't take it lightly if she shames me."

"Fit?" Her father scratched his beard. "Well, she can sew, and, um ... " He looked helplessly at his wife, who started in briskly, as if she'd only been waiting for this cue.

"She can spin, weave and sew like an angel. She can ride and hawk. She can make elegant conversation. She can read and write. And," she added triumphantly, "she can play the rebec, the flute, and the lap harp."

"Wait, back up a bit." Diarmid waved a hand as if brushing away flies. "Did you say *read and write*?"

"I did," Rhianna's mother said proudly.

"What nonsense!" He laughed his musical laugh. "Whatever possessed you to waste such learning on a girl?" Then he frowned. "And she plays, you say?"

"Like an archangel," said Rhianna's mother, a little defiantly now, but still proud.

"All right, let's hear her. Go get her ... hmm ... her flute. Let her play for me."

Play? Rhianna nearly choked. Me play for the king's bard? He smiled back at her, his eyes still cold.

Rhianna's mother sent a servant, an old gray-haired man who hobbled from side to side as he walked, to get the flute. Rhianna couldn't remember ever having seen him before. Perhaps he'd come from one of the farms.

While she was still lulling her mind with these thoughts, the better to keep her courage, the flute lit down in her hands and the old man backed away to the wall. Rhianna took a deep breath, then another, to still her shaking hands. She raised the flute to her lips.

One quavering note, a second sweeter one and a third, strong and true, and she was up and away. The music lifted her on wings and all fear left her. The quick notes chased each other laughing under the high ceiling, and except for Rhianna's playing the hall was silent.

When the last note died into the candlelight, she knew she had never played so well. She looked at Diarmid, hoping to see him warmed and softened.

But his eyes were colder than December seas. "No." He shook his head. "It won't do."

Rhianna's father looked bewildered. "I don't understand," her mother said.

"Of course you don't," Diarmid said. The contempt in his voice lit another spark of anger in Rhianna. "I can't have my own wife showing me up! Can't you hear the jokes? 'The best bard in all the land—except for his wife.' No, there'll be one musician in my household and one only."

"What ...?" Rhianna forgot herself and spoke. "What are you telling me?"

"I'm telling you there'll be no more music from you. Is that understood, my lady Rhianna?"

She shook her head slowly. He might as well have told her there'd be no more air to breathe, no sun to shine tomorrow. Then she knew, all at one blow, what he meant to take from her.

"I know this. I'll never marry you, never!"

She was standing, her bench overturned behind her, and her mother was clucking over her, and her father was shouting, and Alaric was looking from her to Diarmid with tears in his eyes.

In the midst of the uproar came a breath of silence and the whisper of the lame old servant, soft in her ear, "Take heart." It was a brave kindness. She was careful not to look at him.

Diarmid said nothing. He sat and sipped his wine and smiled. When the noise died down he lifted his cup to Rhianna. "I'm still pleased with my bargain. She's headstrong, but I know ways of dealing with that. In a year you won't know the child, I promise." Rhianna's father looked relieved.

Her mother threw an arm around her and walked her to the door. "Go to your room, calm yourself. Yes, I know it's hard, giving up your music. But in a year or two you'll be too busy with babes to spare a thought for anything else."

At midnight Rhianna lay with her eyes wide open. She saw nothing ahead but a darkness darker than the shadows in this room, a darkness that filled tomorrow and next year and all the years of her life.

When the keep was quiet she rose from her bed, dressed and gathered her belongings into a bag.

I'll bring only what I need, she thought. An extra cloak for warmth, a tinderbox, my two gold pins to sell, my flute. I'll live free; I'll marry no man. I'll travel to some great town and lose myself there amongst the people. I'll play the flute for my living, and Diarmid can whistle for me—for all the good it will do him!

She busied herself with these hopeful plans to keep herself from faltering. Down the stairs she crept, and across the great hall, a place of mouse-stirred shadows now, and out into the courtyard. There she stopped, because the gate was closed. Beside it her father's men drowsed but did not sleep. It was the one way out.

At a step behind her she stood still as stone, and thought, I'm done. But no, it was the old servant. Moonlight silvered his hair. "There is another way," he whispered.

"Why would you help me?"

"For pity."

"But you'll be punished."

"Not I. I'll go with you. I know a secret door."

He led her past the stable, where Ned snored in a heap of hay, past the smithy where the smith's boy slept curled up beside the embers. Rhianna stumbled and a stone flew up and rang the anvil like a bell, and her heart sank. But the boy slept on.

The old man laughed softly in the dark. Rhianna felt the feathery touch of fear, but she thought of Diarmid and got her courage back.

They came to a little wooden door in the outer wall of the keep. To Rhianna, who had lived in the keep all her life and knew every stone of it, the door was a fearful thing, for she knew it had not been there before.

"The way out," he said. She looked into his eyes and saw only kindness.

"Who are you?"

He smiled and shook his head.

Rhianna put her hand to the latch and the door swung open. On the other side lay the rocky slopes down to the shore of the loch, and the jetty with its barge and the loch itself, black and silver under the moon.

The door closed behind her. She looked back and it was gone, the wall unbroken. Then she looked at the lame old servant and he was gone too. In his place stood a tall man in black and silver, black of hair and white of face, with eyes that might be blue in daylight.

"Rhianna of the Island Keep, fairest maid in all the west country," he said. "Truly, it was no lie."

"You tricked me!"

"Will you call for help? Will you run back to Diarmid?"

"No." She took a deep breath. "Please, help me to reach a town."

"I'll do better than that, my lady. For I am a prince in my own country. And in that land there is no weeping, and no dying, and never a cruel word. And you shall have a harp of starlight to play, and a flute of moonlight ... forever and ever, my Rhianna."

His words brushed over her like the wings of doves, binding her to his will. She said no word more but walked down to the barge and sat beside him. No man worked the pole, yet the barge moved steadily across the loch. The shores of Rhianna's home moved away, farther and farther, until they were lost in a silver blur.

19

A choice of evils

The silver blur shrank, shaped itself into a rectangle, and became the window of Camrose's room. Mark was still sitting in the desk chair, watching her with a worried look. Miranda was still perched on the dresser, kicking her heels against the drawers. You'd think neither of them had moved in all those hours.

But everything else seemed strange. The room was too bright, the floor was too clean, the air smelled too dry. It took a moment, and then the strangeness backed off a little.

Camrose took a deep breath. "Well, I'm back."

"Back? But—"

"Oh, she's been away," Miranda said. "Far, far away."

Another breeze stirred Camrose's hair. She grabbed the flute and ran to the closet to hide it again before it could take her anyplace else.

"But it's only been a few seconds since—"

"Mark, I was Rhianna."

"You what?"

"I *was* Rhianna! I saw everything from inside her head." She dropped onto the bed and told him the whole story. "So now," she finished, "I can't believe either one of them is the right person to get the flute."

"It's like I thought. Diarmid is just as bad as Terence."

"I don't know. Terence hasn't changed at all since then, but Diarmid has. He's not so proud." Camrose looked at Miranda. "But I didn't see those Wyrde anywhere. What happened?"

"The flute has a will of its own, didn't I say so? It twisted what you said. Fair pay, Keeper, for playing games."

"How could it twist 'Take me to the beginning of the story' to 'Take me to Rhianna'?"

"It took you home."

"Huh?"

"This is how it goes." Miranda spoke with exaggerated patience. "Rhianna's brother? Remember him? He had a daughter when he grew up. His daughter was the first Keeper."

"You mean I'm related to Rhianna?"

"Yes, in a zigzag kind of way." Miranda hopped down from the dresser and began roving around the room. She pulled socks out of a drawer and sniffed them, opened a pencil case and spilled out the pens and pencils, poked the framed photo of Camrose's mother on the shelf above the desk.

"Leave that alone," Camrose said. "No, it seems like too much of a coincidence, Rhianna's niece getting the flute. I mean, how could that just happen?"

"Of course it didn't just happen. It found her."

"It what?"

"There it was, caught in the reeds by the shore of the loch. She picked it up and it sang to her. Hide me, it sang, and keep me safe, until one comes who can lay rightful claim to me. Do this, and prosper. Fail…" Miranda showed her teeth at Camrose. "… And great harm will befall you and your kin."

"Oh, boy," Mark muttered.

"Yeah, how fair is that?" Camrose said. "I mean, who has the right to decide a thing like that for generations and generations of people?"

Miranda picked up the photo and held it close to her eyes. "Some Keepers believed they were chosen by fate. Fate—also known as the Fates, the Parcae, the Norns, the Wyrde. Always three."

Mark rescued the picture and put it back on the shelf. Miranda picked up Camrose's purple pen and tasted the writing tip with a long pink tongue.

"It still doesn't seem fair," Camrose said. "And there's one other thing I can't figure out."

"What, only one thing in all the million million universes? How very wise you must be!"

Camrose simmered quietly while Miranda snickered. "Here's what's been bothering me," she said, after a minute. "How come it took so long for Diarmid and Terence to catch up to the flute? I mean, it seems like those two can feel the thing, somehow. They found me easily enough. They both knew I was the Keeper before I knew it. So why, in all the years since the time of Rhianna, did they not find the flute until 1914?"

"Good question," Mark said.

"*Rrmm* ... You see, truth to tell, that wasn't the first time."
Miranda wasn't snickering now.

"There were other times?"

"*Mmmyess*. Two or three times. Or ten or twelve. Several."

"So, what happened?"

"Things ... went wrong. Each time the Keeper had to hide
the flute again and not decide."

"And?" Camrose prompted. "What aren't you telling us?"

"There's plenty I'm not telling you. Ask another."

"Okay, so what happened when they hid the flute?"

"Well, if you must know, there was once a village in the west
of Ireland that is nothing now but a plain of blackened rocks.
And once there was a great ship like a castle on the sea, and it
sank, and the Keeper was one of a few to escape. And other
things like that."

"Oh, my gosh." Camrose scrambled off the bed. "I've got to
get rid of the thing before it ... " She pulled up just short of
the closet door and looked at Mark. "No good."

He nodded. "That would be the same as not choosing."

She spun around and stabbed a finger at Miranda. "Why
didn't you tell me this before?"

"Because you might have feared to go and get it. Why
else?"

"You'd think those Weirds, Norms, whatever they are,
could've done something to help, wouldn't you? Instead of
sitting on their hands."

"I told you, they—"

"Can't interfere, I know. Lot of good that does me. What the
heck do I do now?"

"Now? The time has come. There's no backing out."

"I wasn't planning on backing out! I just can't decide. And I'm scared." She was mad too. "Get that pen out of your mouth! I'd like to know what use you are, except for messing things up!"

"Use?" Miranda's hair bristled. She went up on her toes and suddenly she towered over Camrose. "I'm your right hand, your eyes and ears, your brains! I tell you, if I'd had the sight, I'd never have made that thrice-cursed bargain all those years ago."

"What bargain?" Camrose narrowed her eyes.

"With that first Keeper, of course, the one who conjured me." She mimicked a plaintive voice. "'Aid me and guard me,' says she, 'and see me through to the ending of this one little task, and then you may go free in the world, provided you swear to harm no human soul.' And I swore to keep that bargain."

"So that's why you're still around. You're tied to the Keepers until one of them—us—gives the flute to the rightful claimant."

"Yesss!" Miranda shook the pen in Camrose's face. "But had I known that my bondage would last so long, then before I'd sworn that oath I'd have thrown myself back into Chaos!"

She jammed her fists skyward, whirled around three times so fast that her rags stood straight out from her body and vanished. The pen fell to the carpet. A smell like burned cinnamon hung on the air.

Mark sniffed. "Have you ever tried to figure out exactly what Miranda is?"

"No, and I don't think I want to know."

After Mark went home for supper, Camrose stayed in her room and ate a chocolate bar out of her desk. Sounds came from below: the television, the fridge door thudding shut.

Sunset flared and faded. She closed and locked her window, wedged the door shut and stuck her desk chair under the knob. She turned on the radio for company. Behind the music she heard stealthy footsteps in the hall outside her door and scratchings at the window screen.

She turned off the radio and the overhead light and lay down in the dim light of her bedside lamp, dressed in her jeans and T-shirt. I'll stay awake till dawn, she promised herself. Maybe by then I'll have figured out what to do.

20

The spell battle

The sky in the east above the park was green-gold, and lights were just starting to come on in the windows of houses, when Mark caught up to Camrose. She was halfway down Grant Street. She looked around when she heard him coming and hoped she didn't look too guilty.

He pointed to the stick shape in her waistband under her T-shirt. "Where're you going with that at this hour?"

"What were you doing, lying in wait?"

"I slept on the shed roof. In case anything tried to get in your window. Figured I'd hear ... whatever. All I saw was you coming out."

"So?"

"Not without me."

"Don't worry, Mark, I'm not planning anything dangerous."

"Tell me about it."

"Well, here's my problem." She walked on briskly and he kept pace beside her. "Yesterday I almost had my mind made up.

g to give Diarmid the flute, and then the Wyrde
ome and take care of Terence."

"And now you can't."

"He'd be the wrong choice. They're both the wrong choice."

"But Miranda says you have to choose."

"Not exactly. She said that terrible things happen when the Keepers don't choose."

"Same thing."

"No. Suppose I never found the flute?"

"But you did."

They were half a block away from the park. The sky was turning peach-colored through the tops of the trees. Camrose walked faster. "Better hurry. I'm going to get back into Ennismor and leave the flute there. It'll be like it was never found. So if it's not found, I can't choose. Or not choose. Can I?"

"Um ... seems to me there's something not right there."

"Got a better plan?" She strode on. Even with his longer legs, he had to trot to catch up.

When they reached the hollow it was blue with the day's first twilight. Camrose searched with her eyes.

"Is it there?" Mark asked.

"Not yet!"

"Maybe we're too early."

But the blue of dusk brightened. Sunlight touched the tops of the trees. Camrose clenched her fists. "It's not coming back!"

"I could have told you that." The voice growled right behind them. Miranda, of course. She leaned against a tree and yawned like a cat, showing the corrugated pink inside of her mouth.

"Then why didn't you?" Camrose snapped. "What's happened?"

"Ennismor is gone. It will never come back."

"But why not?"

"You broke the loop."

"Loop?" echoed Mark and Camrose together.

"The time loop that Gilda made when she first threw you the flute, all those years ago."

"Because she threw it out of her time." Camrose frowned. "Out of hers and into mine."

"Close enough. When you carried the flute out, you closed the loop. See? No more house."

"Then there's no point hanging around here. We'll have to think of something else." Camrose turned and started up the cedar-chip path toward Grant Street as fast as she'd come down it and with a lot more bounce in her step.

She stopped short where the path met the street. Mark ran into her. She pointed a trembling finger.

Grant Street, its cracked pavements, its houses, the cars parked along the curb, were all gone. From this ridge where they stood, the woods swept down into a gorge and up the other side to a higher ridge. Beyond that, forest-covered hills rippled to jagged black mountains on the horizon.

Mark spoke first. "Whatever happened in the woods Saturday night … It's happened again."

"True," Miranda said. "This is not your place."

Camrose found her voice. "Where are we, then?"

"By the smell of it," Miranda snuffled the air, "somewhere near the river of time."

"...an we're in the Otherworld?" Mark's voice

"...o! This is just the borderland. Safe enough, unless you walk the wrong way."

"But how did we get here?" Camrose demanded.

"You were always close to the borderland in that hollow. The bone flute was hidden there so long, it wore a thin spot."

"And when I brought the flute back to the hollow—"

"It was just enough to pull you through."

"So how did *you* get here?"

"I go where I please."

Miranda slouched back toward the hollow. When they came out from under the trees they found that changed too. It was a grassy bowl as big across as a football field. A single tall tree grew in the center.

Only when they came closer to the tree did they see how tall it was. Camrose looked up and up to where the trunk vanished into a stirring dimness.

"Keeper!" Miranda hissed. "Look what came through the hole you made."

Camrose turned. Diarmid walked toward them across the grass from the direction of vanished Grant Street. He stopped three strides away and held out his right hand, palm up.

Camrose backed away a step.

"Come, now. You must choose."

"I'm thinking about it." She took another step back. Her mind darted after ideas like a squirrel after nuts and found none.

"But you know I'm the one. You know how I loved Rhianna."

"I don't know any such thing."

"Well spoken!" came a laughing voice. Terence strolled down
the slope from the opposite side of the hollow. His dark clothes
twinkled with silver. A black velvet cloak was wrapped around
his shoulders and pinned with a golden disc the size of his
hand. Behind him limped a tall red hound.

Camrose backed off again and came up against the tree trunk.
Mark moved so they were shoulder to shoulder. Something
scuttled up the other side and into the branches, and when
Camrose looked around, Miranda was gone.

"Gone while the going's good," she muttered.

But there was no time for bitter thoughts about Miranda.
Terence had stopped about three yards away, with the same
distance between him and Diarmid.

"Well spoken," Terence said again. "You've made the right
choice, Keeper."

"If you mean you, you can forget it."

His smile showed teeth. "It has to be one or the other,
Sweetness."

"Child," Diarmid murmured, "think!" He took a step forward,
held out a hand. "Think of the fate he's promised me."

"And that promise I'll keep!" Terence snatched the gold pin
from his cloak and threw it to the ground, where it bounced
and sent up sparks. He whirled the cloak from his shoulder.

A sudden wind tore at Camrose's hair. Diarmid staggered as
if hit by a fist. The sunlight dimmed.

Diarmid straightened up. He didn't hit back at Terence.
He didn't even look at him. Just lifted his head and began
to sing.

Terence laughed. "Lamenting your doom already, bard?"

Diarmid sang in a language Camrose didn't know, with a lot of liquid sounds mixed up with exhalings from deep in the throat. It didn't sound like a lament. More like a threat. It sent shivers up her spine.

The tree swayed.

Terence glanced up, then smiled. "Give it up! You've left your pipes behind. Besides, this is my country. You can work no spells here."

Diarmid stopped singing. "We're not over the border yet," he said. "And I need no pipes."

The whispering in the branches hadn't stopped. It deepened and spread through the tree and became a wailing on many notes, each chord like the scrape of five fingernails on a chalkboard.

"It's the tree." Mark winced. "He's turned it into a kind of giant harp."

Camrose gritted her teeth against the sound. "He's fighting Terence with music— if you can call that music."

He seemed to be winning too. Terence was kneeling with his hands over his ears. Any minute now he'll break and run, Camrose thought. And then we'll just have Diarmid to deal with.

But Terence didn't break. He lurched to his feet, grabbed his cloak from the ground and whirled it again. Lightning flashed, thunder boomed and the sky went black. A storm wind screamed through the hollow, driving rain sideways into their faces.

Mark grabbed Camrose by the hand. "Next chance we get, run!" he yelled.

Diarmid was singing again. The harping of the tree topped the shriek of the storm. Terence screamed something, and sparks exploded from the tree a few yards over their heads. Smoking leaves and twigs showered down.

Camrose pulled the flute out from under her T-shirt, the better to run. She pulled at Mark's hand. "Now!" They slid around the tree and took three steps away from the battle.

Lightning struck a pine tree at the edge of the hollow. It exploded, and what was left of it burned like a torch. In the sputtering yellow light they saw the red hound limping toward them. Its eyes were fixed on Camrose. She froze.

This was a better view of the beast than she really wanted. Its jaws were wide enough to make one bite of her head. Long yellow eye-teeth curved over its lower lip. Its eyes... No, don't look at its eyes! She remembered hearing that somewhere.

"Okay." Mark's voice in her ear was unnaturally calm. "Here's what we'll do. I can run faster than you, so I'll get it to chase me, and—"

"No! That won't work. If only we had something to distract it. Something we could throw." She looked around wildly. The hound limped nearer. "A piece of meat, or a b—"

She stopped and looked at the bone flute. Mark looked at it. Around them, inside the shriek of the storm and the harping tree and the burning and the smoke, a shell of stillness formed.

Then Mark began, "It's not fair—" and right over him Camrose said, "How come those two have the right...?"

They stopped again. "You first," Camrose said.

"It's not fair they should claim the flute. I mean, where did it come from in the first place?"

"Just what I was thinking."

The hound stood two yards away, silent, watching. Camrose made herself look into its eyes. In the fiery light they should have been blazing red, but they weren't. They were green.

Green as the sea, Camrose thought, and the last piece of the puzzle fell into place.

21

The Wyrde

*C*amrose took a step forward and held out the flute. "I think this belongs to you." She tossed it.

The hound leaped and caught the flute in its teeth. Then it fell to the ground, writhing. At the same moment the rain and wind stopped short. The crackling of the burning tree was the only sound. The wet grass steamed.

In the growing light where the hound had fallen a girl stumbled to her feet. Hair of the true red-gold, Camrose remembered. Eyes like the sea. Fairest maid in all the west country.

She wore a torn, dirty, red gown. The left sleeve was empty. In her right hand she held the flute. Red hair with gold sparks in it fell in tangles to her waist. She looked about fourteen.

"It was you all along!" Camrose hit her forehead with both hands. "Why didn't I see it?"

"You did, at last. I owe you a debt, Keeper." Rhianna looked at Mark, who just then remembered to close his mouth. "And you."

She looked past them, past the tree. Diarmid and Terence were running toward them. But before they could cross half the distance, a sound rolled over the hollow that was like the ocean breaking on a stony shore. Terence and Diarmid froze in mid-step.

On the slope of the hollow, half-hidden in drifting vapor, stood three figures robed in black. "It is done," boomed a voice like three voices woven together. "The Keeper has chosen. The flute is restored to its rightful owner."

Rhianna started. Mark poked Camrose in the side, but she'd already seen. Rhianna's left sleeve was no longer empty.

The triple voice boomed again: "Diarmid the bard, hear your doom."

"Wait!" Diarmid started forward. "What about Rhianna?"

"What about her?" asked one of the black-robed figures.

"She's my promised wife—"

"Liar!" Terence snarled. "She's mine!"

"Sisters, what do you say?"

"I say let the girl choose," snapped the second figure. "It would be the first time in her life she's had the chance to decide anything for herself."

"I agree," said the third in a voice that made the hair stand up on Camrose's neck. "Look at them, girl, and choose."

Rhianna folded her hands together at her waist and studied first Diarmid, then Terence. Then she slowly shook her head.

"That's that, then," said the second sister briskly.

"But I—"

"Diarmid," the first broke in, "you've learned no common sense over the years. But even you have earned something."

"Ask what you would," said the second. "But think well before you condemn yourself out of your own mouth."

He looked angrily at Rhianna, opened his mouth, then closed it. His shoulders slumped, his head bowed. "I'm so tired. All I really want is to rest."

"Done."

Camrose blinked. Diarmid was gone.

"Gwyn, son of Nuadu," said the second sister, "you've overstayed your time in the living lands."

"But—Rhianna?" He reached out a hand. When she looked away, his eyes narrowed. "This is a cheat. The hound was mine!"

The first sister laughed. "Nonsense! This hound was never yours."

"And you hadn't the eyes to see, not in all these years."

"Go!"

He vanished, but unlike Diarmid he faded slowly, until only his eyes glimmered in the air. They moved from Camrose to Mark and back again. "Keeper," said the invisible mouth, "I won't forget. I claim vengeance." Then he was gone.

Camrose went cold. It took a minute before she realized everything wasn't over. The Wyrde were talking to Rhianna.

"What would you have?" asked the first sister. "What would you do, now that you're free to choose?"

Rhianna took a breath, looked up and said, "I would choose to start over. If it can be managed."

The three exchanged glances.

"You see, I haven't lived. Not truly. I was only a child when they told me I was to marry Diarmid. And all the years since

Gwyn—since the hound—seem a bad dream." She looked down at her torn dress and her whole left arm.

The Wyrde exchanged looks again. "You cannot go back," said the second sister.

"Then, let me go forward!"

"Have you the courage?" asked the first.

She knotted her hands together. "I have."

"Done," said all three together.

Sunlight slanted into the hollow. It broke across Rhianna, turned her red hair to a fiery cloud, her body to a golden shimmer. Camrose closed her eyes against the brightness, and when she looked again Rhianna too was gone.

Camrose and Mark were left alone with three dark shapes that never grew any less misty, though the sunlight grew brighter. Camrose wished she knew what to say.

Mark cleared his throat. "Um, Miranda...Is she free now?"

"Wherever she is," Camrose began. Then stepped back as a small, gray-brown shape dropped from the tree to the grass beside her. It rolled over, expanding as it rolled. When it unfolded itself and rose from the grass, it was a ragged young woman with a brown triangular face.

"It's over! I'm free!" She danced on the spot in a whirl of tatters. Camrose expected her to vanish like the others, but instead she stopped dancing and stood biting her nails.

"Well, where would you go?" demanded the second sister.

"Don't know. I've grown used to the Keepers over the years." Miranda darted a glance at Camrose. "Attached, even. Silly creatures though they are. I think I'll stay in their world a while."

"So long as you do no harm," said the first sister. "That part of the oath still holds."

"Oh, yes! I'll be good, Great Ones. I promise!" Miranda swept a bow that grazed the grass, winked at Camrose from under her thicket of hair, leaped into the tree and vanished among the twinkling silver leaves.

"And now you, Keeper." That was the one with the icy voice.

Camrose still couldn't see them clearly, but she knew all their eyes were on her. She shivered.

"Keeper, what would you, now that your burden is laid down?" asked the first sister gently.

Camrose looked at Mark for ideas, but he only shrugged.

"I guess I just want things to be the way they were before. Normal."

"Did you not hear?" said the second sister.

"You cannot go back," said the third in her deep voice.

"But then how are we going to get home?"

"Find your own way," said all three at once.

"But—"

"You were the Keeper. The world will never be the same for you again." The woven voices boomed through the hollow. "You will see truths and find paths hidden to others. And sometimes the sight will be a joy to you and sometimes a grief. That is your gift."

They turned and walked away. In two steps they faded from misty gray to silver. On the third step they were gone.

Camrose stared after them. Then all around the hollow. "Is it really over?" she said. "I can't believe it!"

"Me neither." Mark closed his eyes and rubbed his forehead.

"You okay?"

"I don't feel right. Kind of groggy."

"Breakfast, that's what we need. Let's get out of here!"

They climbed back to the ridge at the edge of the hollow. But nothing had changed. Woods still rippled to the far horizon.

"I guess they want me to use my gift." Camrose set her hands on her hips. "Hidden paths, right? Where should I start looking?"

Mark said nothing. When she looked over her shoulder he wasn't there.

"Mark? Mark! Where'd you go?"

She ran back down the path to the clearing. "Mark!"

He was all the way across the hollow, and he wasn't alone. A tall figure walked beside him, its arm wrapped in a friendly way around his shoulders. They walked into the woods together.

When Camrose reached the spot, breathless, half a minute later, there was no sign of them.

22

The river of time

The path through the woods came out into a meadow of chicory and thistles. Alongside that ran a muddy track beaten into the grass, with more meadow and trees on the other side. "Just like Lynx Landing," Camrose said aloud, not liking the silence of the place. "Only, nothing like it at all."

Eastward—or in the direction that would be east if this were Lynx Landing—two figures passed over the crest of the road. Camrose started running. When she reached the crest, the road on the other side lay empty.

This was the way they'd gone, so this was the way she'd have to go too. If only she didn't have such a feeling of being pulled along on a string.

She walked on. The muddy track turned to gravel, then asphalt. Buildings appeared, but with never a speck of light at the windows, never a human face. The air was cool and wet.

And now the light was draining from the sky. Ten steps more and night fell. There were no stars. Streetlights wore giant halos of mist. The streets glistened black.

Camrose walked into Market Square. The worst of it was, it was almost the same as home. The same stores, the same racks and bins out in front, the same fancy brickwork under the eaves.

But it was all different. The words on the signs were worn away, the awnings were torn, the windows broken.

As she passed the war memorial in the center of the square, movement caught her eye. She whipped around. A scrap of white flicked out of sight around the other side of the granite plinth.

White? Mark had on a white T-shirt. Her heart hammering, she ran around to the other side. Nothing there.

"Eyes playing tricks," she muttered.

She turned around and her heart flipped. There he was, rounding the corner onto Mill Road, on the river side of the square.

"Mark!"

She raced across the square, burst into a short street with inky water gurgling past the end of it and skidded to a halt on the slick pavement. No Mark.

The river wasn't right, either. It was supposed to be fifty feet down at the bottom of the cliff, not up here by the street.

She walked back into the square. "None of this is real. Somebody's jerking me around!"

"Camrose!"

It was the first voice she'd heard in that place besides her own. Mark's voice.

"Cam, help!"

It was coming from the far side of the square, from Mill Street. It sounded scared. Mark never sounded scared! Must be a trick, like the others.

"Cam! Please!"

But suppose it wasn't a trick, this time? Suppose it was really Mark?

Camrose burst into the short street beyond the square. The midnight river gleamed a few strides away. This time a boat rode the water beside a stone curb.

Mark huddled in the bow. Terence sat on the middle thwart with both oars poised above the water. No, not Terence: Gwyn, with his Otherworld face and his darkly glittering clothes.

"You should have come sooner, Keeper. You should have come the first time he called. It's too late now."

The oars dipped. "No! Stop!" Camrose leaped for the boat. The moment her feet hit the boards, the oars bit into the water. The boat shot forward.

When she looked back, the shore was a gray line fading into the night. Ahead and all around lay the river of time.

At first all she could do was hold on to the side. With no land in sight, and nothing but blackness and moving gleams of light all around, the boat seemed to float in a midnight sky. If she fell out she would fall forever.

She closed her eyes. Hearing Gwyn's laughter, she opened them again.

"What are you doing with us?"

"You'll come to no harm, never fear. Not once we're home."

"You mean you're taking us home? Really?"

"Really and truly," he purred.

Mark lifted his head. "Whose home?"

He only smiled.

"Look, I know you want revenge, payment, something!" Camrose said. "What will you take to get us back?"

"You stole my Rhianna. What do you have that could repay me for that?"

"But we didn't *steal* her! And we don't have anything you want."

"Then it will just have to be your own sweet selves, won't it?"

"What for?" Mark demanded. "Camrose was just doing what she was supposed to do."

"That's true enough." He stood up and smiled at them. "But it won't save you." He swept an arm into the darkness, cried, "Look!" and on the word he was gone.

Camrose looked. Where he'd swept his arm the darkness was gone. An oar length away lay a shore of ivory sand, and beyond the shore, soft green meadows rolled back to velvet woods and far blue mountains touched with gold.

The river was clear and gold-shot here. A few feet below their keel lay the sandy bottom, spangled with quivering light from the surface. An eddy carried the boat curving in to shore. The keel grated and stuck.

Mark looked like he'd been bashed on the head and hadn't had time to fall over.

Camrose felt something pulling at her, and realized it was music. She could never have described it, except to say that it made her forget everything else.

Mark was the first to move. He stood up and started to climb over the gunwale. Camrose lurched forward and grabbed him. "No! Don't do that!"

"But…the music! I need to—"

"Don't listen to it!"

"Didn't you hear him? It's too late. We'll never get home."

"Since when do we trust anything he says?"

"It's what the story said: *No mortal flesh may cross that river twice and live.*"

"But so long as we haven't stepped on shore, we haven't crossed—not yet!"

"It hurts me not to go." He set his hands on the gunwale and swung a leg over. Camrose grabbed his shoulders and pulled hard. He sprawled in the bottom of the boat, looking bewildered, then struggled up again.

She wasn't strong enough to hold him. If only she could convince him, make him *see*.

What had the Wyrde said? *You will see truths and find paths hidden to others.* Her gift. Well, this was the time to use it.

"Mark, you always say seeing is believing, right?"

"Right." He gazed at the shore. "Like now."

"Here, hold my hand. I'll take you there. I'll show you."

Her gaze traveled up the ivory shore. Leaving two bodies crouched in the boat, she and Mark skimmed like ghosts across the meadow, hand in hand. They floated inches above the bent tips of the grasses, above fields of sky-blue flowers that turned on threadlike stalks to watch them go by.

They passed through the dark pillars of the woods and on up the mountainside. A gate swung open, and they floated into a wide hall with no roof but the sky.

This was where the music came from. They hovered at the edge of a blur of dancers. The lamps of dawn and moonlight picked out a silken elbow here, a laughing mouth there and over there a crown of living flowers.

Would it be so bad never to go home again? Camrose wondered. Was there anything at home as good as this?

She sank toward the floor, and Mark sank with her.

But in that moment another sound flickered through the music. It slipped past so quickly her ear almost missed it. A cold sound, a whisper like wind in a stony place.

Use your eyes, said a nagging voice in the back of her mind.

She looked again. Darkness veiled the back of the hall. She looked harder, and there stood two rows of seven guards with golden helmets in the shapes of hawks and lions, and all their swords drawn. And beyond them stood the door that had so terrified Miranda.

But now the guards were not standing in front of the door, barring the way. They were lined up on either side, making a pathway like a guard of honor.

And the door stood open. Past the threshold and filling the doorway was nothing. Nothing at all.

The dancers froze. The music fell silent. Heads turned, eyes glittered at Camrose. She looked around and saw Terence standing two paces away, smiling at her. The emptiness in the doorway grew thicker, blacker, began to reach …

"No." The word echoed. A shiver ran through the crowd. She said it again, louder: "No! I see it, and you can't make us."

At that, they were back in the boat. Mark was still blank-faced, still gazing toward the blue and gold mountains.

Camrose pulled one of the oars free of its pins, stuck the paddle end in the sand and pushed. The boat came loose with a jerk that nearly toppled her out of it.

She sat down quickly and pushed with the oar until the boat was floating in deep water. Then she crammed it back in the oarlock, heaved at it to bring the boat around with its bow pointing away from the land and set to work with both oars.

For a few minutes they seemed to make no headway. No matter how hard she rowed, the current pushed the boat back toward shore. When Mark crawled forward and tried to take the oar from her left hand, she held on tight.

"Mark, I'm sorry. But I guess you didn't see what I saw."

"I saw."

She looked at him. The stunned look was gone.

"Let me help."

She shifted along the thwart to give him room.

With the two of them rowing, the ivory shore drew farther away. The green-blue land melted into a glowing mist, then dwindled to a bright line on the water that winked out, and at last they were rowing in the dark.

Reach and pull, reach and pull. The oarlocks creaked and the water slapped the side of the boat, and there were no other sounds except their breathing. Camrose never knew how long they rowed. She began to think this would be Gwyn's real revenge, to keep them laboring in the dark forever, their only light a memory of the Otherworld.

Then Mark stopped rowing. "Smell that?" he said.

She felt it first: a cold wind on her back. It smelled of the spongy wood that collects on the beach after storms, of lime-stone and beached fish and pine trees.

Mark reached with his oar again, and Camrose reached, and they pulled together. The darkness turned gray, then silver and warmed to the glassy pale gold of early morning. Across the river eastward, the hills of Quebec stood black against the morning sky.

Their keel grated on pebbles. Camrose jumped out with a splash and Mark followed her. Towing the boat behind them, they set foot once more upon the shores of home.